Mortal Love

Nine Dark Tales of Love and Obsession

Edward Willoughby

CONTENTS

ACKNOWLEDGMENTS

For Bernadette, who more than anyone believed in me.

Also my children, Luke and Edward, who never once questioned their father's pretentions to write, likewise Octavia, who has always been on hand to help and diligently assisted in the construction and publication of this book.

Warm appreciation and heartfelt affection goes out to my small band of trusted readers who were and always are the first to run a new draft by. My sister-in law, Oonagh, my sister, Jaime B, and two great and loyal friends I have met along the way, Rusty (The Nurse Angel Dolores) and Lorraine.

Some of these stories would never have been written if not for Regan Evers, who pulled me out of the funk and resurrected the author in me when it seemed I had nothing else to give. With love and gratitude.

CANDY STORE

At a very early age I was exposed to the naked male adult form. I was brought up by my Swedish-born father, Otto, who after my older brother got sick and had to go back to Stockholm with my mother because of health care insurance regulations took every opportunity to walk around the house without any clothes on. Cooking, watching TV, doing some DIY. It didn't matter. Long before everybody else became one he'd been a pioneering IT consultant and software engineer and ran his business from home so had got in the habit of sitting at his computer and taking phone calls in his office in total disregard for the clients on the other end of the line who might have felt uncomfortable in the very least dealing with someone who, had they known, happily conversed with them all while in the buff. He did very well out of his job. I went to a prestigious private girls' school and we had a beautiful house in west London and another 'back home' that he rented out on an annual basis until my mother moved back in there for good.

I never understood his need to be unclothed as a naturist thing. He didn't meet with likeminded groups. To my knowledge he'd never been to a nudist beach or anything like that. And though he knew he was handsomely well-endowed I never believed it to be a form of exhibitionism either. Certainly not in front of his own daughter. Why would he? He just enjoyed feeling free in his own home and as a result of that I too have always felt confident in my skin and have to admit to parading my flesh on any given chance when growing up which is not unusual in this day and age. My fifteen-year-old daughter, Megan, tells me her older friends are always getting their boobs out in public or showing off their bottoms. The girls were worse than the boys nowadays and I can say that with some degree of experience.

I was around the age of six when the police knocked on the door for the first time and asked to talk to Otto. A neighbour had complained about seeing him hanging out some washing stark-naked (again) which, he was warned, amounted to indecent exposure and was a criminal offence. But given the affluent neighbourhood and after my father explaining about his Scandinavian upbringing and consequent lifestyle habits along with the promise of confining them between the walls of his own home and behind closed doors they went away and let him off with a caution. However, this was followed up by a visit from the Social Services who were more concerned about my welfare. They sat me down and asked me questions and gave me a doll to play with, telling me to point at the parts of the figure my father liked to touch. I didn't know what they were talking about and Otto just grew angry that they should even be filling my head with such thoughts and threatened to make an official complaint. Nevertheless, they told him they were putting me on the 'at risk' register and would be making regular visits to the house which went on for years to the point I got to know a number of investigators and grew to an age where we could all sit around and laugh about it. My father becoming more of a parody than a threat. But it never stopped him. Not even when after a second and final reprimand from the police sometime later because he had been caught repairing a window latch in full view of a women and her two young children passing in the street. Since that time he began to live his life behind closed curtains, or shutters in our case, which he claimed to nullify his sense of liberty and made him increasingly sullen and moody, likening his existence to that of living in a zoo. As eccentric as his parenting skills sound I grew into thinking that he may have had a point. After all, none of us are born clothed.

"How is the caged bird supposed to fly? Tell me that," he would stomp around and rant, his dozy appendage in constant full swing. Looking back it wasn't so much the elephant in the room as the elephant's trunk, not that he could ever stop drawing attention to the thing.

"Are you talking to me or my penile tremendo?" he would ask with legs and arms akimbo and wearing a comic frown. That's what he called it. Sometimes he could make it twitch in front of my very nose as if it was talking all by itself. It was all a joke to him. And it was to me back then.

Though Otto routinely visited the sunbed boutique to maintain his all-over tan the whole family were fair-skinned and white-blond with eyes like blue ice. I was born in England but it is said in Sweden that one of the biggest tourist attractions are the beautiful girls, although the same could be said for the guys if you like that Nordic look. I had always likened my father to a Norse god but as I grew older he began to lose shape along with his vanity and the inevitable estrangement between my parents after Fredrik, my then nine-year-old brother, fought a long battle against leukaemia and died nearly two years after he and my mother left. She never got over it and as a consequence of all the heartbreak Otto started drinking heavily. His belly began to bulge. He cared less about his daily press-ups and abdominal-obsessed sit-up routine and fitness videos. The dumbbells beneath his bed gathered dust. His once proud definition slowly melted in full view of me as he indifferently succumbed to his lot in life and the onset of middle-age. But the size of his manhood remained impressively intact and without knowing it became something of a phallic yardstick for comparison in my later life.

I shouldn't talk about it so much. I know. But there's not a man I've been out with who hasn't been privy to my unusual upbringing and therefore, at some point, informed of my father's grandeur. Some see it as a challenge. Some are put off. I've always thought of it as an early test of character even if it nearly always ended in some form of disappointment or failure or, in a man's eyes, defeat. In truth most guys just never measured up and sometimes I could see in their expression that I had concocted the whole thing just to intimidate or that I was hiding some deeper issue. And then one day I walked in on my friend's fully-developed fourteen-year-old son getting dressed and I knew then what I was and what my father had done to me. My name is Sally Svensson. You may have heard of me. I am forty-five-years-old and a registered sex offender.

How is the caged bird supposed to fly?

I would have cause to remember those words after that first awakening. I couldn't get the image out of my mind. Worse still I taught biology of all things at the same private school my friend's son attended. David Love. I began to worry that the driving force behind my urge to teach had all the while just been an evil subconscious desire to be around pubescent boys. That's what they say about paedophiles, isn't it? Teachers, clergy, sports coaches and their dubious vocational callings. Like putting kids in charge of a sweet shop. That's how I came to think of it every waking minute of my working day. Driving into school, passing crowds of boys gathered at bus stops, and then of course addressing them in class while seated at their desks and fighting the need to palpitate. The overwhelming distraction was everywhere. But it didn't stop there. As if working at the same school as David didn't put me in enough jeopardy I began to make excuses to visit my friend more and more with the crazy obsession that I could recreate my walking in on him undressing again to whatever weird conclusion I had no idea. Half the time he was in his room anyway. I was sick and disgusted with myself. But I couldn't stop the constant fantasies. Almost overnight it seemed men of my own age no longer interested me and I was only in my late twenties then, my male peers being in their absolute prime or at least should have been. I had imprisoned myself with my thoughts and yearnings. I was in dangerous territory just dreaming about such stuff. I frightened myself. And though I thought all the time about resigning I knew also that I was in the perfect place for me. If cocoa really was the key to increasing the brain's level of serotonin and therefore both elevating and enhancing sexual pleasure especially in women, then I was in the biggest chocolate emporium in the world and it was all I could do to keep my greedy hands from grabbing at the confectionary.

Listen to me. What do I sound like? You would think I would know better after everything that happened. But I met a women in therapy who described it in exactly the same way. Except that it wasn't chocolate it was fruit. Fruit and the fact she'd been entrusted with nursery school children which I obviously disassociated myself from. But she likened them to juicy fruit ripe for plucking. That's right. You heard me the first time. It took many hours of counselling for me to understand there was no difference between us even though her crimes disgusted me as mine in turn did others. My mother in particular who went on to die prematurely shortly after. Both our victims were under the age of sexual consent. Both had been prey to predatory grooming and powerful and persuasive forms of manipulation. When you crave for something so badly it's amazing the lengths to which you go and what you can convince yourself of. Having worked in a secondary school I should tell you that one fourteen-year-old can differentiate very much from another. Both physically and mentally. David looked old enough to know what he was getting into. For instance he had stubble. I still think I gave him the time of his life. But I have been forced to accept the emotional damage done not just to him but ultimately my friend and her husband whose violation of their son took place right under their very watch as it nearly always does in the case of sex offenders. You have to gain everyone's trust as I had Michael and Mary's. People who had at first hired me to babysit David's elder brother, Mark, when I was a little younger and then, David, when I'd been studying hard for my 'A' levels to get to university. Going on to remain a family friend ever since, who of all things asked me to be David's godparent. Not that I'm a particularly religious person but David had been raised a practising Christian and the private school I taught at was of the same denomination. Michael was a devout parishioner and did volunteer work for the same church attended by the school's headmaster and if his recommendation wasn't the defining reason I got the job then it certainly didn't do my application any harm. The definition of a godparent is a person who promises to take responsibility of their godchild's religious not sexual education so it goes without saying that I haven't seen them in a long time. Not since Megan was born anyway. The rumoured grandchild Mary last referred to as an 'abomination' that the family wanted nothing to do with. To make it easy on them and to evade further scandal I assured Mary my pregnancy was down to any number of my online fuck buddies which I in any event had a growing reputation for. At least until I saw David undressed.

I thought I'd put all this behind me. After my conviction I obviously wasn't allowed to teach anymore and for a long time wore an electronic tag on my ankle restricting me to a half-mile radius of areas known to be where older boys might congregate. Schools, obviously. Parks, sports clubs, even shopping malls at certain hours. Thank God Megan was too young to remember but what I hadn't been prepared for was her burgeoning social life as she began to enter her teens in her own right. It was different today. Girls had lots of boyfriends, that is to say boys that are friends, and my daughter was no exception. I had spent years avoiding such situations and began to quietly panic at the thought of her inviting more and more school mates over and my doing nothing to stop it. A condition of my suspended sentence was to be relocated some two hundred miles north by the authorities and to start a new life with my child but even then only under years of strict supervision. No one knew who I was. Especially not Megan who from a very early age began to enquire about her father's origins so I told her he died in a car crash in Sweden and without much thought gave her a picture of some blond, blue-eyed fuck buddy and me to keep even though David's gene pool fought tooth and nail with mine. She has his deep brown eyes which I latterly had to laugh off as a throwback and made something up about an uncle with the same identikit. As you can imagine my life after it happened has been one of fear and fabrication. And yet here I was again faced with the same paralysing temptation coupled with another unspeakably selfish dilemma. A fifteen-year-old boy called Josh who apart from our southern connection I like to think was spending more time in my daughter's company because of the constant eye contact between us and, even if he didn't feel it, a simmering sexual tension. We Swedes have good skin and age well. I am always being complimented about my complexion. People have me down as years younger than I am. Megan even told me some of the boys thought I was a 'yummy mummy' and often referred to me as a MILF. What they didn't know was that I was still on the sex offenders register which was a constant worry to me if anyone really wanted to start sniffing around. But I was also under no more restrictions. No curfews. No more tagging. And there was Josh and any number of my daughter's boyfriends entering and hanging around the flat freely with no lack of encouragement from me. Without contravening a single law it was as if I had been presented my own personal candy store and given the keys to go with it.

I hadn't seen my father in a long time. Not since I'd been forced to move to another town and set up in a council flat and given a job as a cleaner in a care home under a protection programme, as far away from a juvenile boy as could be. Some years after I eventually got a job in a supermarket and still do some private cleaning on the side which enabled me to buy a car and provide a comfortable existence for me and my daughter even if it was a far cry from what I'd envisaged in life. The judge had sympathised with me because I was pregnant and after reading the psychologist's assessment of the family tragedy, subsequent upbringing and my promiscuous lifestyle concluded that although I would be registered as a sex offender he didn't see me as a threat to the public. More than anything else he considered my crime to be 'a gross error of judgement' and one that I would unfortunately pay the rest of my life for and so saw little point in sentencing me to prison. He even wished me a happy future with my child, appearing as keen to believe the baby was just a product of my sleeping around as anyone. No one requested a DNA test. Least of all me. I had taken all I wanted from David. Consequently, it seemed even the press took pity on me as I only made a small column on page five of a couple of national newspapers and after that the media went away and let me get on with it. I don't use the name Svensson anymore. It's Quist, which happens to be my mother's maiden name. There's nothing illegal about that. You can juggle your family names around as much as you want which makes it easier to deceive on an official document. I started by hyphenating the two to no real suspicion which I know a lot of people do. Immigrants I've worked with admit to using all the ancestry at their disposal for more fraudulent reasons especially when all it sometimes took was a simple misspelling to create multiple identities. Also from the very beginning I had started to use my middle name, Freda, which is what Megan knows me as and what my father wanted to call me anyway. He liked the idea of my brother and I having that androgynous connection but my mother just thought it was confusing. Sixteen years on and it appears Sally Svensson had all but disappeared in the eye of the public and yet all the while, the way it must be for the criminally insane, I knew she still lived very much inside of me.

Otto is seventy-years-old now. A shadow of that body-conscious narcissist who reared me and liked to flaunt his big swinging dick in front of his little girl. Yes, I blame him. My mother too who clearly favoured her first born and never came back to get me. It was always my father and me making the trip over to Stockholm to see her. I had no say in where I lived or who I wanted to live with and my father just used his job as an excuse to stay in London even though he could have worked anywhere. They never dealt with the loss and so consequently neither did I. As a biologist I know everything starts from somewhere. Even the sickest minds can be traced back to something. It took me a long time to accept that it wasn't a natural childhood. There were no cookies and milk and bedtime stories. Otto never attended any school events under the protest he would have to wear clothes but which I always understood as an excuse for his dislike of what he called 'pretentious lower-middle-class English parents with too much money'. After Freddy died he became even more wrapped up in himself. I could never invite anyone home for fear he might walk past an open door with that thing. I was left to grow up on my own very quickly where boys were concerned. The irony then being that I was always looking for someone older than me then. Someone with experience. Maybe even someone like my father which isn't unusual in young girls, is it? Just maybe not for the same reason.

In the meantime Otto continued to get into trouble and when I was at teaching college I got a phone call from the police saying he had been arrested and charged for indecent exposure just as they had warned him he would. Some years later I joined him on the sex offenders register which must be some sort of record for father and daughter even if, like the woman in therapy who abused a nursery school child, I didn't think our crimes really compared. An elderly couple out for a walk discovered him sunbathing naked in a quiet piece of woodland one hot summer's day. Apparently, it was a favourite spot of his and he'd been sun-worshipping there for years with no previous incident. Most of the parks in central London are sacred. For the life of me I couldn't think where he was talking about. Certain people just know where to find each other I guess and that certainly turned out to be true in my father's case.

I picked him up at the train station as arranged along with Megan who, with not much of a family to speak about, was ecstatic at the thought of her grandfather coming to stay for a few days. I on the other hand was filled with trepidation at his out-of-the-blue request suspecting most of all that he was terminally ill and was coming to deliver the news first hand and I would be left to deal with the death of my entire family at a still relatively young age. I hadn't seen Otto in years and it made me realise how much I had kept hidden from my daughter. When Megan was little I went back to visit him once or twice after everything died down but he made no effort to reciprocate the gesture and seemed to care little about where Megan and I had been dumped and the impact that had on me or the difficulties that such a massive cultural change involves. To my knowledge my mother had died still very much in the dark about his particular misdemeanours. What happened to us? I can't believe either my father or I would even be on that register if Freddy had never got ill and my mother had stayed. As heinous as my crime might appear to some I have come to think I would have more difficulty trying not to explain away my father as some sort of flasher, which is essentially what he was and had been prosecuted for. So for a long while we just let things drift with just the odd email from him that I still couldn't help but imagine had been written in his birthday suit. The older I get the harder it is to explain any of it. Least of all to Megan who knew absolutely nothing about either of us.

On the ride back from the station I could hardly breathe for the suffocating silence of our skeletons kept buried and my daughter's innocent need-to-know inquiries into my father's life history but that appeared to present themselves to him like booby-traps. She accused me of never talking about him. Of keeping him a secret from her. She wanted to know what her father was like and if he'd ever met him. Had I been a problem child? Had I many boyfriends? Why did I move so far away from him? Of course, I had built a web of stories and excuses over the years but with each potential pitfall Otto would exchange a hesitant glance with me as if we should have made time to get our story straight before slowly answering Megan with a cautious smile that awaited her thoughtful satisfaction. When I could sense my father was starting to panic I told her that she should let him rest. That it had been a long journey for him and there would be lots of time to talk and catch up. Otto still looked in reasonable health but Megan's insistent probing aside there had been a fearful look in his eyes when I met him that seemed to be replaced with an almost immediate sense of relief when he saw me get out of the car and wave. I didn't recognize him at first. I hadn't expected him to bring such a large suitcase for one thing. But for a man who once took so much pride in his appearance (yes, he liked his designer brands as a secondary attire when needs must) his white windcheater and matching flat cap, wide-legged flapping chequered trousers and lurid trainers looked as if he'd been rummaging through a charity shop in a hurried order to disguise himself with the only thing missing being a fake moustache, big plastic-nose and black-rimmed glasses. Even upon hugging after more than ten years apart my father's body had the tense and awkward feel that I sensed was less about our lack of contact and more about a need to go. His obvious agitation began to unsettle me from the moment we got in the car and I thought that perhaps he was just nervous about being in a strange town and not having seen me for so long not to mention Megan's whirlwind interrogation. It certainly didn't cross my mind for a minute that he'd been up to his old tricks and gotten himself in trouble again. Not at the age of seventy.

If my mounting disbelief at Otto's revelations later that night when we had a chance to talk wasn't enough to give him second thoughts about coming to visit, his expression of quiet alarm at seeing two teenage boys sitting on the settee watching TV in my flat as we all entered seemed to test him further. He looked as if he wanted to turn around and walk straight back out. I was momentarily lost for words for how it might appear. The fact being that Josh's stepfather was a violent drunk so I had given him a key to come round whenever the situation became difficult. It wasn't a secret. We all lived on the same estate. Even his mother, Geena, knew and was grateful to me for providing a refuge for her son. She was filing for a restraining order but she'd said that for some months now so I'd begun to believe that it was one of those abusive controlling relationships that would ultimately end badly and that Josh was better off out of it. It was the least I could do for the poor boy who was not only sweet and sensitive with a mop of strawberry-blond hair and soft blue eyes but who Megan admired for being an extremely talented artist. The previous term the school hosted his very own exhibition that had made headlines in the local paper praising the high standard and maturity of his work. Josh's forte was life drawings and although there was no romantic interest between my daughter and him, the other lad, Alfie, made any excuse to come round and seemed smitten with Megan who in turn appeared to enjoy the attention. She had told me that he was the boy all the girls wanted to date. Tall and dark with strong features he could have been several years older but of course by the same hand he wasn't Megan's only admirer. She was a brown-eyed Swede. They could have formed a queue up the stairwell for both of them and in that sense they were the perfect match and I couldn't have been happier for her.

Later, Megan went out to the cinema and for something to eat with a group of friends. I'd put my father up in the little box room that counted as a third bedroom and where sometimes Josh would sleep over. Now that the fuss of his arrival had died down and the presence of teenagers were no longer around Otto visibly began to relax and look around the room, pausing for reflection every now and again as we chitchatted emptily at either end of the corner sofa unit which is where Megan and I usually liked to curl up with a coffee and watch the soaps. She was always catching a nap and would doze intermittently especially after a school day so we would invariably end up watching the recordings again over the weekend just like a couple of besties.

Almost as if we'd only just met my father seemed distracted by every detail of the décor and various mementoes around the place which were mainly photographs of Megan through her growing years, a couple of reproductive prints and a few collectables and knickknacks. It wasn't much to show for a life but I'd made it my little sanctuary. It was clean and cosy and comfortably furnished. I like soft fabrics, lots of cushions and soft lighting and scented candles and things like that. There are far worse flats on far worse estates. It's a tight-knit community where everyone looks out for each other. It was a tough transition in the beginning but it's what Megan grew up knowing so in that sense it became both our home.

"I can hardly understand her accent," he admitted with a soft chuckle.

I had to laugh. I had grown up with some of my friends mimicking my father in what always sounded like B-movie German.

"At least it's native," I said. "These last few years have seen the area become a dumping ground for displaced families. Victims of social cleansing of all cultures and I'm not just talking about immigrants. Josh's family were uprooted from south east London all in the name of gentrification. Two hundred miles away from family and friends. Take it or leave it. Just like me I suppose," I admitted with a shrug. "But for different reasons…"

"Who's Josh?" he asked after a moment.

"You know. The boy that was here earlier," I hesitated, knowing he had been waiting to bring up the subject.

After he continued to look at me I opened my eyes into a cold-ice glare.

"I haven't seen that look in a while," he smiled. My father had so many wrinkles now I couldn't stop staring. So much for the Scandinavian complexion I began to panic.

"It's not what you think, Otto. It's not what it looks like."

"It doesn't matter what it looks like to me," he said.

"Christ," I sighed. "It's my daughter's friend. Give me a break. Should I be worried you're going to flash your cock at her while…I don't know, I get you to change a lightbulb or something?"

And there it was. Within ten minutes of being alone together. The same thing we had seen in each other's eyes the moment we reunited at the station. My father the indecent exposer. His daughter the female pederast. Both carrying our own shame and embarrassment and fear of each other's infamy. At least that's how it felt to me.

"I'm sorry," I said.

"No, you're right," he replied, continuing to look at me openly. "Maybe you should be worried."

"What does that mean? You're not walking around here naked if that's what you think. Let's get that established straight away."

"I haven't done that in a long time. I don't have the physique to feel proud about anymore."

"You're sure about that?" I couldn't help asking with a raised eyebrow.

"That's not what I meant," he said, smiling wryly.

"What's going on, Otto?" I asked in all seriousness.

For a moment it looked as if I had caught him unawares and he wasn't ready to talk about it.

"There's this woman…" he lifted his shoulders in a confessional gesture.

Of all the things I'd been expecting this wasn't it. I could feel the tension since his arrival begin to drain away. My father in a romantic relationship after all this time and at his stage of life. I hadn't seen it coming and began to feel excited for him.

"Susan," he smiled and nodded as if at some happy memory, but something in his eyes told me this story was going somewhere else and that his being here and the big suitcase in the little bedroom that suggested he might be staying some time was a result of it. When you've lived in fear most of your life that feeling of impending sickness is never far away.

"We met in a park. Well, the woods where I go because it's quiet up there and, you know, private."

"No, I don't know, Otto. I thought you went there to sunbathe in the summer and that's where you got caught lying around naked and that was the end of it."

"Well," he shrugged. "I guess walking around the house freely was never going to be enough."

"I'm not sure I understand."

"I go up there every day. It's all I think about every morning. The fresh air. The outdoors."

"And what excites you about it exactly?" I asked hesitantly.

"The meetings with Susan."

I breathed a slight sigh of relief but was still a little confused.

"She understood me," he said, and stared at the floor.

"You say that like you think it's over."

He shifted in his seat and flicked a look at me. His eyes had turned so pale and languid since I last saw him they sometimes appeared lifeless. But then a sudden sharpness would appear. Like a lizard caught dozing.

"The first time we met it was a warm spring day and I was taking a breather on a bench just on the edge of the woodland where the bluebells form a carpet through the trees that turn to a deep cobalt-purple the further you go into the shadows. I could see the glittering stream in snatches as sharp as glass somewhere inside and hear the dog walkers with their Labradors and retrievers and springers splashing around. It's one of my favourite spots, so close to the periphery of…" he seemed to stop himself from going on.

"The periphery of what?" I asked unsurely.

"Danger, I suppose. I don't know. The public. The risk of being caught," he said without drama and shrugged limply as if it was obvious.

My father was one of those people who liked to tell a story in detail, causing me to remember overhearing many a conversation over the phone from his office as a child where it was not only apparent he was enjoying the sound of his own voice but sitting there naked and no doubt casually strumming his cock and configuring his balls as he did so. He would sit there like a king. Revolutionary computer technicians were in demand then.

"Susan came walking along with her little dog, a Jack Russel called 'Skip', and sat down next to me and for a while we admired the view and started to talk about the weather and other trivial things. We didn't even know each other's names when without knowing why I slowly pulled down my joggers and exposed myself to her."

I brought my hands up to my face in horror. Feeling both an urge to burst into tears and to slap him.

"Oh God, no," I uttered.

"So she asked me what I thought I was doing and to put it away and stop being so silly. That's what she said."

"Jesus Christ, Otto," I whispered into my cupped palms before running my hands through my hair and digging my nails into my scalp. "What were you thinking? Are you fucking insane? After everything that's happened."

"I know," he conceded with a nod. "I know."

"You're seventy-years-old for Christ's sake."

"And still a caged bird it seems," he looked at me as if I should know.

It took a moment for me to realise I had risen to the edge of my seat and was at the point of tipping off. I blinked in disbelief and steadied myself and sat back and reorganised some cushions. Crossing my legs and arms and looking at him from every corner of my being in an effort to remove myself from his sordid little tale.

"So what happened?" I couldn't help but show my revulsion. "She's reported you and you're in trouble again? Is that why you're here?

"No," he laughed emptily and frowned as if I had totally missed the point. "That meeting with Susan was over two years ago."

"I don't get it. Are you telling me she continued to meet you after that?" I immediately sat forward again.

"Mostly," he said. "She's... she was always busy at the weekends with family commitments. She's got her own life. She attends church and has grandchildren."

"Does she have a husband? Is that what all this is about?"

"She's a widow," he corrected me quickly.

"Okay, so, you say she has her own life but..."

"She let me be myself, Sally," he waved his hand tiredly and began to rub at his temple.

"Freda," I corrected him instantly, "My name is Freda Quist now. You of all people should be able to remember that."

"What about Megan?"

"What about her? She has the same name, of course."

"Quist?"

"Yes. I had to think about her future. I had to protect her from the past."

He looked momentarily disappointed but what could he expect? It was only my mother who wasn't on the sex offenders' register.

"You don't think she'll ever know?"

"Just tell me about Susan," I said, beginning to grow impatient that he should sit there and judge me.

He sat back and washed his face with his hands and sighed.

"You can't begin to imagine what it felt like. To have someone understand and not...not go crazy. She didn't run. She didn't scream. She didn't call the police or tell anybody. It became just between us."

"Hang on a minute. Are you saying, I mean..." I began to struggle and catch my breath, holding up my hands. "I'm sorry. I'm starting to panic here a little bit. You mean, you continued to meet her and you would expose yourself every time? Is that what you're saying? That she would meet you and let you expose yourself to her in the woods or wherever?"

"Yes."

"But I thought..." I began to shake my head. "All these years I thought you were just eccentric. I thought the police, the authorities had all got it wrong about you. That it was some sort of misunderstanding. And now, what you're telling me is...is, well, it's not good, Otto. You're telling me that you're a menace. You know that don't you? You're talking like you've done it before. That you've always done it and somehow got away with it. You might think you don't mean any harm but you're a public menace. A threat to society. That's what people would say. You know that, don't you? Of course you know it. You've always known it."

"Susan didn't think so. The Christian in her didn't think so. And that's saying something."

"I'm sorry," I laughed. "But I don't understand her behaviour either. Did anything else ever happen between you both?"

"No," he said emphatically. "We never even knew where each other lived. We only addressed each other by our first names. Sometimes we never even spoke at all. I would just wait for her and Skip. It was always around the same time. Sometimes I would just reveal myself from the bushes. Other times openly flash myself to her while walking in the oncoming direction or just sit and masturbate next to her on the bench while she, well, I guess she sort of kept a look-out. She was never phased. She took it all in her stride. She would sometimes feign shock because she knew I liked that. She would reprimand me like a little boy. Sometimes she would openly laugh at me as if to humiliate. I never knew what reaction to expect and that was part of the excitement. Those meetings were all I needed to stay on track and to keep me out of trouble and I know she knew that. She was helping me, you see. She became responsible for me. She knew I meant no harm but also that I couldn't help it. She was doing a good thing."

"Can you really not help it?"

"No," he replied with a hint of exasperation that it should have taken me so long to understand.

"So what happened? I'm assuming this isn't a social visit. Are you running from something? Are the police looking for you?"

"It wasn't how it looked," Otto's voice began to shake and tremble. He gripped his hands as if he was about to slide from his seat and fall to his knees and pray. I could only look at him and frown. He looked close to tears but with what seemed more like anger than self-pity. "It wasn't how it was meant to be."

I wasn't sure I wanted to know any more graphic details. I wished he would just leave. I could feel a familiar dread returning that could be initiated by the tiniest thing. I was haunted by anyone staring at me for too long when out in public, if I stumbled incoherently over some innocently asked question about my past, or was invited to an event where there would be people I didn't know and all for the same reasons. I only ever really felt safe in the comfort of my own home which is what I meant by calling it my sanctuary. The world stopped closing in on me when I shut the door. I felt the same relief when I entered at the end of every single day. It was just me and Megan. It had always just been me and Megan. What had my father brought over the threshold to threaten us after all this time?

"You're really starting to scare me, Otto," I said.

His look did nothing to reassure me. As if he was bracing himself for my reaction.

"It felt like any other day but looking back...looking back perhaps I should have read the warning signs. Susan was a lot later than usual and it was the school holidays so there were a few more people about but it was still only mid-morning. She knew the more dangerous it was for me to be around the public the more excited I got. Over the course of time Skip got in the habit of finding me first if I decided to hide from her. It was all fun and games to him and I knew she was never far behind, play-acting at calling the dog innocently as if all unsuspecting. It was one of our little fantasies. I could hear her but now when I think about it I can hear the panic in her voice as well, the seriousness in her tone as if she thought Skip was in peril. But I could already feel the blood surging through me. I just thought it was part of the role-play that day…" he shook his head.

I sat there spellbound impossible as the scene was to imagine. My father. My seventy-year-old father ready to jump out and expose himself to an old woman and her dog walking in the woods? I thought I'd heard the last of it. But it was worse than I thought. Much worse.

When Megan came back that night with Josh I had to explain to him that my father was staying for a while and there was no room to sleep over. Megan quickly ushered me out into the kitchen and told me Josh's stepfather was drunk and causing problems at home and his mother had advised him to keep away and so my daughter suggested Josh might sleep on the sofa. I have to admit to letting Megan's friends' crash out now and again but with Otto there I couldn't help but sense his disapproval in spite of his own shocking admittance to me that evening.

"I'm sorry," I half-whispered. "But not tonight, sweetheart. I'm a bit overwhelmed emotionally with my own father being here. It really is Geena's problem to sort out. I wouldn't put some man living in this house before you. Ever."

She nodded as if she understood but wasn't used to not getting her own way and made her feelings felt with those big brown eyes as if I had let her down.

"Otto won't be here long," I cupped her beautiful, perfect face and smiled. I nuzzled her nose which is something we'd always done as a sign of reassurance. "I just need a few days, okay? And then we can all go back to normal."

"I don't mind Otto being here," she said, kicking her heel against the floor.

"Huh, we Scandinavians have a saying about being around family too long."

"What's that?" she lifted her head, her eyes brightening to anything remotely genealogical.

"They start to smell of fish," I pulled a face.

We both snorted laughter. It took a few attempts to return to the living-room with straight faces which could have only added to the discomfort of Josh and my father being left on their own to talk. When I tried explaining the situation again to Josh so that he fully understood he didn't look too happy and dropped his gaze from mine before silently leaving. I shared a sympathetic look with Megan and shrugged as she followed him out. When your daughter becomes your best friend at that age it's a tough balancing act but for once I was pleased with myself for not so quickly accommodating her which I had grown into an unhealthy habit of doing for lots of reasons. One day soon I would have to tell her everything. I was prepared for that. But she was still my little girl. She didn't ask for any of this. My job was to look after her for as long as I could. But the truth was out there. And I knew it was coming.

I couldn't sleep those first few nights in fear of what my father had told me. Worse still, I began to wonder if I could trust him around Megan. He was getting old. He warned me he had to go to the toilet a lot in the night which was adjacent in the hallway to all the bedrooms but which I read as an excuse to find him wandering around and possibly exposed. We had an agreement that he was to keep his jogging bottoms on that he liked to wear around the flat at all times. Even in bed. But each time I heard his door open I was on tenterhooks that something should take over him and that he might enter my daughter's bedroom feigning innocence. Then in the day when I was at work I would have to worry about him entertaining himself. Was he walking around naked in the flat? Had he found some nearby parkland to cruise? I still couldn't be sure if he was a pervert or going senile or just plain stupid. Then there was the simple choice. Should I just talk him into giving himself up to the police who must surely be looking for him rather than have a detective turn up at my door in front of Megan and the neighbours? If he explained the story as he did to me, with Susan being his willing accomplice, perhaps he might be charged with a lesser crime. But I was starting to sound like him. Ready to make-up and believe anything than the truly awful and disturbing reality of his actions. Things that he'd been getting away with for as long as I could remember under the guise of some bohemian lifestyle which made me both wonder what my mother had really known about him or if his behaviour had been motivated by her absence and therefore far more calculating and sinister means.

What Otto hadn't known that morning upon meeting Susan was that her grandson had called in to see her and knowing her routine decided to go looking for his grandmother up in the woods with his four-year-old son, Susan's great grandson, Matthew. When he caught up with her Skip was already on the trail of Otto's hiding-place and seeing the dog up ahead the little boy began to set off in chase. That's when my father could later reflect upon the panic he had heard in Susan's voice, but as he had already admitted in his heady state of arousal he'd given it no thought. While he continued talking I found myself thinking about what he'd said earlier about playing with himself on the bench while she kept watch. Had Susan also got what was coming to her? He had made it sound like a harmless fantasy between them but given the length of time it went on and the tacit understanding of their rendezvous it sounded more like an addiction to me. In the chaos that followed Otto assured me the boy never saw anything. But the Dad instinctively knew my father's intentions and was immediately enraged, chasing after him and calling out that he knew who he was and where he lived and was coming to get him. Despite his age my father knew the woods well enough to evade him and felt sure the man wouldn't just leave his son alone in the woods for long. Then a couple of days later Otto received a card through his door from Susan explaining what had happened but said that they should not meet in the woods anymore. Their strange tryst had come to an end it appeared.

"But I thought neither of you knew where each other lived. I thought that was part of the deal," I sat there trembling and hugging myself at his horror story.

"She didn't but the man did," he answered slowly.

"How?"

"It was David Love," he finally admitted.

Not only did I know of David's grandmother I had met the woman several times handing over babysitting duties between us when he was little. Of course, that had been a long time ago and who was I to speak but there was nothing about her then that suggested she had a deviant side if that's what you call it. At least they have a category for me. But this seemingly harmless and lifelong married churchgoer encouraging my father to expose himself in broad daylight through every season of the year left me shaking my head for days in disbelief every time I looked at him.

"What are you going to do?" I asked him at the end of the week because he couldn't stay with me forever and I was starting to believe Susan had talked David round into not reporting the incident. Being devout Christians the family obviously had a forgiving nature but given her involvement it made sense she wouldn't want the police coming to the house and asking awkward questions.

"He said he was coming to get me. Is that what you want?" Otto looked up from reading the paper and eyed me nervously. He had one foot up on the coffee table and complained all the time about his right knee. He left his bed unmade. He always waited for me to make the coffee. He finished the crossword before I could get to it.

My father was starting to smell of fish.

"David wouldn't hurt anyone," I scoffed. "He's as gentle as a baby."

"He's not a fourteen-year-old boy anymore, Sally. I mean, he's a man. He's a father."

Over time Otto had allowed himself to believe Megan was a result of my promiscuous past as that was the story I'd stuck to. But you only had to look at my daughter's dreamy dark eyes to see David.

"You should have heard him," he continued, playing the frail old man which was starting to grate on me as well. There was nothing wrong with my father if he could outrun a man under half his age in the woods. "He was going to rip me apart. He said he knew who I was and where I lived and was coming to get me."

A small part of me had always expected David to knock on my door one day and ask to see Megan. That we could all sit down and work something out.

"Did the kid see anything, Otto?"

"No," he went back to reading the paper. "I told you."

"Are you sure? Because that would be different. That would be completely different. That thing is like a fucking hosepipe."

"I don't know. Maybe," he shrugged.

"Jesus Christ," I shook my head again and left the room.

David was never knocking on my door, I thought. At least not for the reasons I had always hoped. Instead he decided to spray-paint it.

"Mum, you should come and look at this," Megan came home later that night with Josh and Alfie while my father and I had sat in watching television. I'd been waiting to see my favourite chat show for most of the evening and so was a bit annoyed about being interrupted. All three of the kids stood around looking a little sheepish. I could tell the boys were red-eyed from drinking.

"What is it?" I asked.

"Somebody's painted something on the door," she said.

"What do you mean?" I sat up immediately and exchanged a look with Otto who shrank back into his seat with what looked to be genuine fear. I got up and my father followed. The door was still open. I could feel my heart sink at the sight of what at first looked like just random graffiti but when I got close the word hit me like a blow to my chest and I staggered backwards as near close to fainting as I had ever been. My father's sins had chased him all the way two hundred miles north and perhaps mine also from even further back. Anger never really goes away and I know that only because the fear of it doesn't either. I had given David's family the benefit of having a forgiving heart but I had never forgotten Mary's instant rejection of Megan each time I allowed myself to ponder over the miracle of her forbidden conception. If any one of them could have just seen past their outrage they would have known David had fathered a beautiful and perfect girl whose existence bore no relevance to the atrocity they deemed her to be. I had been waiting for something like this for a long time. I just couldn't be entirely sure who it was directed at. It just read: PAEDO.

Of course, I wanted to blame my father. There was no doubt in my mind that his twisted behaviour had ultimately brought this upon us all and that in doing so had opened up a whole other can of worms. Paedo. Had David meant that for me or my father? Perhaps it wasn't David at all. He would have no doubt told his parents. Good Christians or not I remember Michael in particular always quoting the Old Testament. He believed in an eye for an eye. He'd been there every day during the trial glowering hellfire at me each time I looked across the court room. First their son corrupted by not only a family friend and teacher in the same school but his godmother, and now their grandson exposed to the degenerate conduct of the father from the same family. It was understandable. I'd read of sex offenders under similar acts of victimisation being driven out of their locations by vigilante groups taking the law into their own hands. Family orientated communities just didn't want people like me living among them which is why I had kept my head down, rarely socialised and didn't go within a mile of social media anymore despite the constant pressure from my daughter. I worried every time she posted a picture of us on Facebook. I lived in terror of being Googled despite my carefully constructed alias. Did he, David, Michael, they, have other plans to unveil me and that this was all just the start of some persecution campaign? Was he sitting in a car somewhere watching? It was a long way to drive for one act of revenge. As if I hadn't lived through enough trepidation I had to worry now about venturing out in fear of what I might return to.

Megan was talking in my face about calling the police but for the very same reasons Susan didn't want them involved the thought of being questioned and where it might lead to terrified me. No. This was personal and had to stay that way for now. I just needed a bit of time to calm down and think straight.

"Clearly, whoever it was has the wrong house," I said shakily. "I don't want to make enemies."

"What?" Megan shrieked. She had her mobile in her hand and I could tell that her fingers were itching to make the call. There was a selfie of her and Alfie on the screen posing that made me ache for my youth and start all over again. "What does that matter? It's still vandalism. It's still a violation. I'm not sleeping here with that on the door."

"I can get some leftover paint from my Dad's shed," Alfie stepped forward and said. "He's got all colours. I can do it now."

My whole body shook with gratitude. Alfie never seemed to say a lot in my presence but that was the sort of thing I needed to hear not Megan's hysterics or Otto's stone cold, guilt-ridden silence standing somewhere behind me.

"Oh, Alfie, would you?"

All the while he was gone I stood guard by the open door with my arms crossed and shivering while Megan and Josh and my father went to watch my chat show. I remained covering the word with my body in case a neighbour should pass even though it could have been there any number of hours and anyone might have seen it. I was clutching at straws letting the boy paint my door. Just buying time. I knew that. I had always known that if for no other reason than I had been here before. When it starts to feel like the beginning of the end and there is nothing you can do to stop it.

We all sat up into the early hours watching a movie and because I for one still half- expected another act of recrimination. A brick through the window. Some dog shit posted through the letter flap. God forbid a petrol bomb. And as the intended intimidation of the crime began to sink in Megan's initial injustice also turned to one of fearful questioning.

"Why 'paedo'?" she asked. "Do you think it was meant for next door? Do you think Tom is a kiddie fiddler or something?"

Alfie snorted laughter.

"Don't start pointing fingers, Megan. That's how these things escalate," I said.

"What if it happens again?"

"It won't."

"Or something worse."

"Try to forget about it." Alfie said caringly and put his arm round her.

I thanked Alfie with a look but had to tear my eyes from him when he continued to gaze at me intently.

"It's not you, is it, Otto?" she joked, nudging her boyfriend and causing Alfie to snicker. "You didn't leave the bathroom door open again did you?"

"What do you mean?" I sat up and looked at my father.

"Chill, Mum. It was just a joke."

"I keep forgetting to lock it," Otto shrank back behind a table lamp so I couldn't see him.

"What do you mean?" I said again, and stood up.

"I'm not used to locking doors in my house."

"It was an accident, Mum. Get off his case."

"Who forgets to lock a bathroom door?" I looked From Megan to my father.

"I have to go in there a lot," he replied timidly.

"Christ, Mum. Leave him alone."

My mind was filling up with images so grotesque I wanted to throw up in his face. "Well, did you see anything?" I kept my eyes fixed on him.

"Mom! That's rank," she pulled a face and Alfie and Josh started to giggle.

I sat back down barely able to catch a breath. I wanted to tell my father to get out there and then. To go back to his perverted little life and get caught and be locked up so I never had to see him again. As if he hadn't done enough. As if he hadn't damaged me enough he had to lead his insidious snail trail all the way into my home and infect my family with his disgusting behaviour. I didn't believe for a second he forgot to lock the bathroom door. He just couldn't help himself. Couldn't not show the revolting, malformed thing off even at his ridiculous age. It was a laughable and pathetic obsession.

Maybe the message was meant for him after all, I began thinking. Maybe it wasn't David or Michael or anyone to do with the Love family. I didn't know what he'd got up to in the week I'd been working. Was it possible he'd already been out exposing himself to some local like he had my daughter and now I had that horrifying ignominy to be concerned about?

"Mum, what is it? What's going on?" Megan asked worriedly.

I gave my father a sharp look as if to say that he should explain. Out of the corner of my eye I could see both the boys start to shift uncomfortably.

"What have you done?" I asked him slowly.

"Mum?"

I slowly rose from my seat and stood over him. My breath controlled into short shallow puffs like a bodybuilder about to go through a set of a huge chest-lifts. I could feel my own powerful and palpable menace beginning to suffocate the room and everyone in it. Even Megan had stopped talking and watched on with wide-eyed uncertainty. I looked my father up and down with a barely concealed sneer. Nodding as if I could see inside him and what he was capable of and what he had possibly done. As if I was ready to spill out all the sordid secrets between us. That dead-weight of unmentionables that kept our heads barely above water and breathing.

Otto coiled up in his chair, his eyes had a look of pleading and he could all but shake his head at me to stop. To not say the words. The damning words that were on the verge of utterance and would be out there forever once spoken.

"I don't understand," he began to gibber.

"What?" I snapped impatiently.

"How could David know where you live?"

"Shut up, Otto," I could feel my face redden.

"Who's David, Mum?" Megan asked.

"He's probably always known," I said, to stop him talking.

"But you said Susan wouldn't want anyone to know so why would he do it?"

"Do what, Mum? The graffiti? Is he talking about the graffiti?"

"I'm warning you, Otto," I said.

"Is it happening again?" he looked across at Alfie and Josh in dawning horror.

"Shut your stinking fucking pie-hole, Otto!" I screamed.

"Mom!" Megan's voice rose in shock.

"Shut your stinking perverted cock-flashing mouth, Otto! You hear me? Shut your fucking mouth or so help me God I will cut your fucking dick off and shove it up your fucking anus you twisted sick fucking creep!"

Everything I had held back. Everything I had ever thought about him erupted out of me at the speed of vomit. And almost as if I really had thrown up a shocked and barely-concealed repellent look began to spread across the faces of everyone in the room. Megan choked back a stifled cry as I tore my angry gaze from her. Alfie and Josh stared silently on. Not daring to look me in the eye anymore. Only Otto continued to try and see beyond the shield of defiance in my bone-hard glare. The compassionate and still caring father in spite of everything.

David had been falling behind with his science so I offered to help with some extra tuition twice a week after school. He was predicted to get top grades in all subjects by his tutors which only raised his parents' expectations. Most of the kids were under pressure to learn what they would only be taught at the start of the next year anyway which is when David would be in my class. But I couldn't wait until then. So I told Michael and Mary I taught a number of students from other schools to supplement my savings but in reality there were none. I just wanted to get David on his own. It had been several months after I'd seen him peeling off his rugby kit in the utility room of their house where the washing machine and dryer were stored along with a small shower cubicle and downstairs toilet. I knew the place as if it was my own and moved around as such which is how I managed to walk in on him when taking a trip to the loo. He looked up in fright and struggled to reach and cover himself with a towel but not before he registered my appreciation of the sight. I wouldn't say we started to look at each other differently after that. If anything he tried avoiding me for weeks. But the next time we met and from then on in David began to gain confidence and would stare into my eyes that one moment longer just the way I would catch Josh and Alfie doing. That's when I knew that he'd been thinking about the same thing. I'd like to tell you it was some heady romance where I dreamed of us being together for the rest of our lives despite the age gap and all the other difficulties ahead, but it was nothing of the kind. This was no love affair. I knew what I was doing. I wanted him. I stalked him like prey. I was licking my lips at the thought of it. The illicitness and danger involved only exciting me further. Before I knew it we had naked pictures of each other on our phones. He skipped school. I skipped school. When we were at school we fucked in the toilets, the cupboards. The classroom. We fucked in my flat. In my car. When his parents were at church. We fucked in his bedroom when his brother was in the house. When Susan was in the house. I took him in my mouth. I taught him to pleasure me with his tongue. I taught him everything except the thing Michael and Mary were paying me to do. And then one day he asked if one of his friends could join in and I suddenly came to my senses realising he'd been talking. But by then it was all too late.

The night after my father left Megan asked if Josh could have his room back. I didn't like the way that sounded so I told her I thought it was for the best that he try and make things work at home. As difficult as it was for Josh's domestic situation I also felt let-down by his reaction to having Otto stay. He'd remained quiet and sullen all week and had barely acknowledged me to the point of rudeness which was not only strangely out-of-character but totally uncalled for given my hospitality to date and in very sensitive circumstances where I could have been seen as interfering and so I couldn't help but feel a little aggrieved. In trying to do a good thing it seemed I had only made him more dependent upon me and the pressure of that unwanted responsibility had never felt so cloying after my father had gone. For some time at least I just wanted my space back. To walk into my flat the way I had left it. To be able to wallow in a softly-scented, candlelit bath after work without the worry of walking out with just a towel wrapped tight around my cleavage and not have some young boy in the house ogle me or report back to his parents and how that might look. The ball spring latch on my bedroom door can sometimes open by itself and it was on Alfie's first stop-over that I caught sight of him silently standing outside in the darkened hallway as I was getting out of my clothes. So as not to embarrass the boy I pretended not to see but that didn't stop him watching from the shadows as I continued to take my time undressing in order to give him a chance to leave. But he just carried on watching so I eventually stripped naked before turning off the light and climbing into bed. In a flat as small as mine privacy is at a premium and that was just with me and Megan living there. Otto's visit had only reaffirmed that. It wasn't so much the physical as the character presence that had left me gasping for air. My daughter was growing into an opinionated woman with a forceful nature and just a week living with my father and everything that transpired had left me feeling like a prisoner in my own home. So I stuck to my guns and said Josh couldn't stay which would at least eliminate the risk of his presence in my company. But there was little I could do about my daughter's new boyfriend, Alfie. By the time they were officially 'going out' he must have watched me through the doorway at least a dozen times and it still didn't stop then.

When Megan asked why I had said those things about Otto I sat her down and told her about my upbringing and how my father would walk naked around the house which is why I had freaked out about him leaving the bathroom door unlocked.

"I lived my entire childhood without inviting a single friend round for fear of him exposing himself. I shouldn't have to worry about my father being around my daughter. I suppose I didn't realise how angry I was with him even after all this time," I smiled.

"Mum, I have never seen you that angry. You're scary," she said. "So is Otto a pervert like you said? Is that what that thing on the door was about? Is that why we never see him?"

"Remember what I said about Josh's Mum and how I would never put a man before you? Well, it's the same thing. I really don't know what Otto gets up to and I don't want to. We've been estranged for a long time. There's nothing there. I don't even know why he came."

"But what about David. Who's he and who's Susan?"

It felt strange to hear Megan's father's name come out of her mouth, causing me to realise only then how delighted she would have been to hear she had a baby step-brother.

"His neighbours or something. He was warned by the police when I was a child for hanging out his washing without any clothes on. There were always complaints."

She covered her hand with her mouth and started to giggle.

I nodded and raised my eyebrows.

"But he's seventy. That's just gross if he's still doing it."

"I know," I said.

"I'm glad things are back to normal," she hugged my neck. "I'm glad he's gone and it's just us again. He was starting to smell of fish."

She pulled back and we both laughed and then later when Alfie came round I chose my moment when my daughter was asleep on the sofa to go and get undressed for a bath and as always ignored the presence of her boyfriend in the darkened hallway while I lay on the bed and masturbated under his eager eye to a shuddering climax within a matter of minutes.

I don't know why I allowed myself to think that was the end of it all. I worked half-day on Wednesdays which was the only real time in the week I got to myself. Megan stayed late after school for swimming practice and usually went out for some fast food with her team mates after training which gave me a night off from cooking. I would normally indulge myself with a bit of spa treatment and still get home early enough to relax and open a glass of wine and put my feet up before she got home. What I hadn't expected was to find was Josh sitting on the sofa watching TV.

"Hi, Mrs Q," he sprung from his seat as I entered and stood there smiling nervously.

All the boys had got in the habit of calling me that and I never bothered to correct them. The more layers concealing my former self the better. However, they were the first words he'd spoken to me for over a week and I couldn't help but show my irritation.

"What are you doing here, Josh?"

His skin was pale and for a boy that liked to sketch nudes his face coloured easily when embarrassed which appeared to be most of the time.

We looked at each other for a moment longer while I awaited an answer. When nothing was forthcoming I felt him follow me into the kitchen where I set down my keys with a deliberate sigh and began to put away a bag of shopping.

"You smell nice," he said.

I stopped what I was doing and stared at him in all seriousness.

"How is it at home?" I asked.

He shrugged.

"Well, in any event I think it's time I had the key to my flat back. I can't have you just walking in here when you feel like it."

"But…"

"What is it, Josh?"

"But how will I see you?" he protested.

"What do you mean?"

"You know…"

"What are you talking about, Josh?" I put a hand on my hip and tried to keep the frustration from my voice. "You can see me anytime. All Megan's friends are welcome here. You know that."

"No, I mean…"

"What?" I said. "What are you trying to say?"

"Aren't you going to take a bath?" he stammered.

I looked at him openly and laughed. "What? You want me to take a bath when I've just been to the spa and had a massage? You just said I smelt nice for Christ's sake."

"Sorry. I didn't mean it like that," he said, looking a little confused.

"What is it, Josh? What's on your mind?"

"It's nothing. It doesn't matter."

"Look, having my father here made me realise I just want some time to myself, that's all. It's nothing personal. Then there was that thing on the door. You wouldn't know anything about that would you, Josh?"

"No," he frowned and fell sullen as if I had insulted him.

"Well, I'm going to get changed," I said.

I went to my bedroom and pushed the door shut and it immediately sprung back a little way open with a faint chime-like ping. The sound of the door closing was always good enough for me. As if I was in complete ignorance of the faulty ball latch even if the boys did see it as an invitation to voyeur. I was down to my underwear when I caught sight of him using his phone to take a picture of me getting undressed as if for the first time. I marched towards the door and opened it wide.

"What the hell are you doing, Josh?" I glared at him. "Are you spying on me?"

He went white-faced with shock.

"Are you taking pictures of me you little fucking pervert!" I screamed.

"I…" he began to back-pedal down the dark and narrow hallway and tripped over his own feet, falling flat on his back.

"Give me that thing," I snatched the mobile from his grasp and began to pant heavily as if from a mounting anger as I looked at a series of shots of me taking off my clothes. But it was all I could do to contain a powerful sense of arousal at the very idea of it.

I was standing over him with my legs apart. He couldn't keep his eyes from looking between so I pretended to shift my feet and widened my legs a little more, making myself tingle in expectation. If Josh had been bold enough to reach up and touch me I might not have been able to stop myself.

"What is this? Have you done this before? Have you showed anyone pictures of me?"

"No!" he insisted. "I thought…"

"Thought what?"

"I thought you knew," he began to look very frightened.

"You could get arrested for this," I shook the phone at him. "You might be a juvenile but they have prisons for kids like you. I should tell your parents," my eyes bore down upon him judgementally. "Is that what you want?"

"No," he brought a hand to his mouth and wailed. "Please," his whole body was trembling as if he'd been dragged from a freezing river.

"What do you do with this, eh? Do you take it home and play with yourself? Is that what you do you disgusting little boy? Do you go home and beat your meat over me? Is that what you do?"

Just the suggestion was enough to make my heart pound. I was precariously close to the edge, I knew. Images of David came flooding back. I imagined myself standing over Alfie who I felt sure wouldn't have hesitated upon finger-fucking me and making me beg for more. The thought made my knees buckle and I began struggling for breath. I was on the brink of euphoria. Of an explosive self-induced orgasm. My hair had fallen over my face. I was nothing short of salivating over him like a dog guarding a choice piece of meat.

"Delete it all now," I thrust the phone back at him in a last-ditch attempt to save us both from danger. "Delete it now and whatever else you have or so help me God I will tell your mother what a dirty little pervert of a son she has."

"You're wrong!" he yelled back, suddenly emboldened but with what looked like tears of hurt and heartbreak. He scrambled back from under me and got onto his feet. His glittering eyes both fixed and accusatory. "You're wrong about all of that. I…I think you're beautiful. I think your body is beautiful. I use the pictures to sketch you. I can show you. I can prove it. I have a whole book of drawings of you. I thought you knew. I thought you were being my model, my muse. I thought you were letting me because…because, well, I thought you believed in me and that you loved me like I love you. And before you say it I know I'm too young. I know we can't be together yet. I know it can't happen now but…but I want to be

36

with you. I love you, Freda," he said, his first ever use of my name just making me even more uncomfortable and rousing me from my fugue state so that I could barely make sense of his words. "I love you and I can't help it," he dropped his chin into his chest and began to sob uncontrollably. "I'm sorry…I'm so sorry that you didn't know about the pictures."

All at once I felt that craven hunger leaving my body and recognized him for what he was. An innocent young under-aged boy mixed-up by my ravening thirst for the taboo. My borderline behaviour that I had somehow convinced myself of as being unsuspecting and guilt-free. I couldn't be blamed for boys spying on me in the privacy of my own bedroom. At least that was the story I had been prepared to tell. The premeditated lie. I had allowed it to take control. Again. It had to stop.

"You can't come here anymore, Josh," I said, with as much cold heart as I could muster. "You delete those pictures and get the hell out of my flat before I go to the police."

Two days later Josh killed himself by jumping from a bridge in front of a train.

I had no doubt after Josh had left that he would have deleted the pictures of me. But upon hearing about his suicide I somehow instantly had the presence of mind to remember about the sketch book he spoke about. I had to assume it was just one drawing pad among many but I still worried if any of the pencil figures were so obviously me or if they just looked like any of the loosely depicted anatomical forms I had seen at his exhibition. Sometimes a limb or the head wasn't even included and the only photos he could have copied would have been of me with my face turned as I pretended not to notice him. It was only my daughter's boyfriend I had started to put on a performance for in the bedroom and the craving to be left alone in the flat with him began to take an ever-deeper hold as I did my best to attempt a display of upset in the days leading up to Josh's funeral when in reality I felt very little remorse, only an oddly cold, detached and selfish relief that the whole problem had gone away. Standing at the graveside, attending the memorial, even his practical help around the flat when the school closed down for a few days after it happened and I took some time off work to be with Megan, Alfie rose to the plate like a man in terms of both his attentive and emotional support for me and my daughter. In that time we kept our eye-contact to a minimum, instead being allowed the publically open display of physical affection where we got to hug and cling to each other like any would-be grievers, except that I could always feel his swelling when pressing up against him.

It was in one of those embraces at the wake held in Geena's flat that I saw his stepfather, Kenny, watching me through the modest congregation of neighbours and friends with a strange smile on his face far removed from one of mourning or even guilt that Josh's death was rumoured to have been a result of his constant bullying and over-bearance. I'd only met the man on a couple of occasions and his reputation preceded him even then. But instead of the big burly brute I had been expecting he turned out to be a short, rat-faced and wiry little man with bad teeth and mean squinty eyes. He lived in tracksuits and trainers and would turn up smelling of drink at parent evenings without removing his baseball cap. He ridiculed Josh on the touchline for his lack of prowess at sporting events and had openly questioned his stepson's sexual preference at the school exhibition when laughing and making crude jokes about Josh's male life drawings. In truth he scared me a little and I had crossed the road to avoid him many times. But it was only after Megan befriended Josh and he started to stay around the flat that I began to learn not only about Kenny's violent and controlling ways but also his serious criminal convictions.

Kenny's idea of funeral attire was a black Nike tracksuit, matching trainers and cap. The entire ensemble looked to have been newly acquired and at the first opportunity of finding me alone he appeared at my side as I had a feeling he would. I only talked to Geena at school because we were both from London but I knew Kenny was a local lad who commanded a fearful respect in the area and was used to being fawned over rather than ignored so I had always tried to keep my distance. I was standing on the third-floor balcony of the flat overlooking the green on the estate for a bit of fresh air estimating the height from which Josh would have jumped. His mother was so clearly on some sort of powerful sedative that she barely responded to the trickle of condolences from the gathering during the day which made it easier for me not to look her in the eye. As hard as I tried to relate to her I just couldn't despite my involvement which makes me sound like some sort of sociopath. Maybe I am. I never once considered the feelings of David's parents before or after despite their kindness towards me over the years. I just took what I wanted because I could and because I still can.

"I don't think we've ever been properly introduced," Kenny blew his cigarette smoke into the wind only for it to waft back in my face. He waved a hand to try and disperse it before laughing at himself. Brushing the ash from his joggers. "Man," he muttered.

"I'm sorry about Josh," I said flatly, hearing the lack of empathy in my voice.

"Hmm," he leant over the balcony and spat directly down as if he was aiming at something.

"He was very talented."

"You think?"

"Don't you?"

"I used to draw dicks on the covers of my schoolmates texts books when I was a kid," he sniffed. "We all did. Big spiky hairy balls and all. Some with blobs of cum spurting out. No one called us talented," he turned and looked at me with that rodent grin.

"Josh didn't draw cartoons."

"My point is I grew out of it. Anyone at his age who wants to spend hours and hours looking and sketching pictures of the 'male genitalia'," he used his fingers as quotation marks, "well, there has to be something going on, right?" he shifted on his feet and scratched himself. "Perhaps you can tell me as he seemed to spend so much time round your place of late."

"He didn't just draw men," I sighed, as if already bored with the conversation.

I could feel him looking me up and down.

"That's right. Maybe he wasn't such a little faggot after all. I used to think he liked to sleep over because of his crush on the daughter not the Mum." Before I could answer he said: "That's Megan's, boyfriend, right? The big guy, Alfie. The one you were cosying up to?"

"You should be consoling Geena," I continued staring straight ahead.

"What makes you think I don't need consoling?" he sidled in and rubbed his leg against me.

I gave him my best cold glare and looked down at him as if he disgusted me. He was cupping his cigarette by his side like a concealed weapon. Someone had put on some music and the mood began to change to a party atmosphere. Kenny stood humming and gyrating beside me with a knowing look on his face like someone who thought they had the upper hand in a game and was awaiting their opponent's turn. I could feel my worst nightmare coming true. Josh had told me Kenny's most recent stretch in prison had been for extortion and it was known on the estate that he still operated several little rackets involving money lending at inordinate rates. He was used to preying on people in desperate situations and making a profit. It was his instinct. I began to feel sick with fear wondering what he had in mind.

"You know, you're right. I can't draw for shit and Josh, well, he might have been dumb enough to believe you were modelling for him or whatever, but they have legit classes for that where a whole bunch of losers gets to sketch some geriatric in the buff." He sniffed back a pile of mucus that made his throat swell like a reptile before launching it over the balcony in one horrid stringy projectile. "Fore!" he shouted, looking over and croaking laughter. He took a last drag of his cigarette and flicked that into oblivion too. "Maybe that's what you and your old man should have done to keep yourselves out of trouble, eh? Posing naked for some wannabee De Vinci or something instead of going around and getting yourselves in all sorts of trouble flashing your cocks and tits all the time. What's wrong with you Swedes, anyway?"

"What do you want?" I closed my eyes and heard myself ask.

"You know, I'm being cast in a bad light over what happened to Josh. People aren't saying it to my face, of course. But still, that can't be right, can it? All I ever did was try and crush the fairy inside and make a man out of him. But you…" he goadingly began to wag a finger under my nose, "you toyed with a fifteen-year-old boy's emotions because, well, that's what you do, isn't it, Sally? That's your thing. Josh didn't jump off that bridge because of me. You had your fun with him and now you're fucking your own daughter's under-age boyfriend just like you did that other schoolboy years ago."

"I'm not fu-" I gripped the balcony, feeling my shoulders hunch and my body go rigid.

"What if I was to invite Megan round and start taking my clothes off in front of her and everyone got to hear of it? What do you think I would be labelled as, eh? You know the word, Sally. Say it."

He leant in close and reached inside the white blouse I had bought just the day before the funeral and began squeezing my breast.

"Say the word, Sally Svensson," he whispered.

I could smell the nicotine and alcohol on his breath.

"Paedo," I said, my newly pedicured nails digging into the concrete edge.

"And again," he searched deeper inside my bra, pinching my nipple hard. There was nothing remotely sexual about it. He was showing me who was in charge. That he could do anything he wanted.

"Paedo," I choked on the word.

"That's right," he said. "Nobody wants a paedo as a neighbour, Sally. We should both have a good long think about what it's going to take to keep that a secret. Especially from young Megan in there."

He twisted my nipple hard one last time, making me flinch in pain.

"Nice talking," he said, removing his hand and laying it on my back before returning to the room. For a long time I could hear his voice above the music, laughing and chatting as if nothing had happened. I continued to stand there paralysed with fear. Not knowing if I was to stay or go or what he even expected of me.

For the next few days I lived in terror of Kenny paying a visit either in person or by some other means of persecution that I would no longer be able to palm off or even convince myself of as being a result of my father's twisted transgressions. The judge had been right to serve a strict supervision order upon me all those years ago. It had never gone away. I could never trust myself. In the care home where I first worked as a cleaner I made friends with a young lad who'd been serving an apprenticeship under his father as a joiner. He was a beautiful mixed-race boy with unusually bright blue eyes and dark curly hair. His name was Rudy and he'd dropped out of school at the age of fifteen and was still learning the trade. His father had been sub-contracted to work on a kitchen extension at the home and when they came to the end of the job I took his dad aside and asked if he thought Rudy would like to do a few little repairs for cash in my flat. One of them being a faulty latch on my bedroom door. I told him that I couldn't pay much but that it might inspire Rudy to stick at it if he knew he could make a little money on the side from his skills. With no immediate work coming up his father couldn't have been more appreciative and I told myself I really did want the lock looking at in the same way it couldn't be argued that David needed help with his studies or that it was Megan who'd suggested we give Josh a safe haven from his stepfather. No one could point the finger at me if it came to light the kid turned out to be a peeping tom and the same went for Rudy. Only with calculating step-by-step self-justification could I argue against that little voice inside that was telling me to stop, that this time I would go to prison, that Megan would be taken away from me. That it was wrong. It makes me sound out of control but I felt far from it and still do. Not once have I let my urges precipitate the moment. I've never forced any boy into doing something against their will or didn't want to do. It had to feel right for the both of us and even then I was still battling against my own cunning till the very last. Except to leave a bra and panties lying on the bed as if I'd just slipped out of them I just sat around reading a magazine the first time Rudy came over and performed the tasks requested. So what if I read out an agony aunt's column to him that involved a married woman having an affair with a teenage boy? No one believed those letters and anyway what would a young lad like Rudy see in a woman twice his age living alone in a flat with a baby even if I did catch him looking up my skirt once or twice? I like to take off my underwear as soon as I get home. You can't get arrested for that. And I only invited him round after for a cup of tea whenever he was passing out of politeness. I was lonely at the time living so far from home. I never expected him to turn up the next day and for months after that. It was his father who grew suspicious and stopped him from coming over. But of course it didn't stop there.

I received a phone call from my father telling me he'd been arrested later that week. He said he'd been charged with indecent exposure and had been placed on remand at Wormwood Scrubs awaiting bail but that I shouldn't worry about it as his solicitor was organising his release. Perhaps David had reported him after all because he'd been caught in his favourite haunt back up in the woods flashing himself to an undercover policewoman. He didn't sound anything like Otto on the phone and spoke so softly I had to strain my ears as if he was calling from halfway round the world. He appeared frail and frightened but I thought I detected something else in his voice. It wasn't so much acceptance as relief.

"I need help," he admitted for the first time.

His words echoed through me. I realised that even now I hadn't fully accepted the seriousness of his condition. That I still believed it was more to do with vanity than degeneracy. That he was a joke figure rather than a threat. This was Otto the flaunter not a beast who terrorised women. The man who could twitch his penis like a puppet in front of his daughter as if it was talking. But of course there must be a reason I had never told anyone that. I'd seen my mother walking around naked too but would Otto have carried on in the same way had she returned? I was starting to think the situation of my sick older brother being in Sweden had brought about some sort of dormant devilment in him and that my audience alone had been enough at the time.

"Why do you do it?" I asked, thinking about those times. "What are you hoping will happen? Did you want her to touch it? Did you want Susan to touch it? Did you want me to touch it?"

"Don't talk that way, Sally," he quietly reprimanded me.

"I don't understand you," I felt myself wanting to cry. "I don't understand why you have done this to us. To me."

"I know. I'm sorry, Sally," he said. "I'm sorry for everything."

"Jesus fucking Christ," I breathed, feeling suddenly overwhelmed. "Do you know what you've done? I mean, really?"

"Sally?"

"I fucking hate you," I whispered, as the tears began to spill.

"Sally? I heard about the boy."

"Huh? What boy?"

"Josh. The boy that slept at your house. Was that anything to do with you?"

"Fuck you, Otto," I answered tiredly.

"Megan writes to me. You know. Email. She's pretty concerned."

My tears dried up almost instantly. Cold fear began to seep through my stomach.

"What are you talking about?"

He sighed and a long silence followed.

"You know why she's split up with Alfie?"

"You'd better shut your fucking mouth right now, Otto. You hear me? You better shut that fucking cake-hole or you can fucking rot in prison you dirty fucking pervert!"

"She says Alfie told her you've been behaving inappropriately with him."

"Here we fucking go again."

"Of course, she doesn't want to believe it or any of the other rumours."

"La, la, la, la, la, la, la. I'm not even listening to you, Otto. I'm putting the phone down."

"I think you need help too."

"Go wave your talking dick in front of a prison guard. I hope it gets bitten off you filthy, disgusting cunt!"

"It's my fault. It's all my fault, I know. And now I have a suicide on my conscience."

"What?" I raged. "You wait until you get caught by a policewoman at the age of seventy to have a fucking epiphany and now you want to take me down with you? Go fuck yourself Otto you fucking disgusting freak! The kid was being abused by his stepfather. End of story. I know. I've met him. He's a fucking disgusting pikey pig."

"I don't know, Sally. I've got a bad feeling about this. I didn't like the set up there when I turned up. Then there was that message painted on the door. And now...now Alfie is saying this. You shouldn't be putting yourself in these situations. You know that."

"Let me tell you something about, Alfie," I took a deep breath. "I caught him spying on me getting undressed and now he's embarrassed about it. A bit like Megan walking in on you with the toilet door unlocked. You want to explain that to me, Otto? Eh? You want to explain to the police about exposing yourself to my under-age daughter?"

"You know I would never do that."

"You did it to a four-year-old boy."

"That was an acc-"

"YOU DID IT TO ME!" I roared.

"I...I don't remember much about that."

"Really? How convenient."

"What I mean is I'm not sure your memories are the same as mine."

"Either it's all your fault or it isn't, Otto."

"I meant about your brother and your mother. We should have gone with them. I know that now. I should have taken you back with them. We should have all stayed together as a family. We should have been with Freddy. I don't know how I let it happen. I was a coward. I hid behind my business and the fact you were in a good school and some blind, stupid belief that Freddy would pull out of it even though the doctors had said that he wouldn't. I just let Ingrid deal with it. I let you grow up without a mother. I wasn't equipped to be a father. Not when I was left to my own devices. It's more than what you just think. So much more."

"It still wouldn't have stopped you. Not in the end. It's time would have come."

"I'm talking about you as well as me. I'm talking about both of us. That's why I don't understand why you would put yourself at risk again when you have everything to lose. It's not the real you, Sally. I've always believed that. It's not the real you. I'm so sorry."

Megan hadn't mentioned her break-up with Alfie and I was reluctant to ask about her correspondence with my father in case the subject came up so I thought it best to ignore her recent moodiness in the hope it would all blow over. What had really happened between Alfie and me anyway? Outside of my fantasies of him watching me masturbate on the bed I think he had only once seen me naked when I deliberately dropped my towel coming out of the bathroom while he'd been sitting on the sofa waiting for Megan to come home. I squealed and laughed to get his attention and brought my arms across my breasts but I still had to turn and bend over to pick it up. I didn't have to see to feel him looking and after that when I would kiss and hug him hello and goodbye I could always feel his manhood when pressing up hard. Sometimes the kiss lingered and if he pulled away it was just because he was nervous about Megan walking in. You would have thought he was married to her the way he tried to resist all the time and I very much doubt my daughter could give the boy a better blowjob. Probably he'd turn out to be gay or something.

As distractions go the night Geena took her revenge on Kenny couldn't have been more auspiciously timed. Megan burst through the door in a flurry calling my name but by then I had already been alerted to the sounds of sirens which wasn't uncommon on the estate and usually a time when I closed the curtains and kept to myself.

"What's going on?" I asked.

"You've got to come," she said, sounding just like her old self. "It's Kenny. Geena's stabbed him."

We emerged out onto the communal green along with everyone else. It was dusk and a whirlitzer of lights played along the high-rise walls and shadowed warrens of the surrounding blocks. Those with a prime view were gathering on their illuminated balconies exchanging gossip with neighbours down below. Voices echoed everywhere. The stairwell leading up to Geena's flat had been cordoned off with incident tape. A small film crew were already setting up. Police cars continued to descend upon the place with sirens blaring. I noted that some of the officers were armed. There was a rumour flooding through the gathering that Kenny was already dead. Could it be true, I kept hoping? I had lived night after restless night since the wake in dread of what he expected from me. Had thought about fleeing back to my father. Starting a new life in Sweden. If it hadn't been for Megan I might have already gone. I'd like to think a guardian angel was looking on but I doubt they watch over someone like me unless I was considered the lesser evil. I began to see it as my absolute last chance. That Otto was right. I needed help. Something that I had ignored from the moment I saw David undressed. How could I let it go on for so long and consume my life to the point I couldn't even have a proper relationship with someone my own age, with shared little dreams of living out a happy existence? I was weak. I was as weak as my father.

Everyone was talking about Josh's suicide. It had all come to a head, they were saying. That Kenny had finally got his comeuppance. "Way to go, Geena!" someone called. Nearby I could overhear a reporter milling through the crowd asking questions with a little recording device in his hand. A Kenny advocate said the police would use any excuse to arrest him and that it was just a domestic and none of their business. Another said they were always arguing. The reporter asked if anyone knew what the row was about and as he neared I felt myself shrink behind Megan. Then a young female voice piped up and said Josh hadn't taken his own life because of Kenny but that it was all over a girl. I couldn't see who it was. I didn't want to. Megan was scowling in the direction of the reporter and appeared almost on the verge of saying something herself. She gave me a quick glance as if irritated by my studying her.

"Why don't you just go, Mum," she suddenly said.

As much as I wanted to I didn't know what she meant by that so I just shook my head and continued to hide in the darkness. If people were saying stuff I needed to hear it and get my story straight.

"Go, Mum," she insisted.

And then all at once I realised that my daughter was trying to protect me. She had been exposed to so much recently. Not least of all what she may have witnessed through my behaviour. If I could take it back, I thought. If I could just take it all back. I began to panic that my father had shared everything with her. People who hide things will continue to do so even at the most ridiculous odds of denial. Until they can't even see it anymore. Alfie had told Megan about me. Kenny knew about my past. Josh's suicide was now rumoured to have been over a girl. And my daughter's new confidante Otto was in prison for exposing himself again. There were only so many fingers that could plug a leaking dyke. Yet still I found myself turning every which way like a cornered rat looking for a way out.

As the reporter approached I whispered in Megan's ear that I would see her back home. She nodded distractedly and I heard her immediately go into a diatribe with him about how she was Josh's best friend and that he had been forced to stay at our home because of his stepfather's violence. I couldn't help but smile to myself as I hurried away. As much as Megan was trying to defend and help our cause she was only drawing more attention to the fact. It was starting to feel like the day they came and arrested me over David. I tried to end it. I truly did. I told Michael and Mary I couldn't give their son extra tuition anymore because I was planning to move away. I applied for other positions in different parts of the country with the honest intention of making a fresh start. But the other boy who I later learned had been blackmailing David into having a threesome was still out there. I couldn't shut down or control that. I didn't even know who he was at the time. In the end it didn't matter. The whole school new by then, of course. Even the headmaster who had had already accepted my resignation but by the way once made an improper pass at me when I was up for promotion as year head. No one wanted a scandal. I still believe David would have kept it to himself with no real harm done. In those days my stats where that of a centrefold. Other members of staff never stopped hitting on me. Married, young, old, and in one case, female, who only in my first year followed me into a toilet cubicle and asked if she could lick my clit. It was a young boy's dream to be introduced to sex by someone like me, wasn't it? Any grown man would admit that. I don't care what denomination he is. I could have told Mary a few things about Michael when I was just a young girl babysitting their older son, Mark. He couldn't stop with the innuendoes. But I never did. Maybe that's why he turned up at my trial every day giving me the glare of Mephistopheles and preached the Good Book all the time. Who knew what else he got up to? Like father like son. Probably he thought he was going to be part of my testimony. But it was too late by then. I could have been making anything up.

I couldn't remember leaving the television on. But it was the first thing I heard when I opened the door. Also, I wouldn't have left it on a news channel. I was always scared to hear what had happened in the world which is why I religiously watched all the soaps. But it suddenly sounded like I was in two places at once. Everything was as I had left it. Low-lit and with scented candles burning. Except that the local news channel was reporting on the very thing that was happening outside and Geena was sitting on my sofa, her T-shirt and shorts covered in blood. My first instinct was that she should have got it on the furniture.

"I used Josh's key," she said, continuing to stare at the television.

I could only blink and shake myself. She looked like she'd staggered from a multiple car pile-up. I was on the verge of suggesting an ambulance but then I realised she wasn't bleeding from anywhere. That it was all Kenny's blood.

"They're outside," I pointed towards the door, not really knowing who I was talking about. "They're everywhere."

"I know," she nodded.

"They'll find you," I said.

"I know. It's alright. I just came to talk."

Geena lifted her head and smiled pleasantly. She had the same pasty features as Josh. Her hair was always pulled back into a ponytail. She could have done more for herself but she had that worn-down look that a lot of women on the estate had. I'd always thought her fairly plain and unremarkable but something was shining inside her. She seemed calm and detached. Almost serene.

I edged towards the other end of the sofa and sat down.

"Geena, what happened?" I said.

She shrugged and began hugging herself.

"It's over," she said.

I nodded and listened and waited.

"Didn't you ever just want for all the shit to be over?"

"Yes," I said.

"I mean, really?" she looked at me.

"Yes."

"This place," she said. "This world. This fucking shitty world. They dumped us like trash. You, me, Josh. Like human landfill. None of this would have happened where I was. Really. I didn't realise it then but I was happy."

I wanted to agree. I wanted to feel the same. But it was her bad luck she'd been moved to the same estate as me. Hers and Josh's and perhaps Kenny's, too.

"It wasn't much but it was a community. We all came from the same place. There was a strange comfort and safety in that. But this has always felt just like some giant prison to me. And I didn't even do anything wrong."

I knew what she meant. Except that unlike Geena I realised the terms of my sentence.

"You've done a good job on Megan. Do you know there are gangs of men here passing round under-age girls for sex with just the lure of a few treats? Runaways or kids from children's homes or just left to roam the streets. Kids starved of affection. They prey on them with gifts of perfume, alcohol, drugs. Sometimes all it takes is a free McDonald's. Of course, money changes hands. They're called train gangs because the girls just get passed on to the next man. Some of them have had sex with a hundred men before they're even of a legal age. What do you think happens to them? I mean, when they're not wanted anymore? When they realise they've just been used for someone else's own perverted purposes? I thought I was safe with a boy. A decent, kind, hard-working and talented boy like Josh who just liked to draw. The irony is," she said after a long pause, "you look like you wouldn't even hurt a fly."

"Geena," my voice croaked. "It was all just a misunderstanding. A tragic misunderstanding. I didn't know he was spying on me and...and taking pictures and going home and sketching me. I really didn't. There's a faulty latch on my bedroom door and-"

"Did you have sex with my son?" she looked at me sharply.

"No," I reared back and pulled a face.

"What about Alfie?"

"Geena, I don't know what Kenny told you…"

"You'll go away for longer than me. You realise that, don't you? I'm glad Kenny's dead but I want you to suffer."

Her words struck terror through me.

"Megan will have to go into some sort of care. The sort of places Kenny's men prey upon."

"Wait a minute. Kenny's behind the train gangs?"

"He had his eye on Megan for a long time. He just needed some bargaining power. I've saved you a lot of heartache."

"I would have killed him myself," I said. And meant it.

"There's always someone else ready to take over," she warned. "I guess that makes you just like the rest of us now. Living in fear for our children."

"You think I don't care about Megan?"

"Well, you can't do. Can you?" she looked at me openly.

But I hadn't murdered anyone, I thought. It couldn't be proved Josh had committed suicide over me. People were far more likely to believe it had been because of Kenny otherwise why would Geena have killed him? And I assumed Josh's sketches were harmless even if I had posed for him. That there was nothing even remotely erotic about them. As for Alfie, well, it was just his word against mine. And even if they really did want to get into it I always had the excuse of my father's unconventional form of parenthood as a reason for any would-be crimes. Maybe I'd even blocked some stuff out. Even in our last conversation over the phone when he called me from prison Otto was desperate to take the blame for everything. Everything that is except the genetics. Who would want to admit they had passed on something as insidious as that to their own child?

It's not the real you, Sally. I've always believed that.

But he was seventy-years-old now and the regrets were inevitably starting to pile up when he of all should know. You don't just become. You are.

FLOWER GIRL

Recent statistics say among others that you have more chance of having identical quadruplets (1 in 15 million) or being attacked by a shark (1 in 11.5 million) than you have of winning the lottery.

Ben had never bought a ticket in his life but he knew what one looked like. So when a woman he recognized as a visitor to the care home came out of the supermarket encumbered with her two demanding young children and giving off that same sassy little wiggle in her strapless top and tight-fitting shorts he tried not to be obvious about any eye contact as she hurriedly stuffed the ticket into her purse. The younger of the kids, a girl sitting in the trolley seat tried snatching the little pink slip from her mother for a game, causing the woman to scream out in admonishment before glaring at any would-be interfering onlookers, the glint of her nose piercing seeming to send off an extra warning. She saved a particularly spiteful look for Ben when she caught him staring and appeared to grab the older child's hand, a boy, a little tighter and pull him to her side. But the compassion in Ben's eyes only seemed to make her falter. The ticket suddenly becoming a source of apparent embarrassment to her and not the trivial, spur-of-the-moment purchase brought about by another rollover campaign that anyone else might consider it to be. *People like you don't win the lottery. People like you and me don't win the lottery,* she read his thoughts entirely before tearing her gaze from him. There was an air of desperation about the way she was trying to keep the ticket out of eyes view. As if she had been caught stealing. As if he had interrupted her rifling through someone's belongings.

Ben knew what that felt like.

Even so, the Samaritan in him felt inclined to follow her just in case she needed assistance with her shopping. He could tell she had her hands full. That she looked under stress. She kept trying to hitch her handbag over her bare shoulder while negotiating the shopping cart down a kerb, barking at the boy to keep hold of her hand. Tattooed down the length of her thin right bicep was the silhouette of a flower the type of which you saw at funerals. Ben kept his distance until she arrived at her car. An old green, two-door Clio. She bundled the boy into the back between the flip-down seat and then tried hoisting the girl from the cart while holding it all at the same time. The bags spilled over with family provisions. Kids' cereals. Fizzy drinks. Crisps. Oven chips. A sealed tray of dog food. The cheaper end of the market. The opportunist in Ben hesitated. Trying not to draw attention to himself. Feeling like one of the big cats stalking in the long grass of some African plain. It would have to be a slick move. With little cause for her to remember or take in any details. He held back just enough as she bent over and lifted the last shopping bag into the boot, her clinging pink terrycloth shorts exclusively capturing the peach-curved shape of her buttocks and revealing another ornately flowered tattoo at the base of her spine. For a moment he felt his heart stop when the rubbish in the bottom of the cart began to flutter and lift in the breeze. Old elongated receipts stirred. An empty packet of *Walker's* cheese and onion tried to take off and fly. As she turned to find a trolley park Ben swept up her beside and took it away all in one movement.

"Finished with that?" he smiled pleasantly.

A flicker of confused recognition crossed her face but he turned away instantly and began walking ahead without looking back, waiting to hear her call. But she never did. Keeping his cool and for the purpose of the security cameras Ben made his way into the supermarket and did a little shopping of his own which had been his intention anyway, but never enough to warrant a trolley. He ate for one.

Once back outside he was still half-expecting to see the woman come running up in a whirlwind of panic, red-faced and tearful, and he, pre-prepared to play the innocent hero. Her saviour, in effect. Her superhero.

That might have been a better way to get to know her.

But the coast remained gloriously clear to the point the criminal in him cautiously began to break into a casual whistle as he ambled along and stopped to park the trolley before leaning in to reach for his shopping bag.

Then, and only then, under the protection of the glass trolley station did his thin, long, spider-fingered hand scuttle and seize upon the purse he'd seen her drop and that had remained half-hidden all the while amongst the litter.

The year before there had been a scandal at Acorn Springs care home that resulted in the place nearly being closed down. The case related to ten residents between the ages of 85 and 100 suffering from dementia or other long-standing mental health issues who were left lying for hours on painful bed sores and fed on a diet of mainly porridge. A series of three deaths over the course of two months prompted an investigation and it was concluded that the residents died of causes consistent with the effects of severe neglect. Though the manager and owner (who was not brought to court and spent most of his time at his house in the Caribbean) denied any wrongdoing three night staff nurses admitted to the charges, conceding that their fitness to practice had been impaired. Subsequent inspections by regulators had highlighted poor record keeping but there were no more concerns about maltreatment.

Lily only came across the information weeks after committing her grandmother to the home, but by then it was too late for any reservations. Her meetings with the newly-employed manager had been positive and friendly. Lily even got a good feel about the place when being shown around. Sitting in the middle of the expansive parquet-floored entrance hall there was a white grand piano almost magically illuminated in glittering dust modes by an overhead skylight and when Lily explained that her grandmother had once been a concert pianist Margo, the manager, had clapped her hands in exaltation, going on to explain that the home had a number of instruments that the residents were encouraged to play, but apart from the piano Lily had yet to see one. It didn't matter. She hadn't heard Nana play since she was a child and as her grandmother's condition was now lending towards stage three Alzheimer's Lily doubted if she could even remember where middle 'C' was most of the time. 'Concert pianist' had been an exaggeration anyway to say the least. It wasn't until Lily was older that she realised Nana's only real claim to fame was that she had played in the local community chamber orchestra performing in the church halls of neighbouring towns under the 'stage name', Poppy, a pet name coined by Lily's grandfather at an early stage of their relationship because of Nana's rosy red cheeks. Her birth name was Edith which she despised and far preferred the diminutive 'Edie'. "Nevertheless," Lily's grandfather was apt to remind her, "Poppy really is the star of the group. One or two I could mention can barely blow a candle out let alone a woodwind," he bellowed laughter at his own joke which he was often apt to do. With his unconventional shoulder-length curly grey hair and big silver beard he began to physically expand into a larger-than-life Santa Claus figure down the years and Lily adored him.

Despite her ostensibly happy home life however from a very early age Lily had been prone to embellishment. She was always trying to impress and uphold the family name which could turn harmless imaginative exaggeration into bald-faced lies. Something that she earned a reputation for when growing up. Perhaps it all started when her single-parent mother had happily handed her two-and-a-half-year child over to Lily's maternal grandparents to bring up before going off to live another life in Spain, turning her back not just on Lily but her parents too as contact between them all became less and less frequent down the years. As for Lily's father he remained a mystery. Her mother had once attended a music festival over a long weekend only to discover a few months later she was pregnant.

When Grandpa Fats died her mother was uncontactable. Lily had lost interest long before and Poppy just found her absence harder and harder to explain. It was Lily's grandparents who had brought her up. Despite the family musical pretensions Grandpa's name paid no relevance to the jazz and blues geniuses of yesteryear, even though Lily thought he not only secretly enjoyed the association but grew into it as Poppy became more locally known. His birth name was Fitzhugh but the baby name 'Fats' had stuck because as an early learning child it was the nearest he could get to pronouncing it. Fitzhugh and Edith. Fitz and Edie. Fats and Poppy. They must have had a hard time of it just when they thought they'd got their own daughter off their hands. But all Lily remembered was fun and happiness in an eccentric environment. Outside of their passion for music Grandpa Fats had held a number of positions in some of the biggest and most eminent gardens in the south of England, and Poppy loved her job as a primary school teacher and eventual deputy head. In those days they were regarded upon as the golden age silver-haired couple you saw in retirement ads, the downside being that it only took an outsider to remind Lily it wasn't the most natural of upbringings which is when the lies would start to creep in. Inevitably, questions led to the whereabouts of her mother and father. A subject Lily grew up trying to avoid because the truth was she just didn't know and to admit to that made her feel both hurt and ashamed so she found herself making up all manner of stories just to avoid the fact. It seemed her mother had inherited a double-dose of Fats and Poppy's free-spiritedness, paying scant regard for her daughter's wellbeing and continuing to do so with carefree abandon. To this very day Lily didn't know if she was dead or alive.

With Lily's predicament growing evermore desperate it seemed imperative that she should get Poppy into the home. There had been a space and it was only a mile from where Lily lived and she couldn't continue checking in on her grandmother four times a day with two young children to look after and provide for. A percentage of the fees were funded by an NHS contribution scheme but Lily still had to find the rest of the money. It was that or hand her over to the complete care of the authorities which meant Poppy might not only be placed in a different town or even county but subjected to who knows what kind of treatment with all the horror stories going around? Care homes were being shut down all over the country and for far worst crimes of neglect and abuse than Acorn Springs had been found guilty of.

But it still didn't stop her going in once a day to visit and check on her grandmother before going to work for the rest of the day. Lily would look for bed sores and signs of undernourishment and poor health. She was in constant contact with the head nurse regarding Poppy's medication, hygiene and diet. And unlike many other homes a GP made regular weekly visits to check on residents with even the slightest ailment. Lily liked to think she had the staff on their toes or that Acorn Springs' level of care had upped its game since last year's investigation. Probably they were on a final warning or something. Lily found no cause for complaint. What she hadn't been prepared for was the sudden and rapid decline of her grandmother's mental illness and in that respect it was sometimes hard to tell if Poppy was happy there or not.

When he first came to see her he had called himself Clark. This wasn't unusual. Punters often had good reasons to hide their identity. Mainly because they were married or in long-term relationships. She of course used an alias for different reasons and went by the name of Azalea just to keep it in the family. "Paying to have cold and clinical sex under false names is a strange way of getting to know someone," he had said after the facades had been dropped and they had begun dating. By dating she meant it became less about the loveless act he spoke about and more a need for mutual companionship and - she hated admitting to this, his money. She didn't mind having sex with him but by continuing the practice outside of their relationship just made her indifferent and unresponsive to his affections. All men were the same in the end anyway. You just had to give them what they needed. So she lied. Something she was good at. She lied the way she had lied to him the first time. And all the other times he had come to see her. Making him feel special. Making him feel like he was her favourite customer. That she thought about him when he was gone. That he wasn't just any old trick. She lied the way she lied each and every day she went into work. The real trick being that he never saw through it.

That said he was a kind and generous and decent guy who because of that could make her feel bad about herself without even trying. She had been able to move her hours because he worked at night but which also meant he was happy to help with the kids and the school run and the housework and walking the dog. His job intrigued her. He couldn't say much about it he told her as he was sworn by the Official Secrets Act but he managed what was called a 'ghost building' should disaster strike.

"What sort of building?" she wanted to know.

"Huge," he said. "Fully equipped and already to go in the event of an emergency relocation."

"So it's a government building," she said.

He couldn't say.

"What kind of disaster?"

"Falling aircraft," he shrugged. "Chemical or nuclear pollution, disease, but most of all the threat of terrorism."

"I had no idea there were such places," she pondered.

"Planning means surviving," he said, as if the phrase had been drummed into him.

He was obviously smarter than he appeared. The only thing that didn't make sense was that he still lived with his stroke-ridden mother and who by his own admittance was inevitably becoming the carer of. She certainly knew what that felt like so at least they had something in common. Everything else can wait, he had said. The big house, the flashy cars. Even though it was hard to see him with either and that she would sometimes have liked nothing more than to give him a radical make-over. To throw out those geeky T-shirts he sometimes favoured endorsed with the sort of comic book figure branded upon her four-year-old son's lunchbox. *Transformers, X-Men, Spider-Man.* He was thin and reedy and looked starved of Vitamin D. His jeans hung off his paddle-flat arse revealing the washed-out waistband of his threadbare underpants. Even to change his hair from that oily schoolboy side-parting might represent some modicum of improvement. But his answer was always the same. Prosaic and unambitious for someone so young. The answer of a person set in their ways for life. A creature of habit. He said that he didn't have to dress up or think about his appearance for the work he did. What happened to planning means surviving, she thought? Anyone with an outlook like that didn't have a future despite what he said about big houses and flashy cars. And yet she couldn't help but think about his job as, if not slightly glamourous in its mystery, then almost certainly hugely responsible. Sometimes she genuinely wondered what they saw in him. Whoever 'they' were.

"How does someone even get a job like that?" she wanted to know.

"I literally applied to MI5," he laughed as if embarrassed. "The process took up to about a year. It was all very clandestine. They look into your complete family history. There were tests after tests. You were only allowed to tell one close relative or friend."

"You sound like a secret agent. You're not a spook, are you, 'Clark'?"

She liked to tease him about that after she had explained the connection to the flower girls behind her working name but he on the other hand was a little less forthcoming. You could have called yourself anything. 'Dave', 'Bob'. Why *Clark*, she had insisted upon knowing? Is that your code name?

And then one day watching a Superman film with her son she suddenly worked it out and spent the rest of the day laughing to herself whenever she thought about it.

"Just think of me as a glorified janitor," he would reply whenever it came up. If he wasn't sworn to secrecy she might have got the feeling he was avoiding the subject which would have raised her suspicions. But he was good at self-deprecation, if, in fact, that was a good thing. Sometimes she thought that if she didn't know him better, if he hadn't set up a monthly direct debit to help her out, given her access to his credit card details and seen him write her cheques without batting an eye she might not have believed any of it.

There was always that frightening moment when Poppy woke up and she didn't recognise her surroundings. Sometimes it could be a slow and sleepy realisation that she was not where her mind told her she was. Other times a sudden, heart-stopping jolt from sleep. As if she had woken up on a train. In a way the fear was a good thing. Because her instant reaction was to tell herself *not* to be afraid. That this happened every time she'd fall asleep if only for a nap and that it was just a process of reconstruction. *Think Poppy*, she would tell herself. Then everything would start to fall into place and she would calmly try and go through the sequence of remembering and quell the fluttering in her chest and throat. Fats wasn't lying in the bed next to her. That was a long time ago. He hadn't lay next to her in… But it was no use obsessing about numbers or dates. She always awoke in the past.

Trying to summon up what she'd forgotten just made it worse and even more upsetting because Poppy was made to think about her condition. Not that she wanted to forget about that. Being aware of what was happening to her was vitally important. She must hold on to the knowledge of her disease for as long as she could. It may have occurred more than once but when the fog came, when she hadn't the ability to realise what was happening to her and why, it felt like she was being smothered.

Worst of all were the times she would be startled by total strangers speaking her name or moving her around or taking her blood pressure. She couldn't keep up with the staff attending her so would just stay silent and pretend until it wasn't till after they'd left that she began to recall them from the day before. Sometimes she confused them with the flower girls. Marigold and Lily. It made her wary that so many visitors to her room seemed to know her name and so much about her when she spent half the time wondering who they were and what they were doing there.

"Hello, Poppy," one of them was saying to her now. "It's me, Colin. I've been hearing all about you from one of the other residents. You're famous in these parts I'm told."

Poppy looked around the room without moving her head. It was night time. She complained all the time to Lily about being woken at night but Lily said it was necessary to keep her from getting bed sores.

"She says she played in the same orchestra as you, is that right?" he said, holding Poppy's wrist and checking her pulse.

Poppy nodded, but only at the fact she had played in an orchestra.

After he left Poppy lay there a long while trying to remember who he was. Had he said his name was Keith? It was confusing at night because that's when all the support workers came in. They woke you up in your dreams or when you were drifting peacefully through an old memory. Poppy had been thinking about when one of the flower girls was just a toddler. Fitz had at first coined the term when naming their own child after a flower which he had absolutely insisted upon. Then of course their daughter did the same with hers creating a floral lineage that excited them all even if Poppy's real name was only Edith, which she hated to the point of family secrecy. Did she just call him Fitz? Huh. She hadn't used that name in a long time. Now Poppy prompted herself to remember the flower girls for different reasons. When she confused one with the other she told herself M not only stood for Marigold but Mother. L stood for Lily and 'little', the younger of the two. Marigold was Lily's mother which meant she was also Poppy's daughter. Perhaps the confusion lay in all of them being named after flowers and it hadn't been such a good idea after all. Or the fact she had brought Lily Little up as her own. But she was satisfied the memory had been of Marigold playing in a sandpit Fats had built out of old railway sleepers at the back of the garden with them both looking on from the patio and sharing a bottle of wine. Rising up from the pit were tiered flower beds that Marigold spent most of her childhood cultivating through the seasons. It had been such a success that Fats volunteered to build one at the school Poppy had been working in at the time much to the delight of all the staff and parents and children. Poppy had never felt so proud. She had been lucky to marry someone so compatible and with whom to have spent so many long and loyal years together. There had been many evenings like that sitting outside with a drink and taking in the splendour and sheer majesty of Fats' horticultural eye. They both enjoyed the theatre and going to concerts but rarely entertained. Not even with other members of the orchestra. Poppy had been on the point of dozing when she felt herself being stirred by a strange voice. When they woke you too quickly like that the memory could dissolve as rapidly as a dream into a kaleidoscope of life fragments. The way they say it is when you're drowning.

The support workers weren't allowed to administer any medicine. She didn't know how she knew that but it seemed important not to forget it in case one of them tried to. They were only there to check your vital statistics and make a record of the results but Poppy had heard complaints that some of them couldn't even do that properly. Consequently, she regarded them all with suspicion. Colin, Keith, or whoever.

Everyone has a story. This was Lily's. One early summer day at the age of sixteen she was supposed to be playing netball for her school in the afternoon when the match was cancelled due to their opponents going down with a sudden bout of food poisoning after their lunch break. She and the girls were already on the team bus when they got the news so the teacher offered to drop any of them home who lived en route back to the school. It was that last image of seeing her friends and teacher waving from the school bus as she entered her grandparents' house that her memory insisted on summoning up whenever she thought about what happened. As if it was trying to tell her something still. Had she a hankering to stay on the bus that day and make the normal journey home with her friends and so would never have witnessed what she had? A life-changing discovery so shocking to her almost virtuous pubescent mind it sickened her to this very day. She had been brought up by her grandparents after all. There life was a simple, orderly old-fashioned one of regular meal times and limited television and reading hours and strict bedtimes that would overrun with the most wonderfully animated stories told by Grandpa Fats from her mother's very own childhood book collection and that would leave Lily giggling or dreaming or half-scared out of her wits going to sleep curled up in the comfort of her clean-smelling bed every night. It was easy now to think she had been struck by a sense of foreboding. Everything about the day seemed unnaturally perfect looking back. It had been a warm, still afternoon. She'd gotten off early. She was looking forward to some chocolate chip ice cream from out of the freezer. She could still hear the buzz of bees around the lavender pots sentried either side of the front door. Could still see and smell the herbaceous border along the drive. A riot of flame-lit red and yellow Rudbeckia. She remembered everything before as if she'd been saying goodbye to it. Which she did of course. She was still innocent then. Nothing would ever be the same again.

Grandpa Fats had been working an early shift that week so Lily was cautious of letting herself in quietly lest he should have fallen asleep on the settee. If so she would surprise him with a cup of tea and slice of Victoria sponge made by Nana and she the previous weekend which was just another of the many traditions Lily loved about her alternative upbringing. She even waited until the school bus had pulled away, silently urging her friends to stop their raucous. But as soon as she entered the house she knew something wasn't right. She could hear a murmur from the kitchen that sounded like someone was in pain and Lily's first thought was that her grandfather had fallen. He was always doing odd jobs around the house and very often on step ladders. But a deeper instinct held her there in the hallway. Not daring to reveal herself but without knowing why. Everything about the house was as it should have been. Poppy kept a tidy home. Fats tended the garden of course but the house was her domain. The carpet still had brush marks where it had been hoovered. A vase of freshly cut peonies sat on the telephone table, the day's post propped between awaiting the incision of the gleaming silver letter opener that lay beside. The only thing that didn't belong there were the noises. Lily's sixteen-year-old mind couldn't put an act to the sounds she was hearing. There were two people behind the frosted glass door of the kitchen which was slightly ajar. In the gloom of the hallway the door was illuminated with sunlight from the kitchen windows beyond and from where she could just make out the shape of two figures in close contact with each other. She knew it must be her grandfather even though she had yet to recognise his voice in all the wet muffled slobbering invading her ears. It sounded like a big dog was in there eating its dinner. Lily wanted to cry out for them to stop. To not make her see. But before she knew it she was slowly pushing open the door and peering in. Grandpa Fats was leaning against the kitchen side with his head thrown back and his eyes squeezed shut. His hands gripped the edge of the work surface. Tense and white-knuckled. He hadn't even washed from work because there was still dirt beneath his fingernails. Something Poppy would never abide. His chequered work shirt with its leather elbow patches was undone to reveal his big Father Christmas belly and tumbling mat of curly grey hair. The same belly he had allowed her to climb and play on not only as a proper granddaughter but his own child in effect and not some intruder into his secret world as she then felt. Lily could feel herself wanting to cry. Her life as she knew it was sinking in front of her. It had taken years to understand her errant mother was never coming back. What was she being forced to confront now? It felt like the ground was opening up beneath her feet and she was slip-sliding towards a dark portal of unwanted images and grown-up's knowledge. Without knowing it she had felt safe and protected in that clean, neat-as-a-pin, efficiently well-regulated house. There had been nothing more solid-based. No one as dependable as Fats and Poppy. The happily-married golden age couple.

Her grandfather's pants and trousers were nestled around his ankles. Knelt in front of him was an old woman Lily had never seen before. She had discarded her top onto the shiny tiled floor that had no doubt been mopped by Poppy that very morning and her flaccid breasts with overly large nipples the colour of old coffee-stains spilled over the cups of her powder-blue bra. They seemed oblivious to the fact the back door yawned open to the delightful cacophony of birdsong that on any other day her charlatan grandfather might have encouraged her to step out and observe or listen to. The exotically-coloured finches and tits and warblers encouraged into the garden with their many tables and trays and hanging perch rings. She had learnt so much from him. It had been her duty to fill up those bird stations every morning before school with nuts and sunflower seeds that many an acrobatic and roguishly-natured grey squirrel could devour in a day. Poppy had been too house-proud to own a pet but outside was like Lily's personal menagerie. Seeing that little vista through the doorway would stay with her forever. As if she was about to be taken away to a place and knowing she would never be coming back. The raised crazy-pave patio where she had once rode her tricycle and its panoply of pots and troughs over-spilling with geraniums and bergonia and lobelia and other summer bedding plants. The His 'n Hers striped weathered deckchairs that had remained outside since the weekend. Yellow one Nana's. Blue one Gramps. And Grandpa Fats' immaculately rolled emerald lawn with its bountiful multi-coloured borders that throughout her entire childhood she had assisted in attending.

It had been the old woman's low manly voice Lily had heard all the while. Groaning and moaning as she twisted and tugged and feasted upon her grandfather's enormously erect penis.

She had never told anyone that before. Not even her children's fathers. Not even Poppy. Especially not Poppy. But with her constant teasing about calling him Clark he caught her off-guard one day with a question he'd appeared to be thinking about for a long while.

"So why didn't you carry on the tradition?"

She'd known what he'd meant immediately. She had been half- expecting it and had been asked the same thing a few times in the past when the subject of the flower girls came up. Lily had deliberately sought an androgynous name and so had called her daughter Charley. She hadn't even wanted a girl. Or even a child in the second case.

"From a very early age I made up my mind. It was going to be a surprise. When my mum was around I had these great memories of Grandpa sweeping us up in his big arms, Nana and me and my Mum. 'My beautiful bouquet!' he would call us. And snuffle his nose into our necks as if we really were a big bunch of flowers. Through his knowledge I of course grew to know a lot about plants. So I had a plan that when I got married and had a baby girl I was going to call her Honeysuckle."

He nodded but appeared dissatisfied with that.

"So why call yourself Azalea now?"

She hesitated because she knew it would lead to the story she had just shared with him. The story she had never told a single soul about.

"To deflower myself and to continue to deflower myself," she shrugged simply and stared stonily ahead. "Above all the acid-lovers were his favourite. In particular Azaleas."

Among his few attributes he was a good listener. Women like that, she told him. As if she was giving advice for some impending date he was preparing to go on. She realised that she was always trying to let him down gently and spoke frivolously about their future together as if it was all just a passing phase. As if to warn him it wasn't forever. A woman with two kids? A working prostitute? Surely he could do better. But with each derisory comment she would confuse him by accepting his acts of help and kindness and overwhelming generosity, but most significantly, of course, the obligation she felt to give in to him for sex. She knew more than most that you shouldn't play with people's emotions when it came to that. Bad stuff could come out of that. It didn't help that in their first meeting he'd confided in her he had no real experience of carnal knowledge. That's how he put it. And so, seeing a regular in her midst, she had made sure to give him a good time in order to keep him coming back. She could never have envisaged them in a relationship back then. If that's what it really was. Sometimes she felt like the bully. The frustrated adult. She tried to separate herself from him when they were out even though to all intents and purposes they looked like any other young family. That wasn't right. But he had started to visit two to three times a week and never failed to make a point of asking for her. He was always loaded with cash and tipped her handsomely. Then when he told her about his job she grew more curious, suspecting him to be a dark horse of sorts when she had taken it for granted he did long shifts in one of the big stores on the nearby retail park where a lot of her clients worked and so could barely afford the money he was laying out. The charge was one hundred pounds for the hour but by then what with all the excessive tipping he was blowing nearly two thousand a month on her.

The next time Lily went to visit her grandmother Margo was waiting to greet her. She was what people meant by calling a woman handsome, Lily supposed. She was tall and big-boned with a prominent nose and a thick head of dark hair styled from another era and that curled at her shoulders. Her eyes were large and made slightly bulbous by her thick-lens, tortoiseshell-framed glasses. Margo wore a lot of costume jewellery and was always in a trouser suit. Today's being a sort of country check. She looked outdoorsy, like she might live on a farm or go riding. She was also very animated which always put Lily slightly on edge. By the very nature of Lily's job she tried not to draw much attention to herself. She never really knew who knew.

Margo's 'office' was a converted space under the large dog-legged staircase leading up from the entrance hall with barely enough room for two. The care home itself was an adjoining of four large Edwardian houses. Where possible most original features had been preserved. Ceiling roses and cornices, picture and dado rails, foot-high skirting etched in detail and huge marble fireplaces were still all intact. It was one of the things that swung it for Lily. It didn't have that clinical purpose-built utility feel where everything felt the same. Its period somehow reflected the residents. Yes, the house had been converted for practical reasons. Health and Safety issues mostly. Fire doors and such. But wherever possible it had also been lovingly and respectfully restored.

"I felt it my duty to tell you that your grandmother has been getting a little agitated at nights," Margo said in a confiding whisper. Margo lifted her eyes to the floor above indicating her grandmother's whereabouts as if she herself might be listening.

"About what?" Lily asked. "Does she say?"

"Does the name Marlene de Carlo mean anything to you?" Margo grinned tightly revealing her horse teeth as if she suspected it might be a sensitive issue. She began to tiptoe around and clear a space appearing to try and not make a noise. Her desk was just a bit of work surface cluttered in paper and files. There were two office chairs. One panelled wall was slanted to accommodate the staircase. To increase the claustrophobia Margo also smelt like a cheap perfume rep. "Please, sit," she offered.

Lily pulled her handbag into her chest, blinking in surprise and sitting down slowly. Not just because she had only recently been talking about the woman to Clark but that she couldn't remember when her grandmother had last spoken her name.

"Well…what has she been saying?" Lily asked.

"Poppy has become very agitated that this Marlene woman is staying in the home."

"Well, *is* she?" Lily's expression revealed horror at the thought.

"No, no, of course not," Margo laughed tritely as if that wasn't the point. "May I ask who she is?"

"Marlene? She…she played in the same orchestra as my grandmother," Lily said distractedly, wondering where all this had come from. "I haven't heard the name in years. Not spoken out loud, anyway."

"Well, obviously you are very aware of the stage of Poppy's condition. They can live on many parallels which is where the confusion comes. I just wanted to give you a head's up before you saw her today."

"'L' is for   little," Poppy said, awakening sleepily to feel her granddaughter's hand on hers and sitting at her bedside.

"How are you, Nana?" Lily asked.

Lily had been a good name for her, Poppy smiled inside. She had been born with such a beautiful complexion. Skin the colour of milk and eyes like raisins. She moved without sound as a child and could surprise you many a time when turning around just to find her standing there politely waiting with that little pinched grin. Elegant and delicate and nothing like her mother who had inherited Fitz's wild strawberry blonde curls and watery blue eyes. Marigold had been coltish and wayward from the very beginning. Poppy had known they would have problems further down the line. But Lily. Poppy never saw that one coming. It was a shame how the onset of hormones could change a child's personality so irrevocably. There really could have been no other explanation for it. Her granddaughter's character changed almost overnight. Poppy and Fats agonised many times after over the years. But that one beautiful summer in her budding adolescent prime they lost Lily completely to what even now appeared to be some sort of other body inhabitant they had never been exposed to before. An alter-ego. A manifest demon inside her.

Lily gently lifted the bedclothes and did her usual inspections. Checking for bedsores. She stood up and looked around the room. There was a fresh jug of water by the bedside. Everything was neat and clean. She moved to the window and let in a little more light through the blinds. She hesitated upon bringing up the subject of Marlene for fear of upsetting her grandmother and putting something inside her head that may have already gone away. Maybe she'd had a dream.

"'L' is for Lily," Poppy said.

"That's right, Nana," Lily looked over her shoulder and smiled sweetly.

"'M' is for Marigold and…mother."

"Huh, debatable," Lily uttered and moved to the little dresser where she noticed one of her grandmother's photograph albums had been taken out of its place in the drawer. Such mementoes were encouraged along with all number of things sentimental to the residents. The woman in the adjoining room who, like Poppy, had also been a teacher had her children's early primary school drawings dating back fifty years taped to her walls and in all probability could name half the pupils in her class. But it was the seemingly absent-minded ritual of making notes to remind yourself of what you needed to do in the days ahead or forgetting where your car was parked or being unable to remember what you did the week before that was the start of things.

"'A' is for…Azalea."

Lily frowned and turned around. For a strange moment she thought her grandmother was going to echo her thoughts and say 'Alzheimer's'. Sometimes just the thought of Poppy's condition could send shivers through her. It must be like falling backwards into an abyss.

"That's right, Nana," she felt herself falter. "That was Grandpa's favourite, wasn't it?"

Poppy's mouth appeared to be trying to work. Lily could see she was getting visibly agitated. Her grandmother's hands were worrying above the bedclothes. There had been a shift in her pale blue eyes. Lily moved quickly to her side and tried to calm her. Brushing at her forehead. There was a point where she could bring her grandmother back into focus or that terrible lost look took over when she became unreachable. What sometimes worked was to go back out of the room and start the whole conversation again verbatim. As if she had learnt a script but only so far. What's the next line, Nana? Can you remember? Lily had heard stories about sitting by the bedside of loved ones dying from organ failure. The systematic shut down of the body and the horrifying visual experience of seeing that person transform into a fading corpse. But seeing her grandmother retreating in such a way. Into an irretrievable shell where she would be locked like a prisoner in some eternal void seemed somehow crueller.

Lily had Poppy's hands squeezed tight in hers. Nodding encouragement as her grandmother's head bobbed and her thin pinched lips trembled.

"What is it, Nana? We were talking about flowers, can you remember?"

Her grandmother gave her a curious sidelong glance that could have been taken for mistrust. An expression Lily had been on the end of once or twice recently. Such a look could be extremely hurtful. As if she didn't even recognise Lily anymore. As if her grandmother's last impressions would be that of a total stranger by her bedside.

"Demon child," Poppy's mouth tremored as her eyes grew misty. "You broke our hearts. Running away to Spain and leaving us with your demon child."

"Shush, Nana," Lily moved to pour some water.

"Is Marigold here?"

"No, Nana. Here, come on."

Lily helped tip her grandmother's head towards the cup where she sipped at it like a bird.

Poppy laid her head back. Only the day care were allowed to give you medicine, she reminded herself.

"You're not in uniform," she told the nurse. "You shouldn't be in here."

"I'm not a nurse. It's me, Nana. It's Lily."

Poppy lay there scrutinising every feature of the nurse's face. Her name would come back to her once she left the room. Just like when you stop trying to think of a word you couldn't remember. Sometimes she just had to pretend.

"Do you want to watch a little bit of telly, Nana?" Lily asked, trying not to appear upset. She picked up the remote control and went through the channels. Turning her back and wiping at a tear with her sleeve. What upset Lily more than anything was that her grandmother's condition wasn't like any other illness. She was never going to get any better or stabilise or, God forbid, even be put out of her misery. It was just going to get worse until one day Lily would walk in here and her grandmother would be gone. Alive and in the same bed. The same features, the same voice, the same name. Edie. Poppy. Nana. All of them. All of them still living but gone.

The changes started to happen a little while after. Firstly, there had been a problem with his credit. She was ordering some clothes for the kids online when the transaction wouldn't go through. When she confronted him about it he said there had been some fraudulent activity in his account and was awaiting a new card. Then when she did her weekly supermarket shop he told her he didn't have time to draw any cash from the bank. It felt strange having to pay for the shop herself. It wasn't that she couldn't afford it. She'd started to save from the minute she'd met him. But a dark stirring panic lurked somewhere deep in her stomach that she should have become so reliant on him and with it a strange sense of self-loathing. Was he in trouble? Had he blown all his money on her? Had all the talk about the big house and the flashy cars been just casual bravado? Of course, there had been no reason for him to pay for the weekly shopping bill anyway. They didn't live together. He stayed two nights a week at the most. With all the other things he did for her she should have been happy to pay and cook a meal for him a couple of times a week. It made her realise she'd just taken at every opportunity on the assumption it would never last. Who wouldn't? She wasn't stupid. It was his money.

Then he started blaming work commitments for the reason he wasn't able to pick the kids up from school as much anymore or babysit or walk the dog. Something was going on. If he wasn't such a hapless freak she might have thought he'd met someone else. But with that thought in mind she made sure to give him what he wanted the next few times he came round. The same thing that every man wanted. That every customer who came through the door wanted. That even her perverted dirty old man of a grandfather wanted. Men were disgusting.

Even so his behaviour continued. The money dried up. He became more absent. She realised that apart from his phone she had no real access to him. She only knew the area where he lived with his mother and had deliberately never shown any interest in his domestic affairs in case she should get dragged into helping him out the same way he did her. And then of course he wasn't allowed to talk about his work. She had been selfish, she knew. And she would have to hire some help. It had been good while it lasted. But she would miss his support and talking to him. He was the only person she had shared her deepest secrets with.

To this date she hadn't heard from him in weeks.

Someone was in the room again. Poppy held her breath hoping to see a female form in the half-light of the open toilet door but it wasn't. The man was back busying himself at the end of the bed making notes or pretending to. He had on the green smock of the other night staff but there was something different about the way he conducted himself. It was as if he could come and go as he pleased. As if he was in charge. Sometimes he would enter just when another member of staff had left and go through the process of checking her over again.

"Hello, Poppy. It's Carl, remember?"

No, she didn't. She was sure she had never met anyone called Carl in her life.

He pulled up a chair and sat beside her, taking one of her hands in his. They were large and soft and warm as an oven glove.

She could barely make out his features in the shadows but she thought it might be the same person as before. She just got confused with the names. Maybe he was called Carl after all. Colin and Keith and Carl all sounded the same. Or was that the flower girls?

"Guess who I've been talking to earlier?" he asked. "That's right. Your old friend, Marlene. Do you remember me telling you she's staying here?"

Poppy tried ever so slowly to remove her hand from his but he held it there with minimum effort as if she should listen.

"You should hear her holding court down there sometimes," he chuckled. "My, that woman can tell some stories. You really should come down and join in some more. Don't you enjoy a game of bingo or a round of cards?

And then of course there's that big old piano sitting in the hall just doing nothing. I bet you could get everyone going with a good old sing-song. Wouldn't you like that, to feel the ivories beneath your fingertips again? Someone told me you were a concert pianist but that isn't true, is it, Poppy?" It was dark but she could tell by his voice that he was pulling a face as if it was just their little secret. "That would mean you'd be able to play something like 'The Warsaw Concerto'. Can you play that, Poppy? Can you play 'Canon in D' or Rachmaninov's 'Rhapsody on a Theme of Paganini'? No, I didn't think so. Marlene says you're a fake. She says you only used to be able to play about six pieces and that the orchestra had to fall in line with what you knew. She says you couldn't even read music. That's okay. I read once that Paul McCartney couldn't either. The fact is there's lots of half-truths in your family just like there is in any other and that's the real truth, isn't it, Poppy? Half-truths and secrets and lies that no one ever speaks about or worse – worse, Poppy. Worse to be the protagonist of such malicious gossip and not ever knowing, don't you think? The *never* knowing what went on without your knowledge when everyone else does. Behind your *back*, Poppy. With people closest to you withholding sensitive and deeply-personal goings-on and probably for all the best intentions. But, even so. Who in this world gets to be the self-appointed secret keeper? Where is that written? People like that are as guilty as the guilty, wouldn't you say? By what law do they get to keep a secret from you that you are ultimately entitled to know?" He slid his long trailing fingers from hers and sat back and clapped his hands once. "I think you'll agree, Poppy," his voice carried a smile of consolation. "It's a conundrum."

Lily must have stood there for over a minute before they noticed her. The woman let out a strangled shriek and immediately tried to cover herself. Grandpa Fats made a strange *humph* sound as if Lily had interrupted him doing something in need of concentration and that she should have announced herself.

"Lily, for God's sake," his face coloured with anger which in itself was a rare sight and made Lily feel instantly confused and ashamed.

Her grandfather turned away from her but had to gingerly bend to pull up his trousers. He had hip problems in the end and his first few hurried attempts were to no avail, leaving Lily to stare upon his big broad backside peering openly at her like some one-eyed ogre through the rampant cloud of misty white hair enveloping his body. Swaying between his legs his giant testicles hung like stones in a drooping sack made from turkey's neck. With each movement Lily became mesmerised as they shifted between his inner-thighs as if stirred by a gathering breeze. Like the most grotesque form of wind-chimes made by some undiscovered native tribe she imagined them clicking to the sound of billiard balls. She had never felt her feet so rooted. It was as if she would never be able to move from that spot again.

"Creeping up on people all the time…" her grandfather began to huff and puff, but his voice broke as if he was on the point of tears. "Why aren't you at school?"

"Fats," the woman said in a voice of warning. She was dressed and standing on her feet adjusting her hair. She offered Lily a tight, almost sympathetic smile. Woman to woman.

For a moment Lily had forgotten she was even there so transfixed had she become by the sight of her grandfather's genitals. She knew full well what she was looking at. She'd had sex education classes two years before. A girl in her class had shown her some disgusting porn pictures on her phone. She knew what she was seeing. But the living sight of it shocked her. On a school outing to the zoo an elephant had once turned in front of her and defecated in almighty steaming proportions. She didn't know why it had horrified her so much when all the other kids had thought it hysterical and burst into laughter. She knew animals had to go to the toilet in primitive fashion in the same way she knew her grandfather must have reproductive organs. It was just something that she never consciously thought about or ever expected to see.

She became very aware she didn't belong to the scene and for the first time in her life felt rather foolish and naïve standing there in her school uniform as if she had mistaken a dress code and wanted nothing more than to take the moment back. Inside the sudden stifling restrictive attire of her red and gold striped blazer and tie, her sharp white high-buttoned blouse, her pleated grey kilt and white cotton socks pulled up just below her knees she could feel her skin begin to crawl. Even her regulation Alice band for girls with shoulder-length hair or longer seemed to pinch at her head and she fought down an urge to rip it off and stamp on it in front of them in a show of outrage. But she didn't. She just continued to stand stiff and upright as if addressing morning assembly which as house captain it was her duty to do once a month. She had always taken pride in her appearance. It was often commented upon in her school reports. She had Poppy to thank for that. But now it seemed the joke was on her. That everything had been a lie and that she should prepare herself for a very real and ugly world that had been happening right in front of her. That her grandfather in particular had done his hypercritical best to protect her from. He wouldn't even let her watch the evening news.

What Grandpa Fats revealed to her in the ensuing months would distort her trust in human nature forever. Poppy knew instantly something was up the night she came home but before her arrival Fats had brought up a cup of hot chocolate to Lily's bedroom and sat on the edge of the bed with the look of a chagrined basset hound. The only thing that didn't fit was his eyes which had all the feral cunning of a street thief. In the small space between she could tell he had been doing some fast thinking.

"There are two ways to look at this, Lily," he sighed. "Either you can tell your grandmother what you saw and destroy a forty-five marriage that will end up in heartbreak and upheaval and probably divorce and where God only knows that leaves you. Or...you can say nothing for now. Just for now. That's all I'm asking. And think it through. Think of the consequences I just mentioned and ask yourself if it's worth it. Because I tell you now, flower girl, once it's done, it's done. Do you understand?"

It was like a man she had never known before had entered her room. He hadn't time to make up a story or appeal to her that it had all been in a moment of weakness. He knew she wasn't stupid. He knew she knew what she had witnessed. An act of the most terrible betrayal in his marital home with someone Lily would eventually learn to be a friend of Poppy's from the orchestra. Marlene de Carlo. Couldn't he at least have done it with someone who was a stranger to the family? An adoring visitor to one of his prestigious gardens? Grandpa Fats sat there sweating and wringing his hands. Picking at the dirt in his fingernails. His expression ever-alert to the sound of a car pulling up and the front door opening as if he was planning a surprise and was yet to have everything in place. But he wasn't. Instead he was in a panic to get a deal brokered with his sixteen-year-old granddaughter. An inexorable guilt-ridden alliance that with each passing day made Lily not only question her silence on the matter but making it ever harder to come clean about.

"What if I hadn't come home?" Lily heard herself ask him flatly.

"What?" he snapped, seemingly irritated by the interruption to his whirling thoughts.

"It would have been like any other night. It's Thursday so... fish fingers and chips."

"Yes, yes," he said hurriedly. "You can have anything, Lily. Anything you want. Just say."

But she hadn't meant that.

"You've done this before," she said.

He went to lie but thought better of it. There was not time. She could tell he had no time.

"You know...the worst thing that could happen would be for people to think you were making things up again," his sidelong look was sharp and wolf-like. "Remember all those stories you invented when you were younger that got you into trouble at school? Stories about your mother and father dying in a car crash and that you were an orphan? Or your father being a millionaire businessman who died of cancer? That Marigold was a missionary worker in Africa? And they were just the tall tales. It takes a long time to get rid of a reputation like that. If ever. Mud sticks, flower girl. You see what I'm saying? No one trusts a liar."

But she only looked at him as if he should know.

"What do you want?" he asked.

"What do you mean?"

"Anything, you can have anything," he smiled falsely. "Just say the word, flower girl. And it's yours."

The over-use of his pet name for her displayed far more guilt than anything he had tried twisting her mind about.

"I want to be left alone," she said. "I don't feel well."

"Yes, yes," he stood up, seeming pleased with her response. "I'll tell Poppy you're resting. That's good," he said, as if they were suddenly in cahoots. He automatically went to feel her brow and she flinched back, her eyes growing wide in revulsion.

There was no undoing any of it. He knew. And so nodded and silently left the room.

They never spoke about it again.

She didn't mind the bravado of the young boys. Apart from the fact their bodies were sometimes nice to look at they didn't take the seedy conditions too seriously and invariably came fast and were back out the door in half the time. In general the middle-aged men, the married and the lonely were okay too. Though some of them had deep-lying impotency issues that could make the hour seem twice as long. They complimented her. They became infatuated or fell in love and saw a future. Some of them brought gifts. Others came to talk about their relationships, their wives and families, or just wanted the human contact that was being denied them. To be touched and to be held. To be loved in exchange, really. One man liked to strip naked and just spoon with her for the hour. Sometimes falling into a deep slumber. She was always wary of new customers and their needs. She didn't mind the fetish types who usually brought their own accoutrements or were found to be dressed in their mother or wife's underwear or in one case an adult diaper. It was the misogynists who worried her. In particular men of different cultures. Men of all ages who were aroused by verbally degrading her during rough sex. Who paid a lot extra for face-fucking or 'A' or to simulate being taken by force and have her pretend to fight back while calling herself a 'cum slut' who loved it, a 'dirty cock-sucking whore'. Another punter liked to write those very words across her breasts in lipstick before ejaculating over them. And then there were the old men who reminded her of Grandpa Fats. They were usually harmless and just wanted oral or hand relief but if she could get another girl to swap then usually she would. Yet one twinkly-eyed pensioner by the name of Dennis had recently taken a shine to her and you weren't allowed to turn anyone down unless they were threatening or violent towards you least of all a seemingly innocuous old man. In the early part of getting to know each other he told of how his wife had suffered a spinal cord injury in a car accident some fifteen years before which had not only left her paralyzed from the waist down and in a wheelchair but had effectively ended their sex life. Knowing his drive was still strong and after much discussion she had given her consent for him to find 'his needs' elsewhere but she hadn't wanted to know with whom or how or where or when. Not long after that Dennis admitted to his 'free pass' soon becoming an addiction and whose boundaries he still sometimes craved to push. What he liked was for them to use 'sex talk' during her efforts to bring him to a climax which wouldn't have been that unusual except that with each visit he requested she act out increasingly bizarre little scenarios where she undertook the part of an innocent young girl in a short skirt and pigtails and he played some sort of mentor figure. A teacher, a doctor or clergy or some profession that relied upon a position of trust. It was just a bit of role-playing or so she thought. And then one day he handed her a crumpled carrier bag to open and asked her to call him 'Papa Bear'.

The flat she worked out of was a dingy two-floor dwelling above a newsagents in a little parade of shops off a busy main road leading to a motorway junction and whose constant flow of heavy haulage traffic could send shudders through the walls and rattle the window frames. The first floor comprised of a basically furnished living-room where the girls sat around watching TV in exotic underwear awaiting phone appointments, a barely functional kitchen and bathroom and a scuffed and grubby narrow staircase that led upstairs to three small dimly-lit bedrooms. Just inside the ground floor entrance squeezed between two shop fronts a door-sized metal gate was chained and padlocked to keep out undesirables. Punters were made to ring a bell and wait inside the little downstairs hallway for the madam to come and unlock the gate before inviting them up. In Lily's case the 'madam' was a relative of the owner of the flat who took a fifty-per-cent cut of all the girls' earnings. Tips were their own business which is where it paid to accommodate a customer's particular wants. It was rumoured the landlord owned two hundred such properties or more across the UK. Some people might be surprised to learn that in nearly every place all over the country there were at least three brothels or more operating with virtual anonymity under the guise of massage parlours or escort agencies and that didn't include the independent ones or the girls forced to sell themselves on the streets. Then of course there were the towns and cities. Consider the fact each working prostitute was entertaining ten clients or more on a good day and Lily began to get a scale of the need for paid sex. The numbers were mind-boggling. You could probably say that at least one man in five at some point in his life had paid for sex of some description. It didn't matter the occupation or social standing. It didn't matter the lifestyle or income. It didn't matter the risk of reputation or disease. Moral, family and religious values didn't matter. Love and all its life-committing loyalties didn't matter. Paid-for sex was the biggest recidivist of them all. Men were base. Men were disgusting.

"What's this?" Lily asked.

"I hope it fits," Dennis purred. It was usually at the point of excitement that he began breathing heavily through his nose. He seemed in a hurry to get going. He'd already discarded his walking stick and unbuttoned his shirt to reveal his painfully thin skeletal frame, stripping down to his large white Y-Fronts pulled up high above his jutting pelvis. There was an old gold pee stain that hadn't washed out properly. His little sack had been caught to the left.

"Where did you get these?" she asked, slowly pulling out each garment and laying them on the bed.

"Oh, er…"

She didn't mind dressing up if that's what the client wanted. The brothel even supplied a small wardrobe of outfits. Typically a French maid costume, a WPC, a nurse, secretary and schoolgirl. Demand didn't usually get much more imaginative than that. But the difference between the school uniform they supplied and what Dennis had brought was that his wasn't a mock fancy-dress representation but a real second-hand, teenage schoolgirl's uniform. Lily caught a reflection of herself in the half-light of the smoke-mirrored wardrobe opposite the room. She had on a short little black see-through nightie laced with white pom-poms and already had her hair tied up in a high pony-tail. She had tiny tits which had been one of Dennis's original requests over the phone at the first time of calling. It was customary for the madam to give a detailed description of the girls' statistics to cold callers. Now and then an inquirer would ejaculate before she had finished and the line would go dead. To the girls these were known as 'spunkers'.

"A charity shop," he coughed.

"I don't believe you," she looked up at him. "I don't believe any man let alone one of your age would go into a charity shop and buy a second-hand schoolgirl's uniform. It just doesn't look right. I don't even believe they would sell it to you."

He coughed again. His pale, waxen skin reddening in the dim watery pink light of the room.

"What's going on, Dennis?" she laid out the last of the clothing. A long pair of white knee-length socks. "Who's is this? Where did you get it?"

"They were my granddaughter's," he admitted.

Lily felt herself stiffen.

"Why have you got them?"

"My daughter really was giving away some clothing for charity. Some of her husband's old shirts were in there. I told her I would have a look through and take it myself."

"And all the time you were thinking of your granddaughter's school uniform?"

"I…"

"Who's Papa Bear? Don't fucking lie to me, Dennis," she warned, speaking to him for the better like a friend. She picked up the blazer. It still had his granddaughter's name-tag sewn inside the collar. "Milly?" she looked at him.

He nodded.

"Did Milly call you Papa Bear, Dennis? Is that what all this is about?"

"Look, we don't have to do this," he said, appearing a little shaken. He began to look around for his stick and trousers. The folds of his pasty flaccid arse cheeks hung out of the back of his pants like melting pancakes. He still had his black ankle socks on. Lily began to feel a little light-headed. This room, she thought. This room and all its sordid little meetings. She knew every scuff and chip on the paintwork. Knew every stain on the walls and where the paper peeled away at the seams on the ceiling. She had seen them from every angle. Were indelibly printed in her thoughts and dreams along with a myriad names and faces and cocks of all shapes and sizes. Some of the cocks she had trained to respond with all the hypnotic precision a ringmaster might his performing animals. Much like Dennis's. It was a side of the job that most of the girls had a laugh about. Men and their pathetic appendage. It really was a joke to have so much power at your fingertips. Yet rarely had she ever developed any sort of feeling for a customer and it was in that moment Lily realised she'd warmed to Dennis a little and what she'd considered to be just a harmless old man's fading sexual fancies. She'd come to think of herself as almost doing him a service. Much like a nurse. Much like the carers in Acorn Springs. Really, where was the harm in attending to an old man's occasional longing? But she had clearly underestimated the darker side of his desires and her fan-flaming participation in keeping them very much ignited if only for that apparently playful but fantasy-fuelled hour.

Lily could hear the change jingling in his pockets as he fought to put on his trousers without her usual caring assistance when after they were done she would tenderly mop up his little puddle of semen with baby wipes and kitchen towel and the mood quickly changed to one of almost officious departure that would invariably end with him offering her a laughably robust handshake. Business concluded. As if she had done nothing more than to trim his hair instead of engaging in what she now believed to be the warped and calculating world of a would-be paedophile.

"Did you ever touch your granddaughter?" Lily heard herself ask.

"Don't be absurd," he scoffed at her over his shoulder.

"You touched her, didn't you?" she said, feeling sickened and thinking of her exposure to Grandpa Fats's dark and dirty secret and have her silence ever since somehow make her complicit in the fact. Is that how Milly had been made to feel? That by keeping her mouth shut to whatever threats or promises somehow implicated her? "You touched her and no one ever knew. Just you and her. That's the truth, isn't it? There'll be consequences to pay for that. You think stuff like that just goes away? That you can just put a lid on it?"

Lily realised she knew nothing about him even though it felt to her like they had shared a trust of sorts. He seemed like a useful person to know which is why she may have been more careless with her personal confidences and willing to overlook his increasingly troubling peccadilloes. He'd told her he worked in local government all his life but always with an air of intrigue. As if he'd held some high position or was some sort of local dignitary and that her discretion should go without saying. Now it just made her wonder what authority he'd had during his career and over whom? How many more secrets? It felt like the burden of responsibility in exposing her own grandfather's sins had returned to haunt her. Yet there had been good reason not to speak out then. Even now. Even more so. There had been good reason to have protected Poppy from the devastating truth.

You can destroy a forty-five year marriage that will end up in heartbreak and upheaval and probably divorce where God only knows that leaves you. Or…you can say nothing…

"I should report you," she said, feeling a wave of pent-up revenge towards him for crimes she didn't even know to be true. For something that wasn't even connected to him.

"*Really?*" Dennis turned on her. A nasty sneer had distorted his normally avuncular expression into that of a sadist. He was visibly shaking with rage while trying to maintain his balance, the point of his stick seeming suddenly futile as he held it up and pointed at her despotically. "I could have this place shut down in a second. Don't you worry about that, young lady, I still have friends in high places on the council. I wonder what your pimp of a landlord would have to say about that. I wonder what the Social Services would have to say about claiming benefits while moonlighting as a sex worker. I wonder how quick the NHS would be to subsidise your grandmother's care home fees once they knew about that. I could crush you like a bug. I could get your kids taken away from you tomorrow so that you would never see them again and don't you fucking forget it!"

From behind the bedroom door a timid little knock came. It was one of the other girls looking out for her. They must have heard Dennis's raised voice.

"Is everything okay in there, Azalea?" came a voice.

Dennis was still in his shirt and pants. He was breathing heavily but his initial panic and disturbingly telling quick-fire temper had been replaced by a strange mastery emanating from his eyes that she had never seen in him before. Lily was left stunned by his outburst. His change in character. It frightened her that she'd had no sense of this side to him in the same way she still couldn't believe she had lived all her childhood years in ignorance of the guiltless, conniving, self-preservationist in Grandpa Fats until he'd bit back with all the fear and aggression of a cornered rat. This false-faced friendly old man with a wheelchair-ridden wife. Was that even true? Was anything he had told her even true except the thing he didn't want known?

"You know you really shouldn't turn business away while you can get it," Dennis dropped his voice to a breathless rasp. "Those care home fees soon mount up and, well, you can live forever with a mental illness. You think you'll always be young, that you'll have the body of a nubile?"

A thick silence began to grow from behind the bedroom door.

"Yeah, we're fine," Lily faltered, clearing her throat. They were staring at each other from across the bed. She could see he had worked himself up into a state of arousal. "It's just...you know, me and Dennis playing games," her voice sung.

A croaky smoker's laugh rattled down the stairway as she heard her friend turn away and leave them to it.

"Now, young lady," Dennis breathed. "It's about time you understood that what Papa Bear wants Papa Bear gets."

It bestowed in you a strange sense of power to come into the belongings of someone else. Even something as defunct as an out-of-date driving licence. Some of the residents held on to the most useless of possessions. Old greeting cards with hand-written sentiments from dead loved-ones. Wedding anniversaries and birthdays mostly. Then there were the seemingly moribund dog-eared address books that read like obituaries and some diaries dating back decades with only the occasional entry of interest, though Ben had convinced himself they were sometimes coded. For instance, one woman called Gloria around the years of 1977 to 1982 put an asterisk in the corner of a day of the week of every month except, Ben was to eventually deduce, the school holidays. There was enough evidence in the pages to tell Ben she had been an ostensibly happily-married woman with a full family life. But it didn't explain the asterisk. So at night when he went in to check her vitals he would bring the subject up in a bid to unearth the truth and watch her getting slowly distressed. Suggesting that the asterisk represented a rendezvous or tryst she'd had with another man that must have existed for at least five years.

"Is that what you were doing when you were playing happily families, Gloria? Fucking another man all the while when your husband was going out to work to provide for you and your three kids? Is that why only one of your children comes to see you? The loyal one. Is that why you keep those diaries and no other? The boring ones with the banal entries when your life was humdrum doing the school run and your sex life had dried up and your husband was off fucking his secretary in revenge for what you did to him? Is that why you keep them, Gloria? To remember what it was like to feel loved and adored and wanted? Why didn't you just leave if you were unhappy? Why do people stay if they are unhappy?" he would sometimes grow angry, thinking of his own parents.

Gloria died a little later like some of the others he had driven into self-confrontation. There was no medical explanation for that but he had seen it happen enough times to believe they had simply wished death upon themselves rather than remain living with the inescapable truths he felt duty-bound to remind them of. He liked to draw it out. He liked to plant some seeds of doubt and let them work it out for themselves. To have them agonise over the rose-tinted illusion of their lives and all their special memories. He was only telling them what they knew deep down inside to be true. Just to have them question it proved it to be true. It was easy to confuse the mentally ill. But every now and then he would lose one completely to the tunnel of Alzheimer's before he could bring them to accountability and that's when Ben would be left feeling a little cheated. It really didn't matter what you told them after that.

It was a policy of the care home that residents should spend at least two hours in the day 'socialising'. As far as Lily could tell this meant assisting them down to the expansive but overly-furnished living area where they were encouraged to sit, doze or watch one of the many barely-audible TV channels. Any individual care or attention was at a premium as this was also the time of day staff used to clean the rooms and prepare and serve lunch so those of the residents who knew they were there were largely left to mingle and chat amongst themselves for recreation. It was just such an afternoon that Lily came to visit and found Poppy out in the sun-streaked conservatory overlooking the garden engaged in conversation with some old charmer who introduced himself as Bernard. He was surprisingly light on his feet as he sprung up to greet Lily and looked quite dapper in his brass-buttoned blazer and maroon silk cravat (most residents never got out of their dressing gowns) but given her recently-awakened abhorrence of all things to do with old men Lily couldn't help but regard him with suspicion however innocently ancient he claimed to be. His cool-blooded, almost featherweight hand had the thin-skin feel of a cheap weathered purse when she shook it and Lily was barely able to conceal her repulsion.

…what Papa Bear wants Papa Bear gets.

Apparently, Bernard had been trying to convince her grandmother that a woman by the name of Marlene de Carlo wasn't a resident at the care home and been spreading rumours that she couldn't play the piano and other such gossip.

"Not this again, Nana," Lily pulled up a chair and sat down opposite her. For a moment Lily could see that Poppy was trying to register who she was. "I've told you all this. Where are you getting these ideas from after all this time?"

But her grandmother seemed not to be listening. Lily followed Poppy's distant gaze out towards the garden which might have been her point of reflection. It was sometimes hard to tell what she saw. But it was always the same look. Like someone yearning for the sky between the bars of a prison. It wasn't the sky but what it represented. The garden wasn't quite up to Grandpa Fats' standards but it was a late spring day and most of the climbers and flowering shrubs were out on display.

"Are you looking at the clematis, Nana? Do you want to go out and smell the jasmine and the mock orange?"

"So you must be the third generation flower girl," Bernard took his time in interjecting when it became clear that Poppy either hadn't heard or wasn't going to answer.

"She told you that?" Lily smiled quizzically. His little black pencil-thin moustache didn't match the last of his thinning grey hair and looked to have been coloured in by eye-liner. She had the feeling he might have been a former dancer.

"I'm more of a Hybrid Tea rose man myself."

"What other gossip?" Lily suddenly found herself asking.

Bernard looked momentarily confused. Lily glanced back at Poppy whose eyes were now tearfully locked on hers as if everything was coming back to her.

"You said other gossip. What other gossip has she been hearing?"

Poppy suddenly gripped Lily's hand as if to stop her from talking.

"It's, okay, Nana," Lily hushed her.

"But…that's just it. There *is* no gossip," Bernard assured her. "That's what I've been trying to explain to Poppy. No one is talking about your grandmother. No one knows anything about your grandmother except that I think Margo said she was a concert pianist."

Lily had herself to blame for that. Of course there was no gossip. What had she been thinking? It was sending her crazy just being in the place.

"Listen," Bernard leaned in to confide with her as if Poppy wasn't even there. "I've been in this home for nearly five years. I am the eyes and ears of this place and I can tell you there is nothing for your grandmother to upset herself about other than what she's getting mixed up in her head. I used to work for the Security Service. That's MI5. Truly," he nodded. "You can ask Margo. And believe it or not even at our ripe old ages you can still get the odd personality clash. We're just back in the school playground again. That's the cycle of it. Back into the playground then back into our nappies. Dementia is just returning to the same uninformed state we start out in."

Lily smiled falsely. She wanted to like Bernard. She really did.

"But somebody still has to be the monitor," he laughed.

"I thought you weren't supposed to talk about being in MI5," she surprised herself by saying, giving him a doubting look.

"You think it matters now what I did way back then? When they can release archives on Burgess and McLean? On the Cambridge Five?" he chuckled.

Lily didn't know what he was talking about.

"Anyway, I was just a glorified janitor in those days," he sighed.

"Doing what?" Lily asked hesitantly.

"Looking after fully-equipped but empty buildings in the event of emergency relocation," he replied.

Lily felt her heart slow to a steady pace. She must be spending too much time visiting the place to start imagining she'd had the same extraordinary conversation with two entirely different people. It didn't make sense.

"You know, the nuclear threat and all that," he shrugged, but looked as if he thought he might be losing her attention.

Poppy's hand was still squeezed tight around hers.

"So who monitor's you, Bernard?" Lily finally asked.

"*Ahh...* who guard's the guard, you mean?" he sat back and smiled self-importantly.

"Well, you don't appear to be dependant. What are *you* doing here?"

"You know, back in the Cold War they used to say careless talk costs lives. If I told you that Lily I might have to kill you," he winked, stood up, straightened his blazer and sauntered off into the lounge.

For a while Lily sat watching him make a special case of everyone. At one point he stopped to engage with a seemingly crippled and shrunken-bodied old lady with a hoist above her armchair who might have been a hundred-years-old or more. There came a point when you just couldn't tell. Lily waited and waited for him to look back and give her some sort of sign that he'd been joking. But he didn't.

"Don't listen to him. He's as daft as a brush," Poppy suddenly piped up in a moment of such clarity that Lily felt her jaw drop before erupting into a bout of snorting laughter.

Poppy didn't say anything else all the time Lily remained. But her warm, soft eyes glowed all the while as if she had found a place of temporary contentment so Lily just stayed holding her hand looking out at the garden bloom thinking about her own secret agent and wondering where he was and what he was doing. Clark. Why had he stopped calling? Had she driven him away with her indifference and inability to love? She never thought she'd say it but she missed having him around sometimes and it wasn't just because she was paying for her own shopping bills again or doing the school run or walking the dog. She had tried ringing him several times since but the number was always out of service so Lily convinced herself that his undercover work had taken him elsewhere or demanded he assume a new identity if, indeed, any of what he'd told her had been true. It had been his money and generosity she'd allowed to cloud the doubts she'd always had about that. Preferring to believe his talk of flashy cars and big houses as if he had grander plans than to take notice of her inner voice. The one that said it just didn't fit.

And so, mental illness or not Lily was more inclined to believe Bernard's almost word-for-word account of the self-same secretly held position of managing a government ghost building than she did Clark's. So what did that mean? That they were simply both cloak-and-dagger fantasists? Clark. It had been hard for her to break the habit of calling him that and to the very end he still responded to it as a pet name as if he privately liked it. Maybe he and Bernard just read the same stupid comic books, Lily tried laughing off the notion. But Bernard had all but quoted Clark verbatim. Or vice versa. It just seemed too much of a coincidence that two people apparently sworn by the Official Secrets Act to independently claim to have held such a position unless there was some sort of connection between them. Could they be in some way related and if so why hadn't Clark ever mentioned it? There seemed no other explanation and the thought left Lily feeling suddenly ill at ease in the surroundings of the care home the way some of the residents appeared to be. The way Poppy sometimes appeared to be. As if some of them knew things about her.

He didn't like Margo. Things had been different since she'd been hired. After last year's maltreatment scandal she had been brought in to manage the place and although he still held the position of 'head' night support worker she was always on his case about accurate record keeping. Of course, Ben wasn't authorised to administer any medication but he was good enough to clean up the residents' shit in the night when they soiled themselves. Gone were the days when he could leave them to sit in it and pass on the vomit-inducing chore to the day staff who lived in fear of their jobs should they say anything against him. His father only hired immigrants on minimum wages who could barely speak English anyway and it came to light during the hearing last year that one of the three night staff nurses who were charged unfit to practice not only had a criminal conviction but was suspected of making unauthorised withdrawals from one of the residents' bank accounts. Enter the multi-credentialed Margo who not only spoke the perfectly clipped English of one-hundredth-in-line-to-the-throne royalty but who Ben's father paid double the salary of the previous manager, a seemingly unassuming and obsequious ex-headmaster called Barney but who Ben was to discover had the same like-minded attitude towards any truculent or trouble-making skull-head. Before the big hoo-ha of last year there were a few unproven complaints from family members of residents being mistreated, unexplained evidence of bruising and claims of psychological cruelty, but it was easy enough for the old dodderers to hurt themselves just turning over in their sleep and as for messing with their heads, well, they were all half-mad anyway. It made him laugh when family tried to get involved. If they cared so much why consign their cherished mums or grandparents to a home in the first place? In truth most of them just turned a blind eye as did the other members of staff who knew what was good for them. No one ever spoke out about the manager and the owner's son.

Now Margo would inspect every room and every skull-head first thing and with her bloodhound nose would know if and how long a resident had been cleaned and check it in accordance with the records. Then she had brought in a GP to make regular inspections. It wasn't as much fun without Barney around and just recently Ben found himself growing more resentful towards one of the residents in particular. The obstinate and seemingly unreachable Poppy. As if she should be so special. The grandmother of a cock-sucking whore. It was only a matter of time before she became privy to that more than noteworthy titbit. But first she needed to know the truth about her cheating husband and what had made her granddaughter suddenly go off the rails without a word of warning. An 'A' student whose grades dive-bombed almost overnight. Who got in with a crowd of drug-addicted squatters and disappeared for years before returning with two babies by two different men once her grandfather had died. Ben didn't believe Poppy hadn't drawn parallels with her own daughter who had done pretty much the same thing. What did Marigold know to make her want to leave and never come back and furthermore what possible explanation could there be for her to have abandoned her own child on her parents other than to have a reason to blame them for it?

Papa Bear never did get what Papa Bear wanted.

There was always that moment upon genuflection when she had to break through the image of having her own grandfather stood in front of her. To block out the sounds of Marlene de Carlo's animal-like gorging and fight down the regurgitative belch of a thousand different blow jobs that no amount of mouthwash over no amount of time could eradicate. It was never far away like the worst kind of indigestion. Heartburn pills didn't work. All the gum and mints in the world didn't work. The most up-to-date dual rotating heads of her electric toothbrush didn't work. Neither did scrubbing the inside of her mouth manually until her gums bled. If she tried bringing it up. If she stifled it. It was always there like the lingering bacterial stench of halitosis or so she convinced herself. As if it lived in her pores. As if it was laying eggs in the crevices of her molars. That taste. There was no escaping the association of that off-sweet, near-rancid taste. The taste of her grandfather that he'd all but addicted her to. Like the most disgusting form of self-harm. That taste. The taste of his odious poison and all and everything she'd imagined it to be upon entering the kitchen that day on a still warm summer's afternoon at the age of sixteen.

Ben lived in a little self-contained flat in the converted attic of one of the amalgamated properties that made up the care home. In the beginning his father had great plans for him to manage the place but that never materialised once it became clear that Ben couldn't be trusted with the responsibility and so for him to pay his way he'd been given the job of head of the night support who normally worked for next to nothing and were always under-staffed. Ben didn't care. By giving him a position and a place to live and a monthly allowance his father was only alleviating his conscience. The care home was so profitable he could afford to buy a place in the Caribbean where he lived most of the time with his much younger gold-digger of a girlfriend. It was Ben who had been with his mother when she suffered a devastating stroke just weeks after his father had walked out and left them. It was Ben who sat all night talking with her not knowing what was happening, seeing the terror and the pleading in his mother's one working eye, it was Ben who was blamed for not calling an ambulance quick enough. How could he possibly be expected to run a care home?

Those hours spent alone with his mother suddenly incapacitated and not being able to talk gave Ben a strange sense of empowerment. The only sound he ever heard from her mouth again was an occasional and unexplainably disconcerting hiccup. As if she was mocking him still. He'd known it was serious. That things were never going to be the same. That she would never be able to hurt or bully or criticise him again and he could see that she knew that too. He could see even by her half-twisted face that she knew her time had come. That this was it. Yet still it seemed she was being held under some sort of suspended death-sentence, a living purgatory like so many of the residents in the home. Only the truly terrified would choose to die that way. To live and yet not live in exchange for another breath. What made them hang on? What had made his mother hang on? Did they even know?

At first he began to remind his mother of the terrifying regime she had put him under all his life. Her cruelty towards him. The hours spent locked in a cupboard 'for his own good'. As if she wasn't safe to be around. The stony silences that could last for weeks and made him feel sick in the stomach wondering what he'd done wrong and how best to fix it. And the missed meal times that seemed to go on forever while left to starve in his room to the point of passing out where all he had was his comic collection. His father's response was to blame it on the menopause. But Ben only remembered him away on business. If his father ever ended up in the care home with a mental illness Ben would have a few home truths to remind him of too. His dereliction of duty. His abject neglect. Like Poppy and her refusal to see what had been going on in front of her, his father was guilty of if nothing else then surely by association. Ben was left screaming and crying at his mother in the first few critical hours of her interruption of blood flow in the back of her neck and brain as if he had waited all his life to say it. He hadn't realised how angry he was. But all she ever managed was a hiccup and an accusatory eye that he should have let her suffer for so long without calling for help. She was good at that. Even after all this time. Two years on and it still unnerved him entering her private room in the home where she received twenty-four-hour personal care and which was the main reason his father kept away. Ben knew. He wasn't fooled. He saw it all the time in the faces of the relations of other residents. The visits would get shorter. The excuses to leave more hurried and insistent. Some didn't even bother to take off their coats. Just die. You could see it in their barely-concealed expressions when they looked around. How much longer? The place was a walking morgue. Just die, Ben wanted to say. Why didn't his mother just die? WHY DIDN'T THEY ALL JUST FUCKING DIE?

Ben wasn't used to having people knock on his door. Had he been shouting again? He had the window wide open that looked down on the garden. Anyone might have heard. He stood with his hand in his mouth uncertainly, his instinct to remain deathly still and hope whoever it was went away. But then came another, louder knock.

"What is it?" he shouted irritably, realising how worked up he was.

"Clark?" came a voice from behind the door that made him freeze in terror. "Ben is that you? It's me, Lily."

Ben's mind whirled. *How?* How was this happening? He threw his hands to his head and felt himself drop into a crouch. He didn't usually get up until early afternoon and was still dressed in his sleeping attire of T-shirt and underpants. He hadn't washed. His breath stank.

"I just want to talk," Lily said in a friendly tone.

Had she heard him shouting? He began to shake at the thought of his unmasking. The lies, the lies upon lies. He couldn't keep it up after he realised all the money was going to run out. He hadn't planned on a story for that. Now what was he expected to say? He looked around the room. His mind already trying to invent a reason he should be there. But it was hopeless. He felt trapped.

"I'm...I was on the phone," he called back hesitantly by way of explaining his raised voice should she have heard it.

"It's okay," she said softly. "I spoke to Margo. None of it matters. I'm...I'm just a bit confused. Can't we at least please talk?"

"I...er, I just got up. I'm not even dressed."

"So go change in a telephone box," she tried joking. "C'mon, Clark. Just for five minutes."

Lily heard the turn of several locks before the door opened and wondered in that moment why he should feel the need to be so protected within a property clearly geared towards the security of its residents. At night the home was lit up like a palace and visiting hours were over by eight-thirty when the place was locked down and the final third of the shifts changed hands and the night staff took over.

Ben invited her in and offered her a seat in a huge leather recliner while he sat on a stool by a corner unit that appeared to function as a work station. She wasn't surprised to see the place was set up like a teenager's playroom with its big flat-screen TV, game consoles, scattered video software and shelves of what she knew through him to be graphic novels but which just really meant grown-up comic books. For what it was worth, she wanted to tell him, heading a night support operation in a care home of around seventy mostly mentally ill residents was a far more responsible and admirable job than working for MI5 managing a silly government ghost building that probably only existed inside the head of a senile. It also helped that Margo had told her Ben was an only child to a father who not only owned Acorn Springs but by all accounts drove a flashy Bentley and spent most of his time living in a flashy house sailing around in his flashy boat in the Caribbean. Why the hell wouldn't Ben have told her that instead?

"I guess I didn't want to put you off by letting you know your grandmother was a resident in my father's home," he said in answer to that very question, though Lily's mind was a bit cloudy on the chronology of their early conversations. It would have been unlike her to reveal something so confidential before she'd gotten to know the client or thought there might at least be some personal advantage to gain out of it. Like Dennis and his high position on the council.

Sensing her scepticism Ben pressed on. "I thought, I don't know, that for you it might constitute some sort of conflict of interest. So I borrowed Bernard's story," he admitted sheepishly.

It was true. For all the girls there was always that moment when you feared a punter might walk through the door that you knew. A neighbour or friend of a friend. There was no going back for either person after that. One young girl who recently started had a customer select her above the others after her age and statistics had been described to him over the phone only for it to be the father of one of her best school friends. A man whose car she'd been given rides home in not so long before and been present at sleepovers. Of course, Lily already knew him and what he liked as did the others. In fact, she'd been told he'd been a regular for years and was always asking for younger girls.

"Do you see her? I mean, do you attend to her? What do you say?" Lily asked in a gush. The very idea was still so new in her head it was something she was trying to resist being angry about. That she had talked about Poppy and her upbringing and Grandpa Fats and he would just listen in the same way he was now like a faceless counsellor with no real empathy or connection except the fact that nearly every evening he would leave and go back to the home and spend the night tending to her grandmother without ever saying a word. It worried her that she'd had no sense of that. But then men were good at hiding things.

"I talk to all the residents. That's part of the job. Whether they can understand or hear me or not," he rubbed his hands between his legs and smiled fixedly, looking around the room as if he wanted nothing more than to get off the subject.

"But…I don't understand why you would hide this caring side of you. I mean, I know you're shy and a little introvert. We both know you're shy," she sat back and laughed as if it should mean something, but then added seriously: "You do a good thing do you know that?"

He offered a diffident shrug as if embarrassed.

"I mean it, Clark. Huh, I always said you were a good listener." She clapped her hands in self-appreciation and pointed at him. "Didn't I always say that?"

"I should get washed and dressed," he said.

"Why did you stop coming, Clark? Why did you never say anything? Don't you love me anymore?" she tried coaxing him with a little minx-like smile normally reserved for customers upon leaving and when counting out a tip.

Did you enjoy yourself, Hon? You gonna come back and see me?

"We never spoke about love," he frowned and stared hard at the floor, as if he knew that smile.

It was true. She'd never said the three little words to anyone. Not even the fathers of her children the second of which was the product of group sex. If that hadn't happened. If that hadn't been a big enough wake-up call she might still be living in a squat with her firstborn existing in the same underwear for weeks in one giant family of 'brothers' and 'sisters' with adopted monikers such as 'Rags' and 'T-Rex'. Of course, she'd been known as Azalea even then. She'd do anything to make her feel disgusted about herself. The difference now was that she was in control of it. It all suddenly seemed like a long time ago.

"I didn't think we had to," she heard herself say softly.

"Can you tell me what love is? What it feels like?" he looked at her intently.

She felt her mouth move but no words came out.

"I didn't think so," he said. "It's safer to pretend, isn't it? To tell yourself otherwise."

Lily felt herself moved to tears. Something she would never give up to anyone. He spoke as if he knew.

"Why don't you get ready," she offered with a hesitant smile. "You don't start for hours and I haven't got to pick the kids up until four. Maybe we could go and get a coffee or something. Sort of, I don't know, start anew. What do you think?"

Ben's soaring sense of elation at the suggestion was gripped by a moment of chilling uncertainty. As if he suspected her of tricking him.

"It's a nice day," she persisted. "All the flowers are out."

At first she thought he looked a little panic-stricken at the idea but then he seemed to change his mind and began to nod furiously and look around the room as if in a hurry to get out. He stood up and gave her a crooked smile, holding out his hands in a gesture of appeal that she should have discovered him still in his *Incredible Hulk* underpants and in that moment it felt like their eyes met for the first time.

"Take your time," she smiled warmly, which seemed to visibly relax him.

"I just thought of something," Lily called out to him as she heard a shower run from the adjoining room. "Wouldn't it be great to see Nana together some time? Wouldn't that be nice for her to know that we're friends? Well, more than friends."

Not waiting for an answer she began to pick up some of his discarded clothes from around the room. She couldn't remember having such a good feeling about something in a long time. It was like coming out on the first real day of spring and realising you didn't need your coat. She suddenly felt lighter. She held up a washed-out T-shirt with a *Lord of the Rings* print on it and pulled a face before folding it up and putting it in a pile on the work desk along with a crumpled sweatshirt and some joggers and a pair of the same *Marvel Heroes* socks she had put in her son's Christmas stocking. Beside the PC there was a game disc out of its cover and she began to look around for the box. She read along the shelved rack of fantasy and war and shoot-em-up titles and was about to give up looking when her attention was drawn to the barely-open top drawer of the desk and something inside that she thought she recognized. As she slowly pulled it open she told herself that of course there must be a number of reasons why Ben should have one of Poppy's photograph albums hidden away, but it didn't explain everything else. The diaries and notebooks and cards and other possessions that were clearly or had at least once been the personal property of some of the residents. What possible use could he have for them? Her heart was sinking that something like this should be happening to her again. Another dark side revealed to her at the point of giving in to trust, of daring to hope. She wanted to believe that it was part of his job to have custody of such items and that there was a simple explanation that he should be in ownership of something so intensely private as a collection of someone's old love letters wrapped in gold ribbon and written in ink on parchment dating back eighty years, but the simple fact was that she couldn't.

The lower two drawers revealed much of the same thing except that at the back of the bottom one and far more seriously incriminating she discovered a stack of credit and debit cards held fast in a thick rubber band. Shuffling through them she saw that not only did they belong to other people and that many were long expired but that the pack also contained a collection of seemingly worthless forms of varying ID, senior citizens' travel passes and library cards and, Lily felt her mind go blank, her very own driving licence that she thought to have lost some time ago. As she slowly shifted her way back through the pile she came across several other items in her name. Her old bank card. A gym membership she hadn't bothered to replace after it had gone missing. Asda. M&S. But most significant of all perhaps, Azalea's 'Escort and Massage Services' business card.

How long ago had she thought she'd lost that purse? Nine months, a year? It didn't make sense that he should have them. She hadn't even known him then.

"I found them," he said casually as if she had spoken aloud. "They were in a little wallet thing in a shopping trolley."

Lily started at the sound of his voice. He was standing in the doorway towel-drying his hair wearing a clean pair of *Simpson's* boxers.

"Why are you snooping around my stuff?" he wanted to know.

For a moment Lily couldn't believe what she'd heard.

"Excuse me, Clark. But I don't see anything of yours here," she held up her cards. "Why have you got my driving licence?"

"I told you I found it," he lifted a shoulder unconvincingly and dropped his gaze. He disappeared back into the room and returned shortly after in a *Game of Thrones* T-shirt and jeans.

"Jesus fucking Christ those shirts," she said exasperatedly.

"What?" he looked down at himself.

It didn't matter. They were never going out for a coffee. They were never starting anew.

"What's going on here, Clark?"

"I told you I..."

"Yeah, you told me you found my purse in a fucking shopping trolley so why didn't you return it?"

"I brought it that first day I came to see you."

"When?" she frowned, wanting to punch him. She didn't know what he was talking about.

"Well, the only phone number I had to go on was…was well, your business card. And when I asked for you they said I had to make an appointment. So I did."

Lily blinked in astonishment at the idea.

"And what did you think you were making an appointment for?"

"Well, I don't know. To see you. To give you back your stuff."

Lily slumped down on the stool, giving him a sidelong look, both nodding and shaking her head unsurely.

"So why didn't you give it back to me?"

"I…"

"Well?" she began to lose patience.

"I thought…I thought that if I gave it to you…then that would be it. I wouldn't have a reason to go back. But as long as I had your stuff I had a reason. I wanted to tell you. I wanted to give it back every time. I wanted to give everything back."

"What do you mean 'everything'?" she looked around the desk and began scattering the contents angrily, sending his weird treasure trove of collectables everywhere. "What, Clark? What else is there?"

"There was a lottery ticket," he said after a moment and hung his head.

When their eyes eventually met he nodded as if she should know.

"I don't…I don't know what you're saying." Lily looked at him confusedly. She couldn't remember the last time she'd even bought a ticket. And if she did it was only ever on the whim of a huge rollover.

"It's okay. You didn't win the jackpot or anything. You're more likely to be eaten by a shark or something. Anyway, there are runner-up prizes."

"How much?" she asked instantly. "How fucking much, Clark?"

"Fifty-thousand," he spoke quietly.

"Fifty-thousand pounds?"

He nodded.

"That's a lot of money, Clark."

"I know."

"That's a fucking lot of money in anyone's book."

He began to chew the inside of his cheek.

"So where is it?" she breathed.

"That's what I'm trying to tell you. That's why I kept coming back to see you."

Lily could feel her heart thudding in her throat. Did he mean what she thought he meant? She took him to be smart. But deep down inside she had always known there was a part of him that was stunted and childlike and underdeveloped.

"You thought that by coming to see me every week and paying me with my own money was somehow giving it back to me?" Lily tried hard to control the emotion in her voice.

"Not just that," he said. "There was the direct debit. The shopping bills. The kids' stuff."

"*It was my fucking money, Clark!*" she erupted, leaping from the stool and clawing at his face. He yelped and shrank back into the doorway in fear, burying his head in his arms.

Lily's eyes were on fire. She began circling the room. The drawers were still open revealing the contents of his plundering.

"And what about all this? Why have you got all this? What are you anyway a...a fucking magpie or something?" She snatched at Poppy's photograph album and thrust it in his face. "Why have you got my grandmother's stuff, Clark? Does she know? Did she give you permission to take it or have you stolen it like you stole my fucking money? My God," she suddenly realised. "That's what you do isn't it? All those debit and credit cards. You're just a fucking thief. A thief of the worst kind. A thief in a position of trust. I trusted you, Clark! Do you understand? I wanted to trust you. You made me believe in flashy houses. In something outside of this...this fucking bullshit life. You made me believe in goodness and in kindness and in generosity like I'd never known because it's so much safer to pretend. Isn't that right, Clark? Than to believe otherwise. Isn't that what you said? But there is no goodness or kindness is there?" she spat at him breathlessly and threw the book down. "No one's who they say they are. It's just fucking lies. It's always fucking lies."

After a long silence he peered between his arms and saw that she had returned to sit on the stool. Her expression blank.

"What are you going to do?" he asked.

She looked over at him as if she'd forgotten he was there.

"There'll shut the place down," he warned her.

"What do you talk to them about?" she said with a strange calm. "What do you talk to my grandmother about?"

"She's stage three Alzheimer's. She needs special care. If they shut this place down then-"

"She never used to mention Marlene de Carlo's name even when they played in the same orchestra together. Maybe she knew all along," Lily finally accepted with an exhaustive shrug and looked up at him. "Maybe I was keeping her from something she already knew."

Ben felt his mouth twitch. He entered the room hesitantly, wringing his hands and trying to think of the right words.

"She knows things doesn't she?" Lily said. "She knows why my mother left me with them. She knows why my mother disappeared. And she knew all about Grandpa Fats. It seems we have been protecting each other all this time."

"But she doesn't know what you saw," he tried reaching her.

"No, that would be the worst kind of knowledge to take with her," Lily pondered.

"And the repercussions of that."

"My being a prostitute you mean? No, she doesn't know that either. Not yet anyway," she smiled cynically to herself and looked at him. "Isn't that right, Clark?"

From the open window came what Lily first took to be the almost euphonious sound of tinkling glass drifting out into the sunny afternoon air, like a crystal chandelier stirred by a change in the wind, but then came a familiar brushing together of melodic notes followed by a delicate pony trot of rising piano keys through an achingly soft meadow of accompanying chords. She could hear every arresting fingertip step tumbling over the edge as if into a pure and resounding flowing golden waterfall of music.

"Listen," Lily cocked her head. "I know that song."

"It's Canon in D," Ben said after a moment. He frowned and shifted on his feet uncertainly.

Lily stood up as if in a trance. She brushed past him and headed out the door and down the narrow staircase that led up to his room. Once she reached the first floor others were drifting towards the source of the sound too. Residents. Staff. Residents helped by staff. The acoustics becoming infinitely clearer. Both heavenly and secular. The big entrance hall and its parquet stage and hard furnishings provided an almost chapel-like chamber for the slowly gathering and seemingly spellbound crowd appearing from every doorway. Margo. Bernard. Perhaps even Marlene de Carlo somewhere inside her grandmother's mind. Residents still in dressing gowns and carpet slippers held up by walking sticks or seated in wheelchairs looked on in wistful memory. The stick-woman woman who needed a hoist was being held like a baby in the arms of one burly member of staff who was smiling radiantly and nodding in appreciation as everyone continued to exchange glances in both surprise and wonderment. Lily stopped before the stairs and peered over the banister rail still unbelieving of what she had already prepared herself to see. She recalled how Poppy's soft pastel forget-me-not eyes would grow wide and vacant upon playing but now they were somehow different. They had the look of a blind person. Lily hadn't known the piece then and she still wouldn't. It had taken Clark to tell her. But she remembered Nana playing it and how as a child it would sometimes send her off to sleep in Grandpa Fats' fat cosy lap as he looked on at Poppy adoringly. His flower girl. That part had been true. Lily hadn't exaggerated that part just because it was easier to pretend. The way he looked at her when she played had been true. As true as the sound being created by the tender stroke of her grandmother's fingers as they danced across the keys of the great grand piano brought to life in the shaft of sunlight created by the overhead skylight. As true as wherever Poppy had taken herself off to be.

GIRL IN A SUITCASE

There was an urban myth once doing the rounds that was told to me at a dinner party apropos of the story-teller not knowing who I was. He spoke of a man who carried his young daughter around in a suitcase because of her love of it and that he was one day waiting at a train station when surrounded by a group of teenagers who began to harass him to the point of demanding money. A mugging in effect. One of them pulled a knife. The situation became quite serious. Then they started to question if there was anything valuable in the suitcase. The case had been specifically designed so that the man's daughter could open it from the inside in the event that something went wrong and she was left trapped. When the girl heard the commotion she slowly began to unzip from the interior and clambered out, screaming that they should leave her father alone. As you might imagine the gang fled in terror at the sight of a little girl struggling from out of a suitcase and screeching at them like some raging banshee. God only knows what they must have imagined in the after event. The stuff of parents' age-old warnings about talking to strangers probably. A kidnapped child gone crazy with confinement that to this very day must still haunt their collective conscience and something I can't help but feel strangely guilty about even though I am pretty sure not one of them has ever acted upon such bravado again. So maybe it all turned out for the best. The dinner party gathering laughed dubiously amongst themselves and moved on to other conversations. But even though some of the details of the story had clearly become distorted through hand-me-down exchanges over the course of time (it was a bus stop not a train station) only I, the aforementioned boys, and of course, Emily, my daughter, knew the tale to be true.

I met someone long before Emily was born who, as it turned out, had a similar condition, with no idea what that experience was preparing me for. It didn't feel like we were just passing through each other's lives. At least not to me. Not then. I was head-over-heels. Gemma was my first real love. Probably my only. I can say that with some degree of certainty now. We were nineteen-years-old and eventual graduates from the same university. We thought we knew everything back then. We thought we had our futures planned out. She wanted to teach. I had ambitions to be a journalist. We talked about living together. Marriage. Kids. Even the names of our kids. Or at least our two chocolate brown Labradors. Rosencrantz and Guildenstern. Don't laugh. We were young and believe it or not nowhere near as pretentious as some. Not that either of us had any reason to be. We both came from humble backgrounds. We were both geeky and awkward. We both struggled to fit in which is how the relationship developed. Jerry and Gemma probably says it all. But once we became a couple everything got easier. And then to Gemma's credit I saw on her Facebook profile when I eventually tracked her down that she went on to own two pet pythons by those very names which I couldn't help thinking were far more suited to ophidians than canines. Rosencranthhhhtzzz and Guildensssssterrrn. What was it Hamlet said? "I trust them like adders fang'd." So maybe we had known something after all.

All that might have been true if we had put our resulting English degrees into practice. I went on to do a City & Guilds in carpentry and Gemma is an 'exotic dancer' among other things. And so, many years on and, Shakespeare aside, it seemed our lives had turned out very differently all but for the one strange connection that I not only never forgot but had cause to remember when I first found my daughter asleep one morning buried under a toy shelf in her bedroom cupboard around the age of two. When I asked her what she was doing Emily told me she just felt safe being there. To my knowledge I hadn't given her any reason not to be. Until we split her mother and I rowed every day throughout our daughter's childhood but it was usually Sharon doing the shouting and slamming. And then I remembered Gemma.

The first time I slept with Gemma I woke to find her happily curled up beneath the bed with all the blankets and pillows. At the time I put this down to the amount of alcohol we had consumed the evening before. I had woken to find myself in a bath entangled in a shower curtain on such nights which was pretty harmless compared to the morning I emerged from a drunken stupor at the sound of a lorry about to load the half-empty skip of garden waste I was lying in with only the hazy recollection of being thrown in there by a group of so-called friends and not having the required modicum of sobriety to clamber out. What can I tell you? We were students. And despite the weird and wonderful makeshift lairs I would go on to discover Gemma snuggled away in I very quickly came to learn that our excessive drinking habit bore no relevance to her abnormal desire for confinement in enclosed spaces and is the reason I eventually ended up getting in touch with her through social media. Before I met Gemma I'd never even heard of the very little known condition that is claustrophilia. And now it seemed my daughter was starting to display those same tendencies.

During that first university year Gemma's craving to seek small quiet places to sleep or even just to be alone became unnervingly apparent. I just thought it was a childhood thing she'd still yet to grow out of. I came from a big inner city and had two step-siblings from two different fathers. She was an only child from a single-parent family in a small village 'somewhere up north' as she used to put it in the conviction no one would ever have heard of it. I certainly hadn't. Nevertheless, she painted a nostalgic picture of uneven cobbled streets undulating like stone streams between rows of quaint little two-up-and-two-down cottages and a handful of essential shops set against a backdrop of rolling Derbyshire countryside, but sounding to me more like the sort of tight-knit, almost TV soap opera community that couldn't help but know each other's business. And so it turned out.

The village, its bed and breakfast facilities and inn and gift shop and other modest enterprises were also largely dependent upon its potholing tourist trade, she told me, for which enthusiasts came far and wide to spend long weekends. Potholing is an extremely dangerous sport and should never be undertaken without a group leader of great experience, Gemma explained in all seriousness. Some of the old mines that were still accessible where she lived were very unstable because of the miners' habit of stacking up tons of rock above wooden stakes that had often calcified. Other cave systems could go on forever but despite the fact it was easy to get very wet and very tired underground the feeling of being so deep below the surface not only excited her but was where she re-discovered her love for tight dark places and had her first orgasm. That heady erotic feeling of being almost immovably restricted stirring something in her that had been long been virtuously quiescent.

"Sometimes it was as if I wanted to stay down there forever. As if it was where I belonged."

Her words, that same darkening of her eyes she would have when we were on the point of sex, the way her breathing became shallow at the thought not only frightened but roused in me unexplainably naive and jealous feelings of inadequacy that have not only remained but more recently been exacerbated by the fact my daughter had long been demonstrating similar characteristics. Gemma went on to tell me of a young Australian guy who worked as a group leader one summer and who had potholed all over the world. He told wonderfully perilous stories about sliding down black helter-skelter tunnels seeing millions of fossils illuminated by his headlamp, or how that in New Zealand he had waded through cave water prompting glowing insects to light up the cavern ceiling like another zodiac. He spoke of a subterranean world of natural water courses, crawling through mud dating back to the Jurassic period, pitches and drops so deep you had to abseil, 'squeezes' and 'letterboxes' so narrow you had to relax your entire body just to make it through. Gemma spoke of making those same adventures one day. But she never did. Her desire for confinement eventually took a darker, much more disconcerting turn.

Apparently, from a very early age Gemma's father would allow her to snuggle deep down below the covers of the bed and sleep between his legs until such a time he deemed it no longer appropriate. Furthermore, he banned her from taking a nap behind the sofa or any other of her preferred cramped and cozy crawlspaces where you might have found a cat curled up and something she had been allowed to do ever since she was a baby. She had also taken to stealing away into her school locker which was not only attracting the attention of the other kids but was seriously concerning the headmistress. Gemma couldn't remember how old she was at the time, maybe seven or eight, but he might as well have been taking away her favourite childhood toy, she told me. Consequently, she had taken to her own closed-curtained bedroom to find the solace she needed. And that was either in the form of her wardrobe, a blanket box at the end of her bed or the bed itself, where for every night after she had continued to sleep at the bottom buried under the duvet and pillows or anything else she could find to weigh down upon her and close out the light. If her father came to her room he would knock hesitantly and wait until she answered but not with the discretion that any other parent might for their daughter's modesty lest she was changing, but in the worry he didn't know where he might find her. Sometimes she would hide herself in the bathroom for hours where there was at least a lock. He didn't understand, she told me. He fretted for her but seemed more concerned about the neighbours gossiping that his daughter was mentally ill and liked to crawl inside a box for hours. She said these things with an infectious smile and a little tweak of her nose and an ever-growing and all-too-familiar incomprehensible shrug that said it was the rest of the world that was weird and endeared me so much to her I just wanted to sweep her up and never let her go.

"But…why?" I asked her in all earnest, because I still didn't understand it and couldn't help thinking she must have some morbid disposition about wanting to die or be in a coffin or at the very least just be left alone and that made me feel both isolated and excluded. "How does it make you feel?"

"Calm, Jerry," she said after much contemplation. "Calm and protected."

She had never spoken about it before with anyone, she confided. Even now her father wore a look of guilt in his eyes every time she went back home and they said goodnight. He still blamed himself, Gemma said. All those years of letting her sleep where she wanted and then taking it away from her. "How dare he!" she would erupt. He thought he had been doing it for the best. No doubt he thought he had somehow enabled her condition. He persecuted himself over it. But more than that he must have known in doing what he did was as good as cutting off her arm. Gemma narrowed her eyes at the memory and looked at me. "He severed our connection from that moment on", she said. "He lost his only little girl forever and all for what? Because he cared too much about what the village were saying? He should have stuck up for me. For himself, if anything. Was I hurting anyone? Was I breaking the law? No. It's because I was different and that frightens small-minded people."

Waking up with her after that revelation, or coming home to find her napping in the afternoon was like a living game of hide-and-seek, especially in the four-floored warren of a converted Victorian house we shared with seven others and who all took her sleeping habits as a sign of being if not a little strange then bordering on the wild and wacky. Not one of them took it seriously, however. If anything it warmed her to people much like the innocent disregard for others that a child playing make-believe might and which is probably why I was so attracted to her. She didn't see any harm in it and the more I got to know her I couldn't either. But that didn't stop my persistence in trying to find a reason.

"Why can't it just be me?" she would tire of my scrutiny. "Stop examining me, Jerry. You remind me of my father keep trying to find some fault in my upbringing. In his parenting. That I never knew my mother or some such post-traumatic bullshit that I haven't dealt with. Why can't it just be me?"

She was right. I couldn't help it. Secretly I had begun to relate Gemma's desire to seek out such places as some sort of subconscious yearning to return to her mother's womb given the tragic circumstances of her birth and there is a part of me that believes it still. Gemma had been 'born' prematurely and spent four months in an incubator after her mother died in a car accident on a bend in the road notorious for being a black spot. Busybodies had spread the rumour that she'd been driving too fast. Her father bore the stigma of ever letting his pregnant wife drive at all. And now the daughter was mad as a result and wanted to climb into anything resembling a concertinaed car. The family name had been defamed one way or another was how her father saw it but you couldn't win under such bigotry. Gemma couldn't wait to get out of there.

Knowing all this brought about a very early paternal instinct in me to protect that has not only never gone away but continued to ruin many other subsequent relationships with women in much the same way it did mine and Gemma's. In trying to give her what I thought she needed by keeping her close. With what I now realise to have been over-the-top and sometimes annoyingly cloying tactile attention that I still confuse with expressions of love. I was in fact accused of smothering her and not giving her the space she wanted. At the time I thought this rather ironic given the fact I had found Gemma cramped into the many different places around the house she had come to discover. But I suppose there must have been something in her accusations because even Emily's mother grew weary of my 'over-attentiveness' in the end and prefers to live with a man who beats her up. (I only suspect this with the bruises she sometimes shows up with). It's none of my business. Perhaps I should have demanded a similar sort of respect from her instead of always doing my best to remain calm and understanding. I've heard it said that some women are just attracted to the bad ones. Not that Sharon ever cared about our daughter the way a mother should. She is quite a few years younger than me which should have been a red flag from the start given my paternalistic disposition. She left school at sixteen and got a job in a fish and chip bar which is where we met. After finishing my education I never did get out much. My qualifications counted for nothing in the end and my nearest attempt at journalism was being made redundant by the local rag after six months which is how and why I became a chippy. Sharon and I used to joke about that. I liked her simple sense of humour. It could still be an intellectual battle meeting up with old uni chums who liked to debate on all things social, economic and political. I'd withdrawn back into my shell. Sharon was easy to be around and her parents thought I was good for her and liked to brag about my 'academia'. But after we married and had Emily she wouldn't stop harping on about the life she was missing out on. Sharon grew bitter of my student days and the stories I told as if she'd been shortchanged. By the time she left she'd been absent for nearly a year anyway. I never knew from one week to the next where she was. I just took the fact that her clothes and belongings remained in the house to be a good sign. That she would grow out of it sooner or later. But in the end she all but left me to deal with being the single father which is another similarity to Gemma's upbringing that I have tried hard not to obsess on. The other was the point at which my old girlfriend's father must have reached. Except that he'd never had to question why he carried his daughter around in a suitcase or a car boot.

Gemma's online profile was not the girl I had known. She had accepted me by invitation but we hardly spoke over the internet after our initial contact except to joke about the pet names. Rosencrantz and Guildenstern. I still couldn't believe it but she sounded disbelieving of my recollection and just laughed it off as if she had thought it her own idea. Perhaps it was. I can't remember who came up with it now. And as for the brown Labradors she sounded equally skeptic. Claiming that dogs were far too messy a domestic pet and much preferred reptiles. One of Gemma's pet pythons has since disappeared. I don't know much about snakes except that they like to curl up in small dark places. In that same conversation she also freely admitted to having a bondage fetish.

To this day I still haven't updated my Facebook page and only had Emily create one so that I could get in touch with Gemma. I also never did broach the subject of claustrophilia with her but instead fell dutifully into rank and became one of her avid Twitter followers by continuing to watch her evolvement from afar even if accompanied by a withheld foreboding. She was - is, very popular and appears to have lots of people in her life. She leads a far more interesting time than me and presumably the gathering hordes of hundreds of other fascinated observers. Virtual friends or otherwise, voyeurs, curious onlookers like myself with not much of a life to speak of. Apparently, exes count for nothing. I'd never felt so insignificant even if it was all a long time ago and that the technological world had left me napping in the process. Sharon used to say I was one of those people who'd grown old before their time and of course she can't help but plaster pictures of herself and her boyfriend and what they are doing all over the internet. The only 'like' I ever received was from my daughter who just seemed pleased that I was putting myself out there and looking up old school friends which is apparently what people of 'my generation' do. And yet by contrast Gemma has invited people into her closed world like an open book which is an oxymoron if ever I heard one. I know. It's the English graduate compounded in me. I never was invited back to another dinner party. Pointing out such figures of speech would drive Sharon crazy. Especially as she had only ever really known me as a carpenter. She would accuse me of being snobbish and superior and boring but by then I could no longer hold back without engaging in verbal warfare and exploiting her mind-numbing ignorance for my personal amusement. Once set loose our stifling incompatibility began to spread like poison. We argued in front of anyone. In public. Her parents. Our baby. Our poor little baby. Could Emily's need to crawl into a place where she felt safe had started then? Gemma's life had become far more compelling to me over the course of time but the longer I followed her the greater the fear for my daughter's state-of-mind became and the mistakes I was making as a consequence given my ex-girlfriend's increasingly troubling lifestyle choices.

The first time I agreed to smuggling Emily into a case was at the age of five and of course it had only seemed like child's play then even if my memories of finding Gemma hidden under beds, inside boiler cupboards and once, an industrial dryer (when we spent a long weekend at a seaside resort with the lure of the laundry room just beneath our first floor apartment), were never far from my mind. Also, given the aroused state I could sometimes find her in was like discovering her with an amorphous lover. An incubus that appeared at will. On more than one occasion I found her going through a series of seemingly unstoppable convulsions, her eyes rolled back in her head, taken to a place she had never been with me. Yet her outrage at being discovered would bring about a feud between us that could last for days. As if I'd been spying when I was only ever concerned for her whereabouts and safe-keeping. I knew by then the thing was bigger than me. That I couldn't hope to compete. Which was probably why that for a very long time, and despite my daughter displaying the same obvious predilections, I dismissed the fact that I could ever have known two such significant people in my life with the same rare affection for something a majority of people would have a phobia about.

It was my daughter's birthday and we had practiced a routine where I was the absent-minded magician and entertained the audience by pretending not to know where any of my props were and so would be given them by the 'disembodied' hand of Emily from inside the suitcase that I became known to ubiquitously trawl around not just to parties but anywhere. Family gatherings. By public transport. A trip to the supermarket. She wanted to be taken everywhere in it. No doubt I made quite a reputation for myself with the neighbours and people alike who had never heard of our 'act' and must have assumed I travelled a lot each time I set out or loaded up the car with the suitcase in the boot. That is, the suitcase inside the boot with my daughter inside it. My greatest fear in that situation was of course in being pulled over by the police which would not only make me drive everywhere as if under rigorous examination but felt like I was leaving the scene of a crime and trying hard not to draw attention to myself. That's how it would make me think. As if I really had kidnapped a child. My legs would tremble against the pedals causing the car to habitually stall. I would break out into a sweat. I worried over the rear-view mirror to see who was following. Even the very first time I agreed to it which was only meant for fun something inside me knew it was wrong. But then after the second and third time I knew there was no going back.

So Emily would hand me a wand from inside the case, a pack of cards or a bunch of plastic flowers. We even ventured as far as a live rabbit whose name was Betty and who seemed to like being in the case with Emily as much as my daughter did. Though with every performance I expected some tittle-tale to inform if not the RSPCA then almost certainly child welfare. But no one ever did. The party performances grew in popularity under the guise of a cack-handed magic show. I would begin by telling the crowd that Emily was running late and on her way. Feigning a state of clumsy confusion because she was supposed to be there to assist me which prompted much giggling and laughter not just from the enraptured toddlers and children gathered but the fixated on-watching parents. Because of course everyone knew where she was. My finale being the pantomime-like invitation to the audience to tell me if anyone had seen Emily.

"She's in the case!" the kids would scream and shout and point until near fever-pitch, which was always a nervous moment for me because I knew how much my daughter loved and wanted to remain in there. But she would eventually clamber out to all the accolades, a little coy and not quite understanding, like an animal in the circus or the zoo must feel. Who was looking at who, I couldn't help but wonder a little over-protectively? Watching the applauding crowd, the laughing faces, the open-mouthed surprise on some of the younger ones, the cheering mums and dads, there was always that point when a sense of shame would creep over me and I had to fight down the urge to just whip my daughter up in my arms and get her out of there. She hadn't known it then of course but in time Emily would come to learn how I had hidden her condition within the barely acceptable social constraints of a child entertainer. I had reverted to the same defence mechanism I used as a schoolboy to ward off playground bullies by instead of sticking up for myself would attempt to make them laugh just to avoid a dead arm, Chinese burn or worse. I would pull faces, talk in funny voices, walk spastically and generally behave like the court jester. Anything. I would do anything in an attempt to hide the fear I felt for myself and the true and burning cowardice buried deeply within. And so it was that my daughter became known as 'The Girl in a Suitcase' and so much so that we were often asked to perform the same routine at many of her other friends' parties, and friends of friends, and that went on for several years after until it obviously had to come to an end. Except that it didn't. Not for Emily anyway.

Gemma had told me she was around the same age when in his ignorance her father thought he could 'cure' her claustrophilia by simply banning it and allowing her to hide away in the limited confines of her bedroom where he could pretend she was just like any other little girl off playing in her room. And then I learnt she slept with snakes and would post Instagram pictures and little videos of herself being tied and gagged. Telling Emily I couldn't carry her around in a case anymore was the hardest thing I had ever done. Especially as most of the time she had taken to living and sleeping in it with the habit of a couch potato slouching down to watch TV at every opportunity. But apart from anything else she was just getting too heavy to drag around anymore and I still feared the day I was reported to some authority or other. How could I ever explain it without her being taken away from me? In my mounting concern I slowly began to realise I may have committed some criminal act and would be arrested and quite possibly imprisoned. And like Emily, who I had overheard many times dismissing the subject as just being a childhood phase whenever one of her friends fondly referred to it, I too had begun to lie about its continuance which suggested not just a sense of embarrassment and guilt in us both but a deeper-rooted complicit acceptance of her secret needs which began to eat into my conscience and left me feeling the way Gemma's father must for ever having encouraged it. Whatever it was. Whatever it had become began to take her over. It manifested in her mood swings. I would hear her talking to herself. Most disturbing of all was when she was in the case. As if there was someone else inside or that my daughter was displaying signs of schizophrenia and that I could lose her forever to it. So I hid the suitcase away and continued to build more cupboards for her to feel safe and protected in instead.

Gemma had openly admitted to her love of tight spaces giving her a sense of arousal once she grew to an age of sexual self-discovery and had found herself in that cave system. It had seemed an innocent enough tale at the time and something that my insecurity had passed off as more of a fantasy given my insight into the unique pleasures of a claustrophile. And yet still I found myself persistently trying to re-enact those same preferred desires with our love-making by cocooning myself around her tightly under covers as if she was still wedged in that pothole. She went along with it for a time. I never fully understood it and I don't think she did too. Not then. I just wanted to make her happy. I could never make her 'see stars'. Or a zodiac for that matter. And then years later I saw her website and everything fell into place.

An eight-year-old pyromaniac, say, wasn't the same as the eighteen-year-old or even the twenty-eight-year-old who might already be doing time in prison for arson. My point being, was I aiding and abetting my daughter towards the same sexual fetish as Gemma or was it already there? Bondage, ligotage, domination and submissiveness. A seemingly sadomasochistic world that I couldn't hope to comprehend. And yet still without ever actually colluding both Emily and I would continue to put on a pretence for her mother whenever she deigned to visit or take our daughter out for the afternoon with always the end result of Emily rushing into my arms at the doorway and holding me tight as if to never let her go again. As if she couldn't breathe for the open places she had been subjected to and leaving her mother standing confused and irritated and who might have been justified in sensing something being afoot if she had been interested or cared enough. No sooner would her mother leave and Emily would scramble like a rodent into one of her many devised comfort zones and not emerge for hours later or until I took her something to eat.

Over the course of time her built-in wardrobe space began to take up more than half her bedroom. What to anyone else must have looked like some overly-ambitious and not particularly professionally designed or well-executed network of cupboard space to house an abundance of childhood clutter was in fact a carefully customized home for a claustrophile with soft interior lighting and cushioned compartments and with barely a toy in sight. Emily's conventional bed and its Disney designs became redundant as did the TV I bought her the Christmas before to try and tempt her into some sort of normality. The wardrobes and its safe-haven 'caverns' could not only help but remind me of Gemma but became such a place of almost honeycomb sanctuary for my daughter that she had taken to permanently sleeping in there. Do her homework, eat her meals, read, and up until and after Betty the bunny died, accommodate the type of small pets who also seemed to relate to a crepuscular confinement. Hamsters and such.

She had yet to ask for a puppy. Or, now I think about it. A snake.

And so it went on. Even though of course it couldn't possibly go on. I had heard this particular train coming a mile down the track just like the suitcase. What had I been thinking? Emily would soon be a teenager. I had high hopes for her academically but I was not only stunting her development by letting it continue I was actively supporting the condition. Rather perversely, I couldn't help thinking, I had built my daughter a prison in the guise of a safe place of refuge that I knew she would scurry into of her own volition. Just like her pet hamster would its cage. Just like Betty and her little corner nest of old blankets and hay. But why? For better or worse I had reached the point of Gemma's father. God help me. It all had to stop.

I put my decision into action the time Emily was to go on a school trip. An outdoor week of team-building in The Peak District with lots of activities; camping, orienteering, abseiling, zip-wire crossings. I can't say it was something she was looking forward to and began to see it as her living anathema approaching. She constantly appealed to me to write to the school and excuse her as the time approached with a sprained ankle or some such story.

"Since when do we lie, Emily?" I asked her. "Since when do we collude to lies?"

But I could see in her face what she was thinking. That we had kept her secret life from everyone else so far and in doing that if we had not technically lied we certainly hadn't told anyone about it either, not since the magic shows had stopped anyway which was a long time ago. The weeks before Emily left, the seemingly frivolous shopping trips to purchase walking boots and all sorts of sporting gear given my usual thrifty husbandry for calling family and friends to see what I could borrow (I even let her talk me into buying a new phone so we could Skype while she was away) were all viewed with suspicion. My inner enthusiasm for seeing the trip as a springboard to getting my daughter out of the habit of her closet existence was being interpreted as an excuse to get rid of her for the week despite my attempts to reassure her otherwise.

"What are you going to do while Emily's away, Daddy? Are you going to be with that woman?" she caught me off-guard one evening by asking. "Is that why you want your little girl out of the way?"

"What woman?" I replied nervously. I always addressed the third person very carefully. It was Emily's way of handling a difficult conversation. She had done it from a very early age but it could still send a chill through me. I still worried that she might have a split-personality disorder.

"The weird one you like on Twitter and Facebook."

"How…?"

"Oh, Daddy. You never turn the computer off properly. You have to log out not just switch it off."

I started to panic at the things she may have read and seen.

"Well, you shouldn't be looking at that stuff anyway."

"Why?"

"It's inappropriate."

"Why do you look at it then?"

"It's just adult stuff. That's all. There's nothing wrong with it. I don't mean that," I stumbled along. "I just don't want you getting any ideas."

"About what?"

"It doesn't matter. Look, you're right. I should know more about computers. You're going to have to show me how this Skip thing works by the way," I deliberately tried to play the fool to get her off the subject. My technological ignorance was one of the few things that made her laugh. The only thing, I was dismayed to think then. When had she suddenly turned so serious? We used to have so much fun planning the magic shows. Those really had been the best days.

"It's 'Skype', Daddy. You're not that much of a moron."

"I'm not a moron at all, actually. I have a BA in English and MA in journalism. But you can just call me Master."

She looked away at this as if I had unsettled her. It wasn't something I hadn't reminded her of before. Though it wasn't something I bragged about either as Emily well knew. I have a friend I am proud to show off as a writer. He's never been published but the work is there. I've read a lot of his manuscripts. But he would never admit to it because he's a delivery driver. It took me some time to know how he feels. Sharon's parents would never stop trying to impress people with my credentials. But I could always see the question hovering on their lips.

"Saying you're a writer when you're a delivery driver is like saying you practise in brain surgery," my friend once told me.

"What is it, Emily?" I asked.

"When I tell the other girls that you went to university and have a degree they always ask then why is your Dad a carpenter."

Always? I don't remember her friends questioning that when we were doing the magic shows. But she was in senior school now and I knew she was getting a hard time of it.

"And what do you say?" I asked.

"Emily says that Jesus was a carpenter," she looked up coyly from between her long parted hair.

"Does she really?" I sat back and folded my arms, shaking my head and looking at her in momentary wonder.

"And so was Joseph."

"How about that," I smiled to myself and felt a warm glow.

Well, my daughter did like to read. But despite my own learnings theology wasn't a strong point. For some reason I'd always thought Jesus was a gardener.

"Well, you be sure to thank Emily for me."

"Don't be stupid, Daddy," she said.

And that was the end of that.

"Do you like her?"

"Who? Oh…" it took me a moment to backtrack. "Well, on the subject of education that's where I met her. We're old friends from university, Emily. That's all."

"Was she your girlfriend?"

"Listen, Emily. No one is ever going to replace you if that's what you're thinking."

Yet how else was she supposed to feel if not suddenly abandoned after having hidden her away all this time? Emily is twelve-years-old. She is growing very tall and at a rate that makes her appear gangly but can still fold herself into a very small space like an Ikea flat-pack. The damage I had done began to make me look at her with new eyes in everything she said and did. So I continued making excuses about not being able to drive her into school. I told her she was a big girl and too old to ride in the boot and that she should get the bus with all the other kids. In an attempt to break the habit of bringing meals to her cupboard cage I took her out to a few fast food restaurants in the guise of a treat. I was going too fast. I knew it. But I had to start breaking some habits. It wasn't like she had a boyfriend addiction or something and her schoolwork was suffering. If anything she was the model child. What am I saying? She is the model child. Apart from her iPhone she had never really been interested in reality TV or computer games or any of the stuff most kids like. But then Emily wasn't like most kids. She liked to read a lot and when she wasn't seeking out some lucifugous relief seemed mainly to live inside her own head. As a young girl she was always singing and talking to herself but more recently had taken to what I can only describe as reciting in unnerving soliloquy and yes of course always in the third person. Like she was auditioning for a part in a play. Half the time I thought she had a friend round without my knowledge. But for one reason or another her friends had stopped coming. It was as if she was deliberately ostracizing herself not just from her peers but the rest of the world. Perhaps even herself. That couldn't be healthy. And now I had to worry about what she might have come across on the computer and if Gemma's increasingly bizarre online revelations resonated anything in her.

The next time I looked at Gemma's Twitter page it read: Would like to chat but muffled by duck tape, hogtied and inside a body bag with orifice zip entry only. Gotta luv the ST more than the SM. (Submission Trust). Lol. Now what the hell was that safe word? WTF??! I can't speak anyway! My mouth's covered in duck tape! Lol lol lol lol.

Not that she would care or think it any of my business but there was a part of me that still felt responsible for Gemma and the world she had succumbed to. It was hard not to look upon ever meeting her as some sort of fatalistic warning or see her progressively disturbing prose as a crystal ball into Emily's future. Even if my daughter didn't develop a penchant for being bound and gagged in order for erotic arousal then what? A life in the circus as The Incredible Folding Woman? I had begun to curse my first ever decision to let Emily continue sleeping under that toy shelf in the cupboard when she was just two-years-old. And all the tens of times I had acquiesced after. Until I was taking her everywhere in a suitcase.

Would like to chat but muffled by duck tape…

Because of my ex-girlfriend I thought that I was somehow qualified to manage it when for the life of me I had never really recognised Gemma's needs sexually or otherwise anyway.

…hogtied…

And so I came to the worst decision of my life.

…and inside a body bag with orifice zip entry only.

In my mounting panic for both Emily's teenage and adult wellbeing I had seen my opportunity. While she was away on her school trip I planned to dismantle her cupboard warren and turn her bedroom into a minimalistic showroom where not even a shadow could hide.

The old suitcase I used to carry my daughter around in had been hidden away in a caged storage unit in the basement of my apartment building. Emily knew where it was if only because it was also where we kept our boxes of assorted Christmas decorations. When we went down there I'd catch her looking as if in a trance. Her troubled expression seemingly evoked by memories of wistfulness and pain and guilt. As if the case was an old childhood heirloom that had been discarded and left out years before and in all weathers to fade and fall apart and eventually disintegrate. She never said anything and I can't even remember the last time we spoke about the magic shows which I suppose was the start of the sad and deeper-lying estrangement that had begun to form between us after I took the case away. I don't know how you let something like that happen between you and your own child especially in one as young as Emily. It's easy to say now but I should have told her what the suitcase and the shows still meant to me instead of it becoming a taboo subject and leaving her to see the case stuffed back in the shadows redundant and left covered in dust and cobwebs. Just the way we had found it.

The evening before Emily was due to leave I brought the case up and put it down on her bed and left her to pack while I made dinner. I set her equipment out on the floor. Her clothes and personal and cosmetic items all in neat piles. Everything she would need. She looked on in quiet resentment as I did this. Her arms crossed her chest like a folded deckchair. I knew that look. Had seen it many times when confronted with something she didn't want to do. And because I never really knew the full potential of what Emily was capable I sometimes feared she might disappear in a puff of smoke if she didn't get her own way. In the early days Sharon was always losing her around the house and point-blank refused to take her on any more shopping expeditions after twice losing her in malls. The latter of which had the whole place sealed-off and made headlines in all the local papers when Emily was eventually spotted on relayed CCTV by security crawling into one of those giant overhead air-conditioning conduits. And even though I convinced myself this could have been as much a result of my ex-wife's negligence as anything else and used it as a source of blame and one-upmanship in our continuing rows I can't say I was surprised when they found my daughter where she was. Unlike Sharon's over-the-top hysterics I must have been the only parent in the world who never worried when their child suddenly went missing. I knew she'd be somewhere just like I knew I would eventually find Gemma. I say that but it was really what I just told myself in an effort to excuse and laugh away my daughter's behaviour to friends and family who I couldn't blame for thinking was just becoming naughty and recalcitrant. But what they didn't know is that the deeper truth lay in a crayon-written note Emily had left me at a very young age when I had given her a severe telling off for what I saw as 'hiding' when we were in a hurry to leave to get to Sharon's brother's wedding of which Emily was to be a bridesmaid. At the time we were living in a modest two-bedroomed terraced house and the ceremony happened to coincide with our neighbours moving which only added to the chaos of the day. A big removal lorry turned up early in the morning and was already blocking the road. Then our new neighbours arrived with another big removal lorry. Apparently, there had been a mix-up about the exchange of keys. You could hear the arguments outside from our open bedroom window as Sharon and I were getting ready. At the weekend if everyone was home the street would usually be lined with cars bumped up on both sides of the kerb which meant it was give-way traffic only and as time began to tick I knew it would be left to me to initiate some strategy of getting us out of our blocked-in parking space if we were ever going to make it in time for the big day.

And then Emily went missing.

She was still only at the sleeping in her cupboard stage then but what with the huge yawning removal doors left open all the while and umpteen items of furniture stacked deep inside the cavernous maws of both trailers I should have sensed that the stowaway in her might have been tempted to find a place to burrow. But in the end she wasn't in either. Emily had taken it upon herself to wander into next door's house and steal inside a little carpeted cupboard under the stairs where the hoover was normally kept. It took over an hour to find her. Needless to say we were late for the wedding. Emily's dress was crumpled and her hair needed tidying. Sharon was incandescent with rage so it was left to me to reprimand our daughter who just gave me a blank-eyed stare all the while I was knelt in front of her and doing my best to make her understand. But she didn't. In the same way an awoken dozing dog might not. In all the commotion of the day she had simply found a place to lie. Was she breaking the law? Was she hurting anyone?

Stop examining me, Jerry. Why can't it just be me?

Gemma's plea would start to haunt me as Emily grew older to the point I would dream about my daughter asking the same thing in her still-childlike voice. Would become to fear the words if she ever did because even after all these years I still didn't have an answer.

Why can't it just be me?

The wedding photographer couldn't coax a smile out of her. She wouldn't talk for the rest of the day. Emily made sure she stole the show in that respect. And then I woke to find the note the following day under my pillow and have kept it all this time as a reminder if only because it was the first time she began to refer to herself in the third person. It read: Emily is going away Daddy so do not try looking becawze you will <u>never ever</u> find her.

Of course, packing Emily's case was normally the sort of thing I would have done for her. She was still only twelve after all but I had convinced myself she needed to know the seriousness of my intentions in making her go and taking the first steps towards a new and independent life. I wouldn't be there forever, I wanted to tell her. I couldn't drive her around in the boot of my car forever just like I couldn't drag her around in a suitcase. I wanted to tell her these things but I never did. Like Gemma's father, I just let my actions speak for themselves and hoped she would work the rest of it out for herself so I really shouldn't have been surprised to return to her room after preparing our meal to find that she wasn't there and that she hadn't packed the case. After a cursory search of her wardrobes I called out her name and went to check the rest of the flat. It goes without saying that I knew every place she'd ever hidden and she wasn't getting any smaller. I raised my voice in annoyance. Demanding that she come out that very instant and feeling like we were playing one of our old games. I went to the front door and looked down the corridor. Then I went to the living-room window and gazed down at the dark and yellow-lit gloom of the car park. There was a last, gossamer-thin autumnal mist in the air. I could feel and hear my wrestling, thumping heart giving way to the whole idea. I wanted to remain stuck in time like everyone does at least one point in their life. For it just to be me and Emily and nothing ever change. Living with my daughter had always been a bit like owning a precious pet in that if it got outside without your notice it was probably gone forever. It must have been thirty minutes since I'd started preparing dinner. If she really had just silently let herself out of the front door she could be anywhere. The thought made me panic for the first time. I paced around the rooms again. Pulling off sofa cushions. Looking behind curtains. Even peering behind the dusty fur-ball backs of appliances. The sort of stupid places you look when you've lost a set of keys and exhausted all hope and logic. Emily's coat and scarf were still hanging by the door. It was cold outside. She had to be in the apartment. Against all my better instincts I thought about ringing her mother. But then in that moment heard myself on the end of the phone asking the same question I had asked our magic show gatherings all those times and of which you are no doubt bursting to tell me at this very point, dear reader. And so, I will accommodate you by asking: Has anyone seen Emily?

She's in the case! I hear you roar gleefully at the pages.

And, of course, you are right. Just like the audience was always right because that was the point of the show. I just couldn't believe that for a short time I had been hoisted by my own petard, my meticulously planned coup de grace of yesteryear - or, most incomprehensibly, duped by my daughter's particularly special double-jointed talents that had, after all, begun with the very suitcase I went back to the bedroom and found her in.

Emily is five-foot four already. A rising, bony, beanpole and awkward colt of a girl with protruding nuts-and-bolts for limb-joints and a long mane of wavy brown hair half-way down her back. Yet could collapse into a tight space like a pleated-skirt. When I quietly peeled back the suitcase lid her circumvoluted form reminded me of one of those perfectly preserved archaeological discoveries buried in a hundred-of-thousands-of-year-old ice tomb. She had dragged a cushion and blanket into the case from her wardrobe and lay sleeping with the impossibly slow and steady breathing of an animal in hibernation. She was in her preferred habitat. One of which would have induced panic in most but not only seemed to relax her further but had an almost immediate effect, reducing her heart-rate to within three times less in a minute than the average human being. I softly took my daughter's wrist and felt her pulse. She had regressed. I know all this as a fact from clinical tests Sharon insisted on putting her through when she began to display such tendencies. Emily could slow her heart-beat at will like a Tibetan monk. It was a gift, they said. And joked that she would live long. Apparently, it wasn't even that unusual. As for her strange sleeping habits, well, children had been hiding in cupboards for centuries, a child psychologist assured us. There was never any mention of claustrophilia. Probably they hadn't wanted to scare us or jump the gun. Especially if Emily had been displaying early signs of something a lot deeper and more complex. And I might have been inclined to go along with it and believe them all if I had never known Gemma.

I had only ever come across the term 'autoerotic asphyxiation' when reading about the accidental deaths of certain celebrities down the years found hanged by themselves with a ligature of some description around a door knob or other fixture. For the less well-educated the idea of this particular practice is the intentional restriction of oxygen to the brain for the desired achievement of increasing sexual excitement and a higher and more prolonged orgasm. Famous people aside this fetish averages around five hundred deaths each year in America, albeit most of them male and usually connected to one sexual persuasion or another. Cross-dressing typically, transvestism, sadomasochism. But not always. In most cases the details of these fatalities had often been recorded by the coroner as an accidental death or one of misadventure, especially in the cases of teenagers. Real statistics were only just coming to light in recent years of a dual dilemma facing parents and authorities upon discovery of such tragedies. On the mother or father's side it was the inability to cope with the 'shame' of finding their child, more often than not, naked, and surrounded by sex toys, pornographic literature, lubrication or some other stimulatory material which the parent in their shock and panic felt inclined to remove in an act now known as 'sanatising' before calling the police. Better to let the world think of their cherubs harbouring miserable and self-torturing suicidal thoughts than comparatively normal sexual ones, it seemed. Not to mention the parents risking incriminating themselves by tampering with crucial evidence. Yet however dangerous and life-threatening the act turned out to be, I doubt anyone ever expects to kill themselves. On how many occasions have we read about such cases being a mystery to the parents, of them always being a 'happy child' with no clue to the apparent torment going on within? Half the time the authorities were going along with the story anyway. Or it was being 'sensitively' concealed from the parents by the police if they were the first to happen upon the discovery on the basis that psychologists and forensic scientists didn't like to talk about the practice outside of their professional circles for fear of giving kids ideas. But then along came the advancement of technology. Smart phones and ipads and histories in hard-drives and a particular individual's sexual interests were not only more difficult to conceal, but much more likely to be openly shared through some form of social media. Chatrooms, mostly.

The morning I took Emily to board the coach for her trip the miserable weather seemed to reflect her mood. The journey north was around nine hours away and the school had instructed everyone that they were setting off early at six. Emily stood watching disconsolately under the still-black sky as I heaved her suitcase into the car boot, seemingly oblivious to the swirling rainstorm that lifted her clothing and chased a discarded fast-food bag and drink carton across the street. A neighbour peered out through a lit window. For the first time probably seeing my daughter in the presence of the case. Though I could tell what Emily was thinking. As she could I. Which is why she turned away with a slight stamp of her foot and got in the back seat where she lay down in the shadows pretending to sleep all the way there and muttering about how much 'Emily' didn't want to go.

The coach was a huge double-decker. When we arrived I could see all the parents standing around shifting on their feet and talking under a swaying panoply of rain-slickened umbrellas illuminated by the coach's interior lights. One or two bore corporate names. Some of my daughter's more privileged friends had moved on to private schools and over the course of the year a new influx of senior school pupils had begun teasing Emily for talking in the third person. They had also learnt about the time she had crawled into the air-conditioning duct and even the magic shows had become a subject of ridicule. It saddened me to think that the source of these whispers probably came from the very same girls who not so long before had marveled at her emergence from the suitcase at the end of our performance and indeed the ever-expanding cupboard warrens where they would come and play until one by one they all grew out of it. In a moment of weakness that little bullied boy in me who'd deflected a beating by acting as the class clown wanted to scoop my daughter up and bundle her into the car boot and just take her home and I swear I would have if Emily hadn't already been registered by one of the teachers standing by the coach and braving the elements whilst trying to protect the sodden pages of her clipboard.

Emily.

I gave the suitcase to the driver who was working hard stacking the luggage into a deep black hold that ran the length of the entire coach beneath the first deck of seats. For a long while she just stood there almost transfixed. Looking into that large gloomy space where I knew she imagined to be lying snuggled between suitcases and backpacks.

Why can't it just be me?

And even though I had long convinced myself that everything I had in mind to do was in my daughter's best interests I all at once became gripped by an overwhelming anxiety as I and the other parents stood watching our children file up into the stairwell of the coach. No doubt the other mums and dads' fears would have been a lot more rational. Homesickness. Supervision concerns. Even danger to their offspring given the activities. No one, I felt sure, was about to commit a very cruel act in their child's absence. One which they would probably never be forgiven for. Gemma had likened it to taking away her favourite childhood toy. That her father might as well have been cutting off her arm. I saw it as a betrayal of trust and knew Emily would, too. And almost as if hearing my thoughts she turned to look back at me over her shoulder upon boarding. Giving me that 'other' Emily look. That third person girl whose power over my daughter could sometimes frighten me deep down. "You're leaving me with her?" she seemed to be asking. But even then I couldn't tell which one of them was saying it. I tried offering a reassuring smile and went to raise a hand to wave but she only swished that long brown pony-tail in a last defiant gesture at being made to go and disappeared up inside the coach for good. We never even kissed.

I had begun to worry about Gemma's growing absence when her last tweet remained the same for over forty-eight hours. I would normally only visit her site every now and then and quite expected some quip about how she had locked herself in a safe for a day or wriggled out of some sexual contraption or other, Houdini-like, and lived to tell the tale. But her last comment continued to have a disturbing effect on me to the point I began checking in every few hours. What had happened to her? In my experience she was never far away from her online world. My concern grew to the point of even messaging her a few times which might have seemed strange from Gemma's point of view after our initial re-connection years before and with no contact since apart from my distant voyeurism. Not only that. Most of her followers were growing worried too and had begun chattering feverishly amongst themselves as to her whereabouts.

Don't try this at home, folks!

I was getting a bad feeling.

Gemma was of course referring to the dangers of erotic asphyxiation which was how the subject had been brought to my attention. After that I went off and did some research that only alarmed me further in the unveiling light of hitherto teenage tragedies and had begun to take this as a sign of sorts. The only difference being that as far as I knew Gemma practiced it with a partner. The dangers of doing it alone is that if something goes wrong there is no one to help. I read about a case of a 23-year-old man who had strung a length of boat rope through an eye hook he'd driven into the floor, looped it around his neck in a way that allowed him to control the tension and threaded it into a second eye hook which he'd affixed to the archway above his head. Then he just took the free end in his hand and pulled. When the police discovered his body he was slumped in a cat's cradle of ropes in his obvious struggle to break free, within arm's reach of his laptop computer that was flashing pornography. Clearly, this was not an intended suicide even though the case was recorded as such until the mother and father began to probe and came across the more grisly details and decided to publish the article as a warning to other parents in particular. According to one expert I subsequently read, when pressure is put on the vagus nerve instant death can happen. The sudden increase in pressure sends a message to the heart to shut down and a cardiac arrest will inevitably result. If I had never met Gemma I don't know at what point I would be with my daughter. As intolerant to Emily's condition as her mother perhaps. As unreceptive as Gemma's father? But more importantly, where would Emily be? I am not a particularly spiritual person but I have long come to think of that university romance as if not a strange twist of fate then almost certainly an omen to be heeded.

I went about dismantling Emily's room as soon as I got back home. I set down my toolbox and surveyed the surroundings with new eyes. My daughter and I had never been apart. Not for one single day. Her absence brought about a whole new reality to the room that for all my good intentions I now saw as some sort of prison and even had me questioning my own motives. Outside of Emily's claustrophilia, was there a condition in a parent similar to, say, Munchhausen's syndrome, whereby instead of deliberately keeping a child permanently sick to draw attention to yourself you created a world for them that they would never want to leave, and that therefore, would never leave you? If her mother had been interested enough to venture over the threshold of the flat let alone Emily's bedroom, and likewise anyone else, who knows what conclusions they may have drawn. Only Emily's friends had ever visited and now I have to ask myself why I was always a little nervous about that and what they might have gone back and reported to their parents. In any event, the friends eventually stopped coming as my daughter's expanding warren became more and more difficult to explain for the both of us.

Two thirds of Emily's bedroom had been built to accommodate her wants. The converted flat we lived in was much like the house I had shared as a student except that Emily and I had the whole upper floor, incorporating big rooms with high ceilings. What to anyone else just looked like a run of elaborate wardrobe space along two walls hid a mini supersystem of various dens and cubbyholes flanked at each end by two tall shaft-like spaces with just enough room for her to crouch or stand and wriggle into tunnel entrances that led to rat-runs both above and below, all of which had been added upon over the years. Every little extra idea had only seemed exactly that at the time. Her conventional wardrobe had long been shared with mine. Likewise, her discarded or outgrown childhood memorabilia that I always felt a moral obligation to hang on to, like someone whose kid had gone missing years before and still prayed for their return – is that how I saw my child, that someone, something had taken her and I was still waiting for the real Emily, the normal Emily to come back?

For the first of a thousand times and more I would see my daughter standing on the steps to the coach, the rain and wind tugging and stirring at everything around except her expression which remained stony-faced, hard-eyed and pocketed by the shadow of the stranger inside her.

Emily had always collected torches but I had no notion of how many she actually owned until I began emptying out every hiding-hole. In the process I became very aware I was not only invading but violating her private sanctuary and began to feel a little nauseous at the thought yet at the same time a deep, self-loathing anger set in. In my hurry to eradicate the madness, to wipe out the evidence and pretend it had never happened I was torn by thoughts of Emily and what I was doing to her. But it was too late. As if I had put my daughter to the stake I heard her scream with each savage hammer blow or rent of hinges as I smashed and ripped the whole thing down in an hour of pent-up resentment for myself and the distorted upbringing I had encouraged my child into instead of perhaps trying to make her understand the dangers of it. I had destroyed her world. The result was a carnage of piled timber ready for burning. Peppered drill holes and great gouges of plaster spilled from the walls as if an AK-47 had been taken to them. Wiring lay tangled and hanging. Shelving brackets and light and plug sockets that my skilled-labourer mind told me might still be worth something or put to another use lay everywhere. All of it. I remembered building every section of it. Years of careful dismantling, re-designing and perfecting with great fun and gusto and all with a warm sense of attachment for my daughter's desires that now seemed to have been reneged overnight. Standing amongst the debris I came to realise I had lost all control when gazing around in my near-dumbfounded state at the damage that had been done. If I had just walked in then, it looked as though a lunatic had been let loose in the place. I stood there panting and heaving. Spitting out the floating modes of stirred-up dust. My clothes soaked in sweat and my eyes red and tear-stained and emotions torn to shreds at the surrounding devastation. There was no going back then.

The day after the trip up the kids had been allowed to contact their families by phone between eight and eight-thirty every night before bed for the rest of the week. With painstaking deliberation and fingers that felt like fat chips I at last managed to master my new phone and text Emily in advance telling her I would be waiting for her to call but she   never responded. By eight-thirty I texted her again to see if she was okay but she didn't answer so by nine I called the teacher's emergency number and to my dismay it was Miss Anders who answered, Emily's bane of an athletics teacher and someone with whom I had obviously had a few run-ins over the years given my daughter's 'indoor' disposition. She also had a habit of calling me by full Christian name as if I was one of the children but which I found to be a passive-aggressive way of reminding me who was in charge. Miss Anders told me Emily hadn't been feeling well during the coach trip up and hadn't participated in the next day's events, which had been river-crossing, so had spent the afternoon and evening shut off in her shared room. Miss Anders had the same, hard, barely-concealed and infuriatingly patronising tone of exasperation in her voice that I had come to know through more recent conversations between us. As if we shared a mutual frustration at Emily's apparent 'shenanigans' and that we were better off ignoring them. They had called in a doctor but of course he couldn't find anything wrong, she said with cemented satisfaction. "Well, you know, Emily," she concluded by saying in a high-pitched tone, as if she was already feeling the pressures of the whole excursion.

Yes, I did, I continued to think deep into the night. I got up around three and entered my daughter's bedroom. I had cleared everything out during the afternoon she left and then the next day set about repairing the walls with filler and rubbing down the woodwork. The old carpet and curtains were gone. Emily's childhood wallpaper stripped. There wasn't a semblance of her old room that I could see which brought about a deep and familiar sense of change in me. It was the same feeling I had when I knew Sharon had finally left me for good. You get an endless amount of clues and warnings and threats and false leavings in a long, declining relationship. Feeling constantly torn between panic for something you are habitually attached to and yet relief for finally being rid of it. And then one day you wake up and realise that something has gone and is never coming back and you feel different. You feel okay. But I shouldn't have been feeling like that about my daughter. Worse still, I shouldn't have been fighting an unshakeable sense of foreboding for ever having agreed to a trip she was so against.

Of course, I could have put it all back or designed something new. Or maybe just created at least one space where she could go and be herself. But wouldn't that just be the start of everything happening again? Nevertheless, the thought constantly occurred to me over the next day or so as I papered and painted her room in a soft apple white, exchanging the heavy curtains of old for smart, bright Venetian blinds that even when closed couldn't quite keep out the probing daylight. I intended to sand down the floorboards and varnish them. There was to be nothing hidden under the carpet anymore. Metaphorically or otherwise. I wanted the walls to be flat and bare and without depth, as if suspecting my daughter of somehow being able to camouflage or submerge into them chameleon-like, a shape-shifting sprite. I wanted a natural airy ambience and not one that was more suited to a vampire. I use these analogies freely because I had always felt there to be something almost paranormal about my daughter. From the moment I had discovered her as a toddler hidden under the toy shelf outside her bed and every morning of every day since, a held-back panic existed in me each time I went to wake her in the belief that one day I would find that she had simply vanished to somewhere no one could find her. I used to think about it all the time. A child with an inclination to contort and hide. Who felt safe in small, dark spaces? Was it any wonder I lived with this irrational fear that she might one day ball herself up into nothingness? That she would disappear down a rabbit hole of her own making. Lost to me forever in some parallel equivalent of Narnia much the way Gemma seemed to have done? After the mall incident and at Sharon's insistence I put locks on all the windows and doors. Imprisoning Emily inside her own prison. But now I had removed all those too. It was the only way. I had opened the birdcage.

Gemma's absence grew to a fevered concern amongst her Twitter followers over the days I worked on the bedroom. Don't try this at home, folks! Something about that flippant sign-off made me suspect it to be some sort of attention-seeking stunt and as a consequence I began to wonder if I had misread the signs from the very beginning and in doing so had ultimately misinterpreted my own daughter's condition? That long-ago fresher year when what I took to be a deep and insecure psychological illness in needing to hide away from the world now seemed in Gemma's case a complete turn-around towards an almost narcissistic desire to create concern. I remember how Gemma seemed oblivious to my worries for her wellbeing whenever I fretted over her disappearances, fearing that she could have crawled into a hiding-hole with no escape, or somehow entrapped herself and suffocated, much like Emily's stunt at the mall when surely some small part of my daughter must have known of the distress she would cause her mother and I by doing such a thing.

Well, you know Emily.

Sharon would often use that same exasperated tone. Constantly accusing me of being manipulated and pandering to Emily's affectations. By then our daughter had regularly taken to sleeping in cupboards even though her mother threatened to ban her bedtime story read or some such punishment when of course Emily knew I would always argue her cause. Most of the arguments we ever had were about her. We'd been told by so-called experts she would grow out of it which was good enough for me despite my lingering reservations but the mall incident not only freaked Sharon out but seemed to trigger my wife's increasingly derelict duties as a mother. In the end I was getting Emily dressed in the morning and packing her lunchbox and doing the school runs and helping with her homework. But I was also doing other things without Sharon's knowledge. I'd let Emily ride in the boot of the car. At weekends when the supervisor wasn't around I took her to work with me and let her play and hide in the empty office building my company had been contracted to renovate. There were lots of rooms and cupboards and stairwells and a basement packed with crates and boxes full of old files. It was also piled high with discarded office furniture and buried within is where Emily found the suitcase. I've always called it a suitcase but it really has the capacity of a trunk. Its cracked leather exterior had a cherry finish and was decorated in faded travel stickers from the far continents. Countries from all over Asia, Africa and South America which only added to its mystique and prompted the question why someone should have left it down there with all the other second-hand junk that was to be sold off as a job lot unless it had some darker, inauspicious origin. But once I found Emily sleeping contentedly inside I somehow knew it had a place in our lives even if I could never have envisaged how much. In my naivety I had at first seen it as an alternative place for her to sleep like the old solution of using a cabinet drawer for a baby's crib not the bogus accessory of a charlatan magician. Stuffed with a blanket and pillow I thought it could act as a sort of middle-ground between her own bed and the cupboard. But it wasn't long before she wanted to be entombed in the thing and so I customized it with a couple of casters and a zip that could be opened from the inside and pretty soon I was taking her everywhere in it.

I got a text that Thursday from Emily offering to FaceTime me later in the evening which was all new to me. Don't worry, Daddy. Just pick up when I call, ok? I missed my good old reliable gadget-less Nokia. But she sounded in good spirits and it would be the first time we had spoken since she left. I also hadn't heard from Miss Anders for a couple of days by then which I took to be a good thing and was eager to hear what pursuits Emily had taken part in. When I picked up the call later I had just got out of the shower and wandered absently into Emily's room thinking about the next day's project. I answered it naturally and put the phone to my ear before hearing Emily, screaming with laughter, telling me to look at the screen. Apart from the instant tug at my heart I felt at seeing her beaming face I found myself rearing in confused surprise at this technological marvel, much to my daughter's delight, who went on to share with her friends in booming audio my ignorance of all things post-millennium.

"You don't have to do anything. Remember me telling you? Just answer the call."

"I'm scared to touch the thing," I admitted.

"Oh, Daddy. Stop pretending. I've seen you on Twitter and Facebook stalking women."

"I don't stalk- Hey, can your friends here me – I mean, can they hear what I'm saying?"

"Of course, we're on FaceTime, silly. They can also see you so put on some clothes, Daddy!" she giggled and covered her mouth in mock disgust.

I heard her other friends laugh too. It was a joy to think of her in the company of girls who may well have been the same ones labelling her as some sort of freak and my heart soared to imagine her spending days outdoors just like any other budding teenager. In doing what I thought was best had I instead just held her back? The self-persecuting thoughts wouldn't go away. I should have made her get outside herself. Learn a sport. Have an interest. Join a club. Anything.

In my momentary reverie Emily's words suddenly filtered through and gave me cause to look down at myself and realise I was still in my underpants after the shower. Though they could only see my head and shoulders I began to quizzically observe myself in the little window in the corner of the screen the way someone might a bug and playing up to it as if I was still the bumbling magician which only prompted even more hysterics from Emily and her friends in the background. Nevertheless, I didn't want to be the subject of investigation from Miss Anders for parading half-naked in front of underage girls so I propped the phone very gingerly on Emily's dresser lest it should turn itself into a toaster or something and told her to wait a second while I went to put on a shirt. But by the time I returned her mood had completely changed to one I knew all too well.

One of the few things Emily inherited from her mother was the unspoken, accusatory glare. This was first brought to my attention when she was only young and if I deviously dared try avoiding taking her to see friends or family in the suitcase when I had already promised to do so. As she grew older she would come home from school and march straight back out of her room again claiming that I had 'been touching her stuff', which may have meant anything from my tidying up or opening her curtains. God forbid I should so much as even peer into one of her crawlspaces. "I like the way it looks!" she would scream. "It's my nest!"

"Where are you?" she said, once I had come back wearing a T-shirt with tracksuit bottoms and a bounce in my step for making her friends laugh even if it was at my own expense. I was used to being mocked. But Emily had lowered her voice and taken up a position elsewhere. By the way the wind snatched at her words and buffeted the phone's speaker I could tell she was outside.

"What do you mean? At home of course."

"What is that room you are in? That is Emily's room, Daddy. What have you done to the room your daughter sleeps in?"

Another thing the third person would do when angry was to drop all abbreviations. For a long time I told myself it was just a habit she'd picked up at an early age. As a little girl I'd found it almost engaging and might even have encouraged it. As if she had an imaginary friend by the same name. But then I supported a lot of things Emily did in defiance of Sharon that I probably shouldn't have.

I looked around and for the first time saw Emily's bedroom in all its refurbished entirety. I had worked non-stop on it. Fighting my reservations. Not daring to stand back and look at it for any longer than was necessary before getting on with the next immediate task.

She was glaring at me intently on the phone, the wind whipping her hair, pulling at strands, her lower lip trembling and appearing to hyperventilate. I hated that hitching sound she would make between sobs more than anything, especially with us being so far apart. At least twice a year she would go into some sort of breakdown about herself, questioning her condition and needing a father's reassurance until we got to a place where it was us against the world and she would walk off happily after a few hugs and kisses.

"It was going to be a surprise," I offered meekly.

"What have you done to her nest?" she asked again. Her voice rattled demonically, as if the phone was coming apart.

"You're older now," I said. "You're getting older, Emily. You are going to need a big girl's room."

"There is nothing in-," but the last words were lost in the gathering storm.

Something near her was flapping wildly. An awning. A tent. Making it hard to hear.

"No, I know, I mean, not yet," I began to shout, offering up a fake laugh and preparing to lie. To tell her anything rather than have her find out like this.

"Where is everything?" she yelled, beginning to cry. "Where are Emily's safe places? Where is she going to hide?"

"We can talk about it when you get home, okay?" I tried appeasing her. "We can talk about that stuff."

"That was my home, Daddy," she said, in dawning horror. "And now there is nothing there. You have destroyed my home. You have destroyed Emily's home without her permission. You have destroyed my fucking home, Daddy! How could you?"

"Emily, listen," I started to panic. I had never heard her swear. Not even in the third person when it always seemed like I was talking to someone much older. As if that side of her could see right through me. "We can talk about it when you get back, okay? That room – your room, Emily's room… it, it hasn't seen a lick of paint since you were born. It was supposed to be a surprise. A nice surprise. You're growing up and-"

"Stop saying that," she snarled. "Emily does not want to grow up. You can't make me. No one can make me. Where will I go when I'm grown up? Where can I feel safe?"

"You're right," I said. "That's a long way off. You don't have to think about that right now. But, you know, Emily. You can't…you can't just hide away forever."

"Why not?" she sounded a little deflated. "Why not, Daddy? Why can't I just be me?"

And there it was. The all but same question as Gemma's that I had feared answering for so long.

Why can't it just be me?

I wanted to tell her about Gemma muffled by duck tape inside a body bag and how I hadn't heard from her since. Or the young man found in a cat's cradle of ropes in search of erotic stimulation.

Don't try this at home, folks!

"Why not, 'Daddy?'" Emily insisted, but I could tell by the slight change in her tone I was talking to the other Emily. The third person never addressed me by name and it left me feeling uncomfortable and strangely powerless.

"Because…"

"Do you think there is something wrong with Emily?"

"Listen, we can talk about this when-"

"Do you love your daughter or not?"

"Emily, listen to me…"

"Your little girl?"

"Stop it. Stop talking like that. I hate you talking in that other voice. You should have grown out of it by now."

"Emily is going away, 'Daddy'. So do not try looking because you will never, ever find her."

"Oh, God, please don't say that."

"Ever…ever…" she trailed off in a sing-song voice.

"Stop it! This all has to stop! Do you hear me Emily? I mean it. It just has to stop!" I suddenly yelled. I hadn't raised my voice to her in a long, long time. Not since the hoover cupboard incident. "It just has to stop, Emily," I said, reigning in my frustration and trying to sound calm and authoritative which was a joke because she'd always had me round her little finger. Sharon was right. Everyone was right. Why would I have gone to such lengths to keep her claustrophilia a secret after the magic shows had stopped? Knowing what I knew. Why couldn't it have just stayed with the magic shows? That should have been enough.

"Hey," I said, feeling suddenly desperately nostalgic. "Didn't we have some fun with those magic shows?"

But the phone had disconnected. I tried calling back but she must have turned it off. It was the last time we ever spoke.

When Gemma finally re-emerged it wasn't from being entrapped in a body bag or by some rope-bound ligature suspended from the inside of a wardrobe but a spur-of-the-moment yoga holiday in Thailand she had been talked into by a woman called Jasmine she'd met at a party only days before, one of the rules being that all technology was banned. This was not just a form of discipline and physical commitment but one of 'emotional tranquility and spiritual enlightenment', Gemma informed her audience, which would not only be the first of many of her new-found guru's quotes but eventually see Gemma lose almost half her following over the ensuing months. It seems posted pics of the cobra, pigeon or downward-facing dog position did little to stimulate the interest of those used to seeing her in far more darkly erotic poses of sexual confinement. Nevertheless, Gemma went on to inform us that Jasmine had seen an instant connection between the inner yearnings of a claustrophile to find one's 'own space and calm' to that of which deep yoga traditions were founded and that everything she had been seeking from the comfort of the space between her father's legs to being hogtied in a body bag was already within her. She just needed to find it.

Humph, I said to myself. Hogwash more like. Much more of that and I would eventually become another of Gemma's Twitter renegades.

And yet it hadn't escaped my attention since I had 'reunited' with Gemma that there was never a mention of any significant man in her life, unless you included Rosencrantz, the remaining python, and I had only ever assumed her deviant partner in crime, her 'safe word' buddy, was a male. Rather pathetically, along with this slow realisation was an urge to let myself off the hook for never being able to satisfy Gemma sexually. She appeared to live a single and fickle existence but something about her over-enthusiastic prose told me she was quite smitten with Jasmine. I really don't know why I should think that has anything to do with me after all this time. Except that of course I couldn't help but see Gemma as the trailblazer for Emily's forthcoming years. And if that was true all I had to apparently worry about was my daughter turning out to be a lesbian with a yoga addiction. There are worse things for a father to get upset about. I just found myself wishing that Gemma could have discovered this about herself a year earlier, or even months before when I had begun to plot the mindless destruction of Emily's safe-house. And now all the fight had gone out of me. I stood looking around her new room and wished it back together the way it had been the morning she left. It now looked to be awaiting some anonymous renter. I had changed things forever. I had ripped out my daughter's soul. What had I been thinking?

The call came later that next day. The day before Emily was supposed to come home. It was Miss Anders and I immediately braced myself for some reprimand over my daughter's behaviour. In truth, I had been expecting it – but Miss Anders sounded a little funny and hesitant. As if she had called me in the middle of the night seeking a desperate favour and as a consequence I found myself taking command.

"What is it, Miss Anders?" I asked. "What's happened?"

"Emily's lost," she said.

I felt myself turn instantly cold. Those words.

"Lost? What does that mean? Is she lost or did you lose her?"

"If you'll just let me explain…"

Here it was. Here it was, I began to panic. The news I has waited for all my life.

"To lose is not the same meaning as lost. So which one is it, Miss Anders? The verb or the adjective?" I said, trying to be clever and assert even greater control.

Emily is going away Daddy…

In her increasing fluster Miss Anders went on to explain that there had been a potholing expedition and-

"Whoa, whoa," I interrupted her, because that was the last thing I had been preparing myself to hear. "There was no mention of potholing in the itinerary of pursuits."

"I know," Miss Anders took a tremulous pause before her long, ensuing silence seemed to suggest she was taking a moment to consider Emily's history – the infamous mall incident, the magic shows. Emily's general otherworldliness. And so here was Miss Anders now, talking to the very man who once carried his daughter round in a suitcase. Who knows what the school thought not just of Emily, but of me? Mad, probably. Eccentric in the very least. Was it any wonder I'd always felt Miss Anders didn't take me seriously? The carpenter with a Master's.

Well, now she knows, I thought.

"The weather has been so bad here that…well, we've had to come up with other pursuits to keep them occupied."

"That's a dangerous sport," I said flatly. I could feel my mind slowing down. Imagining that underworld Gemma had talked about so vividly. The Australian instructor and his talk of subterranean zodiacs. Natural aqua-zooms. The tiniest gaps and fissures where a person had to slow their breathing just to squeeze through. It was more than possible that Emily had found her haven.

"I'm sure she'll turn up. There's a rescue team down there at this very moment looking for her," Miss Anders hurried on. "She can't have gotten far. I mean, there's really nowhere to go."

"Then how did you lose her?" I asked, quelling an anger that wouldn't quite come because I knew my daughter and the reasons she had done it. A madding voice was chattering in my head. Making it hard to concentrate. They would never find her. They would never find her and it's all your fault. You severed her arm. You destroyed her home while her back was turned. It had been a wicked, cowardly act. A betrayal of Shakespearean proportions. And now they would never find her. She had slinked away just like the python Guildenstern. Because she could. Because some things are just not meant to be imprisoned. They would never find her. Not if she didn't want them to.

"Jeremy, just try and stay calm. She was with a trained prof-"

"Then how did you lose her, 'Belinda'?" I said again, feeling something between rage and fear and the most terrible, sickening, gut-churning cesspit of guilt in my stomach. But there was something else, too. A stirring sense of justification for the way I had handled my daughter all these years. See! Do you see now? I wanted to say. Do you now understand what I have been dealing with all these years? Why there were locks on the windows and doors? Why I had to build her a virtual indoor city? Because my wife couldn't. Oh, no. She didn't want to know. She just gave up and walked out and left. But Miss Anders silence was deafening.

The same way you lost her in the mall.

"How…how long has she been missing?" I spun on the spot and covered my mouth with my hand in some sort of new dull appreciation of the situation. It still wouldn't sink in. It was just Emily trying to frighten me again by hiding, or at least the constant threat of it. She had done it to me all her life.

"It happened this afternoon. I…I don't know. It all got a bit frantic down there. Some of the other children were panicking and growing claustrophobic. We had to get them out."

…never ever find her.

"Jesus Christ…" I uttered. "You left her all alone down there?"

"We…no, we never left her. Another leader came down and then the other children were guided up."

"You don't know my daughter, Miss Anders," I began to whine.

"Please, please try and stay calm, Jeremy. I'm sure…"

"She could crawl into a fucking keyhole!" I yelled. "What the hell were you thinking even taking her down there? Do you hear me? You have no idea what you're dealing with. She could crawl right up that fat fucking cellulite arse of yours and pluck that big bug you've always had for her right out of it! Do you hear me, Belinda? Do you now understand?"

"Well, I…" Miss Anders gasped.

I emitted a manic burst of laughter in a spray of saliva at my own outburst which was so completely out of character I suddenly stood stock still in shock at myself. Staring at my reflection in the black-night sheen of the living room window in a moment of suspended curiosity. For a moment it was as if I couldn't even identify the person in front of me. Not even my eyes.

"You don't know what you've done," I began to utter quietly, shaking my head and resolving that I should go up there. "I can't sit here," I said. "I can't just sit here."

"Please, Jeremy," she urged. "Just wait by your phone and we will contact you as soon as she is found."

But they wouldn't find her. I had known even then that they wouldn't find her. How long could she survive down there without water, two – three days? Unless she had found a natural source. Of course she had. Emily wasn't stupid. There must be hundreds of rivulets and streams and great pools of it big enough to swim in. Perhaps seeing that had been part of the allure. Food, then? Who knew what was edible down there. And, anyway, a human could go a long while without food. So she was safe for now. For quite some time, in fact. I paced through the rooms, beginning to feel a little better. She could survive at least. Just like Gemma's python. Guildenstern wasn't dead. My daughter wasn't dead. I had to remain calm.

But the blackness, I suddenly thought. The dark and the damp and the wet. Once her torch battery died would she panic? It was one thing to climb inside the cosy crypt of a darkened wardrobe or snuggle herself into the reassuring tunnel-light inside a conduit where you knew there was a beginning and end. But an underground cavern with no sure route back? In my mind's eye I chose to imagine great luminous glowing-green stalactites and stalagmites and eerily lit grottos with fairy-tale rock formations looking like something out of Oz's Emerald City. It felt strangely comforting to think Emily had found such a place even if it wasn't true. I had to imagine something positive. That my daughter was in her natural habitat and should not be hunted down like a lion in the bush. Call off the search! I felt like screaming. Leave her alone! Everyone just leave her alone! But of course it was only a fleeting romantic illusion and one I still find myself clinging to even after all this time rather than face the far more real horror. That Emily had crept off of her own accord because of what I had done and died a terrible death down there. Exhausted, shivering, cold and alone and waiting for her Daddy to come and rescue her. My heart was left broken at the thought.

It's been six months since it happened. The old mine entrance is still closed to the public and the television crews who got good mileage out of the story have long since gone. The chief fire officer in charge of the operation began 'scaling down' the search after six weeks claiming it "highly unlikely that any individual could have survived the conditions of such a challenging environment for so long", before shutting it down completely a fortnight after and seemingly entombing Emily forever. Last month yet another team of professional rescue workers with experience in such South American catastrophes as collapsed mine shafts and earthquakes and landslides volunteered to venture down claiming that while there is always hope they were realistically looking to bring up Emily's body. It seems my daughter has either become the subterranean equivalent of an elusive shipwreck full of treasures for pothole enthusiasts or there is some spurious publicity money-making mischief behind such stunts. Probably organized by some shadowy local cartel looking to promote the mine's increased commercial potential if and when it is eventually re-opened to the public. It has certainly put the area on the map much like Huntingdon and Lockerbie's crimes and tragedies did, but not quite for the reasons you might think. The internet has been rife with conspiracy theories about her 'disappearance' once the press got wind of Emily's penchant for confined spaces and the suitcase story inevitably came out. Sharon sure got her fifteen minutes of fame out of that one, I can tell you. Selling her side of things to the Sunday tabloids and absolving herself of all responsibility whilst laying the blame squarely at my door. She even tried to inculpate me in the mall incident and I wasn't even there! But it wasn't long before she was being vilified by female columnists nationwide once the real story had been unearthed courtesy of just about any penny-grabbing parasite that knew her. That she had walked out on her daughter when she was only six-years-old and happily left me with the job of bringing her up alone and not even bothering to fight for custody. I, of course, have maintained my silence on the matter. Not just in the belief that Emily chose or still chooses not to be found but that she might one day miraculously return by route of some elaborate sewer system or some such miracle and that I should find her curled up in the empty suitcase that sits on her bed every day awaiting her return just the way I had discovered her in the basement of the office block. Looking back I'm not sure who found who. This mysterious transporter from the past that by chance had been buried away in the bowels of my place of work brought back to life by my daughter's enquiring disposition to seek out a hiding place. I have no doubt they were meant to be. Without the suitcase there would be no story. Quite possibly no cupboard warren. Even no missing Emily. And yet I can't help but think of the case as some sort of loyal old dog mourning my daughter's absence as much as I do. Boy, we had some fun with that case. Why couldn't she just be her?

In the months since she has been gone I simply have no answer and the penance is mine alone to bear not the worlds' who have already made out my precious, ever-so-special gift of a daughter to be some sort of oddity. A recent theory even stated that it was possible for Emily to survive in the right cavern given her exposure to an overdose of natural minerals alone, but that it would almost definitely mutate her, and that she could become England's answer to Bigfoot or The Himalayan Yeti the longer she wasn't found. I had to laugh out loud at that because over the course of time I have grown to think that my daughter has had one over on everyone. That she is exactly where she wants to be and will come out of her own accord. A father - any loving parent, I believe deep down would know if their child was lost to them forever if they had gone missing for as long as Emily has. But the truth is I just don't feel it.

I really don't.

.

MY NAME IS MIA

Staying at the guest house had been a mistake. It was a shame because one of the things Art had enjoyed most about planning his retirement trip was booking the overnight accommodation along the way. The inns and lodges and farmhouses. The historic and the modern. But from now on it would have to be strictly faceless motels and cheap diners so as not to draw any more attention to himself, what Art liked to call 'real' America.

He plunged his foot down on the accelerator and checked his rear view mirror to see the portly form of the proprietor, Earl Hammer, still standing at the edge of his property under a sleepily stirring stars and stripes banner as he watched Art go. He had one hand tucked into his waistband and the other shielding his eyes like he might linger there for a while. But for Art one sharp wink of Earl's big, brass, bald eagle belt buckle against the morning sunlight and he had disappeared for good in the swirling dust trail left by Art's rental, a shiny black Chevy SUV. He had insisted on an American manufacturer more out of reminiscence than anything else but apart from that he had no respect for what he was driving. Cars of today were just a means of getting from A to B to Art, or in this case the entire route of interstate 75. He didn't know what it was but growing up as an only child and being left largely to his own devices there was something about the American pop culture that had always attracted him. Television, magazines and of course movies had all left an impression on Art but not in the way some might think. He cared less about such iconic monuments as The Statue of Liberty or Mount Rushmore. He hadn't come to the USA for that. The glitz and glamour of Hollywood and Vegas were anathema to him and he wouldn't dream of wasting his money on a theme park let along spending a night in some mock-up hotel and served breakfast by some cartoon-caped character. Art wasn't even particularly interested in American history such as it was or anything remotely political. It was the nostalgic lure of a Happy Days diner that took him back in time. The sound of the Beach Boys. The open roads in Easy Rider even if he still found the plot ambiguous and nonsensical. As a kid he was always looking at the backdrops in films and photographs. Art was always imaging a life so different from his inner-city council flat upbringing where just the thought of venturing out on a shopping errand for his mother filled him with anxiety. So he bought into the world of the American dream where he would one day move and get a good job and work hard and get married and have children who could ride the mustard-coloured buses safely to and from school instead of running the gauntlet of the dismal concrete underpasses on his estate where teenage gangs loitered. A land of brightly exposed fire hydrants and picket fences and mail boxes at the end of rolling lawns with house numbers that reached into the thousands. And then there were the cars. Gloriously-named futuristic vehicles like the Thunderbird and Studebaker and of course the mean-grilled, shark-finned Plymouth Fury made famous by Stephen King of which Art grew up being a devout fan. But even then it was the settings and characters of the novelist that would often capture Art's imagination more than the stories themselves. Yet despite his hopes and dreams it was only now Art got to finally experience that 'land of the free' feeling and in his excitement he had already made a list of driving through some of the little-known, bizarrely-named towns on this or other trips that might well have been fictionally invented by the great horror writer himself. Places called Accident, Cut and Shoot, Embarrass, Experiment, Frankenstein, Intercourse, Money, Nothing, Pee Pee, Truth or Consequences, War, Whynot and perhaps the most dauntingly enticing of all, a town called Hell in Michigan, which Art had made sure was on this year's route. Not that he had anyone to go back home and tell it to. But just to say he had driven through Hell and back made Art chuckle.

Art had flown in from Heathrow and picked the car up in Miami ten days before and apart from a two-day detour down to the Keys had driven over the Florida border through Georgia, Tennessee, Kentucky and Ohio with the intention of continuing up through the Great Lakes and all the way to Canada. He liked the idea of passing through different landscapes and climates. It was another one of America's big appeals. He could see himself driving around with his wife and kids in a big Winnebago and camping out. But Art had never married or even had a girlfriend. There had never been anyone to share his deep sense of adventure with.

Anyone, that is, until now.

Art looked sheepishly in Mia's direction and gave out a huge sigh of relief accompanied by a false, shuddering laugh once the guest house was out of view. It was hard to read her expression behind her huge sunglasses and silk headscarf (Art liked to drive with the windows down) but her silence said everything.

You should never have left me, Art.

"I know, Mia. I know…" he spoke out, patting her on the knee and daring to let his hand linger there for longer than was comfortably necessary. "But it's all over now."

Do you promise?

As Art had been checking out at the desk manned by Earl's wife, Bunny, his "doll", Earl had made an excuse to go busy himself in the front yard driveway where Mia could be seen waiting in the car. Art had already been forced to explain her absence around the breakfast table, claiming that she had been feeling unwell after dining out the night before and so had spent the morning in bed. Art had tried desperately deflecting the subject by appearing overly interested in a couple of young antique dealers who'd also stayed overnight. They had been introduced to him by Earl as Jesse and Laurie and Art had noticed their truck parked out the front earlier overloaded and strapped down with 'collectables'. He'd seen an old gasoline pump. A beat-up motor cycle without handle bars. Some rusted oil cans and weathered commercial advertisements that even Art could have dated back to the fifties and sixties. 'Pickers', they called themselves. 'Looking to turn other people's junk into a dollar,' or so read the subtext on their business card. At that Earl had wanted to know how much a framed photograph holding pride and place over the mantle would be worth. He took it down explaining that an astronaut had once stayed and later sent him a signed picture of a view of earth taken from the window of his space capsule. But every time Bunny would enter with yet another course of her dynamic breakfast spread she would turn the attention back to Art's sick wife, pressing him constantly for details of what she'd eaten the night before and insisting on all sorts of remedies. Art could feel himself burning at having to spontaneously invent a fictitious menu and a local restaurant no one had ever heard of.

"You could do worse than listen to Bunny, you know, Art," Earl persisted. "She's never steered me wrong. You ever get the feeling you were someone else in a former life? Has anyone?" he looked around the table, but his attention had been lost by Jesse who had begun closely examining the silverware with the reading glasses he wore around his neck. "It's okay," he chuckled at Art's blank expression, "me neither. We're religious folk. But Bunny, my doll, I gotta tell you. Sometimes I think she must have been a doctor or physician or something. That's what I tell her. I've never even seen the inside of a hospital and I can't remember the last time I went to a walk-in. That's all down to my baby doll."

"Aww…hear that, Jess?" Laurie crooned, and squeezed her man's arm tightly in an effort to stop him working.

Art couldn't help but admire the couple as Laurie went on to explain how they not only responded to clients of their own ads but would very often 'freestyle', as she called it, and stop off at any home or outbuilding on their interstate travels that looked interesting. "You'd be amazed what's buried in some people's garages and barns," she engaged Art enthusiastically.

"How much for the photograph?" Jesse suddenly piped up and wanted to know. His darting rodent eyes, his obvious restlessness to be back on the road and almost continuing assessment of every knickknack in the room suggested he was the real evaluator of the two. Art began to avoid his gaze fearing that he might be next to fall under the man's instinctive appraisal for anything of worth.

What's that you got in your car, Art?

Pleeeeease…

"Oh, it's not for sale," Earl smiled lovingly at the picture he had carefully set back above the large open fireplace and shared a look with Art as if he should know. "I'm sorry, Art," he seemed to make a point of saying for everyone's benefit. "But I've forgotten your wife's name."

"Mia. It's Mia," Art said, nodding to everyone at the table. He looked down, feeling suddenly overwhelmed at the sight of his plate piled high with pancakes and syrup and fruit.

"That's pretty," Laurie chimed in.

Art tilted his head uncertainly, feeling an unexplainable hesitation. "Thank you," he said, and blushed a little.

"And, well, it doesn't matter, of course. You are a fully paid up member of Her Majesty's kingdom. You have verified that. But you say her - your wife's, Mia's passport is in some sort of transit?"

"Yes," Art dropped his head.

"Mia? Now is that Oriental or something?" Earl persisted.

Art thought Earl must have seen him sneaking Mia in after dark to have made such a wildly accurate assumption and that for some reason he was trying to trip Art up. He had told Earl upon arrival that he had left his wife shopping and was going back out to pick her up and go for a meal before returning late so he would need a key. Art had sat outside in the car until way past midnight waiting for the upstairs lights to go off before quietly venturing in. The house was a classic colonial design. Built in the mid-1800s. A big front porch with swing chairs, six bedrooms and sitting in an acre of land dominated by an enormous oak and that giant flag. But apart from the creaking boards everywhere you trod and the ticking of the great grandfather clock in the hall you could literally hear a pin drop. He'd had to wait until everyone was seated for breakfast before he could smuggle Mia back out again.

You're ashamed of me.

"That's rubbish," he scoffed.

I'm damaged goods.

"I told you. Never say that again."

"So what part of the east is she from, Art?" Earl wanted to know.

"Japan," Art said, which at least was true.

"Yeah?" Jesse's curiosity had been aroused. "Is that where you met then? In Japan?"

"No," Art shook his head furiously, forking some food into his mouth and failing to elaborate because he hadn't had time to think about a cover story.

"I've always wanted to go to Japan," Laurie said dreamily.

"Don't tell me you met on the internet!" Earl exclaimed with a laugh and looked around the table. But the pickers only shrank away in shock and unease lest it might be true. "Is that right, Art, eh? Asian Brides Dot Com, eh? Is that where you met her you lucky old so-and-so." He brushed at Art's shoulder.

"Earl Hammer, that's enough!" Bunny admonished him as she brought in a giant platter of cakes and buns. "You're embarrassing the poor man."

"Why should he be embarrassed? You told me she was young and gorgeous. Good luck to the old devil is what I say," he reached round and slapped Art's back and began roaring heartily whilst massaging Art's neck. Art wasn't used to being on the receiving end of such demonstrative gestures. He couldn't remember the last time he'd been touched in such a way. Probably by his mother. He would spend the rest of the day wiping and shrugging off Earl's imaginary bear-paw imprint.

"I'm sorry, Art," Bunny looked a little guilty. She wore a lot of make-up for early morning and her hair was held up in pig-tails by baby-blue ribbon. "I couldn't help but see you helping her into the car through the kitchen window. She did look a little frail the poor thing but my, she really is a beauty from what I could tell."

"Thank you," Art reddened. He dabbed at his mouth with a napkin. "I probably should explain that apart from not feeling well she is also really quite shy. She…Mia, doesn't talk much. By that I mean English, of course. I hope you understand."

"Of course, Art. Of course. Aww, the precious little thing," Bunny screwed up her nose as if to wish him all the happiness in the world.

"Yes, she is, as you say, quite precious," Art agreed, his eyes shining as he looked at each person in turn and began nodding resolutely.

The pickers gazed upon him fondly as he left, wishing him luck on the rest of his journey. "Take it easy, man," Jesse said. He lifted his head but looked Art up and down as if for one final consideration. Art was taken by surprise when Laurie stepped forward to give him a hug and kiss. "That's how we do it in these parts," she beamed, bouncing up and down. "Say goodbye to your wife from us. Or however you say it in Japanese. How do you say it, Art?"

"Huh?" Art stood looking at them all.

"How do you say 'goodbye' in Japanese?" she wanted to know.

"Why it's sayonara of course," the vaunt in Earl couldn't stop himself from interjecting.

Art almost collapsed with relief and was still shaking by the time he'd reached the turnpike. Rolling his neck this way and that and shrugging off the impression of Earl's hand still rubbing at his sinews, as if he'd meant to pin Art there for answers. Of all of them it was Earl who'd suspected something wasn't right about Art's story and yet despite his probing it had felt strangely exciting to talk about Mia in such a way. That there was someone in his life he should care about and that who others presumably thought cared for him. It gave him a social status he had never known before. Something that most people in a relationship just took for granted but that Art could only ever dream of, a sudden sense of belonging that in Art's experience as a singleton could be a very lonely and unforgiving world. Many times he had found himself envying even the most innocent public displays of affection between couples.

"They all thought you were gorgeous," he said, smiling over at her, though Mia remained unconvinced.

Where are we going?

"On an adventure and then far, far away," he replied. "Somewhere you can feel safe from harm."

Just don't take me back there.

"I won't," he assured her.

To him.

"I won't."

You promise?

He reached over and squeezed her baby-soft hand. He toyed with each tiny finger in turn, thinking that a ring wouldn't go amiss, or at the very least a bracelet. Some claim to her. "Do you want to hear some music?" he suggested. Ten minutes of trawling through religious and country-and-western channels passed before he reluctantly settled on a political phone-in. All the talk was about Trump. He checked with Mia but she didn't seem to care or even to be listening. He'd wrapped her in his short coat that he'd packed in anticipation of some cooler weather upstate and a pair of unsightly oversized jogging pants he would normally wear for lounging around, but it was clear he was going to have to stop at a department store and buy her a couple of outfits and a few other necessities. The only shoes she had were white heels. Apart from that she possessed one item of underwear and a short frilly negligee. He'd only bought the sunglasses and headscarf as a disguise. She didn't even own a handbag. The next state was Michigan. He wriggled down into his seat for a comfortable position in preparation for the long drive ahead feeling unbelievably content. He had found a discreet little motel with all the mod cons on the outskirts of Detroit.

"Famed for its auto industry and the Tamla Motown record label," he told Mia cheerily with a nod. "Motown is in fact a combination of the words motor and town," he continued. It was quite possible that she knew these things already and he was just being boring. But Art couldn't help but feel excited at the prospect of now having someone to share the rest of the journey with. When he next stole a look at her he was sure he saw a softening in her expression so allowed himself another tender touch of her hand, gently stroking the silky pad of her open palm and encouraged by the fact that she didn't pull away. He wouldn't have blamed her if she did. He wouldn't have blamed her for never trusting anyone again after being made to suffer the most unspeakable degradation the night before.

Next to the sex shop that displayed two strikingly mega-busted shop-window mannequins in provocative underwear – one of whom at second glance was seen to have a perkily-shaped penile object tucked down the front of its garish red panties – Art had noticed a felt-tipped, hand-scrawled sign on cardboard tied to a wire-mesh fence that read: FREE BIKINI WASH. A barely legible subtext went on to explain that you could bring your cat, bike or car there for a 'free' bikini wash in order that you make a charitable donation to some local cause but which not only went on to lose the plot of its own appeal, but the space with which to write it in. This 'unique' service was taking place early Sunday morning in the neighbouring forecourt of next door's bar where a space had been cleared for two foaming buckets of water, a scattering of sponges and a dribbling hose at the ready, all presumably awaiting custom.

Art, in a moment of hesitancy, crossed the road to avoid entering the sex shop in front of a group of boisterous bikers congregating up ahead. They were laughing and joking and drinking from beer cans. For a long while Art stood distracted by the glint and gleam of their dismounted motorcycles. Those pristine chromed dragons had always provoked an irrational longing in him that appealed to his sense of wanderlust. He recalled how a work colleague had once hired one and toured the Amalfi on it Dennis Hopper style. Art could only imagine ever doing such a thing. But he often asked himself: Was there ever as gloriously vain an inanimate object as a Harley Davidson?

The charity appeal seemed at first to Art to be a small, almost humbling and somewhat admirable attempt at raising money, not that much different from the children's lemonade stalls he had passed on his off-route travels. That was until it became slowly apparent that the raucous, aged bikers spilling into the road, stripped bare to their flabby flesh and largely emblazoned with tattoos and assorted styles of peppered facial hair, were, in fact, the bikini washers and not a pair of nubile off-duty volunteers from some nearby Hooters bar as the makeshift advertisement had subliminally suggested. But not only that. The bikers had traded the proposed beachwear (which might have gone some way to bringing a comical aspect to the scene) for the same sort of women's undergarments displayed by the dummies in the sex shop window.

It took a moment for Art to behold the sight. As if the still luridly debauched events of the evening before hadn't already been enough. His one night in Dayton. Yet nothing seemed to surprise the average passer-by, making the whole spectacle even more bizarre. The sex shop owner casually came out to chit-chat and share a smoke with locals like he was the mayor of the town, even taking the time to lift a hand from across the road in acknowledgement of Art as if campaigning for votes. Art quickly looked away, but not before noticing his shop still had a CLOSED sign on the door. Being shut out of a sex shop in front of such a crowd didn't bear thinking about so Art thought he would give himself at least another hour before wandering down the strip again. As he set off two of the bikers drove past on a Harley. "I'm still a man!" the passenger called out to Art over the bike's clattering roar, seemingly on a spontaneous tour of the place or to possibly drum up business.

He'd been wearing a powder-blue bra and matching French knickers.

It seemed too soon to be drunk but more than that the whole occasion and its general acceptance of the outrageous early morning parade appeared to have an almost Mardi Gras feel about it. No one was really having their car cleaned and Art doubted if any of the bikers cared that they would. The almost ubiquitous decline of Dayton's once heavy manufacturing industry didn't seem to bother them in the slightest even if for Art it seemed to sit like a dark shadow over the surviving populous. As if it had once been subject to an endemic virus and left to survive by itself not only by an otherwise indifferent government but quite possibly the rest of the world. Even on the outskirts of neighbouring Cincinnati, not an hour's drive away and albeit linked by a stretch of route 75 with the most ridiculous and gruesomely large amounts of roadkill, disaffected locals gathered early in the streets, quietly chatting or more often than not just sitting or shuffling aimlessly on their own and staring into space. Winters can be harsh in the mid-west so perhaps everyone was just enjoying the last of the summer weather, but it was the purposelessness about them that so affected Art. No one looked to be going about their business. No one looked to have any business to be going about. The mazy, faceless and dull grimy streets leading towards the presumably prosperous financial district where a few office tower blocks loomed large and gleaming (and from where there was the only hope of finding an ATM), were colourless even of the omnipresent fast food corporations that one might still expect to find in parts of the Third World. There were no Starbucks, no Dunkin' Donuts', not even a golden arch on the horizon. The only coffee Art could find was from a percolator in a plastic cup at a convenient store that sold cigarettes and liquor and other basic needs. Like the once famed 'Gem City' of Dayton, a proclaimed diadem of the area not so many years before and the home of the Wright Brothers and the Model T-Ford, Cincinnati appeared to exist only as a sad and sorry shell of itself.

It wasn't like Art to frequent bars. Almost every night of the trip he had been safely tucked up in bed by ten with the TV on and researching the next few days' places of interest, looking for scenic detours of note and adequately-rated dining establishments. Art had read that nowadays the Dayton area's economy relied much upon defence and aerospace research along with insurance, legal and healthcare sectors. Yet apart from its grim though strangely alluring architectural backdrop of abandoned factories and disused warehouses that were just crying out for restoration and redevelopment Dayton didn't offer much in the way of culture for the passing tourist so Art found himself wandering the area in the early evening of Saturday night until he came across a particularly lively downtown strip consisting mostly of crowded bars and boutique restaurants but most noticeable of all, a flagrantly stocked sex shop that not only spanned the width of two adjacent premises, but afforded about as uninhibitedly central and mainstay a position in the road as, say, the local library or town hall might.

Late afternoon and early evening revelers, most of whom Art took to be the young at heart, were already staggering into the road regardless of any slow-moving traffic. Art smiled back at everyone before finding himself uncharacteristically tapping his toe alongside a street musician in an effort not to appear self-conscious as he casually perused the exhibits in the sex shop window. He jiggled some change in his trouser pockets, trying to relax into the carnival atmosphere and feeling an almost liberating light of foot that he had never before experienced not only in all his years spent commuting back and forth to work in London, but in the workplace itself. Art's career had been spent in the civil service which had been a good place to remain nondescript given his inherently reticent nature. Apart from sometimes being the object of a work colleague's joke no one really bothered or asked much of him. As the only child of a single working mother Art was used to being marginalised. He was made to stay in his room or keep out of the way if she ever brought anyone home. When she introduced Art to visitors it always came by way of an excuse or apology, as if he was a dog with disgusting habits or that might turn. Even at an early age he sensed her embarrassment of him which only deepened his feelings of social impotence. He was always knocking things over or spilling stuff. He stammered. He reddened in conversation and still did. Yet she saw her constant criticism of him as encouragement, her anxiety that he should find some friends, any friend, as wholehearted concern and not the inhibiting infection it really was and came to be. Consequently, Art had never dated or brought anyone home. Social events terrified him. And when Art took a sick day it was the prospect of entering the agoraphobic arena of daily life that would set off a psychosomatic reaction in him and in turn, the very real and all-consuming fear that those same childhood afflictions he had fought so hard to conquer were only ever a formal handshake away.

From the bar next door some live music broke out, calling to Art's attention a little outdoor balcony above where drinkers and smokers could overlook the strip. Hanging over the corner nearest to Art were a group of women calling and waving to someone across the road. Art felt an unfamiliar roll of excitement when one of them caught his eye and blew him a kiss. She was plump and piggy-eyed with a tattoo on her left breast that threatened to spill out of her top and almost definitely drunk by the sounds, but Art lifted his head and smiled in acknowledgement.

"Hello," he called back.

The woman stared open-mouthed for a moment before clapping her hands just once as if to scare off a small creature.

"Oh my God," she drawled. "Are you English?"

"I...I am, yes," Art felt himself flush a little.

"Say something else," she insisted, her eyes widened like a child's before a magician.

"Like what?" he asked, smiling awkwardly and shifting his feet. He made what felt like one deliberate giant stride away from the sex shop window as if to pay her more attention.

"What?" she shouted over the music belting out of the bar.

The street musician packed up his things and walked off, giving Art a last look.

"Er...how are you?" he shouted with all the gusto he could muster, feeling rather like a poor man's Romeo.

"Wait!" she held up a hand to him, turning to her friends.

Art tried another subtle side-shoe shuffle into the street but blocked off a thin, scraggy-looking guy with a cigarette stuck to his lower lip and who instantly took offence. His snarl revealed a few missing teeth but more than that the age of the mouth didn't fit the face.

"What the fuck, man?" he screwed up his eyes and held out his hands as if it was the last thing he needed.

"Sorry, sorry," Art stuttered, pin-wheeling his way back to where he'd started before finding himself under the dull but strangely judgmental gaze of the mannequins.

See anything you like, Art?

"Listen!" the woman shouted, trying to get her friends' attention but who were being held court by someone else amidst much laughter.

At that moment a couple came out of the shop swinging a bag, nodding at Art as they walked by. Art's smile felt like a leer and when he next looked up at the balcony the woman had turned away and begun talking loudly to her friends while animatedly waving a cigarette. More laughter broke out. Art could see that her backless top was held together by a single tied cord revealing deep creases of sagging flesh where her shoulder blades should have been. It took a moment for Art to realise that no one seemed to care that he was loitering outside a sex shop with the obvious intention of entering for reasons still not quite known even to him. In Art's mind he felt like a gunman on the brink of indecision as to whether to go in and rob the place. Such an establishment at home would normally have him crossing the road for fear of being seen to show even a covert interest - or worse, to be harangued into entering like some of the women in massage shop doorways often did. Art always felt it was something given away by his gait that made them call out. Like he had suddenly forgotten how to walk. Is that what the woman on the balcony had sensed in him and so had turned away? His awkwardness? His crushingly abject inhibition? There had been no reason at all to ever walk through that district after work on his way home to the station. But Art always did.

Art bought a beer before trying to push his way through the loud, sweaty-faced throng monopolising the bar to get a vantage point on a small platform halfway up the stairway to the balcony where he could overlook the stage and dance floor. A young female singer fronted the otherwise aged band of old rockers and could have been plucked from any of the scantily-clad, caterwauling crowd of mostly overweight women and who seemed to outnumber the men in droves. They appeared generically dressed for the night. Squeezed into tight brightly-coloured tops and short skirts with pounds upon pounds of tattooed flesh on display. They danced in little groups, holding beer bottles by the neck and pointing their fingers in the air, jiggling and wiggling their collective wobbly bits, all seemingly in search of a good time. Art leant closer against the handrail as he watched a scrawny-looking guy get dragged from the peripheral shadows and made to perform some sort of ritualistic dance inside a quickly gathering corral of women who had descended upon him like bees. The man shimmied round in a circle with his eyes closed and a stupid, serenely-drunk smile on his face, playing up to the applause of his adoring audience with his jeans halfway down his legs and revealing a pair of washed-out chequered boxers. Art thought then that the women were probably younger than he had first given them credit for. He didn't know if it was the heavily-applied make-up or the almost palpable desperation in them to be noticed at the expense of their own clearly diminishing self-worth, but one thing was evident, like the man he had bumped into with the rotten gums, everyone seemed to be abusing their bodies way ahead of time in some shape or form.

A short while later and to a tune and dance they all seemed to know the girls lined up to form a strangely reluctant and half-hearted parade. Some talked among themselves as they moved and swayed indifferently, others were already lost to the alcohol and stumbled through. One or two hungrily scanned the now partially interested crowd of men for takers. Was the girl on the floor looking directly at Art the same woman from the balcony? Art couldn't be sure. In a place like this probably everyone had been with everyone so for the first time in his life Art allowed himself the luxury of thinking he stood out if only because he was a stranger in town. Now the woman stepped forward from the would-be pageant and made an attempt at puckering her lips and fluttering her eyes. Art watched slightly agog as her giant breasts bounced around like inflatable playthings.

"You're like raw meat to this crowd," a man standing next to him echoed Art's thoughts colourfully. Certainly Art thought he had just seen the girl licking her lips but in any case, Art didn't even think the man had been talking to him until he felt a nudge to his arm.

A huge cherubic-cheeked man with a long pointed ginger beard and wearing a denim waistcoat was holding out two bottles of beer to Art in one giant fist. Art looked down, momentarily studying the snarling snake's head tattooed on the back of his hand and followed its coiling body all the way up the man's trunk-like forearm and ballooning bicep to where its rattle tail nested quivering in cartooned double parenthesis on his left jugular. It was inked in a marvelous myriad of tiny black scales that Art found himself hypnotically beginning to count.

"You're from the UK, right?" the big man shouted over the music. He had sharp green eyes and a wide friendly grin but Art could already feel himself begin to clam up. "I heard you ordering a beer at the bar," he went on to explain. "So I thought to myself anyone who comes in here with an accent like that is going to get some attention. Here, I bought you a beer and figured I'd hang on to your coat tails a bit. My name's Mitch. Go ahead," he urged.

"Thank you," Art responded with a deft nod. "Thank you very much. I'm…Arthur. Art. Call me Art."

There was an awkward moment when Art took the bottle with his right hand, switched his own beer to under his left armpit and then jerked out his left hand to be shaken.

"Ohhh, man," Mitch threw back his head and laughed uproariously, clapping Art on the shoulder. "Just what I thought. Straight out of Downton Abbey," he hooted. "I think me and you are gonna have some fun, Arthur."

Art was beginning to regret his choice of accommodation once he reached Detroit and had checked them in at the motel office. The 'mod cons' described on the website amounted to wi-fi only being available in the office building, and twenty-four hour room service a plaza of fast food restaurants across the highway that were prepared to deliver. But he hadn't wanted to deal with any identification problems and so had paid cash for the night which the owner was happy to take from him without a bill of sale. Art hesitated upon signing his and Mia's name into the guest register as man and wife like he had at Earl and Bunny's but thought it more than likely that the book wasn't worth the paper he was writing on anyway. In any event, Art had no idea of Mia's surname and she didn't seem to want to tell him either.

My name is Mia.

For the first real time since secreting her away he was able to look at Mia without the sunglasses and headscarf and coat he had shawled her in. She sat on the edge of the bed in the lamplight watching him take out the clothes he had stopped to buy her at an outlet store along the way. Her hair was dark and shoulder length with natural looking kinks and waves. Her skin glowed like honey. She leant provocatively on one arm, her green eyes fixed on him. Her other hand was draped between her slightly parted legs.

She was still wearing the same skimpy see-through white nightie edged with frills and bows. Beneath this sexy apparel Art could clearly see that she was naked and perfectly formed. He felt his heart pound at the sight.

What are you thinking?

"Nothing," Art shook his head. "Nothing."

You're staring at me.

"I...I don't mean to," he looked away, fumbling through the shopping bags. He held up some items. Plain, simple, knee-length dresses like the shop assistant had been wearing. She'd been young and petite just like Mia and after Art had complimented the girl on her style she had been happy to help pick out some clothes along with a pair of flat ballet-type shoes and some sandals.

What about underwear?

Art felt himself begin to flush.

Do you expect me to sit around like this?

"All in good time, Mia," Art said, growing agitated. "I'll tell you what. We...we should make a list."

You'd like that, wouldn't you?

"I'll get my notebook," he stammered, going to his laptop bag by the door. He could feel himself breaking out into a terrible sweat. His throat turned dry.

Are you trying to see between my legs?

And it was true. He had looked. Just then. And before.

My bush?

He could feel himself shaking.

What's to stop you, Art?

"Stop it!" he suddenly admonished her. "Stop talking like that."

But she only continued to stare at him. At the spittle that foamed inside the creases of his mouth. He wiped at it with the back of his trembling hand, taking a deep breath. After a moment he walked over and tenderly stroked her hair. Moving her head slightly.

"You don't have to talk like that," he whispered, and leant to kiss her cheek.

I know what you want to do, Art.

But Art didn't answer. Knowing how easy it could be. Her lips, that deeply seductive, slightly-parted, second-hand hole for a mouth was only a few tempting inches away. He gazed down at her dark brown nipple exposed to him by the parting in her negligee. Her exquisitely shaped bun-sized breast.

Put it in my mouth if you want to.

But he couldn't. Not just yet. Not after what she'd been put through the night before.

Don't you want to put it in my mouth, Art?

Art stood up and reeled away. Is that all she thought she was good for? Perhaps he should sleep on the floor for another night, he told himself. He didn't want to rush things and besides he had no experience in such matters. It didn't help that his continuing sense of arousal only served to confuse and frighten him especially in the wake of the previous night's ordeal where he had witnessed the most deplorable and depraved sexual behavior and filling his head with images so sickening he feared me might never get over it. If he took advantage of Mia now then he was no better than the rest of them. It was important to Art that he gained her respect. And so he helped her into the bed and lay down her head to sleep feeling a weight off his mind for having made the decision in the same way he did when resisting the siren calls of the women in the doorways of the strip clubs and massage parlours.

Don't you want to come inside my mouth?

He turned off the light and sat in a chair from across the room watching her still form slowly come to life in the dark. Art thought he could see the covers gently rising with each shallow breath, could hear the troubled murmur of her sub conscious as she fell into a dccpcr and deeper sleep.

It was probably the fact Art had got no further than lingering outside the sex shop window the night before that he had failed to see the leaflet of what looked to be Mia on the inside of the door beneath the heading: 'MODEL G FOR HIRE. ENQUIRE WITHIN.' Art pretended not to see the owner beckoning him from behind the counter, likewise the bikers still clad in women's underwear, staggering around in a drunk and disorderly state, some of whom were now clearly soaked in the aftermath of a water fight and one or two of which didn't appear to realise their genitals were, if not quite fully exposed, then leaving little or nothing to the imagination.

Art had wandered aimlessly up and down the strip until noon waiting for the sex shop to open and even then had no confidence in himself that he would ever be able to enter let alone somehow bring up the subject of Mia. And yet there she was for all to see (a different style and colour of hair but most definitely her) on a small poster on the inside of a door of a sex shop just like any other stickers he had wasted time reading over up and down the road: a travelling circus was coming to town, the Dayton Playhouse was performing the musical Camelot, and, of course, a free bikini wash was being offered for a good cause by bikers in women's underwear.

Only in America!

MODEL G FOR HIRE. ENQUIRE WITHIN.

A car rolled slowly by honking at the bikers who had ambled a little too close to Art for his liking. One of them had already called out and urged Art on about something or so he thought. He was starting to feel cornered. It was now or never, he decided. The easiest thing would have been to walk away and forget about Mia but Art wasn't sure he could do that. He had the wherewithal to get her out of the place and the degeneracy to which she'd been subjected. They had used her as a vessel for sex in every vile way possible and would do again, he was in no doubt. Was he really going to let that happen? At that moment a man brushed past him and pushed open the door to the shop and Art instinctively followed him in.

Feeling momentarily bewildered at the egregious display of merchandise Art found himself wandering down an aisle stacked with pornographic DVDs and fetish magazines as the man and the sex shop owner began to engage in conversation. Art overheard the man enquiring about Viagra. At the back of the shop there were several display cabinets of lurid sex toys catering for all tastes: vibrators, strap-ons, cock rings and butt plugs.

Help me…

Another was stocked with all sorts of lubricants and lotions, flavoured stimulants, enhancers and massage oils. And then Art had cause to look with closer inspection at a section that appeared dedicated to sado-masochistic paraphernalia. Art felt his mouth go dry at the display of masks and blindfolds behind the glass case, the whips and handcuffs, clamps and clothespins. In truth he didn't know half of what he was looking at or what they were for and had only his now distorted imagination to rely upon.

Pleeeease…

Art felt himself flinch at the image of the woman who had called to him from the balcony, her top rolled down to reveal great pendulous breasts scarred by stretch marks cut deep as tyre tracks, urged on by Mitch and whoever else was there as she mounted Mia from behind with a huge pink rubber penis held in place by a harness that was almost completely concealed by the wobbling overlap of her corpulent waistline and flaccid chunk of drooping mons pubis. Her name was Mercedes, he remembered then. She was the single mother of two children but he vaguely recalled her telling him a story about getting pregnant at fourteen by a family friend and burying the baby in the woods because it was stillborn. She had been sitting on his lap in the back of a car, stroking his brow and calling him a good listener. Every now and then she would probe his mouth with her wet plump tongue, filling his senses with her tobacco breath. At one point Art had felt a pill being exchanged in their mouths and swallowed it without thinking. The next thing he remembered was watching Mercedes swaying to the gravelly tone of Johnny Cash, her head thrown back and her eyes closed dreamily as she tried directing the enormous phallus between Mia's strikingly exposed anus.

Please help…

"For God's sake," Art heard himself whisper and tried sitting forward, but there was a young girl on the floor sitting between his legs who appeared to have passed out.

Another girl in a short denim skirt and skimpy top crawled into the little arena of about thirty people on her hands and knees and began lubricating the strap-on with her saliva, but not before simulating oral sex with the thing and whipping the rabble into a frenzy of excitement. Unlike most of the women back at the bar the girl was just skin and bones. She pulled out a small empty sack of flesh for a breast with dirt-filled fingernails and began licking at her nipple in an inebriated attempt to tease. She could have been no more than about twenty-five but her entire set of front teeth were missing. Art stared around drunkenly at the sea of delirious faces through a hanging smog. He had trouble lifting his head and his eyes stung. Nearly everyone was smoking. They were in somebody's living-room, he began to notice. There were family photographs and sports medals high on a shelf. A cluster of greeting cards adorned a dresser celebrating someone's birthday or anniversary. Music was being played to the point of distortion. He recognized some of the baying mob from earlier in the evening but had no recollection of leaving the bar. The man he had bumped into with the blackened gums was staring at him from across the room as if he should know who Art was. He had just been passed what looked to be an aerosol of some solvent or other and was groggily attempting to bring it to his nostril. The guy who had just passed him the tin then pulled off his T-shirt to reveal a near-skeletal frame decorated in biro-blue tattoos that might have been drawn by a child. He shuffled over on his knees and unzipped his jeans but was met by a roar of derision when he shook at his lifeless penis to no avail and only answered his hecklers with outstretched arms and a wide toothy grin as if he could care less. In a moment of the sickest vaudeville the girl tried accommodating him by putting his dick in her mouth but almost instantly recoiled by pulling away and making a face while holding her nose all for the audience's entertainment. Not to be deterred the man edged his way round towards Mia's remarkably impassive expression, gripping her chin so hard Art could see the shadowed indentations in her soft yellow pallor. With one bleary eye half-closed, as if trying to thread a needle, he attempted to feed his limp and shriveled cock between her roughly cupped lips. The crowd continued to mock him but Art could feel Mitch growing agitated as if the show wasn't going to his liking. The girl between Art's legs woke up. She was pale and thin and her hair had fallen all over her face.

"Fuck her in the ass!" Mitch began shouting at Mercedes above the music. His mouth foamed into his beard, his eyes had turned feral and red. He gave Art a quick, manic grin.

"Yeah," the girl between Art's legs called. "Fuck her in the ass." She pushed back her hair and looked up at Art. "You wanna fuck me in the ass, Daddy?" she licked at her dry, cracked lips. Her eyes were dull and lost. "Eh, Daddy?"

"FUCK HER IN THE ASS! FUCK HER IN THE ASS!" everyone began to pick up the chant.

Daddy?

Art closed his eyes to the ineradicable image of a seemingly hideous hermaphrodite wreathed in a demonic smoke haze burying his/herself into the most beautiful woman he had ever seen.

Daddy…?

Next to a changing room guarded by a female mannequin dressed from head to toe in shimmering black PVC and brandishing a cat o' nine tails was a long rack of role-playing outfits. Art fingered his way through the nurse and French maid uniforms. The nuns, schoolgirls, secretaries and policewomen. He glanced guiltily back towards the shop entrance when the other customer left, catching the eye of the owner.

"Can I help you with anything back there?" he called.

"Er…no, no thank you," Art cleared his throat. "I'm just looking."

"Take your time."

Art did his best to remain out of view and trying not to look overly interested. But of course the owner had seen it all before. It just wasn't possible to feign an act of time-killing in a place that traded in the erotic in the same way you could the travel section of a book shop. No one looked at you disapprovingly in book shops. Art felt his armpits leak at the sudden thump of one the bikers banging on the shop window. The owner called out and swore and laughed then went outside and joined them in a smoke, leaving Art alone in the shop and only heightening his sense of deviancy. Seeing his own shamefaced image in the omnipotent-eyed convex of the security mirror high up in the corner of the ceiling didn't help either. He could have been a suspect ensnared on camera in one of those true-life TV crime programs appealing for witnesses. For the life of him Art didn't think he could go through with it and wished he could just walk out but it seemed he had put himself in a position of no return. A single, older gent such as he seen browsing in a sex shop could only do one of two things now that he had entered. Continue to browse for his own seemingly prurient interest before walking out of the shop empty-handed and risking the silent opprobrium of if not the owner then surely the bikers who remained virtually impassable and would see him skulking into the road, or confidently purchase something and leave the premises happily swinging a bag like he had seen other customers do.

I'm not going out in a bag, Art.

Art inwardly cringed at the thought of being seen as a pervert. His work colleagues often made jokes about spotting him creeping around the red light district but sometimes he just couldn't stop his legs from taking him there. Now, walking out of the shop suddenly seemed harder than walking in. Something that had always prevented him from going into the strip clubs and massage parlours back home. To enter any of those iniquitous dens had always felt to Art like jumping off a cliff-edge.

The next time Art checked himself in the mirror he almost started at the sight of a woman in a baseball cap watching him from a far corner of the shop. He momentarily struggled to find his bearings, turning this way and that and tentatively peering down one aisle then another, trying to keep out of sight. Perhaps the owner had an assistant who was keeping a watchful eye. Of course, he wasn't to be trusted. A twisted degenerate left on his own in a sex shop. Who knew what types frequented such establishments? He had lived all his life fighting against his urges and now here he was feeling exposed and humiliated for having finally given in to them. And not just now but the sickening and shameful temptations of the night before.

Daddy...?

Outside he could hear a gathering of voices and laughter. More bikers dressed in drag. Art began to wonder if there was a way out the back.

In his fluster he walked straight into a display stand of second-hand DVDs and sent the whole lot crashing. Covers of the most lurid sexual detail slid like ice hockey pucks across the polished floor. He tried not to look at them as he scrambled around on his hands and knees in an attempt to pick them all up before the assistant arrived.

Art, pleeeease....

He didn't want to look at the pictures. He wasn't like that. He would never do that. And now the assistant would think he had been searching through them all. Looking for a bargain to take back to a darkened room somewhere.

BUKKAKI BONANZA. VOL V.

Art paused. Momentarily holding the case in his trembling hand. Seeing himself on his knees under the lofty gaze of the security mirror and the assistant who hadn't moved.

He took a furtive look around before taking the time to read a footnote at the back of the cover under a reel of stills of women either willing or forced into an act of the utmost abasement, and which went on to read: Bukkaki. Originated in Tahlequah, Oklahoma by a man named Johnny Bukkaki. Bukkaki is when a woman is ejaculated on by 3 or more men, most women say it's the most intense pleasurable euphoria they've ever experienced, to which leads an addiction.

"I'll give you three for two and you can't say fairer than that," a voice said beside him.

Art jumped, emitting a small whimper. It was the owner. Standing right over him with the same conspiratorial grin he had given Art when entering. The same semi-sneer he gave all his single male customers, Art didn't doubt. Art looked from the owner to the mirror. He could see his own glistening sun-tanned brow even from way up there. The sweat-patches that had broken out all over his shirt. He looked pathetic amidst all the scattered films. Like a kid let loose in a toy shop. As if he hadn't been able to contain his excitement.

The owner continued to leer at him, chewing and making a loud disgusting wet sound with his mouth. He had one hand down the front of his grubby grey jogging bottoms and seemed to be visibly readjusting himself but after a short while it became clear it was just a habit he'd developed. His hand just stayed down there. Fondling and fidgeting.

"I...I knocked it over," Art stammered. "It was...it was an accident."

"Yeah, I know. This place can still get me a little hot under the collar. Good choice," he chuckled and nodded at the DVDs.

"It wasn't-" Art countered, standing to his feet. "It wasn't that."

The owner took a moment to consider him.

"A Brit, eh?"

"Um, yes," Art said, brushing himself down. He still held the DVD and looked around as if not knowing what to do with it.

The owner continued to look at him. His masticating coming to a slow and silent halt like a cow whose attention had been caught.

"Looking for anything in particular?" he finally asked.

Art felt himself twitch involuntarily.

"A playmate perhaps," he continued, jiggling his eyebrows in encouragement and jerking his head towards the corner of the shop. His fiddling suddenly became more animated and he began to drool openly.

Art looked across his shoulder at the assistant in the baseball cap who had been watching him all the time. The assistant who wasn't an assistant at all but was in fact an inflatable doll all but naked beneath a pair of denim dungaree shorts and that cap.

It was at first a surprise to learn that the owner did a roaring trade in sex dolls. Claiming to have sold over ninety. The doll stared back at Art vacuously from under the brim of the cap emblazoned with the words DAYTON DYNAMOES, its glossy red-lipped mouth stretched open in what Art took to be an expression of virtuous surprise, as if it had just been told a filthy joke. And yet there must be nothing that mouth or the mouths of the other ninety hadn't been forced to do that would shock or surprise them, Art thought.

"This one has a nine-inch anal passage," the owner informed him, to which Art could only blink in astonishment, not at the fact but that the owner should even have said it. "Ribbed love tunnel. Cyberskin pussy and ass. I have about five left in boxes and can do you a deal for eighty bucks. They're fully deflated so you could walk out with one now the same way you could a bag of groceries."

Art stepped forward. Its eyes and brows were painted on. Its glaringly golden synthetic wig stuck fast. The longer Art looked the more distress it seemed to be in. The doll's immediate surprise had turned to one of shock, of near horror. As if she was locked in one long silent scream.

Heeeeelp me!

"I know," the owner chuckled at Art's expression. "Makes you want to shove it down her throat right now, eh? Fucking no good whore," he suddenly turned his nose up at it in disgust.

"I was thinking…" Art stuttered.

"Okay, look. Let's call it seventy but that's my bottom line," he offered, growing a little impatient at Art's increasing impediment.

"No!" Art burst as if for air. "The girl, I mean, the one in the window."

The owner looked momentarily puzzled and stopped scratching himself. "You mean the mannequin?"

Art shook his head, feeling his mouth dry up. "The model in the picture."

The owner squinted and looked towards the front of the shop before revealing a slow smile. "You mean the Model G," he gave Art a significant look as if he had totally underestimated him.

"Mia, yes," Art sighed.

"'Mia'? How'd you know about Mia?" the owner's eyes narrowed suspiciously. "It's okay," he tried allaying Art's obvious alarm. "I saw you out on the town last night. Not much goes on without my knowing. Truth is you probably ended up with a relation of mine," he chuckled. "There are a few of us I can tell you and they go mad for an unknown face especially with an accent. Especially with a British accent. Well, well, well," he nodded. "Aren't you a dark horse…eh, what's your name?" he said, pulling his hand out from his bottoms and giving it a cursory wipe down the front of his shirt. He had short stubby fingers with nails chewed down to the skin. "I'm Eric."

"Arthur. Art," Art said, reluctant to take the owner's proffered handshake but sensing at the same time that it might be some sort of test.

"Well, nice to meet you Arthur," Eric seized Art's hand and continued to shake it with a moist but toughening grip. "So you want a date with Mia, eh?"

Art reddened and tilted his head sheepishly, attempting a smile.

"Well, I'll be damned. Mia has a Brit for a fan."

It took a moment for the stock room light to flicker into life. And in those few seconds it could so easily have been a young woman sat imprisoned there amidst a heap of boxes. A large standing fan was directed towards her, fluttering at Mia's dark shoulder length hair. Her faintly Oriental features were beautifully sculpted with a seemingly soft bone structure and a skin that appeared to radiate a mellow nectar light. She leant provocatively on one arm, her other hand draped between her slightly parted legs, exactly the way he would leave her to greet him on his homecomings from there on in.

How was your day, Art?

She wore a skimpy see-through white nightie edged with frills and bows. Beneath this sexy apparel stirred by the artificial breeze Art could clearly see that she was naked and perfectly formed. He would forever feel his heart pound at the sight.

Are you looking at my bush?

In the stuttering, exploding flashes of fluorescent paparazzi light a series of freeze-frame images appeared to bring Mia to life, leaving Art with the impression that her head had moved slightly. The fan continued to awaken the kinks and curls of her hair and flicker teasingly at the shoulder strap of her negligee. Looking at her. Seeing her. Art couldn't believe this perfect creature appeared so untouched by the ordeals of the night before.

"Japanese made," Eric purred. "Pure silicon from head to foot – that's medical grade too, mind. High elasticity, the body is as soft and supple as a fifteen-year-olds and you won't get arrested for touching," he broke into a smoker's cough. "Look at the hands. Feel the hands. It's like holding a fucking baby's hands. And the breasts and the lips, oh man, the breasts are like, well, they're made of a more jelly-like silicon for extra softness and that's exactly how they feel, like fucking jelly, man. Like heaven's fucking jelly in your hands."

"I don't understand…I mean, how does she sit there like that?" Art uttered breathlessly.

"That's the beauty of it. That's where things have moved on. This doll has a hyper-anatomical frame, which to you and me means a skeleton. Her legs and hips can move 140 degrees. See what I'm saying, Arthur?" he breathed into Art's ear. "Mia here can accommodate you any which way. 'Course, you can call her fucking Mildred if you want. She aint gonna answer back. Not when her mouth is full anyways," he broke into another laughing cough.

My name is Mia.

"I like the name Mia," Art said.

"Yeah, well, that's just her head name. The dolls' features are interchangeable. It has four different heads. Let's see now. You have Arisa and-"

"I like the name Mia," he repeated.

"You mean you like Mia," Eric corrected him. "That's okay. I get it. See all I'm saying is that you can customise them the way you want. Wigs, nipples, eye tone."

Art was drawn to her eyes. They looked back at him with compassion and understanding. As soft and languid green as the colour of olives.

"They even do four different kinds of pubic hair if you want the authentic look. Asian girls - the Japanese in particular don't shave because showing the vulva is forbidden by law. But fuck them. I don't know about you but I like a pussy on show. You know? Like it's been sliced by a cleaver. But everyone requests something different. You just so happened to have met Mia because she was hired out last night and I had to clean her up this morning because she has another appointment later."

"Cleaned?" Art repeated dreamily. He slowly began to observe the room. There was a large sink with a long draining board still wet with soapy water in the corner and to which a showerhead was attached. He saw various solutions in large plastic bottles the type of which might have been bought wholesale. Art noted two labels that read: ANTI-BACTERIAL CLEANER and RE-NEWER POWDER. There was something that resembled a pipe brush, a giant Q-tip and a large open tin of clear resin. To the side of the sink was a cupboard whose door was ajar to reveal the doll's other heads on a high shelf staring blandly out as if on pikes. For a moment it felt to Art like he might have either stumbled upon some sort of makeshift mortuary or a maniac's den.

"Yeah, I mean. She's only for hire, Arthur. No one round here is gonna pay for a fucking doll as lifelike as this. She costs thousands so I make my money by hiring her out. Those crazy Hell's Angels outside can only afford her by clubbing together with their 'charity' causes," he broke into laugher as if it was the funniest thing he'd ever heard. "Those crazy guys," he shook his head.

"What do you mean?" Art addressed him soberly, peering out past the stockroom door and looking towards the front window. A few of the bikers were now involved in a piggy-back fight that involved the passenger trying to stab the other's face with a lit cigarette end. The shop glass consistently wobbled as they stumbled against it.

"Well," he pulled out a crumpled tissue from his pocket and coughed into it. "They're the ones who have hired her out tonight."

Have you come to save me, Art?

"So you rent her out like a whore," he said.

"Just like a fucking whore. Yes. Damn, yes. Guess that makes me some sort of pimp, eh, Arthur?" he laughed. But Art could tell he had told the same joke before.

The more Art stared the harder it was not to imagine the doll might at any moment get up and walk over and whisper a husky "hello". Art tilted his head this way and that, trying not to see just a vestige of pleading.

Have you come to save me, Daddy?

"How much do you want for her?" Art heard himself ask.

"Well, now, before we get started on that Arthur, Mia here comes with a few terms and conditions that amounts to a hefty insurance deposit that acts as a guarantee you will bring her back in one piece. For instance, the one I had before. The Model F. I had to track some wacko down who had gotten carried away and destroyed her in cigarette burns. Before that another one had all the cavities ripped out of it. She's just as soft and tender as a human being so has to be treated the same way. She's a sex doll, Arthur. Top grade. Not something to be brutally abused or tortured. Go beat up your wife. Go stick a lampstand up her ass if that's what floats your boat."

Stop them, Art. Pleeeease… I'm begging you.

"I wouldn't hurt her," Art said, turning to look at him. "And I don't want to hire her. I want to buy her."

Art watched Eric's jaw drop, revealing the wad of gum tucked inside his bottom lip that bubbled with saliva.

"That's a fucking joke, right?" he asked, stifling a belch.

"No," Art said.

"The doll costs thousands."

"I know. You said."

"I couldn't let you do it," Eric laughed and shook his head.

"Why not?" Art frowned, feeling a dull stirring anger.

"You mean apart from the fact I've got twenty Hell's Angels out there who have paid up front and ready to show Mia a good time tonight?" he laughed and pointed towards the front of the shop. "Are you fucking kidding me you fucking dumb-ass Brit?"

Art stood with his arms by his side like a boy scout ready for inspection. He didn't know what else to say or do. He had never felt so out of his depth. But there was something else. A feeling of liberation. Some belief in him or excitement that made him stand his ground. Life had been his bully and for the first time he felt like he was standing up to it. For something he wanted. He had jumped off the cliff-edge.

"Jesus," Eric shook his head once he could see Art was serious. "Jesus fucking Christ, Arthur. Look, if you think you can afford to buy this doll from me then you can afford to go and buy a brand new one. See what I'm saying? One all for yourself. I'll even give you the name of the website. You can buy one online and it'll be shipped to you within weeks. I mean, think about it, Arthur. In doll's terms," he began to chuckle at the thought. "In real-life fucking doll's terms, if you get my meaning. Well, this doll's a fucking whore. She's nothing better than a no-good skank. A dirty fucking no-good skank. Look, what I'm trying to tell you is that she's damaged goods, Arthur. Go get yourself a clean one. You seem like a nice respectable guy. What the fuck are you even doing here, anyways?"

"You could say that about most people," Art said after a moment.

"What?"

"If everyone thought like that," Art appeared to be addressing an audience. "I mean, if everyone cared about each other's past. Well, then, no one would get together with anyone."

"But…"

"It's true."

"But we're not talking about real life here, Arthur, are we? I said in 'doll's terms'…you, you…fucking dumb Brit. You have the money to go and buy yourself the same fucking model. Something identical. Same tits. Same eyes and pussy. Hell, call it fucking Mia if you like or by your sister or your fucking mother's name or whatever the hell your fucking problem is. But you can't want this bucket of cum when you could afford a clean one. That's what I'm saying. It's like picking a prostitute over a princess."

Art flinched but resolutely stood his ground. Saying nothing as if he wouldn't leave until the deal was done.

"See, what I'm trying to explain to you is that you can have your own little virgin. Pure and untouched," Eric moved up beside him and purred in his ear. He had his hand down the front of his joggers again and began fondling around. "You do know the doll's not real don't you, Arthur? You're not just a fucking nut job in here wasting my time?"

Don't listen to him, Art.

"Yes, I mean…no." Art cleared his throat. "Of course I know."

"Huh, because you don't sound so sure is all I'm saying. It's starting to sound to me like you think the doll's got feelings or something stupid like that. You wouldn't be going along those lines, would you? I mean, I've told you the thing is made of silicon."

"On the contrary. It's you who seems to think the doll has no self-worth."

Art continued to stand to attention. Moving only his eyes at Eric as the sex shop owner patrolled around him nodding and frowning as if Art was a safe to be unlocked and he was working out how best to go about it.

"Still got a hard-on for Mia have you Art, old boy?"

"No."

"Why don't you tell me what happened last night," Eric turned away and began pacing around. "Something that might help me understand why you're suddenly so infatuated with our Mia."

"What…what do you mean?" Art replied hesitantly.

"Well, you were there weren't you?" Eric grinned, pulling his hand out from his joggers and wagging a sausage finger like a cross-examiner who had placed him at the scene of the crime before instinctively running the smell of his genitals beneath his nostrils for a sniff. "I've spent all morning cleaning her up. And I don't mean just smearing her with a few fucking baby wipes either like I've just cum over her tits because the mood took me. I've washed out every passage for safe measure and now you're here in my shop the very next day wanting to buy her? Who would want to do that after seeing what that whore of a thing was willing to be subjected to? Whatever it was I hope you had protection, Arthur. I hope you didn't get 'lost in the mood'. There were still bodily fluids being exchanged. You know what that means, don't you?" he grinned and winked and nodded.

"It's like you say. If…if it's just a doll to you then what difference does it make? You can buy another one. A new one. Maybe even a Model…eh…" but Art had suddenly lost the capacity to recite the alphabet. "Whatever the next one is."

"Careful there, Arthur," Eric stopped and gave him a sidelong glance. He still had his finger held up and casually picked his nose with it before flicking off the remnant. "Let's not try and get too clever about this. She's still my baby doll, remember. I can do with her whatever I want. She's still my cum bucket. I had her first and I can have her any time I feel like it. Hell, I might slip my pants down right here and now and shove it between those sweet golden lips. How would you feel about that, Arthur, eh? Would you still want to buy your baby doll then? With bubbles of cum in her mouth?"

He's right, Art. Do what he says. Do whatever it takes. You don't know what he's capable of.

Eric walked up to Art until they were almost nose to nose.

"What are you anyway?" he breathed, cocking his head this way and that like a large strutting bird. "Some sort of fucking bleeding heart liberal? Huh? Is that what you are, Arthur? Some fucking Brit suffragette in pants? Go burn your fucking bra somewhere else you fucking Brit faggot. You fucking red coat, because your type is what's wrong with this world. Your type make me want to fucking puke."

Don't listen to him, Art.

"It's…it's not that," Art stammered.

"Sure…sure, it isn't," Eric rolled his shoulders and began teasing him, as if he was trying to make a child cry. "You know where 'Mia' and every fucking whore in this world belongs, Art? Under our fucking shoe. Right under our fucking heel and if you think anything different you're nothing but a no-good faggot. You may think you're better than me with that fucking fancy accent of yours but you and I both know that's what you believe. To have her to yourself. To do with her whatever you want, eh? Aint that the real fucking truth? Say it you fucking red coat. The only difference between me and you is I'm just honest enough to admit it. But don't we all hate them for the fucking hold they have over us? Eh? Every fucking slut in this world? I tell you, Art. If there were no fucking laws…" he trailed off and nodded, as if deep down both he and Art knew. Eric turned away and let out a long whistle.

"I'm sorry I just…I just don't agree…"

"What you gonna do then, Art? Take her on a fucking world cruise?" Eric suddenly spun round and opened his arms and roared with laughter as the darkness appeared to leave him. His eyes lost their cloudiness and his mood lightened. He was back being the mayor of the town. "Get fucking married?" he stooped over and bust a gut at that as Art stood on silently watching.

He had a point. What was Art thinking of?

But then Eric was suddenly in his face again close enough for Art to smell his tobacco-gum breath and corroding his mind with images of Mercedes.

"Or what…?" Eric wanted to know.

Mercedes had been the first to drag him into the ring. He didn't know who had pulled down his trousers and pants or who was masturbating him from behind to the hoot and howl of the crowd. To his chagrin it could quite conceivably have been a man. There had been an argument about the music. Someone changed it to early rock-and-roll. Chuck Berry was singing Route 66. Then there was Elvis and Buddy Holly. A sweet smoke scent filled his head, relaxing him. When he looked round he saw other men being pleasured by a sea of half-naked women on their hands and knees. By then most of them were kissing and having sex with each other. Art foggily observed how it was that only Mia created the female attention of the men. Some tottered up beside him and ejaculated over the doll by themselves. At one point her every orifice was being raped as if by some giant human squid.

Pleeeease…

"How much?" Art said. "I'll pay you the price of two dolls. That way you can double your income."

They had arrived at the guest house late afternoon. It was still light so Mia had to lie down under a blanket on the back seat. After making a deal with the sex shop owner Art still had to go back and check out of his overnight accommodation and put his case together and get his car. In the meantime Eric said he would finish getting Mia ready. There was a small parking space at the back of the shop. Art picked her up two hours later but as soon as he got Mia in the car and drove away he could tell something was wrong.

You shouldn't have left me, Art.

Art knew he was going to have to conceal her at least until late when everyone had gone to bed so he only continued to drive in silence even though inside his heart was fit to burst. She was with him now and would be forever.

Upon meeting the proprietors Bunny appeared fine at first but it was Earl who seemed frustrated at not being able to impose a rigid set of house rules when Art asked for a front door key and explained that he wouldn't be back until late.

"So what restaurant are you taking your wife out to?" he wanted to know. "Be sure to get back early enough for a nightcap. Baby doll here turns in at ten-thirty regular as clockwork."

"I need my beauty sleep, Earl," she played up to him, sharing a look with Art as if Earl didn't mean anything by it. "When he lets me get it that is," she added flirtatiously.

Art smiled sickly and made his excuses, dropping his case off in the room before going back out.

Later, sitting outside the house and waiting for the lights to go off Art couldn't resist any longer and quietly stepped out of the car, opening the back door and reaching beneath the blanket. It was a clear night and when he sat Mia up his breath was taken away by her beauty. He ran his trembling fingertips down the silk-like skin of her arm and adjusted her hair by fluffing it so it fell in front of her shoulders. Only her eyes seemed different. They stared ahead. Opaque and unblinking. As resistant to the floodlights coming from the house as a sheet of glass. Perhaps he had seen something of his own emotions in her silent observation of him back in the storeroom. That the compassion he'd imagined was merely a reflection of his personal feelings for her predicament the way one might feel sorry when seeing a wild animal in the zoo but that in actuality no one could know what that animal was feeling just by looking into its eyes.

Nevertheless, Art couldn't help but imagine she appeared a little cold sitting there half-dressed so he reached down and pulled at the blanket with the intention of draping it over her naked shoulders when he noticed the little puddle appearing beneath her on the back seat. He inadvertently felt its sticky touch before reeling back and wiping at the blanket, looking at Mia in horror and disgust. But her gaze just remained blank and unmoved. Like the lifeless doll that she was.

"Mia...I..." but there was nothing to say and Art could only hang his head, playing back the sequence of the afternoon in his mind.

You should never have left me, Art.

"Oh, Mia," he said.

I'm damaged goods.

"Don't say that!" he shouted. "Never say that again," he tried lowering his voice, shoving his fist into his mouth and stifling a cry. "I should go back and burn his bloody shop down. That's what I should do if I had anything about me."

But Art never did that.

Art also never got to say he had driven through Hell and back. He and Mia continued their adventure up around the Great Lakes, staying in cabins and touring through Indiana and Illinois and Wisconsin, Minnesota and Ontario. Art extended his trip an extra week before spending their last day at Niagra Falls. He had already driven the Seven Mile Bridge in Florida but on the flight home began researching about The Million Dollar Highway, The Going-to-the-Sun Road, the 100-mile White Rim Road, and, of course, Highway 1, California. Those weirdly named towns he had so diligently researched had become of no interest to him because Art would never have imagined that at his stage of life he would ever get to drive through such beautiful scenery and breathtaking landscapes, or that he had finally found someone to share it all with. Just like that family in the Winnebago that he never got to be.

YOU SHOULD LISTEN TO THIS (PARTS 1 AND 2)

(PART 1)

When he first set out to write the letter with a knowing trepidation for his two sons' future wellbeing he entitled it: A Message from Dad. By the time he had finished scripting everything he wanted to say, he decided to visually record it on his laptop so there could be no misunderstanding. He wanted to look his children in the eye and tell them everything. Even if it was to be from beyond the grave.

You Should Listen to This: He ultimately filed it under name on his computer, and forwarded the document to the only person he trusted in the impending eventuality of his death.

Three months later and he still wasn't dead. Not as the doctors had precisely predicted he would be anyway. In fact, he hadn't felt better in what…eighteen months since the first diagnosis of an innocuous looking purple bump on his thigh that he had originally likened to a blood blister and all the ongoing treatment after? In particular, the first dose study of a new drug he had signed on for. What did he have to lose? Creeping past that first calendar date of his personal doomsday prognosis seemed like he had entered onto some higher mortal plane. Especially with the return of some of his fading faculties. His sense of taste and smell mostly. That's how it felt. Like he was seeing the world from a higher view. Oncologists rarely got it wrong. So why was he still here? It should have been something to celebrate. And it was, of course. But the old university friend he had entrusted the document to had rightly assumed the worst and before going off radar and proceeding to spend the remainder of his own years in some technology-forbidden commune in Asia at the age of sixty-six in the belief they would meet up in Nirvana anyway the idiot went and posted the thing off to his sons before he left regardless.

Fucking pot-smoking hippy.

"Have you got this document from Uncle Anton?" Brad called his brother. Since the family break-up he had been working in a call centre. A six-by-six cubicle with barely enough room for a coffee mug on his desk space and a framed picture of his biological mother.

"Yeah, I haven't opened it," Ivan admitted. "I assumed it was just another conspiracy theory. 'You Should Listen to This'? What the fuck?" he mocked loudly, for the purpose of his work colleagues who looked up and grinned and were listening in by courtesy of speaker phone. "What's the mad old bohemian going on about now? That it was really Elvis flying a UFO into the twin towers?"

He sat back and steepled his fingers and spun round in his swivel office chair, enjoying the spotlight.

"It's not from Uncle Anton it's from Dad," Brad said after a long pause.

Neither had spoken to their father since he had come out of prison.

"And Dad's...well, it seems Dad died, at some point, somewhere..." Brad continued. "Uncle Anton was just the messenger."

Ivan ceased spinning and gripped the edge of his desk as if seized by vertigo. He heard the words but they wouldn't filter through. The way he could stare at a page layout sometimes for half an hour and process nothing. Ivan was a marketing consultant but he often found his mind elsewhere. Up until that point he had been showing off a bit. He didn't know why. He was sometimes filled with an irrational pride about having a younger brother. Brad was somewhat of a family miracle. His mother's pregnancy had been kept a secret from Ivan throughout because of complications. Then one day she just turned up with him in her arms much like someone does a surprise puppy. It was only later he learnt that Brad was his mother's dead sister's baby.

"How can you be sure?" Ivan asked lowly. He switched off the speaker and picked up the phone and slunk down in his chair.

"Just watch the beginning of it," Brad said. "It's pretty clear. I don't know how long it goes on. I had to switch it off after a couple of minutes."

"Hello boys. If you are listening to this then it means Uncle Anton has sent you the document and I am already dead. I'm sorry to have to break it to you this way and I don't want you to feel bad about anything. All the funeral arrangements have been made. Everything has been paid for and of course there is the Will that at some point my solicitor will be contacting you about. It's not much after the flat is divided up between you and your mother but I hope it helps. The truth is I was diagnosed with melanoma...when was it? Oh, well, I guess it doesn't matter. Time is irrelevant now and my memory is in and out. But suffice to say I have been given a very short time to live which is the purpose of this video..."

Looking at the recording now made Don feel like he was watching his own funeral. That he was somehow a fraud who had faked death not for some personal gain but more bizarrely, to emit some sort of warped sympathy from it. Hadn't we all wondered at some point what would be said at our wake and who would attend? Didn't we all hanker for some sort of life accolade from friends and family? The thought that it was now in the hands of Bradley and John, or Ivan, as his older son had become more popularly known through his mother's insistence, and that he was still alive, made Don inexplicably want to run and hide. It was rare to say but he felt sure given the recent history between them all that they might even feel better about their father in death than if alive even if it was based upon the basic human condition to forgive and forget in times of grief.

It was in the last few months of Don's prison term that doctors had diagnosed melanoma. After a full body scan it was revealed that the cancer had spread to his intestines, with other traces visible on his bladder and stomach. Chemotherapy had little reaction. During the six months of treatments other tumours appeared in his lungs, liver and pancreas. Surgeons removed parts of Don's colon, liver, lung and his entire lower bowel. But still the cancer seemed intent on spreading upwards towards his brain. In just over a year Don dropped half his body weight. That's when he got his doomsday date and decided to write a letter to his sons.

It wasn't what his father had to say so much as the shock of seeing him looking like skin and bones beneath his drawn and melting mustard-like pallor that made Brad stop listening. Moving past the subject of his death Brad was barely interested in what he had to say for himself in the weird after-event experience of his passing. It seemed somehow vain but was also hard and intensely troubling to watch. For a start he looked like a talking corpse. His eyes had sunken into hollows where barely a light of his former dark bronze passion and potency burnt. In seemingly no time at all his teeth had taken on the look of old piano keys and his neck hung like strips of streaky bacon. He had always been a big man. In stature and in life. An ostensibly successful self-made entrepreneur with his fingers in a number of businesses until a series of bad investments coupled with the crash of 2008 saw his empire reduced to next to nothing which had been the start of his tax fraud investigations. The police confiscated his work and home computers. Their six-bedroom house was repossessed. Cars were taken off the drive. Even Brad's eighteenth birthday Porsche Cayenne. The boys and their mother were to learn that everything had been bought on credit and maxed to the absolute hilt. The astronomical interest rates soon became unaffordable. He took out loans. Jewellery was pawned. Bailiffs turned up at six in the morning. From a very early age Brad and his brother had enjoyed the good life. Exotic holidays, private schools, lavish celebrations. Their father had covered himself in glory yet he possessed nothing of substance when it all came crashing down. There were no savings to fall back on. No protection. Only his life insurance which the brothers were to later learn had been insisted upon by their mother because of their parents' vast difference in age. Their father had played with every penny they had as well as the Inland Revenue's. He lived life carpe diem. Like a devil-may-care lottery winner. Then when he was sentenced to prison for two years Brad and Ivan and their mother were left to stand on their own two feet. Ivan moved in with his girlfriend who subsequently left him after a matter of months. Brad got a job in a call centre and rented a flat above a shop. And their mother returned to her native Croatia with the intention of thinking things through. The place where it had all begun. The story being that she had met their father over there during the conflict on one of his spurious-sounding business trips promoting some sort of shady body-guard security operation for war correspondents.

As it turned out there were many stories.

That their mother had never returned didn't sit too well with Brad and his brother either. She had never fully settled in England. Brad could remember a time when she went back regularly to visit family and friends. But she only ever went alone and none of her relations ever came to visit which was strange because both Brad and his brother had been born there. Brad had never got to meet his maternal grandparents or aunts and uncles or cousins or all the people she spoke about with heartfelt enthusiasm on her returns. In fact, outside of their father and Brad and Ivan and Anton, no one even knew of her exact origins. Only that she had escaped Serbian occupation as a young woman from the small coastal town she had grown up in. Just one of some estimated 220,000 displaced Croats during the Homeland War. Anything else Brad wanted to know about those times he would come to learn from history books because his mother never, ever spoke about her experience of it.

His mother's name was Nina, or at least, the mother he thought he knew at the time. She was twenty years younger than their father but sometimes Brad would catch her out lying about their dates of birth. Usually to conceal the difference rather than laud over it. She could have been doing it to hide his father's insecurity of the fact or her own embarrassment of it. Brad never knew. To this day he still couldn't say with any conviction how old they were. It just seemed a stupid thing to be dishonest about when their disparity in age was so obvious. That and the fact you would never have put them together anyway. His mother was snake-thin and exotic with eyes like black pearls and a mane of tumbling curly hair to match that she was prepossessed to wash and brush and groom every single morning beyond anything of trivially equal or comparatively major importance. His father on the other hand was rotund and bald and drank and smoked and ate too much. Growing up all Brad's friends teased him about how hot his mother was. That his father was just her sugar daddy. His online bride. His mother was always getting attention. And the comparisons only got worse as his father continued to enjoy the high life.

"I suppose I should start by telling you a little bit about your mother, or at least the bits you think you know, or don't, as the case may be. What I have to say will be both upsetting and harrowing but there are reasons for my telling you and which I hope you can forgive me for and understand, if not now, then one day. It was something that Nina and I discussed at great length and that we both agreed to although upon reflection I'm not sure how sincere she was about it at the time and probably only went along with to it to shut me up even if she knew I was one-hundred-per-cent morally and ethically right. You were kids then, babies, in fact. Being old enough to know the truth even if you ended up hating us for it seemed a long, way away. I have had little contact with your mother since she went back to Croatia accept to receive a letter from her solicitor asking for a divorce. Well, now it seems she will get her decree absolute sooner than she thinks so perhaps everything worked out for the best. If we still had the house and the holidays and the cars and all the rest of it you would have only inherited debts. I never wanted that. I always thought I could fix it. I'm sorry I put you through all the embarrassment of prison boys. I don't know if that means anything to you but I'm glad it all came out in the end and I got to serve my time for it. I just wanted the best for you all. For your mother. And well, you know Nina. She had me round her little finger from day one. She could have talked me into anything… Not that any of that matters now which is what I meant by everything working out for the best. I could be a millionaire but it doesn't escape the fact that I would still be sitting here in the same position. With a terminal illness and only a short time to unburden my conscience to you before meeting my maker. I want to… I need to sign off with a clean slate, God forgive me…"

His father broke off in an attempt to hide his tears. The recording appeared to be self-made and roughly edited. He had obviously put it together over a short sequence of time. Ivan had never seen his father cry or certainly speak about religion but he supposed death could make you re-think about all that stuff. Dad was an only child who had lost both his parents at an early age to cancer so he had a lot to be angry with God about if you wanted to look at it like that. Not that you would have known. He and Uncle Anton would often light-heartedly debate the authenticity of his old university friend's claims to be a Buddhist and his plans to die in the lotus position so along with his political paranoia no one ever really took Uncle Anton that seriously. Of course, Anton wasn't really their uncle. It was something encouraged by their mother because they were short of family members to the outside world. The 'outside world' being the next door neighbours or Ivan and Brad's school friends' parents mostly. Her determination for social credibility to the point of inverted xenophobia had always frightened Ivan a little growing up. His parents had married at a registry office with only Uncle Anton and a stranger pulled from the street as witnesses. His mother never befriended anyone. No one ever came to the house. He never understood her suspicion of people whereas as a kid he just accepted their position in life. But she sometimes scared him with her frenzied behaviour. As if everyone was an enemy and that something awful was about to happen.

Yet on other days she would speak dreamily about a wealth of relations back in Croatia that Ivan had only ever seen old photographs of on the dressing table in her private bedroom. It was something that always seemed strange to him that their mother had gone to great lengths to have them both born there, but had never taken either back to meet any of their extended family since. In the early days before Brad came along she would tell Ivan it was war-torn and still very dangerous which only compounded Ivan's curiosity about his origins. Yet he remembered her going back under those very conditions to give birth to Brad. Why not just have the baby in England where it was safe, he had grown up wondering? Ivan could have only been one or two by then. His mother and father had kept the pregnancy a secret from him because under the apparent advice of a doctor Ivan had been having regression problems at the time. He wouldn't sleep alone. He consistently wet the bed. He wanted to suckle even though his mother had never breast fed him. Her sudden disappearance and being left with his father for months must have soon put paid to that. Then one day she just returned home with a baby. This time Dad had made sure there was no Croatian translation for the name Bradley, but it didn't stop there. At least, not until the death of Ivan's three-week old baby sister, Gabrijela.

Growing up with that experience always made Ivan fearful that his mother would come back with another sibling every time she returned home or even left the house. He had overheard his parents arguing many times about having another child and it always sounded like it was his father putting his foot down. His mother would fly into rages and withdraw into long moods that could last for weeks. Retreating into the sanctuary of her own bedroom where she kept all things indigenous to her homeland and in particular her childhood collection of wooden toys set high on a mantle and a number of handmade dolls laid down inside Ivan and Brad's old rocking cradle. Entering that room had sometimes seemed like walking into a low-lit fairy-tale grotto of lace and glassware and copious variations of Licitar hearts in all sizes hanging from the dressing table mirror and bedstead and drawer handles inscribed in a language Ivan had never understood in the form of an ornamental gift. Originally made in colourfully decorated biscuit of sweet honey dough it had become part of Croatia's heritage and a traditional symbol of the capital Zagreb on such celebratory days as weddings and St. Valentine's and Christmas to give or exchange the hearts each with their own personal sentiment. Yet without knowing it as a child it seemed to Ivan that there was something achingly forlorn about that room. As if it represented some sort of shrine for heartbreak instead of a tribute to anything good or nostalgic.

That Ivan came to learn his grandfather was a skilled artisan had always intrigued him. But by far the most romantic impression he had of his mother's father when growing up was that he had started out as a toymaker and that nearly everything in her room including Ivan's old rocking cradle had been made with his grandfather's own hands.

As a child it didn't get much better than that.

Three months into Don's death diagnosis a substitute nurse was assigned to him. At the time he thought it was a shame because his regular nurse had been called Angel and he had drawn some small comfort from that every time she attended to him. His new nurse was an American from Louisiana whose name was Dolores but she went on to tell him she had taken care of a parent just as sick as he that was helped by an experimental melanoma drug that was being tested in the University of California, Los Angeles. The City of Angels, Don took note. At that point he had finished the video to his sons and was ready to die. Dolores told him that she knew it was now being trialled upon patients in the UK and implored Don to sign on for it after witnessing what she described as 'the miracle' of her previous patient's recovery. A forty-year-old man in Arizona who'd gone through the almost exact same procedure and of which chemotherapy and radiation treatment had no effect. By then Don had been on a feeding tube. If it hadn't been for Dolores' insistence, he would have happily sailed away on the morphine.

The drug was designed to stimulate the immune system. Within the next thirty days – his penultimate month as far as he had been told – the lesions on Don's skin had almost disappeared. The medical director of oncology and other doctors and researchers and people he'd never met before came to see him, all growing increasingly excited. No one seemed to know why it was working so fast or how. He was told the drug only worked on about ten-per-cent of patients and that he was one of the lucky ones. They just needed to know why the stimulant caused an immune response in him that in turn fought off the cancer, and not others.

"Or you could just thank God and call it a miracle," Dolores suggested.

"The miracle," Don told her, "is that you were sent to me all the way from the USA. Right to this hospital. Right to this very ward when even an Angel couldn't save me."

"The drug didn't work on everyone," she reminded him.

Dolores was right. Sometimes it did seem like divine intervention. That he had been kept alive for a purpose. And with it came a whole new appreciation for life.

But by the time the treatment was finished and Don had been allowed to leave hospital Anton had set off for Nirvana and sent both Ivan and Brad the recording.

"Your mother came from a small village on the Dalmatian coast that was eventually taken over by Serbian troops during the war. She grew up in a peace-loving community. Many of the other villagers were ethnic Serbians as were some of her family's friends. But the war quickly divided people. Stories spread of homes being looted and burned and atrocities being committed on ethnic Croats living in Serbia and Bosnia and Montenegro. Fighting broke out almost immediately as the threat of invasion spread. Neighbour fought against neighbour. Friends against friends. Hastily assembled bands of butchers and bakers… and in this instance, toymakers, with no military training were organised into make-shift units to take on the Serbian separatists. But they were quickly overwhelmed by the help of the Serbian-led Yugoslav National Army and the Serbian forces themselves. Planes shelled the area. Churches, schools, hospitals and cemeteries were targeted. Within a year Serbs had gained control of one third of the country. In that time Nina saw almost her entire village of family and friends either killed in the fighting, become victims of war crimes, or had already fled. The place she had grown up in, a beautiful run of coastline of villages and neighbouring towns along the Northern Adriatic belt was left empty and war ravaged…"

Brad paused the recording feeling a mixture of anger and frustration. He stood up and paced the room running a hand over his head. Every now and then staring back at his father's sunken, hollow-eyed features still frozen on the screen. Everywhere he walked it was like his father's stony gaze had him in his crosshairs.

You should listen to this.

But why? Why now when both his parents had spent their entire lives not talking about this stuff. It was just like his baby sister, Gabrijela. Her name was never allowed to come up. He didn't even know where his sister's grave was. Brad hadn't even known his mother was pregnant.

"It's your mother's loss," he remembered his father telling him. "You're too young to understand. Maybe one day…"

And in the ensuing years Nika was if not all but forgotten, then certainly became a taboo subject.

Brad hadn't done as well as expected at school. Not as well as his golden boy brother. Ivan was always saying Brad got it easier than he did and that less had been expected of him. That he, Ivan, was victim of first child syndrome. Brad couldn't argue with that but the one subject he did take an interest in was Modern History and in particular the Yugoslav war. He would go home and start questioning his mother about the Serbian invasion. About the atrocities committed. He had grown up knowing his mother was a refugee from Croatia but that was about it. She never spoke about it. Then he found out that there was a Serbian boy at school in the year above called

Luka who had been adopted from a Bosnian orphanage and given a new life by a wealthy English family.

"Why not a Croat?" he would ask his mother. "I mean, the Serbs were the bad guys, right? Why didn't they pick out a Croatian?"

"It's not that simple," she told him. "Croatians did bad things, too."

"But the Serbs started it, right? Fucking Serbs, I hate them!"

"Don't ever let me hear you talk like that again!" she admonished him. "Do you understand?"

But later on he picked a fight with the Serb boy from school whose temperament he had underestimated and only ended up coming off worse. It seemed Luka had some deep-lying issues of his own. And every time they passed after that a look of mutual hatred was exchanged between them that made Brad want to do him some serious harm so he continued to provoke him by daubing racist graffiti on his locker which got Brad into deep trouble with the school and who threatened him with expulsion.

"Listen to me, Bradley. You don't know what that poor boy went through, okay?" his mother sat him down after.

"How can you call him a 'poor boy'?" he retaliated angrily. "His Dad was probably a soldier."

"Or a toymaker..." she looked at him sagely, pulling him up short. "You see what I am saying, Bradley? Serbian or Croatian the war had nothing to do with children. The children. The innocents. The genocidal massacre of tens of thousands of Muslims were just victims of it."

He hadn't expected his mother to refer to the war with such humanity. He just assumed she couldn't talk about it because it was too painful. Like Gabrijela.

"Why are you always sticking up for them? They were the aggressors. I don't get it."

"Because I don't want you growing up like them!" she suddenly erupted. The whites around her dark stormy eyes shone like moonstone when she grew passionate. She could be an intimidating figure when she stood up. A Medusa-like presence. More often than not dressed in something sensual and figure-hugging and made taller by heels. Her raven-coloured mane seemed to tumble and seethe around her protectively as if restrained only by witchcraft. "I don't want you growing up filled with hate," she said.

And that's when she called Ivan into the room and told them that their father, Don, had adopted them, that both their natural fathers had died fighting in the war and that he, Brad, was the son of her sister, Petra, who had also died. There was no preamble. No sentiment. No more explanation. Just a cold matter-of-factness. "Now you know why I don't want to talk about these things. You would have found out sooner or later in any case. For instance, Petra is named as your mother on your birth certificate, Bradley. And well, your father, the man who has loved and taken care of you, Don, always wanted to tell you one day," she said. "Just maybe not like this."

Until that moment both Brad and he had always been led to believe that her sister Petra was still alive.

It was strange for Ivan to hear his father talk so openly about his mother's experience of the war after all the attempts his parents had made to keep it from both he and Brad when growing up. She had been a volunteer nurse in her local hospital and Ivan only knew that because he came across her uniform one day hanging in the closet of her bedroom along with some other clothes he'd never seen her wear before when playing hide-and-seek with Brad. It looked like a fancy-dress rack with hats and wigs and strange jackets and coats.

So many things were left closed off or unexplained not least of all his baby sister's sudden arrival. Ivan and his brother were quickly sworn to secrecy about it because Gabrijela had been born with an infection that might kill her and they didn't know if she was going to live or die. Ivan didn't question it and Brad was still a little too young to understand. Nevertheless, through all that time the curtains were kept closed. There was no evidence of celebration. Even the TV wasn't allowed on. And then, just when Ivan was getting used to the idea of not resenting another sibling being produced without any forewarning and as if out of a magician's hat, their parents sat him and Brad down and told them their baby sister had died. But that it was the family's business and theirs alone and that they were never, ever to speak about her again.

Gabrijela.

Ivan estimated she would have been about twenty-two by now. Three years younger than him.

When the bailiffs came and started to take away the most expensive pieces of equipment and furniture his mother made sure her bedroom door was locked at all times telling them they should take anything they wanted but not from there. That the possessions were personal and held nothing of worth.

Helping his mother move out Ivan couldn't remember the last time he had even entered her room. It had become sealed off over the years. Yet after all the events of their father being held on remand and eventually jailed for tax evasion offences and suffering the ignominy of the house being repossessed she still clung to those vestiges of her past with a lion-hearted protection.

Among the room's festoonery of chiefly red hearts Ivan came across a black pendant he couldn't remember noticing before hanging from the crib's hood with an unusually simple inscription. It read: PETAR. Nikada nisam zaboravilla.

"Who's Petar?" he asked.

His mother turned to him look at slowly. She had a huge sheet of bubble wrap rolled out on her bed and was meticulously packaging everything individually.

"It's you."

"What do you mean?"

"It's what I wanted to call you."

Her eyes began to glitter. She had her hair pulled from her face and it hung down her back like a thick sable pelt.

"Why didn't you?" he asked softly.

"You know why. Your father insisted you should have an English name to go with your English surname to give you a better chance in life. So he called you John which was stupid because I just translated it anyway. John Best," she shook her body as if to shake off chills, as if it was still an issue.

"So why is this heart black and why isn't there a heart for Brad…or Gabrijela?"

"Don't talk about Gabrijela," she hung her head. "Gabrijela didn't exist."

"Yes she did, Mama. Don't say that. She even slept in the rocking crib. I remember it all. Why won't you talk about her?"

"There's nothing to say," she shrugged. She went back to her task with an added air of efficiency. Cutting through the wrap with a pair of scissors and flashing him a glance to see if he was still watching.

"What happened to her?" he surprised himself by asking when their eyes eventually met. Growing up he had always respected his mother's right to silence on the matter. He'd been young. Years went past without Ivan even thinking about Gabrijela. It wasn't until he got older that he began to grow more curious about the mystery surrounding his baby sister's death.

"Why do you make me think about her, huh?" she began growing angry. She fought with a reel of tape that stuck to her fingers before appearing to give up on it completely and threw it down in frustration. "You think I don't have enough bad things to think about? You think my life has been as easy for me as it has for you?"

"No, Mama, I don't," his eyes fell upon the array of framed photographs of family members on her dressing table. When Ivan was a child she would take him through each one. "This is Mama I Tata." (The toymaker! He would think every time). "I Djed i Baka. Ove je moj brat Marko I sestra Petra…"

"I have uncles and aunts!" he enthused. "And cousins, too?"

"Yes," she would smile down at him, but always with a sense of sadness.

The only picture she had been prepared to give away was one of her sister to Brad who kept it on his bedroom desk until the day they all moved out.

"Do you miss your home, Mama?"

For the first time he'd noticed her closet door open. There was a refuse sack clearly full of unwanted clothes but he saw her old nurse's uniform still draped on a hanger as if saved for the trip.

"All the time, Beba," she would reply.

Given his dearth of paternal relations this no less excited Ivan anyway. But as he started to get a little older and became more inquisitive and demanding about meeting his mother's family she stopped talking about them completely and her room became less a place of warm invitation than of cold and seemingly cruel withdrawal where no one was welcome. "Your mother's in her room," his father would tell Ivan by way of a warning. Over the course of time they all got to know what that meant. Very often the plaintive wail of an aria floated down the hall, or thunderous classical pieces which could be heard shaking the walls. She could go weeks excluding herself from daily activity before he would one morning walk into the kitchen to find her cooking some lavish breakfast and cheerfully greeting them all as if nothing had happened.

His mother seemed to allow him a last moment to absorb the photographs before slowly stacking them up for shipment.

"What are you thinking?" she asked, looking around the room as if she was seeing it for the first time.

"What happened, Mama?" he asked, thinking that he already knew the answer but had waited a lifetime to ask it.

"What are you saying?"

"Your family. Your mother and father. Are they still alive?"

"No," she said.

"What about your brother?"

"Marko is in a psychiatric hospital. He lost both his legs when he stepped on a mine. That's who I go back to see. Not so much these days," she admitted with a shrug.

"How did Petra die?"

But his mother only shook her head as if the subject was off limits.

"Why did you never say?"

"You didn't need to know such things. You were a baby."

"I knew anyway," he said.

She looked at him sharply. Her eyes narrowing into dark splinters.

"This place. This room. I knew they were just…memories. Somewhere you used to go to remember."

"And what do you remember, Ivan?" she asked him. "Sometimes I wonder."

There was a moment when for the first time in his life they looked at each other plainly. Like equal adults.

His sudden licence to speak. To ask questions about the puzzle pieces that had never fit seemed all at once overwhelming. Knowing this to be a last chance. That his mother was going back to her homeland – their homeland, and leaving him here. That it was never to be the same. If it was ever anything. Where was he supposed to go? Ivan suddenly realised the enormity of the situation. So he simply shook his head and said nothing.

"I guess I should start with you, Ivan. I don't know what you shared with your brother when growing up, if anything. I don't know what you remember. I never met your mother in Croatia. That was the first of many lies. I've never even been to Croatia. She came to work for me as a cleaner. Upon opening the door she took my breath away. She was also carrying a baby because she had no one to look after it. That baby was you Ivan. She hadn't been in the country long. She managed to escape Croatia and came here as a refugee claiming political asylum. Her English was limited. But we sat there and managed to understand each other for a whole afternoon. I was smitten. The terrible stories she told. The atrocities. Her journey getting here. You're both old enough now to imagine. You've read the history books. But you also have a right to know. By the end of that first time of meeting I asked her to marry me. Telling her I would look after you both forever. I'm not a stupid man, boys. Apart from the massive age difference I knew that in any other circumstances she wouldn't have looked twice at me. But I fully believed I could make her love me if only by kindness alone. So that's what we did. We married as soon as the authorities told us we could which was some time after. And I have never, ever regretted it..."

What Don was starting to regret however was to have ever made the recording in the first place, in retrospect of his newly extended life it suddenly seemed like a wholly selfish act and completely without thought for the damage done to the relationship between his wife and sons. What good could possibly come out of it after all this time and moreover, have it told in such a way from his deathbed? Hadn't he put them through enough? The plan had always been to sit down together one day and tell Ivan and Bradley the truth. He had absolutely insisted upon that. It was both their guilt to carry.

It was hard to get back to that muddled mindset of reasoning believing you only had a few months left to live. As ridiculous as it sounds he could only liken it to moving home. That's what it felt like. Walking through each empty room one last time to make sure nothing had been left or overlooked. Every cupboard and drawer cleared. Then one last contemplative look out through the windows you had looked out every day of being there before sucking in all the memories and turning the lock of the front door for the final time knowing you were never coming back.

Goodbye old house.

Goodbye life.

In the apparent end he was constantly being advised to 'put his affairs in order' by pastoral care when it had always been in his nature to juggle his business in the belief that it would all one day work out. Why should the onset of death change all that unless he'd been motivated by more malicious means? That deep down he felt he had a score to settle for being made answerable to a broken family when his only incentive had been to provide and not left hung out to dry like some common criminal sent to prison for tax evasion and cruelly ostracised by his two sons when his wife had by far committed the greater sins and that if he was to be held accountable for anything it was for harbouring her dark, hitherto untold secrets all these years. He just never thought he'd live long enough to have an even bigger judgement passed upon him and perhaps therein lied the idiom of 'living your hell on earth'. Nurse Dolores had likened his recovery to an act of God. But Don was beginning to feel like a restless ghost left haunting a place of tragedy. Even now he had to keep reminding himself that he was still alive if only because the people that mattered most to him still didn't know it.

What had he done?

Brad's reaction to being told he was in fact his mother's sister's baby had left a lasting impression on Ivan. Nothing changed. He asked a few questions about Petra and seemed satisfied with the photograph their mother gave him, but if anything appeared even happier in the knowledge that he had been saved by Nina and not left to some orphanage like the boy Luka from his school and prey to the adoption procedure. If that had been the motivation behind their mother's revelations that day then it worked. Brad had no more run-ins with the boy or the headmaster. If anything it looked to make him feel special. And as he went on to tell Ivan after in a number of conversations between them. He had only ever known Nina as his mother anyway. So why should anything be different? For a few months after Ivan could only watch from afar as their mother and he appeared to form an even closer bond than usual which was something Ivan had always been discomfortingly alert to when growing up. It was just that it seemed to make more sense after it came out and not something he should have felt threatened about. Under the most tragic of circumstances Brad had been placed in his Aunt's charge. Ivan just wished he'd known earlier in life however well-intentioned the secret.

Another reason Brad may have taken it all in his stride is because of the diluting effect of both he and Ivan learning at the same time that their fathers were both war heroes. More than blood they had that in common. Or at least that's what they told themselves. Nothing else was ever explained. When their mother stopped talking about the subject it was over so Brad and he were left to try and figure out the rest by themselves. One thing they both agreed upon at the time though was that the real hero in all of this was Don, the man they had only ever known as their father.

"So when the soldiers came. When they took over the village. They singled out individuals into the old and the frail, the men, the women, the Muslims, the ethnic Serbs and then, separated the children into boys and girls. Your mother was put into a school gymnasium where she was made to sleep with the other young women of the village which included Nina's sister, Petra. Nina was seventeen and Petra was fifteen. Over the course of some weeks or maybe months the girls were selected for gang rape. They were taken to a local hotel and plied with drinks and made to do whatever the soldiers wanted which in the history books you would have read as 'ethnic cleansing'. Nina told me each soldier would tell her his name and made her swear to call the child after them. "You will carry a Serbian baby!" they said. The old and the frail were shot. As were the men who hadn't already been killed in the fighting. After the war ended they found a mass grave of the villagers. Nearly all your mother's relatives included. Her mother and father. Uncles and aunts. Simple people…"

"Switch it off," said Brad. "I can't take much more of this. Are you telling me we are the sons of rapist Serbs?"

But Ivan only sat watching the pixelated image of his ailing father in an oversized chequered shirt, looking crumpled and weak. He had suspected something like this was coming which is why he wanted to believe their version of events years before that their fathers had been handsome young beaus who had lost their lives in their country's fight against invasion. That would have been a good father to have inherited attributes from. So why did their real father, their only father, feel the need to tell them the terrible and sickening truth? Ivan would never know who the man was and wouldn't want to. A rapist. A barbarian. Serbian or otherwise. It made him question himself. As if he might have the same pathological inclinations. As if he was carrying some sort of time-bomb inside himself. He had never even thought about such things as mass raping a woman, of course. It was a heinous act. The worst of war crimes. Better to just be shot and killed or so Ivan thought. Which couldn't help but beg the question why his mother had even given birth to him.

Had she just learned to love him?

"Ivan?" Brad reached a hand around his brother's neck. "Whatever it is. We're still brothers, okay?"

Ivan shook his head as if it didn't matter but he couldn't get the image of his conception out of his head.

They had agreed to meet for a drink in a local bar and watch the rest of the recording together, both needing that moral support or some Dutch courage or even a bit of hand-holding, Brad had joked. They'd set themselves up in a little booth in the corner out of the way. Up until that point Brad seemed more surprised than Ivan by the unfolding series of lies. But this one had shaken Ivan to the core.

"Why is he telling us this?" Ivan eventually asked aloud, and got up to get another round of drinks.

Of course, Don wasn't out of the woods yet. At his first check-up the doctor said he should wait two years until it could be safely said he was in remission. Part of him had wanted the doctor to tell him the worst. That it had come back and there was nothing they could do. But that was just the cowardice talking. He felt more removed from his family at this point in time than he'd ever experienced in the steadily darkening valley of his own approaching death. He was alive but he wasn't. He lived but he didn't. There was no undoing any of it. What now then, he wondered? That's when the thought came to him that his life was over anyway. That the best thing was for them to never know he had come through the other side and to leave it as it was and that he should just disappear but this time of his own doing. It seemed that God had wasted his messenger the Angel Dolores and the miracle of their meeting after all.

"One soldier, the officer in charge took a particular liking to your mother's sister. So one night when they came to take away some girls Petra never came back. When Nina got in a fury about this and kept insisting she wanted to know where her sister was the soldiers beat her as a lesson to anyone else who would question them. Can you imagine for a moment, boys, your mother sitting in front of me applying for a cleaner's job and telling me all these horrific stories in the most basic, broken English? I hope you are beginning to understand. And I feel a need to recall every detail and relay it to you chronologically if only because that is the way it all happened and, well, also because you will never get a chance to be able to ask me anything about it again... "

"This is fucked up, man. I don't like this one bit," Brad seemed on the point of panic. He took a long swig of his beer and leant forward and washed his face with his hands. "I don't like the sound of what's coming. If Petra - if my real mother disappeared. If there's a chance she is still alive. Then how the fuck am I here? Tell me that. Can't we just fast forward it and find out what the hell went down?"

"Listen. Brad," Ivan laid an unfamiliar hand on his brother's, tightening his grip. "Whatever it is we can handle it, okay? I'm scared, too. But it's like you say, we're still brothers no matter what."

"I'm not sure I want to know, anyway," Brad rambled, pulling away his hand and appearing not to listen. "I can't watch anymore. It's freaking me out. I mean it. It's like some sick joke. If I couldn't see his face and how gaunt and yellow he looks I'd think someone had put him up to it. Like one of those hostage videos where they're told what to say or someone's standing behind them ready to cut their fucking heads off, you know? Isn't it bad enough that we have to learn that he's dead this way? You watch it, Ivan," he said shaking his head and looking ready to go, rubbing his hands on his thighs. "You can tell me after. Or don't. I don't fucking care."

"There's a reason he sent this to both of us, Brad," Ivan looked at his brother seriously. "Not just me."

"We should contact Mama," Brad suddenly said. "Do you think she knows he's dead? Do you think Anton sent her the tape?"

"I really don't know. Dad's talking to us not her. The whole recording is about her. This whole thing, whatever it is, is about Mama. He is talking to us."

"Why didn't he tell us he was sick?" Brad continued his rant.

Ivan could see his brother was all over the place.

"Because he was a selfless person, Brad. All that trouble he got into. All that debt. It was just to maintain his lifestyle. Our lifestyle. Or at least the illusion of it. Because he loved us. Because he loved Mama."

"He shouldn't have bought me that Porsche on my eighteenth."

"That's what I mean."

"Even if it was second-hand," Brad looked at Ivan slyly and laughed out loud a little manically. "I was a little disappointed by that," he admitted.

"He tried his best."

"I know," said Brad, and hung his head. "I was just angry he drove Mama away after it all happened not...not the embarrassment of prison and the house being repossessed and all that. Everyone else can go take a fucking hike. I went to see him once. I think I told you. It didn't go very well. He told me I didn't have to come visit again. That he'd be out soon and that I shouldn't worry for him. The thing is I was so angry I wanted to punch him. We had everything and then nothing. Not even Mama."

"We're not children anymore, Brad. Whatever he has to tell us we need to deal with. Maybe it will make sense of everything."

"Everything like what?"

Ivan paused. Trying to find the right words. "Listen, we had a great childhood but...didn't you ever at least once get the feeling growing up that something strange was going on?" he asked in all earnest.

"Well, as you know your mother never spoke about Petra because...well, she never knew what happened to her and that was just too painful to talk about because as the older sister she felt responsible. That was one of the reasons you may remember her going back after the war was over. She returned to her village and that's when she found out about her brother. The natural thing would have been for her sister to return to the village too so she kept going back in hope. She met with government officials and aid workers and campaigners who in particular were all doing the same thing. All looking for lost loved ones. But the reality was no one knew what happened to her. I remember her telling me there was this huge board set up by some charity organization in one of the bigger towns with photographs of missing people on it. Literally hundreds and hundreds. Nina never gave up hope. She quite believed Petra would turn up and knock on our door someday. I wouldn't be surprised if she was still searching for her now. It's strange, but something that I kept thinking about in prison. After everything that's happened over here and over there. Nina, your mother, has spent nearly her whole life being or feeling misplaced. She seems to have a different place of abode every time I hear from her nowadays. Which is usually only to send her money. She knew I still had a little bit tucked away that managed to slip under the radar of those IR bloodsucking squids. Huh, listen to me I sound like Uncle Anton…

(Coughing pause)

I set out to tell you this in order. But, you know, what with my drug increase and the worry that I will wake up one day and not be able to make myself understood…that, I am running out of time, basically. I think that while it is on my mind I should explain to you about Gabrijela…"

Ivan had gone home that night with the intention of taking the next day off and tracking down Anton and his father's solicitor. In the middle of the night he got up and watched a bit more of the tape.

Gabrijela.

It seemed somehow wrong to continue watching this new disclosure without his brother and part of him really did want his hand held as Brad had metaphorically joked before. This was their rollercoaster ride and theirs alone. And something else. What could have divided them even further under the weight of discord of the last few years was actually becoming a recognized feeling of brotherly unity that Ivan knew Brad felt too. So Ivan text Brad at three-thirty in the morning and his brother came straight back with a reply saying that he had watched a bit more too and stopped at exactly the same point and for the same reason.

Looks like I'll be seeing you tomorrow. Same time? Same place?

Hold on to your hat, Ivan replied.

There wasn't a reason in the world that Ivan should know who his father's solicitor was so he decided he should just wait to be contacted about whatever 'estate' had been left to them. But if anyone would know it was Uncle Anton. Whenever he thought of Anton a sort of warm glow would come over him. His Dad's best and only friend had been a bit part character in all their time growing up. Flitting in and out of their lives with outrageous stories of public demonstrations and run-ins with authorities and cheating the system and worldwide adventures that took him off for years before suddenly turning up at the door looking another stage older and with a new religion and another strange necklace or bangle on his wrist or even the odd tattoo in latter times. Increasingly grey-bearded, lank-haired and drug-thin and looking like he didn't have a penny to his name but always seemingly somehow drifting through life and surviving. A 'cool cat' as Dad liked to describe him and an unlikely a pair as you could ever meet. Anti-establishment, anti-capitalism, anti-pretty-much-just-about-everything that Dad represented what with Ivan's father's multiple business enterprises and property investments and altogether conservative points of view at the height of his time, or so Ivan remembered. But there was also another reason Anton was hugely popular in the family. No one else ever came to visit yet their mother openly adored him. It was only now Ivan realised that it was probably not just that they were all by their own nature social misfits, but the only two closest people to his Dad, even if Anton did constantly accuse his father of trying to fit it and having middle-class pretentions and worst of all in Anton's eyes, a supporter of the monarchy. Nevertheless, therein lied the alliance. With Anton smoking his pot and Dad slurring over his whiskey and Ivan's teetotal, non-smoking, significantly younger and highly glamourous war refugee of a mother, laughing and enjoying each other's company to the full like partners in crime behind the closed door of Dad's study or more often than not the kitchen where the family dined most nights over a big farmhouse table and with French doors that opened out into an expansive garden which wasn't so much showy as randomly well-established with no off-limits and a haven for two young boys left to their wild imaginations growing up. It seemed strange to think they all knew then that Brad and he were the bastard sons of rapist soldiers. Sometimes Ivan was lured just by Anton's pungent aroma alone which could be likened at any time to some indistinct herb or cat's piss or freshly-mown grass. It was always the same smell but it wasn't. Ivan would creep down the stairs and up to the door and sit down and listen, feeling relaxed and comforted by the sounds and smells and would very often be found later by one of the adults curled up and sleeping in the hall in his pyjamas. But he remembered those times as vividly when Anton was visiting as if the pot still filled his head. That's what it felt like. An exaggerated world where the house appeared full of whispering and scheming but also with sudden bursts of joviality and mutual-appreciation and always a call for another round of drinks by his father. As if the no-go areas inside the house and shut-off rooms and palpable air of secrecy was all for a good cause. As if they were celebrating an advent. Just like the night before Christmas.

"I don't know what memories you have of the night Gabrijela was brought home. But by then Nina had lost all hope of ever seeing Petra again.

She was being treated for depression. It was the not knowing that plagued her. That and the guilt of not being able to protect her baby sister. And then of course she could only imagine the unimaginable having suffered it herself. It was a terrible thing to have to live with. She was haunted by unspeakable horrors. The most evil and deplorable acts of men who probably roam free to this very day and have families of their own. Which is why she needed and spent so much time in her own room alone."

(Pause. Shake of the head).

"The worst, most irreplaceable of losses. I can only explain what she did as some sort of love transference."

(Pause).

"The truth is you never had a baby sister. Your mother, she, well, she stole the baby. There it is."

(Shrugs)

"Gabrijela's disappearance was big news. We had her in the house for two weeks. Of course, her name wasn't really Gabrijela. That was Petra's middle name. The baby's name was Charlotte. It was three-weeks-old. Nina took the baby from a child's playground in the park. It was random. It was reckless. I don't know how she did it. Or at least, how she got away with it. There was an opportunist in her. She had learnt to live on her wits since the war. I can't explain it. She brought the baby home like someone would a stray cat. A spontaneous purchase in a pet store. She didn't even see the wrong in it. Saying that the mother hadn't been paying attention and didn't even deserve a baby if she turned her back on it for so much as five seconds – no mother did…"

(Long pause. Sorrowful shake of the head and sigh).

"Well, we kept the media away from you for obvious reasons. You were still so little. Ivan, you were about three and Brad well, you know you're a year younger. I don't know what you recall. The only other person involved was your Uncle Anton. I needed his help. It was his idea to shut the curtains and keep the TV off and keep you, Ivan, away from your little nursery school in case you started talking about the sudden arrival of a baby in the house. We had to make up a story for you guys. One you would understand and if spoke about no one would come prying. So we pretended she died. But in the meantime, in the two weeks that followed with police presence everywhere in the neighbourhood and people talking about it constantly the baby needed nurturing. It cried. It knew. It needed feeding and changing. Luckily we lived in a big house so no one could hear through the walls or saw us coming and going. Nina slept with the baby every night in her room but the baby just cried and cried. I didn't know what to do. I thought it was over for all of us. But in the end it was your Uncle Anton who talked your mother round to reason. He knew what she'd been through. He knew everything. So one night he snuck out and returned the baby outside a hospital before getting on a plane and travelling the world for six months financed by me and with my blessing in case he should ever have been seen or filmed and stayed away until it felt safe for him to come back. It all died down. The baby's mother even went on television to tell the abductor they had done the right thing by returning her child but that whoever did it needed help. She had the compassion to say that publicly. But Nina never believed any of it. She thought she could have given the baby a better life. And because of that she hardly talked to me for the entire six months Anton was away. It was as if she'd lived through the whole experience of having Petra taken away from her again..."

Ivan had stopped listening towards the end and was looking at his brother from across the booth. It wasn't hard to read Brad's expression. He looked the way Ivan felt. Shocked, disappointed, disturbed and confused. They had grown up with this romantically-painted illusion of their parents union. That they had met in war-torn Croatia and had a whirlwind romance that ended in marriage. With their father some sort of legendary figure for giving their mother a better life. Ivan would have far more wanted to remember things that way than this unravelling drama of elaborately-spun lies and darker truths. And to what end? Ivan began to wonder. Did he and Brad really need to know their mother once stole a baby when nothing had ever come of it? That their mother had turned up at the door applying for a job as a cleaner with him as her babe in arms, the racist spawn of an ugly rapist? The tape suddenly seemed less about some moral need-to-know declaration than a bitter and orchestrated attempt at dividing an already broken family made worse by the fact their father had died without their knowledge and with no hope of any sort of reconciliation or closure.

"He's a cunt," Brad sat back and said, echoing Ivan's thoughts entirely. "I mean, why did he do this? What's the point?"

Ivan shrugged in agreement, continuing to look openly at his brother.

"If he knows…if he knew why she did it - stole the baby, I mean. That it was replacing Petra or whatever he said. If he knew why she did it why tell us? I don't get it. Is he saying she was sick? Is he saying Mama's sick?"

"I don't know what he's saying or why," Ivan admitted. "It seems to me he's unburdening himself before he…" Ivan trailed off.

"It's fucking selfish that's what it is."

"I agree."

"Can we change any of it?" Brad stabbed a finger on the table. "No. So what's the fucking point of knowing? The fucking baby went back to its mother after two weeks, didn't it? So no fucking harm done there. And us. What the fuck are we supposed to do? Even if I wanted to know who my natural father was there's no hope of ever…" he suddenly stopped.

"What is it?" Ivan asked, but he thought knew what was coming.

"Something doesn't make sense. He keeps talking as if Petra, as if my mother might still be alive. As if she's missing not dead. And something else. If we are both bastard sons of the same band of Serbian rapist soldiers how come there's over a year in age difference between us?"

It now seemed to Don he had been in such a hurry to explain to his sons about their true origins he had forgotten to tell them the most important part. That he had always regarded them as his own children no matter what. He knew Ivan and Brad both blamed him for driving Nina away but the reality was she always intended on going back to Croatia. He would never have been able to stop her. Her leaving him had been a fear Don had lived with all his married life. He had always been uncomfortable with the generation difference between them. It festered in him that she would take a lover or might one day meet someone her own age. "There is another life in me!" she would sometimes curse, as if his time was up and he had somehow entrapped her into the bargain. When she spoke like that the implication was clear. That it was only a matter of time. That when the boys were old enough to understand she would be gone which only left Don feeling alone and old and used. At times like that he wished they would have kept Gabrijela. Or at least allowed Nina another child or even more if it meant keeping them all together. But in trying so hard to please her and give his wife everything she wanted he could barely support the family he had in the end. He'd known he was on a runaway train to ruin. He didn't need a financial adviser to tell him that. He had buried his head in the sand in the belief that the right investment was just around the corner, that he was due a lucky break, a lottery win, anything. There had been times of such worry and desperation and the most enormous sense of responsibility that he had even considered faking his own death. His life insurance being the only payment he had kept up with to this very day and something to Don's creeping discomfort and embarrassment Ivan and Brad would soon be expecting a share from. He hadn't thought about any of that when taking the drug. He hadn't thought about what he was saying on the tape. He didn't even believe in the drug. He just wanted to die alone and quietly like an old dog who knows its time has come and find the shade of a big tree to lie under. That's why he'd told Anton to go ahead with his plans to live out his life in Yemen or wherever he went. That his friend shouldn't be around when it all came out because of Anton's peripheral involvement. Upon reflection he didn't blame Anton for forwarding the tape ahead of its time and had never entirely trusted him with the deed anyway knowing his friend's views on the matter. He never stopped reminding Don that he had always said he would one day sit Ivan and Bradley down and tell them everything. And he would have. Don was sure. He'd just never thought it was a decision he would be forced into.

So Don went ahead with arranging a pauper's funeral with his solicitor who knew only of his pastoral wishes. Not the fact Don didn't want his sons mourning over something that didn't exist. That had never existed. Or that they had a right to know the truth and not grieve over a lifelong lie and crimes of such unforgiveable proportions the like of which there was no hope of ever coming back from. That they should really be mourning their own lost lives. In his dying state knowing that had given Don some sort of false solace. Making the tape had seemed like the just and proper thing to do. That it would give them plenty of time for reflection. But he was starting to realise now that some things were just best left alone and that the truth should come out of its own accord not through the vanity of some dying man's request to amend his wrongdoings and who wouldn't be around to face the consequences. That was the coward's way out.

"Boys, you should listen to this…"
(Drifts off and becomes visibly emotional)
"I need to go back to the beginning. I need to talk about you, Ivan. To both of you. I haven't got time to keep going over the recording. I'm a bit groggy half the while, or sleeping. They've got me on a cocktail of drugs. I'm probably repeating myself. It doesn't matter. As long as you know. You have a right to know and I know I should just say it right out in case…in case I just die in the night. But I won't. Not yet… I refuse to die just yet but most of all you both need to understand."
(Coughs. Followed by a long and thoughtful pause)
"And so Nina… was impregnated by one of the Serbian soldiers who raped her. Several months after, once the soldiers had moved on, most of the women who were victims of 'ethnic cleansing' chose to have abortions, but not Nina. Despite the fact the baby would never know its natural father and the circumstances of its conception Nina only saw the baby as a pure thing and most of all that she was the mother of the child and had a duty to protect it. She saw it as some innocent casualty of war but more than that, a replacement for all the loved ones she had lost. She saw it as a gift, hard as you might find it to believe. A divine gift. Perhaps her loss or replacement of Petra had even started then…
I suspect by now you both think you are the sons of rapists. You are not. Hospital conditions were still brutal over there. They were dealing with casualties every day. The war still raged on. Nina's baby was stillborn. It was a boy. She called it Petar for obvious reasons. But worse still there had been complications with the delivery. Nina was told she would never be able to have children again."
(Drops his head. A long silence).
"Boys. I have waited a lifetime to tell you this. I would like to say that you are orphans, that we found you wandering the streets in the rubble. That we

gave you a better life even, but that would be a lie. The truth is I don't know what sort of lives you would have had because, well, we stole them from you. You are both stolen children. Stolen from two different families from two different hospitals with two different names from the ones you grew up with. I am sorry to tell you that you are not even related…"

At that point Brad broke down. Ivan reached across the table and held his brother's hand. His brother who was not his brother. A man who in another life he would have almost certainly never even met. Brad looked up, his eyes broken and soul-searching. Ivan could read his mind. Just when he thought his real mother might still be alive… But it seemed one dark secret just unlocked another. Ivan nodded and then shook his head but was already aware of a distance growing between them. Feeling in that moment his stomach give way to nothing. The gut-churning, stirring acids invoked by the held-breath anticipation of each of his father's revelations suddenly stopped. The man who wasn't even his legally adoptive father. But there was no anger. No emotion. He felt the exact opposite of what Brad appeared to be going through. Because deep down Ivan thought he'd known anyway. That he had always known or at least somehow sensed. Some distant instinct. A faraway yearning ache but for what? He knew now what that was. It made perfect sense and in a small way gave him some small comfort to have at last been enlightened of that final missing jigsaw. That feeling of incompleteness that over the years had left him questioning his sexuality, his sanity, his very normalcy. The few times he tried to speak of it he'd been met with trite philosophical responses. He was reminded by a friend of the works of Plato who said that we were all once androgynous beings and that we spend our entire lives looking for the other part of ourselves. It was clear no one felt like Ivan so he just shut up about it after that but maybe Plato wasn't so far off. For Ivan now recognized that primal lament deep in his inner soul that he had never understood to be the lingering distress of being separated from his mother and furthermore perhaps, her lifelong suffering of being separated from him. Was his mother still out there calling him? Did her belief nevertheless remain like the faintest of heartbeats that they might one day be reunited? Is that what he had felt all these years? He had to believe she still did. Ivan felt suddenly overwhelmed with a conviction that she remained waiting and praying for her son's return.

(Part 2)

Ivan spent his first full day in Dubrovnik sight-seeing. It was really less about tourism and more about trying to get an endemic feel for the place he had been taken from as a five-day-old. It was mid-July and the summer festival was on. At night the gleaming marble streets of the 'old town' came alive with the lustrously-lit facades of baroque architecture. The illuminated palaces and forts, the churches and monasteries, museums and fountains all served as theatrical backdrops to endless open-air venues with acts consisting of classical music, theatre and opera and dance performances. Temperatures were in the mid-eighties. The enormously shadowed walled town punctuated with turrets and towers and gates enclosing the streets teemed with visitors. Strolling amidst the celebrations Ivan ached to connect but the truth was he just didn't feel it. He might have been anywhere at carnival time. Rio. New Orleans. Mexico. Anywhere. His pidgin Croatian was swallowed up by the hurried dialect of the locals. They sounded nothing like his mother. Or, Nina, as he now continually tried reminding himself. Nina and Don. The more he said it the more they began to take on the names of strangers. Nina and Don. They sounded like a cruise ship couple. A ballroom dance team. "And for out next contestants we welcome to the floor Nina and Don doing the foxtrot! Please give a big round of applause to the baby-stealers of Croatia!"

That wasn't fair. It was Nina who stole babies.

Ivan stopped at a café near the port where the sun glittered off the near purple-blue sea. A marina afloat with boats and yachts of all shapes and sizes stretched from end to end, creating a bovine interest from the procession of people making their way along the seafront. He could hear the constant slops and plops against the bows and dock walls. The sight and sound of water was everywhere. A far cry from the English suburbs. The 'pearl of the Adriatic' Lord Byron had called it according to Ivan's guide book. George Bernard Shaw went one better. 'Those who seek paradise on earth should come to Dubrovnik and find it.' Learning that made Ivan rather melancholy and caused him to wonder how very different his life might have been growing up in such a historically romantic place and conjured up a fanciful notion of a childhood spent in perpetual fantasy, a little boy's wonderland, until he went on to read about the damage done to the city walls by shells and mortar attacks in the year he had been born and reminding him of something his brother had said before he left. In the weeks building up to the trip Ivan had done his level best to persuade Brad to come with him, even though Don had told them on the tape that Brad had been stolen from a place in the east, a hospital in Vukovar that resulted in a massacre of some three hundred people who were shot in groups of ten and twenty and buried in mass graves discovered a year after and one of the crimes Serbian President Slobodan Milosevic was tried for.

"That could have been me in one of those graves, Ivan. Croatians were singled out along with other groups," Brad the history-buff said. "Did you ever stop and think about that? Dubrovnik was being bombed when she took you. Did it ever occur to you that she was trying to save us?"

"She might have believed it," Ivan replied. "It might be true if we had been orphaned and she just wanted to get out of there and cut through the red tape. But she didn't. She just took what was not rightfully hers without a second thought for our real parents. We were just substitutes for her loss, Brad. Surrogate children. The family she knew she could never have."

"I only know one set of parents. Good, bad, evil," Brad shrugged. "They looked after us, right? Obviously Mama was…is, well, she's sick, I guess. And Dad, Dad did some bad things but they both tried their hardest. You can't say they didn't love us like real parents. We had a good life up to a point. We can't complain. What's the point of what-might-have-beens? And now we've lost both of them and you think going over there and finding our real ones like some sort of ready-made replacement is going to fix all that? How can you be so sure they even want to know you? How do you know they're even alive? You have no idea where they live or what you're doing. I don't care what they did. I wish Dad was alive and Mama would come home and it could all just go back to the way it was. You should be going over there to bring Mama back not on some wild fucking goose-chase that's never going to fix anything."

And that's where they differed. DNA or otherwise. Because as hard as it was to connect with the surroundings, to think of the old former maritime town as his home, he thought he saw a welcoming warmth in the eyes of its inhabitants as if everyone knew why he was there. Don't give up, the wise old looks seemed to keep telling him. Of course it was only reciprocated friendliness because Ivan couldn't help smiling everywhere he went and for reasons he couldn't quite explain. "Is it you?" he wanted to ask when searching out the soul of every native passer-by. "Do I look familiar to you? Do you know my mother or father?" He felt very close to finding out.

Only the shame of not having already made contact with his sons had Don resisting the urge to call them. The long nights were the worst. His head playing scenarios over and over. And with each passing day the situation only worsened. His plans to move away and disappear lost impetus with the steady realisation that he was never going to return to full fitness. He still lived in the same apartment. All they would have to do is knock on the door. It wouldn't take much investigating to find out there no was record of his death. And then what? As if they hadn't been through enough they then discover he is a hoaxer of the sickest proportions. How else could it look other than he was getting some macabre pleasure out of making them think he was dead? Then he had to keep reminding himself that he wasn't their father anyway and that they must almost definitely hate him. Dead or alive. He had tried many times writing a long letter of explanation, but wasn't that how this whole thing had started? So what should he entitle this one?

But deep down there was also another more self-preserving fear for not making contact. And that was that they should go to the authorities and report them all. Don, Nina. Even Anton. That is if they hadn't already. Maybe Nina was already behind bars and there was an Interpol alert out on Anton. People just didn't steal babies. Apart from anything else maybe he should have thought about the mess he was leaving his wife and friend in when he was so conveniently terminal. So Don continued to go about his business, shuffling to and from the local corner shop under guise as if to avoid being detected by paparazzi and because he could never be far away from the toilet. The removal of his large intestine meant his digestive system worked a lot faster than most despite the copious amount of medication he was on to slow it down. So Don had been operating a little enterprise out of his home by phone. He was buying prescriptive drugs online in bulk and selling them in small amounts at a profit of three or four-hundred percent. Amphetamines, Viagra, ethnobotanicals and other party pills. Zoplicone, which was a sleeping pill, Diazepam (Valium), and a powerful painkiller called Tramadol. The sort of medication you couldn't ask your local GP for in extensive amounts or people didn't want turning up on their credit card statements, but mostly that his average client could only afford to buy piecemeal, albeit at an exorbitant rate which is where Don's middle-man talents came in. His buyers ranged from kids to middle-aged men and women of all descriptions each with their own reasons for Don's discretionary dealings. It was none of Don's business. He was just surprised how easy a way it was to make money. And then one evening he'd agreed to make an exchange at a nearby pub where he felt safe knowing there was a toilet and as he slowly neared he saw Brad seated at an outside table coolly sipping a beer and watching him approach, his eyes narrowed with suspicion. Not for the first time in his life Don had the sinking feeling that his game was up.

There is just one general hospital in Dubrovnik. Ivan wasn't sure why he took a ten minute cab ride out to see it. Only that he'd spent nine months in his mother's womb. That she had carried and delivered him to this very point. And that for five days he had been kissed and nurtured by breast. Don didn't tell him that part. Ivan knew that instinctively to the point he could almost make himself remember it. He had been held and cherished and spoken to in another tongue. Addressed by another name. Sometimes he dreamt that. He could never see the face or understand the words but it was the sound that comforted him. What he understood now to be the warm, soft and loving tones of only a mother's tenderness. And then that love, that life had been taken by Nina in the most calculating of criminal acts by masquerading as a nurse. The very nurse's outfit that had hung in her wardrobe for years when the story had been that she worked as a volunteer during the conflict. She must have known with absolute cold-blooded certainty what she was inflicting on his mother if only because she had lost a child herself. A stillborn. Yet however sorry one could feel for her about that, the tragedies didn't even begin to compare.

So with no particular plan in mind Nina headed for the political sanctuary of England, befriending a lorry driver along the way who agreed to smuggle them over, Don told them. With only the story of what happened to her village as evidence and following government corroboration of the facts, she was eventually granted political asylum and along with Ivan permitted refugee status. Don went on to explain that he lived a year believing Ivan to be her son until one day, after returning from a three-week trip to Croatia ostensibly to visit friends and family, he received a desperate phone call from her followed by a short conversation that would turn his life upside down. She told me she had stolen a baby and needed my help, he said.

Watching Brad's reaction to that had been the hardest thing. His brother just kept nodding his head slowly with his lips pursed and trying to toughen it out as if he'd known all long but until that moment Ivan didn't think he'd fully accepted any of it. It wasn't the same for Brad. Brad just remembered growing up with a brother and in a settled home and being afforded every privilege and in many ways Ivan had always felt that his little brother had been the favourite. Brad loved and trusted the bedrock that was his Mum and Dad. He never doubted it. But Ivan was intuitively alerted to Brad's arrival in much the same way he had been Gabrijela's. There had been no reference to a baby up until that point. Ivan remembered arguments behind closed doors that went on for years after when Nina could be heard screaming uncontrollably at the top of her voice. "I bring a gift to you and this is how you treat me? I bring you a son! I even let you call him stupid film star name!" If Ivan didn't know what he knew now it could still so easily be interpreted as just her referring to giving birth to Don's child even if it had left Ivan feeling confused and suspicious that there was only ever one son being mentioned or argued about. It left Ivan feeling like an outcast. So what had Nina been saying? That she had abducted Brad for him? That they both each had a stolen child and that he was now somehow inextricably implicated? Ivan had always recognized Nina's wiles in trying to get her own way or win Don over. She was striking, headstrong, sensual and full of life. She could turn her husband into mush with a sway of her body, a flash of her onyx eyes or a lingering stroke of her fingertips. But in all the years Ivan had never thought of her as seriously troubled or unhinged.

And so, much like the Gabrijela fabrication, his supposed mother and father sat him down and told Ivan a pack of lies about him having a baby brother. That his mother had to go back to Croatia to a special hospital because there had been complications with the pregnancy that they didn't want to share with him until they knew everything was going to be all right.

If anyone asked then that was the version he was to tell they coerced him until he had learnt to repeat it verbatim and to their satisfaction. Good boy, they said. But being a stolen baby himself must have given Ivan some heightened instinct because despite his tender age at the time, Brad's story, and then the day Gabrijela was brought home, just seemed to stir a familiar memory in him. A sense of deja vu that triggered off an unsettling feeling of dread and of danger from the furthest corners of his being. It was only now that it all made sense. In total Nina had stolen three children. Ivan had to keep reminding himself of that. Who knew how many she had been capable of taking if not for the undying protection of Don and his many misguided loyalties?

Brad had been ready for the sight of his father looking a lot different after the dramatic weight loss seen in the recording. What he hadn't prepared himself for was the shockwave of actually seeing his father alive after believing him to be dead, even though he'd had a few weeks to get used to the idea. He appeared gaunt and frail and a little out of breath. But there was something else in his look when their eyes met. He seemed weighed down and haunted. Brad felt the anger and disappointment he had carried for so long disappear as soon as he saw him. He stood up feeling an overwhelming disbelief that it was all true, that his father was somehow still here, back from the dead, impossible as that was to rewind.

In a moment of impulse Brad stepped forward to hug him which only caused Don to flinch in the thought he was being attacked. Seeing his rapidly-aged father fearful of him only made Brad feel worse. After he had gone to prison the family had pretty much shunned him to the point his father had never even shared his two-year battle with cancer with them. No one should have to face something like that alone. Being a stolen baby had nothing to do with that as Ivan would like to think. His father had done his best to provide and protect them when in reality it had all been his mother's mess. What was his father supposed to have done? Turn her in? Except for the tape Brad wouldn't have changed anything.

Why did you make the fucking tape? Brad wanted to ask.

"I had to be forgiven," Don's lips trembled, reading the question in his son's expression and holding out his hands in a gesture of pleading.

Don felt himself capitulate under a great shuddering wave of relief and tears as Brad reached round and hugged his father tightly. A surge of goodness flooded through him in the same way a religious healing was supposed to work and that no amount of prescription pills were able to produce. It made him think of the Angel Dolores and in that instant he felt like his old self in the days before the insidiousness took hold. That stealthy evil that he still believed and wholly accepted was some sort of righteous punishment for being party to not only the stealing of the lives of two children, but the lives of their natural parents and grandparents in turn. What terrible undeserving shadow had been cast over their remaining time? Ivan and Brad had never known any different but such had been the depth of Don's purgatory over the years that in his darkest hours he sometimes thought his conscience might have been easier appeased had he taken the children from their natural parents in a fatal drink driving accident. At least then in time they might have been able to come to terms with it.

Don had explained Nina's abduction of Brad by coming into the country and going through the exact same story and process she had with Ivan but in this case using her sister's name. Contrary to her previous deception however she claimed to have a place of refuge with an old friend of the family in the UK, namely Don, while the authorities looked into her case. Don was routinely questioned and Anton testified as a witness to the fact and she was eventually granted refugee status (again) along with Brad and assuming her still presumably dead sister's identity into the bargain. Such a scam might not have been possible in today's modern digital age. But Nina's scheming mind clearly stretched way beyond the elementary manipulation of her husband. No doubt there were many immigrants legal or otherwise operating similar frauds for the purposes of claiming benefits or who knows what but Nina's only intention was to smuggle in another baby without jeopardising the asylum already granted her. Don made her promise that she would never do anything like it again and in the belief that the compulsion had been sated forever he agreed to marry her and adopt the children and make everything about as legal as it could be, leaving her sister's alter-ego to disappear under the radar for good. It never bothered her that the boys' legal papers had their mother documented with two different names and that both their fathers were listed as 'unknown', which she would only go on to pass off as clerical errors. There would come a time when they should learn they were adopted and that Brad would have to be told he was Petra's child, she had said. But that wasn't what Don had been worried about. It was still all a pack of lies. One day they will have to know everything, he had warned her. Even if he had to tell them himself.

And that's when Don shakily held up the two little wristbands to the camera like some pathetic peace settlement exchange. Ivan had felt his stomach roll. He watched transfixed as Don started to shudder with emotion and began fighting back tears but tears of what? Guilt, regret, self-pity? Ivan still wasn't sure he knew. They all seemed like luxurious emotions to him in the circumstances and he only began to grow angry. It was clear the entire 45:33 footage of film had been building up to that point. With Don sitting there in bed attached to an IV drip and propped up by pillows looking cadaverous and wax-yellow in his hospital gown. Silently pleading forgiveness with his outstretched offerings. The baby bracelets removed from them at birth by a cold conscience and kept hidden all their lives.

'Boys…these are your real identities. I am going to put them in an envelope now and leave them with my solicitor under the strict instructions that only you are to open them-'

And that was it. Almost as if the video had overrun its length or Don had gone into some sort of seizure and the tape had been cut short. Brad and he were left feeling the sudden vacuum of his passing just the way it would have been. One minute he was there alive and talking. The next gone. With only a strange emptiness residing amidst the devastating impact of his unveilings. Like the eerie silence following an explosion. His words still ringing in their ears.

It was only weeks after that Don's true colours revealed him to be a confidence trickster of the most sick-minded magnitude. Resurrected by some wonder drug but with their charlatan father happy to let Brad and he think otherwise. It just felt like some elaborate joke that had fallen flat but that Ivan was still the victim of not some medical phenomenon as Brad wanted to believe and that he had tried arguing in Don's defence must have given him reasons for keeping his recovery from them. His brother's increasingly diehard conviction that no harm had really been done and that with the miraculous return of their duplicitous father the family was still somehow salvageable left Ivan to reflect on the differing circumstances of their abductions. Was Brad right that Nina may have deliberately targeted the hospital in Vukovar some hundreds of miles east of Dalmatia knowing the desperate situation there and that the stealing of a baby would be made easier despite the obvious danger to herself whether infiltrating as a nurse or not? The eventual massacre and almost certain death of Brad's parents given the harrowing statistics of one of the worst war crimes to come out of the conflict would have explained why his brother didn't feel the same inner yearnings as he to find his birth mother. Especially if she had never been alive to mourn his disappearance.

Ivan had got a good last-minute deal on a contemporary-styled studio apartment overlooking the terracotta rooftops of the old town and the verdant inland hills rising up beyond. The converted three-storey stone building was situated in a tiny cobbled sloping street just off Stradun and was run by a young couple called Dragan and Ana who lived on the ground floor along with Karlo, an extremely docile golden retriever who could usually be found passed-out on the tiled entrance by reception with barely a wag of his tail in acknowledgement to the guests going in and out or who would stop to pet him. Towards the back of the building a dark narrow arched hallway opened up into a little gift shop from where the bright morning light could be seen on the adjacent street, creating the feeling of a virtual thoroughfare between.

In the couple's tiny dining room where breakfast was served Ivan spent an hour browsing over a map and drinking coffee. Ana was cute and petite with big brown eyes and dark elfin hair and spoke good English which was in the interests of all the little enterprises Ivan supposed given that tourism was the old town's main source of economy. She wore a white fitted short-sleeved blouse and tight black trousers and watching her attend to other guests out of the corner of his eye Ivan suspected for the first time since his arrival that she might be pregnant. When she served him some more coffee and enquired what he had planned for the day Ivan felt his hand move to conceal the circled highlights he'd drawn on the map. All he had to go by was the hospital wristband with his name and date of birth. Henrik Domonik Zebitko. As if he didn't have enough names already. According to the research he had done before coming over there were only five families who went by that surname in Dubrovnik and none of them resided in the old town. So he told her he was going to walk the city walls that morning and she advised him to not leave it much longer as it could get really hot up there and that there was no shade, urging him to look in her mother's gift shop before he left where she supplied a number of hats. And water, she urged. Take lots of water. There are vendors up there but they charge twice as much, she smiled sweetly. He smiled back and for a moment their eyes lingered. If she hadn't been married he might have been bold enough to ask for a guided tour.

Feeling an almost childlike inadequacy to do as was suggested Ivan found himself going out through the gift shop entrance for fear of Ana seeing him do otherwise. The tiny emporium was crammed full of tourist merchandise, including to his dismay an array of assorted hats on a stand by the door that his now deepening ineptitude felt obliged to purchase. Yet still the skinflint in him was considering it a waste of money. There was no one at the counter and as he cast an eye back along the hallway to see if he was being watched he saw Ana hurrying down towards him, running stiffly like a young girl with her arms straight by her side and her wrists out-turned. She seemed in a bit of a fluster and he couldn't help but notice one of her blouse buttons had come undone revealing the soft little swelling of her abdomen. She laughed, a little out of breath. Microscopic beads of sweat began to appear along her upper lip. He hadn't been so struck by a woman in a long time. If ever. She hurriedly explained that the shop wasn't open yet but he was to take what he wanted and pay later. Sensing his hesitation she calmed herself and walked over to the stand, pulling a quizzical look and looking back at him over her shoulder. Hmm, she said, blowing a strand of hair from her face out of the side of her mouth. She then pouted her lips and frowned in an act of deep concentration and turned the stand round before picking out a white baseball cap that made him want to turn and run. He'd never worn a baseball cap in his life. As she neared he could see there was an emblem on the front. One half was the red-and-white chequered flag of Croatia and the other half the horizontal tri colours of Serbia.

"Don't think about the colour," she read his thoughts, bending the peak of the cap and looking up at him from under her fringe. "White is the symbol of peace and unity. I am a Croat married to a Serb. Ivan is a Slavic name," she said after a brief pause, cocking her head and awaiting a response with those big, unblinking doe eyes.

"It also means 'John' in English," he replied, a smile appearing at the corners of his mouth.

The intimacy of the moment was making his throat a little dry. She on the other hand seemed in complete control.

"Is your name John, then?"

"My mother was – is Croatian," he said.

"Where is she now?"

"I don't know," he shrugged. "Somewhere. Somewhere over here, I think."

"Is that why you're here John Ivan? Are you looking for your mother?"

"As a matter of fact I am," he said.

She nodded. "I hope very much that you will find her."

She had to stand on her tip-toes to position the cap on his head.

"There," she said, and stepped back and nodded. "Savrsen."

One of the first things Don asked was if Ivan knew. Brad told him it was Ivan who had tracked down Don's solicitor in search of the wristbands. His solicitor was as confused to hear that Don had died as Ivan was to hear that the solicitor had only recently had a phone conversation with his father about a miracle drug he had been taking and that he was still alive and out of hospital. Don suspected as much and had made no attempts to conceal his tracks. He'd known it would only be a matter of time before his sons would find him and he took a perverse pleasure in that if only because it proved some sort of connection still existed between them.

"I just don't understand why you would let us think that all this time. Why you would do that to us," Brad's voice cracked, searching Don's face earnestly. It was hard to be angry. Apart from the dramatic change of appearance his father had a furtive look about him. They were seated outside in the warmth of the early evening sinking sun. But he looked up nervously at every passer-by and wouldn't stop shifting in his seat. Brad had put it down to the dubious operation he had been told his father was running but it was only later that Don explained to him how he lived in perpetual unease at soiling himself.

"You were never meant to see the tape," Don said, shaking his head ruefully. "It was Anton..."

"Do you regret making it?"

"No," Don said instantly, looking Brad straight in the eye. "You had to know. You both deserved to know."

"It was just more convenient telling us after you were dead," Brad nevertheless simmered.

"It wasn't meant to be like that. I was given weeks left to live. Trust me, until you hear those words you always think there's a chance. I'd envisaged a hundred different ways of telling you. But you and your broth- It was like the whole family had disowned me and for what? I didn't want to make matters worse but in the end I was forced into doing it. Maybe it was the coward's way out. Maybe there was even a bit of malice in it. I don't know. You have to remember I was sick. I thought I was running out of time. I couldn't die without telling you. I used to be scared of being killed in a car crash for that very reason because I knew your moth- Nina, would have kept it a secret from you forever."

"Why didn't you tell us you were ill?"

"Why didn't you ask?" Don responded angrily, his body was trembling with upset. "Why didn't you come visit after I got out of prison and see how I was doing? It was bad enough that my wife walked out on me. But my sons..." he trailed off, laughing emptily. "I can't even hold that against you now. Nothing makes sense anymore."

"I am your son, Dad," Brad said.

Don looked away, his eyes shining.

"And you always will be to me, Brad. But...but you know those adoption papers aren't worth the paper they're written on. They're fraudulent."

"You did what you thought best, you did the right thing at the time."

"Yeah, that's what I always tried telling myself. That's why I tried to give you everything. To give you a life that couldn't be compared. But that was never, ever my right to call. Your mother, Nina, had something very bad happen to her. An unimaginable horror. Her moral code. That...that fundamental ethic of what we all know to be what is right and what is wrong was taken from her when she was gang-raped by soldiers. Is it any wonder she saw fit to take something back in return without any thought for the lifelong trauma her actions would cause on others? No. Right or wrong she didn't know any better. At least not in a rational way. And so, taking into account the loss of her parents, her sister and stillborn baby, I don't think there's a jury in the world who would convict her for her crimes. But what's my excuse, Brad? Tell me that."

The first address Ivan arrived at was a modern apartment building off a wide busy road in a soulless financial district and upon pressing the intercom he received no answer. He didn't get a good feeling about the place anyway.

Yet just the sight of the name Edvard Zebitko listed in the directory got his heart racing. It was still more than possible that in a place of just 40,000 inhabitants the man could be a relative of his.

Frederick, the cab driver he'd hired for the morning spoke good English but insisted on pointing out every landmark and taking scenic detours between each destination. He was a big man with an enormous black moustache and habitually hummed between conversation and when Ivan was left wondering what the appeal was about the heavily industrial landscape they were passing through the cab came to a slow, trundling stop in front of a dirt road lined with a row of terraced cottage houses. Frederick nodded gruffly and pointed at the houses, looking at him in the rear-view mirror. Ivan consulted his map and looked around. The gritty backdrop of workshops and warehouses and factories made his heart sink so attached had he become to the idea he hailed from the old walled city overlooking the Adriatic. He stepped out of the cab feeling a sudden lack of enthusiasm for his quest. The air was arid and polluted by a faint smell of sulphur. Scrubland grew all around. There was a constant drone from a distant plant that belched smoke from two tall chimneys. He checked the house number and looked back at the cab driver giving him a gesture that he should stay. Frederick nodded and lit up a thin cigar and pushed his seat back as Ivan set off down the mud road dried rock-hard into shallow criss-crossing ravines made by tyre tracks and making it difficult to walk.

After several knocks on the door Ivan was at the point of walking away when he heard a distant murmur and the shuffling of someone approaching. It was opened by a little old lady in glasses that Ivan's mind was instantly programmed into believing could be his mother. He used his limited Croatian to introduce himself, but it wasn't translating very well so he reached into his pocket and held out the hospital bracelet for her to examine.

"Henrik," she said, and pointed at him.

"Yes," he nodded vigorously, expectantly. For some reason he found himself standing up straight as if for inspection.

"Henrik Dominik Zebitko."

"Da," he said.

She shrugged as if the name meant nothing to her.

He stepped back and checked the house number and the surroundings. It was possible it was the wrong address, he supposed. That there was another road by the same name. But in his heart he knew he didn't want it to be this address. He didn't want the woman to be his mother and felt a sudden yearning for the whole thing to go away just like Brad had said. That everything should go back to the way it was.

You should be going there to bring Mama back not on some wild fucking goose-chase that's never going to fix anything.

"I'm sorry," he said, gently prising the bracelet out of her hand.

"Ne," she said, and suddenly closed her thin fingers around it with surprising strength.

A flicker of uncertainty passed through Ivan's eyes.

"Cekati," she told him, implying with a firm hand that he should stay where he was.

When she shuffled back into the shadows Ivan looked back at the cab driver hesitantly before gesturing at him to come over. Frederick pointed at himself and Ivan nodded and began waving at him hurriedly.

"I might need an interpreter," he called, to which Frederick gave him the thumbs up and threw away his cigar before struggling to get out of the car. He seemed more than happy to be of use.

When the old woman returned she was holding a faded photograph turning at the edges. She held it out to Ivan. Frederick, still wheezing from his sudden exertion, introduced himself and the two began talking. Upon examination Ivan could see the picture looked to be some sort of family gathering that crossed three generations. The Croatian flag was proudly on display strung along a fence in the background.

"She says her son found it down the back of some old furniture left behind when he moved in," said Frederick.

Scrawled on the back was the date: svibanj 1996. It was post-war. Maybe that's what the celebration was about.

Ivan looked at Frederick a little nonplussed and went to hand the picture back.

"She says the woman who lived here before was a widow called Iva. Iva Zebitko."

Ivan searched the photograph again. Not daring to hope. There must have been twenty-five, thirty people in the picture. His eyes scanned the middle generation. He counted four women who might have been around his mother's age at that time, some with children by their side. One holding a baby.

"Does she know where the woman is now?" Ivan felt a tingle of excitement coupled with the more realistic and altogether heavier expectation of braced disappointment.

The old lady continued to shake her head at a continuing line of questioning from Frederick who appeared to be doing his best.

"She moved to be with family is all she knows," Frederick told him. "It's not unusual. This lady lives with her son. I live with my sister and her husband. Nearly all of us lost someone if not more. You can keep the picture," he smiled pleasantly.

Ivan nodded humbly. "Hvala ti," he looked at the old lady warmly and held his hands up as if in prayer. "Hvala vam puno."

"Henrik Dominic Zebitko," she repeated and smiled as if she understood before handing Ivan back the bracelet.

Clearly the online information he had was out of date which was a bit dismaying in the least. One of the other two addresses didn't even exist anymore and had been replaced by a new housing development. And the last one, a semi-detached house in a leafy suburb was occupied by an Asian family who claimed to have lived there for years. Ivan arrived back in the old town in the late afternoon. He went back to his room and changed his clothes before setting out to walk around the city walls which took him almost two hours. Ana had been right. The heat was intense but when he arrived at the southern section he found several cafes and a bar where he was able to sit and have a beer in the shade and admire the view across the sea dotted with sailing boats and kayakers. He took out the photograph and sat there until sundown studying each face over and over in the vain hope of seeing a resemblance and in particular the four women who could have been around the age of his mother. Of course, there was a good chance everyone there might have lost someone close to them. But not in the way his mother had. There was a bravery and unity connecting the whole gathering. A defiance that shone through. All except for one, he began to think. The woman with two little girls by her side had a different loss in her eyes. A faraway look of suspended sadness.

Once back down on Stradum sound tests were already going on. Rows upon rows of chairs were being set out around every turn. Street vendors were out in force. There was another vibe of anticipation about the place and by early evening the festival was in full swing again. Recalling the photograph and the huge family gathering he couldn't escape the feeling that he may have brushed shoulders with a relative. A cousin or uncle. Even a sibling. He found himself constantly searching faces in the crowds even though he had no hope of recognizing anyone. And so, perhaps if he hadn't been looking so hard he would never have even seen her and have cause to feel his heart freeze.

There was a small orchestra playing in a fountained square in front of the steep rising steps of the Jesuit Monastery. The scene was floodlit and most of the seated crowd were thronged by passers-by who had stopped to watch. She was standing at such an angle he could barely see her profile but he could tell by the swing of her body that she was singing to herself as she often had. Then of course there was that dark tumbling mane held loosely in place by a bow-tied red ribbon. He had never seen her in a pair of shorts before and her long tanned legs seemed to go on forever. She had her arms cupped in front of her as if the music was filling her chest, but then he realised that the strap across her back wasn't a bag of some sort as he had first thought but that she appeared to be holding something.

Ivan pulled the brow of his cap down over his eyes in an effort to disguise himself and inched forward for a better view, feeling his blood pound. Was she with someone? But the area was packed with onlookers. Most of the crowd were enraptured by the wavelike sway of the violinists as they went through their movement and the frenzied gesticulations of the conductor. The music drifted up into the still and starry night. For a moment he thought he'd lost her but when she came back into view between the heads of the people in front of him Ivan's initial fear was confirmed. It was Nina and she was holding a baby.

He began to push his way roughly through the crowd, excusing himself and apologizing. His eyes never leaving her. As he neared he could see she was attentively adjusting the hood of the baby's shawl, trying to keep the dazzle of the floodlights from its eyes, cooing and smiling and nuzzling her face into the shadowy recess where Ivan imagined a soft and newborn smell. The baby could have been weeks or several months old. It was hard to tell. He still didn't know what he was going to do. He began to look around for a policeman. Someone official. Was he really going to expose her like this? But he couldn't let it happen again. He couldn't have someone else go through this all over again. Think of the parents, he told himself. Think of the mother. Nina was sick. She was ill. For her own good it had to stop. He recalled their last conversation when she'd been packing things up in her bedroom to leave.

And what do you remember, Ivan? Sometimes I wonder.

He remembered being held by his mother. He remembered suckling at his mother's breast. He had no doubt about that. He remembered it if only because he remembered that first and primal feeling of warmth and security becoming a place of fear and upset as he fed off Nina's anxieties in the ensuing months after his kidnap. He couldn't stand by and let that happen. He couldn't let this baby be torn from that. But in the instant he approached she looked up and saw him and her face flushed with horror as she turned to run, pushing her way into the audience and screaming.

"Mama!" he called. "Nina, stop!"

She looked over her shoulder at him, wide-eyed in terror, pushing and shoving and bulldozing her way through and sending an old couple staggering backwards and sprawling into the road, creating an outcry from the surrounding audience. Heads turned. The man's wallet and change spilled from his pockets. Ivan caught a whiff of pot in the air. A glass smashed. The woman had hit her head and was crawling around dazed and bleeding. Someone else tripped over her. The orchestra played on faultlessly. For a moment Ivan lost her in the mayhem. It was on the tip of his tongue to call out for someone to stop her. That she had someone's baby. But when he saw her fleeting across the street he just continued to silently pursue her. Hopscotching and weaving and darting his way round the oncoming masses.

It didn't have to be this way. He could talk some sense into her. Get her to return the baby just like Gabrijela. The sister he never had. But up ahead he could see a further crowd had gathered for another event. He could hear the operatic boom of a tenor growing ever nearer. He would lose her, he began to panic.

"Stop her!" he suddenly shouted. "Stop that woman she's stolen a baby. That's someone else's baby!" He was pushing his way through the hordes now like a swimmer. Wading and pin-wheeling his arms. "Stop..."

She glanced back at him one last time and darted down a side alley. He reached the darkened entrance just in time to hear the clip-clapping of her sandals as she disappeared out of the other end and into another street teeming with festival goers. He stood at the archway to the narrow little passage panting and shaking his head, realising she'd gone for good when he noticed something lying on the floor halfway down illuminated by a single coach light. It couldn't possibly be what he thought it was but the more he approached the clearer it became. Was she so callous to have discarded the baby to save herself? His heart was thudding. There was no sound coming from the little mound that lay deathly still and tangled up in its shawl on the ground. He could make out a tiny hand clutching lifelessly at nothing. At the other end of the alleyway a group of people entered blowing party favours. "Stand back!" his voice reverberated off the walls, making a woman squeal in fright.

"What is it?" someone's voice echoed.

Ivan slowly knelt down to peel away the hood.

"Is it a baby? Oh my God, is it a baby?" the woman cried out.

For a long while there was only a trapped silence as the cacophony of celebratory sounds went on all around. Ivan was left looking at the blank-eyed stare of a doll. A doll he remembered his mother Nina keeping in their old rocking crib. One of the many dolls her father the toymaker had made her. The toymaker who had died in the fighting. And everyone and everything else that had been taken from her.

In the small reception area by the glass entrance doors where Karlo the retriever liked to sprawl was a little reading corner with two leather chairs and the days' newspapers set out on a low tiled table with plenty of tourist literature comprising of maps and guides and leaflets to what was going on. Ivan wandered out from the breakfast room with a coffee and began to peruse the bookshelves looking for a phone directory and with that the faint hope of seeing Ana on duty at the desk as her mother appeared to be working the kitchen that morning. It was a pointless pursuit, he knew. But seeing her each day had lit up his stay and given their last encounter he felt obliged to speak about his tour of the city walls even if it was just an excuse to take up her time. But there was only Dragan, the Serbian husband talking animatedly on the phone as if relaying good news. Come to think of it even his normally surly mother-in-law whom Ivan had only seen in the shadows of the gift shop when passing through had a sunny disposition about her when serving up coffee that morning. Some family cause for celebration no doubt, Ivan mused. And with that thought Karlo suddenly lifted his head as if even his interest had been roused, pausing to yawn and scratch and stare at his master who put down the phone and whooped for joy before going about his business. When he caught Ivan's eye he nodded.

"How are you enjoying your stay, sir?" he asked.

"I am enjoying it very much," Ivan replied. "Thank you."

"Excellent, excellent," he beamed, then pointed. "You've hurt your head."

"Yes," Ivan touched his temple, he had caught it on a wall chasing Nina. He'd only seen the graze in the mirror this morning.

Dragan went to pick up the phone again.

"You seem excited," Ivan smiled, his curiosity getting the better of him.

"Ana went with her sister to go to the hospital this morning. You know, a routine check-up."

Ivan nodded. The hospital where I was stolen, he couldn't help thinking.

"She had a chance to find out the sex of the baby and asked me if I wanted to know."

"And what is it?" Ivan asked, unable to prevent himself from mirroring Dragan's obvious delight at the outcome.

"It's supposed to be a secret," he burst into laughter at himself. "But I can't stop telling everyone. It's a boy!"

Somehow Ivan knew that anyway.

The phone rang in his hand and Dragan excused himself while Ivan nodded and smiled and went back to the directory. When he found the list of Zebitkos he was dismayed to see there was more than half a column of them. There was even a Henrik. So much for the wonders of the internet, he thought. Time was running out. The trip had been planned for four days and apart from work commitments he couldn't afford to stay any longer. Brad had been trying to reach him on the phone and left several voice messages going into detail about their 'father's' health and expressing concern over his state of mind. Working at a call centre Brad was able to reverse the charge so Ivan went for a stroll at lunchtime looking for a quiet place to talk but in the end couldn't bring himself to do it. He didn't share the same worries for Don in the way his brother appeared to. He could barely be happy for the man that he was still alive. Don's apparent death and the tape he had left had turned Ivan's life on its head. People didn't just walk back into your life after declaring themselves dead. And then of course there was Nina which had been the real cause for his reluctance to call his brother. What sort of fucked-up, distorted pile of wreckage was this to be left to deal with in the after-event of being told you were never who you thought you were? Yet it wasn't until late in the afternoon that it took Ivan to realise his aimless wandering through the old town's mazy streets had in part been a desire to keep looking for her, until he found himself staring back down the alley where she had vanished into the night like a phantom but for the slap of her fleeting soles still heard resonating in his mind. The narrow streets and lingering aromatic cooking smells wafting from open-windowed kitchens together with scented gardens of hidden dwellings from beyond the ancient stone walls created such an air of mysticism about the place that if not for the doll Ivan might have believed the whole thing to be a fantasy of his own making. This time he slowly made his way down the dank and gloomy passage as if looking for clues before emerging out into the blistering sunlight of the street running parallel to the other side, pulling down the peak of his cap to shield his eyes and trying to retrace her steps, looking from left to right, at the tiny pot-planted balconies to apartments up above, wondering where she'd took flight, or why she was even there at all.

Across the road something caught his eye in the window of yet another gift shop. He had to wait for a train of tourists led by a jabbering tour guide holding a sunhat atop an umbrella as a homing beacon to pass before he could cross. All the streets began to look familiar which only heightened his sense of disorientation. Twice he walked into people without looking, as if the object he'd noticed might disappear if he took his eyes from it. He was trying to remember the last time he'd seen one even though of course he knew. It had been when his mother – when Nina was packing to leave. He should have realised the air of finality about it now when looking back. If she'd been intent on ever returning most of her stuff could have gone into storage. But she had taken everything. Had systematically wrapped and packed and all but written down an inventory of each and every item or object d'art precious to her. Everything that is except the two boys she had stolen long before.

As he slowly made his way through another passing throng he could see tucked away in the corner of the window amidst the usual paraphernalia of souvenirs was a stand dripping with cheap costume jewellery. In his reflection he noticed the bump to his head which appeared to have got worse in its bruising so he adjusted his cap a little further before cupping his hands and pushing his face against the glass. Hanging from the display he saw a number of Licitar hearts made from differing materials and in all shapes and sizes. He had seen them in cake and sweet form since being in Dubrovnik but not as a pendant the type of which Nina had collected. A sign in the window said in various languages that engraving was free. He remembered the black heart in Nina's room hanging from the hood of the crib inscribed with the name Petar. It made perfect sense to him now that Petar had been the name of her stillborn.

You think I don't have enough bad things to think about? You think my life has been as easy for me as it has for you?

Squinting through the cluster of hearts into the gloom of the little shop an older woman sat behind a counter gazing into space. At first he thought he recognised her but it was not so much her features as the expression in her eyes. He could see she wore a heart around her neck which might have been to drum up business but he didn't think so. Not the way she gently caressed it in her hand. So personal a moment did it appear to be that he was scared she might catch him spying but he couldn't help himself, something drew him in and for an instant Ivan felt like he had entered her mind and could almost hear what she was thinking.

"Ivan!" someone beside him poked his side and laughed.

Startled from his reverie Ivan turned to see Ana standing in front of him with another attractive girl that might have been her twin. A cab was pulling away from the kerb. Ivan stood blinking in surprise and slight alarm as if he'd been woken from a dream.

"Are you trying to see if my mother's there so you can avoid paying for that hat?" she put a hand on her hip and twitched her nose at him disapprovingly. Her English was disconcertingly perfect.

Ivan stepped back and looked up at the shop in confusion. Coming out of the other end of the alley had caused him to lose his bearings. He'd been peering into the gift shop window of the hotel where he was staying.

"This is my sister, Lorena," she continued to giggle at his addled state. "This is John Ivan. He's here looking for his mother," she told her sister.

"Hi," Ivan smirked, pulling himself together. "I was…I was looking at the hearts," he said.

They looked at each other and giggled.

"She's the unmarried one if you're looking for hearts, John Ivan," Ana jerked her head at her sister and raised her eyebrows.

"Ana!" Lorena slapped her sister's shoulder in embarrassment.

Ana caught him looking at her bump and placed a hand over it protectively.

"I hear it's to be a boy," Ivan said rather clumsily.

Ana's mouth dropped wide-open in shock.

"I'm sorry," Ivan pulled a face. "Dragan's…he's, well, he's happy. Ecstatic, in fact."

"What have you done to your head?" Lorena wanted to know.

"Do you have a name?" Ivan looked distractedly from Ana to Lorena and touched his brow and shook his head as if it was nothing.

"Henrik," she said. "It was always to be Henrik."

"Henrik's a good name," he said, nodding and smiling and feeling a lump in his throat.

"Are you okay John Ivan?" she seemed suddenly concerned.

For the first time he began to take in the sisters' physical appearance without the distortion of pheromones.

"Come on. We have to go," Ana yanked her sister's arm and pulled her into the shop. Lorena looked at Ivan with mock surprise and attempted a shrug. "See you again John Ivan!" she called, and they both fell into the shop snorting laughter.

Ivan continued to stand on the street for a long time. Every now and again looking back through the window to see if Ana's mother was still there. She had begun to busy herself now. That same forlorn look he recognized from the photograph had vanished in the preoccupying self-demand of her little industry. Her daily pause for reflection, or hope, or prayer, put to rest for another sunrise. Even death allowed respite in the end. But the not knowing must never sleep, he thought.

When he entered the shop a little bell went off above the door and she looked up at him and smiled tightly. She was small-framed with her hair pulled up into a greying bun and wore some reading glasses around her neck. She had her daughters' eyes but the softness he had witnessed in her private moment had been replaced by a hard glazed shield of efficiency. He lingered at the front of the shop nervously knowing he was drawing attention to himself. He didn't know why but he had the feeling she had taken an instant dislike to him. Maybe it was because he had yet to pay for the hat as Ana had reminded him. He carefully selected a heart made from stainless steel with a matching ball chain. It had the look of a military dog tag. He made his way towards the counter where she was arranging a little show case of miniature monument replicas. Ivan was familiar enough with the place now to recognize Pile City Gate, Minceta and Bokar Fort, the Onfario fountain. He felt he could live there forever. He laid down the heart on the glass top and they looked at each other in silence. Her rather more delicate silver pendant was still on display and when she caught him looking at it she tucked the curio inside her blouse but not before he had clearly seen the inscription: Henrik.

Unlike Ana her English was limited. "Name?" she asked, and made a gesture with her hand as if to squiggle.

"Mama," he said, and looked at her.

She flickered a smile and lowered her head before writing it down.

"Also," he gestured at the hat.

She looked up from above her glasses and gave out a short sound.

When she began ringing up the till Ivan reached into his trouser pocket and felt his hand grow clammy as it closed around the baby bracelet. At that moment Ana came back into the shop and softly called his name.

"Ivan," she whispered. "There is someone here to see you."

"Me?" he stupidly pointed at himself.

She nodded. "It's the police," she said, and shrugged.

He looked to her mother then back at Ana, feeling his hand loosen.

"I…excuse me," he said, and followed Ana out into the reception.

The two uniformed officers introduced themselves and invited Ivan to sit down. Ana made room with an extra chair and dragged the reluctant Karlo from his spot with what sounded like a bribe in Croatian as she led him off into the kitchen. Meanwhile, Dragan watched on suspiciously whilst trying to occupy himself from behind the front desk.

At first they just took down his details and wanted to know what he was doing there and how long he was staying. Then they told him they were investigating an incident the night before where he matched the description of a man running through the streets chasing a woman with a baby.

Ivan sat back and let out a deep breath, catching Dragan's eye who had turned narrow-eyed and wary. He looked at each officer in turn. Officer Novak had more badges and seemed to be the one in charge doing all the talking.

"Has…has the woman put in a complaint?" Ivan wanted to know. "Because I very much doubt that she has."

"So it was you?" Novak asked.

"It's just that I can't imagine the woman would put in a complaint," he pushed back his cap and looked around agitatedly.

"How you get bruise?" the other officer asked, lifting his chin as if suspecting a lie.

"Well…" Ivan expanded his arms and emitted an empty laugh. "I think you know how."

The officers exchanged something in Croatian and Novak jerked his head and the other one got up and began talking to Dragan in a dull murmur.

"Look," said Ivan, trying to keep his voice low lest Ana or her sister or mother should overhear. "Has the woman-?"

"Why do you keep asking that?" Novak interrupted as the situation suddenly turned serious. "Do you have some reason to know she will not come forward?"

Ivan saw where it was going.

"No," he conceded with open palms and sat back. "Not at all."

"The complaints have come from people. Tourists like you knocked into the road. This is not good for Debrovnik, for the old town."

"I understand," Ivan said.

"Do you always wear a baseball cap at night pulled down over your eyes?"

Ivan slowly shook his head and removed the cap with a look of resignation.

"We will need to search your room," Novak said.

As Ivan led Novak up the stairway into his apartment he saw Ana and her mother being questioned in the hallway by the other officer. There was a faint look of encouragement in Ana's eyes but her mother seemed to have already made up her own mind and was toying nervously now with the heart around her neck as if Ivan was somebody not to be trusted.

The first thing Novak noticed was the doll propped on the writing desk.

"It wasn't a baby," Ivan tried being as honest as he could and sighed. "My grandfather was a toymaker from Dalmatia. He made it. I was chasing...I was chasing my mother," he said with a heavy heart, because he knew his mother was downstairs. "She disappeared from my life two years ago and I came out here to find her."

Novak appeared to understand and began nodding sympathetically as if it all started to make sense. But after closer examination of the doll he looked up with a frown and began to grow angry.

"A toymaker?" he asked.

"Yes," Ivan nodded.

"This doll was made in Thailand," he said, pulling back the clothing and showing Ivan the branding. "It's plastic," he said.

Ivan stepped over and blinked. Last night he had convinced himself he'd recognized its very face but now it just looked like any old doll from a cheap arcade.

"I don't..." he began to shake his head.

But now Novak was taking a particular interest in the photograph left by Ivan's bedside.

"Who are these people and why have you got it?" Novak grew suddenly hostile. "Isn't this the family who run the hotel? Why are you interested in them?"

Novak had seen the similarities immediately. Maybe he knew them. Maybe he even recognized the scene. Ivan went to speak but Novak held up a hand for him to keep his distance. He picked up the phone and begun talking hurriedly. When he'd finished the other officer was already at the door.

"We will need your passport," Novak said. "And then you are to come to the station for further questioning."

He was escorted out of the hotel with the whole family hovering around the reception. The other officer made no attempt to conceal the doll made visible in the plastic bag he carried presumably as some form of evidence. By the bewildered expression on Ana's face he didn't appear to have anyone on his side anymore. The story was out. He had pursued a woman holding a baby through the streets of the old town. With a slow dawning horror Ivan sat in the back of the police car as he was driven away gazing out at the very streets he had chased Nina through and seeing how it might have looked.

He was taken to a small interview room by Novak and made to empty his pockets. The officer took off his cap and jacket and rolled up his sleeves as if they were to be there a while. Ivan reluctantly took out the baby bracelet and set it down on the table between them. Novak turned it over in his hand.

"What is this thing you have with dolls and babies?" he said.

"It's mine. That's my name."

"But your name is…" he consulted the passport again. "John Best."

"I'm adopted. I was born in Croatia just like my passport says. Henrik is my real name."

"You were born in the war."

"Yes."

"And the woman you were chasing. You say it was your mother?"

This was the tricky part, thought Ivan. He didn't want to open that can of worms. Not yet. He hadn't come here to get Nina arrested. He tried to stay as much within the confines of truth as possible if only because he was so near to re-uniting with his real mother. His mother and two sisters, he thought excitedly. Realising then that the attraction between Ana and he hadn't been sexual but genetic. He couldn't wait to explain himself.

"My adoptive mother, yes," Ivan lied.

"And what is her name," he asked.

Ivan swallowed hard and told him the names of both Nina and Don.

Novak slowly wrote everything down and after he'd finished he looked up at Ivan for the first time as if to see inside his soul. Ivan shifted in his seat.

"So tell me John Best," he said deliberately as if he didn't believe the story for a minute. "Why was your adoptive mother running so hard to get away from you in the streets of the old town?"

The longer Ivan didn't answer the more his mind went blank. He could hear himself going into detail about his father's crimes and the resulting disintegration of the family but he didn't want to get into that.

"You'd have to ask her," he finally said. "It's personal."

"It's personal," Novak repeated.

"Yeah, family stuff," he shrugged.

Novak grunted and stood up and took his notes, Ivan's passport and the bracelet and left the room.

They left Ivan there for over three hours. It was nearly eleven p.m. and he had become very agitated. His flight was due out the next day. When was he supposed to tell his mother he had found her? If he hadn't dawdled so long outside the shop he could have handed her the bracelet and then everything could have been explained. But Novak never came back. Ivan was told by an officer on station duty he was being detained overnight and would be escorted to the airport the next day. His belongings would be picked up from the hotel, he was assured. When Ivan said he wanted to talk to someone of a higher authority he was ignored. He had something to say, he said. He wanted to tell the truth. But he was only told it would have to wait until the morning.

The next day around ten his cell door opened and Novak entered dressed in full uniform wearing sunglasses and holding a plastic cup of instant coffee. Ivan had only just fallen to sleep. He sat up blinking on his cot.

"You want to tell me something," Novak said impatiently.

"Yes, yes," Ivan said. "It's very important. You…you should listen to this…"

The jailer stood by the door as if awaiting instructions.

"Do you think I could get a coffee or something?" Ivan asked.

"Dobiti ga na kavu," Novak spoke out loud without taking his hidden eyes from Ivan.

"I didn't come here to find my adoptive mother I came to find my real mother," Ivan began. "I didn't even know she was here. Not in Dubrovnik, anyway. That's why she ran I think. It seems she wants her own life."

The jailer returned and handed Ivan a black coffee. For a contemplative moment he just let the aroma fill his senses.

"What do you want to say to me?" Novak hurried him.

"The woman at the hotel. The mother…"

"Iva?" Novak shrugged, as if to ask what did she have to do with anything.

"Yes!" Ivan looked up brightly. "Iva, Ivan, don't you see? If that's not some sort of sign then, well…"

"Who's Ivan?" Novak shook his head and frowned as if he was running out of patience.

"It doesn't matter," Ivan said, looking at the floor and smiling to himself.

"Are you a drug addict or something, Mr Best? If I took a blood sample from you now would you test positive? Because I could lock you up for that. I could charge you with public disorder. Endangering the lives of others. Do you understand? I could take away your passport and ban you from ever coming to this country again or anywhere else in Europe. The good news for you is that no one has brought charges and I am a busy man and you are going home today. So if you have something to tell me it had better not be a waste of any more of my time."

"That woman, Iva, she's my natural mother. And Ana and Lorena are my sisters," Ivan bit his lip and nodded as if Novak should believe him. "It's true. I was on the point of giving Iva the bracelet before you arrived at the hotel."

Novak seemed to regard him with new suspicion.

"And what makes you think that, Mr Best?"

"You mean Mr Zebitko," he said. "Isn't that right? Isn't her name, Iva Zebitko? Isn't that Ana's maiden name? Didn't Iva have a son taken from her called Henrik? A baby stolen from the hospital here?"

"No, Mr Best. She did not."

For a moment Ivan sat staring into the coffee cup he held with both hands. Novak hadn't been listening. "Well, maybe you should ask her."

"I don't have to," Novak uttered quietly. "I know the family."

Ivan could feel himself starting to shake, realising he was going to have to tell the whole truth after all. That everything was to come out. Their sham of a family life would be exposed to the world. The media would have a field day. He sighed and took a quiet moment.

"She lost a husband called Henrik not a son. And Ana and Lorena lost a father. We all lost someone," he said.

Ivan sat with his head still bowed. He could feel his breathing become shallow and his heart-rate start to accelerate.

"I don't know who you're looking for Mr Best, and I don't think you do either. There were over 200,000 misplaced Croats after the war and if the story you have been told is true then it seems you were one of them."

Novak quietly left the cell and shut the door. Ivan heard the turn of the key in the lock. He rested his head back against the wall and closed his eyes, trying to make sense of the last few days.

Sitting in the back of the police car outside the hotel reception Ivan could see Novak talking to Ana. There was a different, much younger officer behind the wheel who was watching him vigilantly in the rear-view mirror as if he was ready for anything. A few locals had gathered at their doorways to see what was going on. When Novak came out with Ivan's suitcase Ana stood at the entrance steps and lifted her hand in acknowledgement at him, offering a little sympathetic smile. Ivan nodded and looked away, suddenly just wanting to be gone. When Novak got in the car he leant over and offered something to Ivan wrapped in red tissue. He gestured impatiently at Ivan to take it and when he did he slowly unwrapped it to find the heart he was going to buy. It had been engraved with the word: Mama. He looked back through the rear window as the car pulled away but Ana had already disappeared inside.

Ivan sat back, considering the heart for a long time, rubbing his thumb reverentially across each inscribed letter before quietly slipping it around his neck.

Once out of the old town they passed through a place called Gruz which Novak affably informed Ivan was famous for its open-air market by the port. It took Ivan a while to realise that he wasn't being taken on a time-killing sightseeing tour en route to the airport or that police business necessitated they pass through the town but that Novak simply wanted to pick up his shopping. From the start of the journey he had been enthusing about the fresh fish caught every morning by trawlers and the abundance of fruit and seasonal vegetables that was available from local farms, but added with a mischievous wag of his finger that parking spots were at a premium. And so, like a law unto himself his driver positioned the police car as near to the entrance as he could and Novak slid his sunglasses down from the top of his head and got out and ventured into the bustling, vibrant market atmosphere without so much as a backward glance. Ivan thought he might be pushing his luck by asking Novak if he could accompany him and have one last look around. The cluster of vendors' parasols and other shaded stalls fighting for space amidst the more natural cover of native olive trees stretched along the plaza for as far as he could see with just the occasional glimpse of the electric-blue backdrop of the Adriatic in between. The market grew busier by the minute as people poured in from all around, exacerbating Ivan's feeling of incarceration. It was already getting very warm and when he began to grow restless and shifted in his seat his eyes were met by the driver's stony gaze in the rear-view mirror.

Ivan sighed and sat back and turned his attention towards a fresh-flower stall by the entrance that had taken his interest if only for the delightful profusion of rainbow colours and striking variation of genus that appeared to catch the eye of everyone who entered. It looked like a portal to paradise and made Ivan want to get out and run and just keep running. He didn't know much about plants. He didn't know much about trawling for shrimp or carving wood into toys or anything else he might have been able to turn his hand to because the chance of a life like that had been taken from him. Revelation idealists would say it was all part of his spiritual path and the ongoing struggle of the constant tests between good and evil that we are all made to face. But for Ivan he didn't feel like he'd got a fair start. Worse, he felt he'd been cheated. Returning to such a beautiful part of the world and what might have been seemed to Ivan that he had rolled a six in life at the first time of asking. But that it was somehow declared cocked and so had been made to roll it again.

As the crowd thickened and it became clear Novak was going to be a while the driver switched off the engine and opened the windows and got out of the car to have a stretch, giving Ivan a cautious glare to remain where he was. From somewhere inside the busy marketplace a live rendition of The Clog Dance was being played by what sounded to be nothing bigger than a string quartet. Ivan knew the piece from Nina's collection and wistfully recalled how that on more than one occasion she would hitch up her skirt and perform the comic ballet in heels to the adoring applause of Don and who by way of an excuse not to participate would always encourage Ivan and Brad to join in which is how he knew it so well.

Wafting through the air and seemingly on a wave of the music came the pleasurable aroma of meat cooking in spices, bringing Ivan's taste buds to life. It had been a miserable night in the cell and he wanted nothing more now than to wander through the market freely. What harm could it do when they still had his passport and he had no means of travel? So Ivan shuffled along the seat and got out and stood up and stretched, nodding and smiling at the officer that everything was all right. He leant across the car roof with his arms tucked under his chin continuing to watch and savour the ambience when a scene began to develop with a group of people crowded around the flower-seller. A scuffle broke out between two men, one in what looked to be a white linen suit had been pushed to the ground. A woman's voice rang out in Croatian and a baby began to cry. Ivan looked over at the other officer who was taking a mild interest but only to see if he had detected the sweet scent of marijuana that had begun to mingle sickly with the tantalizing fusion of cooking smells. When Ivan sharpened his eyes to the scene it appeared to be the aproned flower-seller who had taken umbrage with the man in the suit and who had now got up and was dusting himself down and holding up his hands in a gesture of supplication. From the back you could see he was one of those older men who had a receding head of hair but still insisted on pulling it back into a little bun. It wasn't until Officer Novak came wading through laden with shopping bags that the crowd began to disperse and everything calmed down.

"You're supposed to be guarding our prisoner," Novak reprimanded his colleague in English for the purpose of Ivan's amusement. He had sweat patches all over his shirt and seemed a little out of breath.

"I watch which goes on," he replied seriously, clearly a little challenged by Novak's fluency.

"Well, if you watch 'which' goes on you'll know a man is walking around with his family openly smoking pot in a public place."

"So we go and arrest him."

"The only place we're going is to put this fresh seafood in my fridge," Novak said. "It's the old hippy's lucky day."

The old hippy.

"Get in the car, John," Novak lifted his sunglasses and looked over the car roof at him when they were all ready to go.

But Ivan was already scouring the thinning crowd. The flower-seller was still ranting and remonstrating in the direction of some people heading out from the market towards a heavily-congested car park.

They must have split up the night he had chased her, Ivan's mind began to race.

"John Best," Novak warned him loudly. "It's none of your business. Get in the car."

But he couldn't. Not until he was absolutely sure. Lots of people were wearing white. White dresses, white shirts. He flicked a glance at Novak, weighing his options.

When the other officer got back out of the car Ivan inched round to the rear end where he could see them both.

"John," Novak tried reasoning. "I don't know what's going on but if you make one more move we will have to restrain you. Do you understand? You will be handcuffed and escorted home and handed over to the authorities in the UK with charges against you. I don't want to do that, John. I can tell you're confused and have been put through something in your life that you didn't ask for, okay? I just want to help you get home."

"This is my home," Ivan's voice cracked. "And my name's not John Best."

"Well, that's the name on your passp-"

At that point he went to bolt but the other officer was too quick for him and brought Ivan crashing to the ground, wedging a knee between his shoulder blades and pulling an arm around his back and cuffing his wrist roughly like he had waited all day to do it.

Ivan lifted his face from the dusty ground and spat out some dirt, seeing Novak's boots come into view.

"So now we have to do things the hard way," he sighed, like a character straight out of Hollywood.

"Wait!" Ivan raved as they bundled him in the back of the car and secured the door locks. "The man in the white suit smoking pot. You said he was with his family?"

As Ivan spoke he bounced around on the seat agitatedly, his head turning every which way. Cars were queueing to leave and enter, creating gridlocks at every turn.

Novak didn't answer.

"Was the woman…did she have a long head of dark hair? About five-ten? Dark eyes, almost black eyes?"

"She was wearing sunglasses," Novak tried to sound disinterested.

He suddenly turned on the siren for five seconds to clear the shuffling masses in front of them.

"Hold on!" Ivan pleaded, growing tearful. "Did you look twice at her? Was she attractive?"

The other officer cast a glance at Novak as Ivan twisted and turned in his seat, jiggling the handcuffs like an escapologist going through his routine.

"Sit back," Novak said tiredly.

"Did you look at her twice?" Ivan insisted.

"Yeah, the old hippy has done well for himself," Novak conceded, he switched the siren on and off again.

"You said family," Ivan pressed.

The cars in front were edging up onto a grass verge to let them through.

Novak shrugged. "They could be the grandparents. I don't know."

Ivan suddenly sat back feeling exhausted. Not daring to ask. Not wanting to know.

"And it wasn't a doll?" he finally uttered, closing his eyes.

Novak looked over his shoulder at him with a crooked grin. "You would have to be a little bit crazy to confuse a doll for a real live baby, eh John?"

Both officers laughed out loud at that even though Ivan thought the younger one didn't really understand.

"My name isn't John," Ivan said quietly to himself as the car sped away from the crowd and turned into the main road. "You don't understand. I'm no one," he said, feeling the heart sway around inside his shirt.

No one.

OUT THERE

Eleven years later, in the same café in the same town they had pledged to meet on the exact date of that following year, Joe saw Ellie tucked away in a corner by the toilets at the back of the shop. She was partly-concealed by shopping bags hooked over the handles of a child's stroller whilst covertly attempting to breastfeed a baby. Of all the countless times he had envisaged seeing her again. Of all the romantic and hope-filled scenarios he had played out. Nursing a baby in full public view hadn't been one of them.

Of course, in between trading under a number of different establishments the original coffee shop had long been taken over by one of the bigger chains. The cheap white plastic chairs of Ozzie's Oasis where they had courted as sweethearts had been replaced with plush, coffee bean-coloured leather sofas. Fuzzy monochrome photographs of nothing in particular positioned along two-tone walls that had once been coated in peeling eggshell and faded azure prints of Ozzie's homeland now lured the newly-affluent coffee culture and its plethora of trendy beverage selections. Smart laminated wooden flooring and strategically designed spotlighting took the place of the old café's spluttering fluorescents and grubby black and white self-adhesive chequered floor tiles that turned up at the edges and of which Health and Safety inspectors were forever warning him about. And Joe often found himself reflecting fondly upon Ozzie's bickering family members that made up his staff each time he was met with the frosty efficiency of the East European baristas seemingly favoured by the anonymous café chain management. Out of interest he had filled out a part-time job application when the place first opened up but then later thought against it.

"Can I help you?"

"Caffe latte please."

"Grande, regular…?"

He always faltered at this juncture, still convinced that 'grande' meant large when he only wanted, well, grande.

"Normal. Small," he said, before reminding Olga and her unpronounceable surname that he preferred a cup to a glass. This was usually met with minor confusion even though he was a regular.

"Cup?"

"Yes."

Same beverage. Different receptacle, Joe thought.

He always reverted to the Englishman abroad at this point and made a little limp, entirely ineffective and self-humiliating gesture with his wrist in an attempt to indicate his difficulty in holding a coffee glass. It stayed hot too long. The handle was stupidly small for his oversized skeletal fingers. You needed two hands just to lift it.

Joe could feel himself begin to redden.

"Anything else?"

"No."

"Club card?"

He produced it.

"Sugar is on the right."

She told him every time.

Whew! Joe made a sweeping gesture with his eyebrows at the other patrons looking on including Ellie who he knew had recognized him some moments earlier in the queue but that he had quite inexplicably continued to maintain his ignorance of. In a show of nerves he found himself begin to whistle silently as he moved to walk past her, feeling his heart race.

"Joe?" she called.

"Ellie?" he feigned a little too quickly, frowning, before slowly releasing a smile. "My God, Ellie Hunt. Is it really you?"

"Yes," she said, all at once appearing self-conscious and withdrawing into the corner of the walls. She pulled the baby and shawl tighter against her chest and began to make soothing sounds, looking up beneath her brow a little bashfully.

Once, in her father's heated swimming pool, she had allowed him to suckle at that same rose-pink nipple, he couldn't help thinking.

Joe continued with his act, looking around the shop and making flabbergasted sounds, hearing himself: "What…what are you doing here?" he asked. The cup and saucer began tottering in his trembling hands, making him glad he didn't have the tall, annoying glass. He looked at the empty seat. "May I?" he asked, setting down his coffee and slowly sliding into the chair with apparent wonderment.

For a moment they just stared, both thinking the same thing.

Eleven years had passed. Eleven years.

"How long has it been?" he asked.

"Eleven years," she said.

"Eleven years," he nodded and shook his head.

"You look great, Joe," she said, and he did. He had created an impression from the moment he'd walked in. Even if it hadn't been Joe. He was tall and slim and wore a shimmering light-grey suit that outlined every shadowed crease and fold like an architect's stick-human drawing. He had on a crisp white shirt and purple and black striped tie. His long fair hair of old was fashionably cropped as if he might be starting to lose it. Only his physique remained the same. Ellie could still make out the hollow in his chest as he'd sat down and unbuttoned his jacket. His wiry frame. He placed his phone and car keys on the table as if he'd been told to empty his pockets. For the first few minutes she couldn't take him seriously. He hadn't filled out at all and didn't look old enough to be this would-be executive or whatever he was now. Married probably with children of his own.

"We made a pact," she laughed, thinking of what might have been. Of the young boy who had been the first to touch her. The only person she had ever allowed to touch her. "Do you remember?"

Joe attempted puzzlement. Then dawning. Then recognition. As if he was auditioning for an acting role. He pointed a finger at her. Drawing out the words. "That's right. You moved to… don't tell me."

She jiggled the baby in her lap, surreptitiously concealing her breast whilst Joe tried not to look and began clicking his fingers several times in a fake attempt to remember. She still seemed to be carrying some extra weight from the pregnancy. There were two folds in her chin. Her eyes were a little piggy. Her hair had faded to something almost neutral and was lank and greasy.

"Devon," she said tiredly, as if seeing through his charade.

"That's right," he said, nodding and smiling and picking at the top of his scalp. "Your Dad was relocated or something."

"How have you been?" she suddenly interjected.

"In the last eleven years?" he sat back in his chair in surprise and joked. "How long have you got?"

She laughed too, chewing on her lip and shaking her head as if it had been a silly thing to say.

"And whooo's this?" he suddenly loomed over the table at the baby and startling it. The baby's face grew in alarm and its head wobbled. For a moment Joe thought he had made it cry. But then it just sat staring intently at him with the glassy brown eyes of its father.

"This is little Jim Jiminy," she cooed into the baby's ear and kissed its cheek.

"Well, hello, little Jimmy Jimmy," Joe said, holding out the back of his hand like you would to someone else's dog and not knowing why he had taken to mimicking Ellie's baby voice. Little Jimmy obliged by closing his tiny fist   around Joe's long lollypop stick index finger and for a moment both he and Ellie felt it. That they could have been taken for any other little family in the coffee shop. They both gazed around smiling at everyone. Enjoying the attention.

"How old is he?" an old lady asked.

"Six months," Ellie said, and Joe nodded in affirmation.

"Ahhh," said the old lady and smiled.

"His name's Jimmy," Joe called out.

They all smiled and nodded until Joe's expression began to sit like a tight mask.

Joe turned back to Ellie, deciding he didn't like being under the spotlight after all as the old woman turned to someone next to her and began whispering behind the back of her hand. Probably they were gossiping about the colour of the baby's eyes, he thought.

"He lost his job a year after that," Ellie dropped her voice as Joe pretended to take further interest in the baby. "He was made redundant so we had to move again."

"Sometimes I think he only agreed to that job to get me out of your life," Joe said without looking up, still tugging at the baby's hand with his finger.

In that one sentence he had undone his whole performance, Joe all at once realised.

"He was made to go," she replied flatly.

"Well," he shrugged, "at least that's what I remember thinking at the time."

"We were fourteen," she said. "Anyway, what about you? What have you been doing?"

Joe took a long time to answer.

"Well, I took a job at Ozzie's waiting tables," he averted his eyes with patent embarrassment, slowly pulling his finger away from the now sleeping baby.

"Ozzie's!" she exclaimed. "But... but wasn't that...?"

"Here, yes. These exact premises," he sat back and laughed.

"I wasn't sure," she said. "When I first walked down the street I couldn't be sure where Ozzie's had been so much has changed."

"No, it was here," he said, grinning. "Can you imagine what your Dad would have said - me waiting tables at Ozzie's? That I'd achieved my station in life or something like that."

"Don't say that," she admonished him. "I never thought of you like that."

"It didn't matter what you thought, Ellie," he replied a little too quickly, settling his gaze upon her.

She looked away. Rocking the baby to sleep. Her face a little flushed.

Joe couldn't help noticing that the carrier bags were from the everything-under-a-pound shop down the road. When he thought she caught him looking Joe instinctively picked up his phone and checked for messages.

"He...he started to go downhill a bit after that second time," she began slowly, her eyes glistening. "He couldn't get a job in Devon. We couldn't afford to move back to London with the property prices. So we had to move out even further."

"Where?"

"Oh, you wouldn't know. Somewhere out in the sticks down there. Somewhere in the middle of nowhere," she spoke into her chest, not looking up. "Every time we moved the situation just got worse. Like we were moving further and further away from... well, everything."

"What about your education?" he frowned.

"It...fizzled out," she shrugged.

"But I thought he wanted you to be a lawyer or a doctor or something."

"He forgot all about that when he couldn't find work. He withdrew. My mother got sick."

"I'm sorry," he said.

"I became her virtual carer," she looked at him as if she wanted to say more but was thinking twice about it.

Joe frowned, not knowing what to say.

"How long did you work at Ozzie's for?" she tried changing the subject, smiling brightly.

"Oh, I don't know," Joe dropped his head.

"Wasn't it strange working there, here, after all the times we used to meet after school? What was the name of that ice cre-?"

"Knickerbocker Glory," Joe said smartly.

"That's right," she reflected.

When their eyes met something warm passed through him. She pulled her gaze away as if she felt it too.

"Don't look at me like that," she said, rocking the baby and avoiding his continued stare.

But Joe only smiled. He couldn't help himself. He had waited so long.

"I don't like being watched," was all she said.

When Joe reluctantly looked away his attention was caught by the sight of the grubby and frayed sleeves of her coat flung across another seat. She caught his critical look as if she could read his thoughts so he pretended to check his phone again in anticipation.

"Are you expecting a call?"

"Who's the father?" he tried asking distractedly, as if some text interested him more. It had been the first question on his lips. But when he looked up she had her head back and her eyes closed. "I'm sorry, it's none of my business, I suppose."

"It's not that," she shook her head.

Joe sipped his coffee, feeling the words drying up.

"Wasn't it strange working here?" she insisted.

"Yes," he said, noticing for the first time that she drank her coffee out of a tall glass.

"What did you do after that?"

Joe chuckled.

"What's funny?" she said, breaking into a slow smile.

"You won't believe it but I tried my hand at hairdressing," he pursed his lips, trying not to break into laughter.

Ellie looked at him blankly, as if the words wouldn't sink in.

He nodded that she had heard him right.

"I started out as an apprentice. Did three days in college and three days here sweeping up and washing hair and watching the professionals," he nodded and smiled. "Then I became a stylist."

"You?"

"Yep."

"Here?" she looked puzzled.

"Huh?"

"You said here."

"Locally," he faltered, sweeping a hand. "I meant, locally."

"But you always said you couldn't wait to get out of this place. This town."

"We both said that," he said, avoiding her studious look.

"Yes, well, I didn't mean for me to end up in a village full of in-breds," she set her jaw, an anger appearing in her eyes. "That wasn't my choice."

"So what happened?"

"What do you mean?"

"Why didn't you leave when you were old enough? Why didn't you just get out of it? You never liked your father. You used to get embarrassed by the way he went on."

"I told you. They became dependant. They both needed me."

"That's not right," he said.

"I cooked, I cleaned…" she bit her lip and looked away. "I wasn't allowed to…"

"Wasn't allowed to what?"

"Aren't you listening? We were… we were… I didn't even know where we were, Joe. We were isolated. I was cut off from my old life."

"I don't get it."

"I became their prisoner," she began to plead his understanding. "The nearest bus stop was miles away. As dependant as they were on me in a strange way I became equally dependant. Almost institutionalised if that's the right word. I started to forget everything else. I had to live by his rules. I had to do everything he said. I had no choice. I lived in terror of the consequences. I lost my confidence. My self-esteem… I became his slave."

Distant memories stretching way beyond the last missing eleven years fed at the edge of Joe's mind like tiny schools of fish. They had been childhood friends. At one time their fathers had been in business together. There had been parties and good times. Ellie had a big house with a swimming pool. For a long time Joe had never known anything else. Then, without any real explanation, everyone fell out. Everyone except for Joe and Ellie.

"So where are they now? Where's your Mum and Dad?"

"My mother has a mental illness," Ellie looked away. "She was always making little notes when she had to remember things. I thought it was just the way she was. The way she had always been. Even when it got much, much worse."

Joe nodded. Even he could remember the little notes.

"She's in a home," Ellie looked at him blankly. "She thinks I'm some girl my father used to…"

Joe frowned, feeling an old stirring. "What girl?"

"Do you still cut hair?" she suddenly asked. Her eyes brightening. She tugged at some loose strands and gave him a coy look. Drawing to Joe's attention the condition of her fingernails which were bitten down to the bare ends. The skin around them gnawed red.

He shook his head and smiled. Habitually touching the hairline receding at his temples. "No, I decided to get a proper job."

"Doing what?" she eagerly repositioned herself as if he had caught her interest. The baby stirred in her lap and blew a perfect bubble from its cherubic, doll-like lips.

Joe thought they could have been hand-painted.

"I…worked in property…" he replied dreamily, still staring at little Jimmy.

"What does that mean?"

"Buying and selling. I bought a flat and renovated it then sold it for a profit. And then I bought two."

"Is that what you're still doing?"

"I rent a number of properties now, yes. But I bought my first house last year. You should see it. You should come and stay," he said a little too quickly. "I don't mean… I mean, I've converted the basement. It's totally self-contained."

"Are you looking for a lodger then?" she laughed.

"Maybe," he shrugged, and sipped at his coffee nervously.

"So, you're well off," she uttered almost disappointedly, her mood suddenly changing.

"I don't know about that," he smiled quirkily.

"Well, it sounds like you've got money coming in from everywhere. I've forgotten what it's like to have money," she said seriously.

Their fathers had fallen out over business matters. That's all Joe remembered. Joe's father had come off worse. He'd had more to lose. He'd been out of his depth was all his mother would argue for years after. Joe's father didn't have a house with a swimming pool in the back garden to fall back on.

"How's your Mum and Dad doing?" she asked tentatively, as if she knew what he was thinking.

"The same," he said with a shrug, wanting to ask her about the tall glass and if she found it difficult to drink from.

"What about your sister?" she ventured carefully. "How's Charley?"

They shared a look.

Joe had never liked his older sister's flirtatious behaviour around Ellie's father. When she went round to the pool parties she would always dress inappropriately in stringed bikinis or wet and braless see-through vests and thongs. She was impressed by his wealth. She liked to tease and joke with him and parade in front of his video camera which Ellie's father was always wielding in those days. Once Ellie had told Joe that she had heard her father playing back the footage of a party in his study one night. He would always lock it from the inside saying he didn't want to be disturbed so she had stood by the door listening, hearing Charley's squeals over and over again as if the video was being replayed. When she challenged him about it the next day in front of her mother her father only said he'd been learning how to edit the tape. But Ellie had never believed him.

"What do you think he was doing?" a naïve young Joe had asked.

"My father can't drive past a bus stop without ogling schoolgirls," was all she said.

"Charley has two kids by two different fathers," Joe leant forward and pulled a face, jiggling his legs and spinning his phone on the table top. "Neither of whom are around."

"Do you still see her?" Ellie asked.

"Only when she wants some money," he said.

Ellie looked away pensively.

"What are you doing here?" he asked, sounding more aggressive than he'd intended. As if he suspected her of having the same agenda.

"What do you mean?" she frowned, tugging at the shawl and draping it over the baby.

"I mean, what's happened? Why are you here after all this time?" he tried softening his voice.

Ellie's face instantly began to crumble. When Joe reached out a hand she shook her head for him to stop, squeezing her features into a tight ball.

"Ellie?" he said kindly. It felt good to utter her name again and not over some old photograph or distant memory. Sometimes he would hear himself calling out for her when waking from a dream. As if she had died tragically. As if she had gone forever and was never come back. But he had never stopped believing. Even after eleven years. Eleven years, he couldn't help thinking.

"I had a stupid idea," she said after a long moment, brushing away a tear and flicking a look at him. "So stupid."

"Oh, yeah?" he smirked.

"Don't toy with me, Joe," she gave him a sharp look. "We made a pact."

"Yeah, you said."

"I know, but did you remember?"

"Did I remember what?"

"Did you remember to come?" she glared at him.

Joe's features froze. Only his eyes moved around the shop as if he feared someone might be listening.

"Did you come?" she asked, almost pleading.

"I was working here," he sighed, looking at her openly.

She nodded quietly to herself. Her eyes beginning to well.

"I worked here because I didn't want to miss a minute," he admitted, "not even one second when you might have walked in that door and walked right out again because you thought I wasn't here waiting."

"I knew it," she looked away again, fighting her tears. "That's all I needed to know."

For a long while they sat in silence. Now and again they would catch each other's stare but despite his feeling of sinking relief her eyes only remained hard and raw as if she might never let him in.

"Do you want another coffee?" he suddenly asked. He stood up as if he intended to get one anyway. "Do you want one in that glass or would you prefer a cup?"

"The glass is fine," Ellie smiled falsely and shook her head as if she didn't understand the reason for his question.

She watched him get behind the queue. Monitoring his every expression and movement as he addressed the girl behind the counter before performing that same limp-wristed gesture thing he had done earlier when ordering his coffee. He looked over at her and shrugged as if to share the joke. When he'd first entered he didn't appear to recognise her and a part deep down inside of Ellie had almost let him walk by even though she had known his face instantly. Had sat waiting and hoping on a miracle for nearly three hours before he entered. She would have heard his nasal tone in the hubbub of a crowded stadium. It was the only thing that had kept her alive.

"You know what I never understood?" Joe sat down and began stirring his coffee for over a minute.

Ellie watched as if mesmerised.

"I didn't call or write."

He looked up. "Yes," he said, after a moment. Seemingly happy for her to have understood. He sucked the froth from the spoon and looked at her while waving it. "I mean, not even a postcard? We agreed to write at least, didn't we?"

"I never knew my address," she said.

"What?" Joe screwed up his face, as if doubting her for the first time.

"Why do you think we made the pact?" she looked at him earnestly. "Why did we make the pact, Joe?"

"In case... I don't know, in case we lost touch," Joe said carefully.

"Yes, because we were moving into rented accommodation at first and my father wouldn't tell me where. Then, when we bought a house in the middle of the moors he took away all my means of communication."

"So he did want me out of your life," he said morosely.

"This isn't about you, Joe. None of it was ever about you. You were a kid. We were kids. You weren't a threat to my father," Ellie pulled a face.

"A threat?"

"Yes, well not then, anyway. He knew he could trust me. With a boyfriend, I mean."

"Trust you not to...?"

"Don't you think I could have been a hairdresser or a property developer?" she moved on. "Don't you think I would have done just about any job to get out? To escape from him? I would have cleaned toilets if I had to. But I wasn't allowed as much as a pen, Joe. He invented a completely different set of rules. I had to go to him for everything. He had keys for every room and every cupboard. I even had to go to him for clean underwear every day. Sometimes he would video me dressing. He said he was making a film for posterity. To show my children. But he never filmed me when I was younger. Only then. Only then did I slowly become aware of all his little spy-holes over the house. In the bathroom, the toilet, my bedroom..." she tailed off. "What are you thinking?" she asked, appearing a little anxious. "Am I making you feel sick? Do you want me to stop talking?"

"I'm thinking that I'd like to kill him," Joe said without a trace of humour.

Ellie laughed nervously. She gingerly reached for her coffee, performing a large sweep so as careful not to spill it over the sleeping tot.

"You should have had it in a cup," Joe fretted.

"I used to pretend to myself it was all because he could never find another job," Ellie said, setting the glass down a little shakily and causing Joe to hesitate upon helping her. "You know, like he couldn't handle his fall from grace or something. The big man. The big man with the heated swimming pool and the Maserati and the 4x4 on the drive. He never stopped going on about what he'd lost. But then sometimes..." she shook her head in a slow, deliberate way. "Sometimes, looking back, I think he mourned the pool for different reasons."

"What do you mean?"

"He couldn't even swim," she shrugged.

Joe's eyes darkened.

After a moment's reflection she let out a loud burst of ironic laughter, as if she had finally seen the joke, reaching for her coffee again and shaking her head. "The disgusting fat blob would have probably sunk anyway," she muttered.

Joe watched her expressionlessly, recalling the parties.

"Who were the other girls?" he suddenly piped up, starting to remember. "There were a few of them around my sister's age then. Who were they? Where did they come from?"

"My mother's extra-tuition pupils mostly," she said, staring at the glass of coffee in her hand as if it would take an incredible feat to lift it.

"That's right. I'd forgotten your mother had been a teacher once," he said, watching the glass.

"He used to invite them to stay after and use the pool. In the end it just became a thing. Like an after-school club. The girls would bring their costumes and the parents would all turn up at the same time and stand there chitchatting with my father like he was some great philanthropist. But he never invited boys or the younger ones it took me a while to realise. They all had to be a certain age - your sister's age," she looked at him. "For a long time after I tried convincing myself my mother must have given it up because she'd known she was suffering from the early stages of her disease. She only did it for some independence. But in reality I just don't think she could control him anymore."

"You said eleven years," Joe's mind had wandered off.

"What?"

"You said eleven years straight off the bat as soon as I asked you how long it had been. You didn't even have to think about it."

"Did I?" she looked at him doubtfully, and made an attempt to shrug it off with a cheery smile. "So, anyway, Mr Property Developer, Mr Hairdresser, what's your situation? Why are you in here 'eleven years' to the day after our pact casually buying a cup of coffee?"

"I come in here all the time," he said, finishing his latte and eyeing her over the brim. "I still haven't heard your excuse."

"Are you married?" she blurted.

Joe took his time answering, enjoying the eye contact. "No," he said, and stared.

"Partner, kids, boyyyfriend?" she shrilled nervously, adopting a strange voice.

Joe pictured himself sucking her nipple at the water's edge of her Dad's swimming pool shortly before she had moved. Cupping her young, puppy-soft undeveloped breasts. Rubbing his huge erection up against her as she writhed and moaned and helped him come for the first time together. They had made their pact then. Pulling each other close. "Swear to me, Joe," she had said, "Swear to me you will wait there." In truth, the memory had hampered the love life he should have had and that Ellie jokingly alluded to. He could have got married. Or at least be seeing someone. He should have moved on. It wasn't like there hadn't been opportunities. But he had never been able to forget her or the pact they had made that day in the pool.

"After Ozzie's place this became a hairdressing salon," he said, eyeing her reaction cautiously.

Once the words sunk in Joe watched Ellie's face turn pale and serious.

"One time, on the day of our pact," he continued, "when I was supposed to be at college, I turned up here pretending I'd got my days mixed up. The manager let me work the whole day."

"Here?" she said, her eyes flitting wildly at the furnishings.

"Yes," he said. "These exact premises."

"But...but how long after was that?"

"How long after was what?" he asked innocently.

"You know what I mean, Joe," she warned, suddenly in no mood for humour.

"That would have been...well, let me see..." Joe looked away into the middle distance, stroking his chin. "That would have been about five years after you left."

Ellie's eyes grew into saucers. She looked both alarmed and confused.

"Five years after our pact?" her voice rose, attracting the attention of the old lady. "You were coming here for five years?"

"No," he corrected her. "I was working here."

"You were working here," she repeated.

"Yes."

"For five years," she stated flatly.

"Yes."

"You couldn't get another job in another place?" she twisted her mouth impishly, as if she might have caught him out.

"I didn't want another job in another place, Ellie," he said.

Ellie collapsed back into her seat, tilting and almost dropping the baby. She gave Joe one last sceptical look out of the corner of her eye, hushing little Jimmy back to sleep. Then she just sat there with her head resting against the wall as if in a state of profound shock.

"I need to think," she said.

"Do you want to go somewhere else?" he asked. "It's a nice day. We could go for a walk."

"No, let's stay here, Jimmy's asleep and..." she looked around and back at him. "Well, I've been waiting a long time."

Joe followed her gaze, envisioning all the old fixtures and fittings the shop had undergone with every change. Ozzie's sizzling hive-of-industry hot stove, the basins of the salon where Joe would wash the customers' hair prior to a cut, the eighteen-month hiatus when the shop had been up for lease, and not least the revolving sale boards in the estate agents where Joe had worked and cut his teeth in the property market.

"Yes, I wonder what little emporium is next in line when everyone starts to realise they're being ripped off for what is just basically…a milky coffee," he remarked, tipping his empty cup towards her as if for proof.

"Did you really work here for five years?" she said, her soft voice carried a tender appreciation that Joe took to be pity.

"Well," he sniffed, "let's not get carried away. It's not as if I slayed a dragon or anything."

"Don't ruin it, Joe," she set her face like a child and kicked him from under the table.

Joe frowned and rubbed his leg. "It's like you said. We were kids."

"I'm sorry I didn't come that day," she turned her eyes away from him.

"Couldn't you have at least written?" he asked.

"So you *are* angry about it," she said with a hint of disappointment.

"Well, you knew my address even if you didn't know yours," he insisted. "You could have told me what was happening."

"With no reply, with no…no thought of what you were making of it all? Haven't you already heard enough?" she leaned forward and beseeched him in a low, fearful tone, trying not to wake the baby. "Haven't I admitted to enough, Joe? How was I supposed to put that on paper even if I had been permitted some? Even if I could have afforded a stamp or knew where the nearest post office was? And what was I supposed to write, Joe, that…that my father is holding me hostage? That he is spying on me whenever I take my clothes off? That he has incestuous desires? That my mother chose to succumb to madness rather than confront it?"

Her words had brought her to tears. At first she tried wiping them away with a trembling hand, before giving in to a stifled series of heart-rending, choking sobs that drew the attention of everyone.

"I'm sorry," she looked away, trying to compose herself whilst dexterously producing some tissues from her baby bag. "I'm sorry to put this on you, but it has to be said."

Joe felt embarrassed. "No, you're right," he said with a heavy sigh. "We all ignored it even back then. Everyone did."

She turned and looked at him, nodding fiercely with relief and appreciation, the tears falling down her face.

"Something was wrong," he shook his head, putting his elbows on the table and peering into his empty cup. "We all knew it."

"That's what people do," she told him, reaching over and touching his arm, their first physical contact for eleven years. "But you know, Joe, I never forgot that date. I mean it."

"Huh, why does that make me feel worse?" he said, looking up at the heavens.

"What do you mean?"

"All I had to do was make sure I was here once a year," he shrugged, looking at her and smiling simply. "It doesn't compare."

"When did you give up?" she inquired tentatively as if she didn't really want to know.

She saw him look at the chewed and reddened edges around her fingertips still resting on his arm.

"Well…" he eyed her mischievously.

"Oh, stop it," she said, not waiting for him to continue and using it as an excuse to withdraw her hand. "I mean, I know you're here today but… Well, you can't tell me you've been coming here for the last eleven years," she scoffed. But seeing the look on his face made her laugh instantly fade.

"Is it any harder to believe than the fact you are sitting here after all that time on this exact date in the exact place we vowed to meet?"

"Don't say 'vow,' Joe," she looked away. "Don't say that word. It just makes me feel worse."

"Well, you're here, aren't you?" he lowered his voice. "It's not a coincidence, is it?"

"No," she replied, dropping her head and taking a sudden interest in the baby.

"Ellie?" he spoke gently.

She kept her head down but acknowledged his voice with a little nod like a reprimanded child.

"You have to tell me what happened. Not now if you don't want to but whenever you're ready."

"No," she mumbled. "I have to tell you now. It wouldn't be fair on you. You might not want me. I'm damaged. I'm used goods."

"You mean Jimmy?"

"What's Jimmy got to do with it?" she snapped. "Jimmy's the innocent in all of this."

"Because it wouldn't matter to me," he said. "That's all I'm saying."

He held off telling her about the nursery he had prepared in his new house for their own children.

"Did you ever wonder what happens to the images of victims of child porn?" she looked at him. "Nothing. Nothing happens. It doesn't matter how many people get caught with downloaded images or illegal sites getting shut down. They are out there, Joe. Forever."

Joe could feel her watching him intently awaiting a response.

"Is Jimmy…? Is he your father's child?" he asked.

"No," she said, but in such a dismissive way that she might have been lying.

"Well, then," he couldn't help hiding his relief, rolling his shoulders and looking at her because nothing could have been as bad as that. "Are you going to tell me?"

She seemed to bristle a little at his forthrightness before looking away, giving Joe a reminder about how carefully he should tread.

"What happened after the hairdresser's?" she said.

"What?" he laughed emptily.

"I want to hear it. What happened to this shop?" she stared at him.

He sat back in his chair feeling slightly bewildered at the turn in conversation. "I don't know," he rubbed at the top of his head and stopped midway to pick at a bristle. "It was up for lease for a while."

"How long?" her eyes sharpened as if suspecting him of lying.

Joe sat forward and repositioned his empty cup on the table. "Exactly eighteen months," he said.

"What did you do?" she asked.

"What did I do?" he raised his eyebrows.

A message came through on his phone, causing it to buzz and tremble on the table surface.

"Yes," she said, trying to keep his attention. "What did you do?"

He looked around and wiped his face and blew a sound with his mouth.

"Did you leave me, Joe?" she asked.

"No," he said, and closed his eyes.

She leaned her head back and closed her eyes too.

"There's a little door out the back that leads to the alley," he began as if confessing to a crime. "They changed all the front locks but the back just stayed the same – it probably still is. I had a key cut long before in case I ever needed to get in."

"Why did you think you would need to get in?" she asked, her eyes still closed.

"I…"

"Did you wait for me?" she spoke drowsily, as if in a dream.

"Yes," he said.

Ellie sighed and opened her eyes.

"I stood at the front window knee-deep in junk mail in the dark and dingy shadows of a ripped-out hairdressing salon watching every passer-by on the day of our pact," he admitted. "But you never came."

"How long would that have been?" she asked, as if calculating her own whereabouts.

"I guess we'd be at about eight years before it was rented again."

"You waited for eight years?"

"Yes," he said.

"Why didn't you just give up?"

"I was in love with you like nothing I've ever known since," he said, giving her a sidelong glance.

"I never forgot you, Joe. You were all the memories I had. Do you believe that?"

"What about the child?" he asked, starting to feel increasingly uncertain of anything. "Who's the father of the child, Ellie?"

"Does it make a difference to you?"

"No, I guess not."

"Well, then," she said. "Tell me about the shop. What happened next?"

"No," he said abruptly. "Not until you tell me something in return. We're at eight years. You would have been twenty-two..."

She looked at him and smiled.

"Okay," she said. "At the time you were standing in that empty shop eight years after our pact my father must have raped me hundreds of times. Maybe a thousand," she added wearily.

For a long moment they both just sat and stared, numbed by the words. Joe had suspected as much, had been bracing himself for the worst, but not that. Not that and whatever else was to come. He felt his body want to slump, he was desperate to offer some crumb of consolation but there was nothing to say.

"It started about a year after he got us in that house. Around the time you must have been working for Ozzie. When I was fifteen," she flickered a smile. "By then my mother had been officially diagnosed. He used to say that if I ever told her they would think her disease had degenerated to such a degree that she would be sent to a psychiatric hospital and never released. He said they would think her confused and mad. I didn't want my Mum to end up that way."

"But she knew," said Joe, "She must have known."

"Well, you said it," Ellie reminded him.

Joe nodded solemnly.

"Remember how he used to call me 'Cookie?'"

"Yes, of course," Joe said. "It was your childhood pet name."

"That's right," she said. "I was a real Daddy's girl. He used to make me feel like I was the only one in the world. 'My little cookie in the oven only half done,' he would whisper into my ear when I was little. It was only when I grew older I started to understand what that meant. I knew the age he liked and so did my mother. There were always going to be problems. And so in anticipation I began locking the bathroom door. I would say my goodnights to him in front of my mother. I used the pool less and less. I was starting to feel him watching me. He didn't take that relocation to get you out of my life, Joe. He'd been inappropriate with a trainee doing work experience. I heard my parents arguing about it later. He had no choice. That's why I made you swear to the pact. I didn't want to admit to you that my father gave me the creeps. But I didn't know where we were going or what was going to happen to us either. I needed somewhere I could come back to. Someone, I should say."

"But then you say he lost his job?" Joe said. "Did it happen again?"

"All I know is that he was made redundant within a year of us moving. He'd lost his appetite for work, anyway. He seemed constantly distracted. Always lingering around late in the mornings or arriving home early or unexpectedly. His attention to me became suffocating. His innuendoes. His lechery. It was like I became his sexual obsession."

"But what about your education? What about school?"

"At first he talked about it. We even went to see one or two. But then he just let it slide telling me I was more use at home looking after my mother. That really was the beginning of it all," she said with bitter resignation. "He worked out that if we lived within our means we could survive on his redundancy payment and pension plans. He didn't need a job. I didn't need to go to school. The house had been paid for outright. We could all live happily enough if we each pulled our weight. But of course I began to fear what was behind it. Sometimes I think my mother even retreated into her illness if that's possible. Just let it swallow her up rather than face the awful reality of the man she had married. This pervert. This molester. She had turned a blind eye to it all her life, but me?" Ellie appealed to Joe. "Her own daughter?"

"Do you blame her?" he asked tentatively.

"Do I blame her?" Ellie repeated, as if she had never thought about it. "I don't know. It's not as if I was a child, is it?"

"What do you mean?"

"Well, I can't explain it. I can't explain why I let it happen or why I stayed. But I did. Because once he moved us into that old remote stone cottage miles from anywhere and set up all his deviant little peep-holes it just became his fantasy playground. His perversion…his twisted lust or love or whatever you want to call it had become fully-blown by then. It completely took him over. He was out of control. I honestly don't think he had a particular plan worked out when we first relocated. He had just been following his urges. But after that, after we moved into that house, that's how it stayed for a long, long time. Yes, I could blame my mother. Yes, of course he was a monster. But neither of those things explain why I let it happen to me. Not after the first time or the second or even the hundredth."

Joe sat back and blew out his cheeks.

"But you seem, I don't know, remarkably level-headed about it all," he said. "Almost understanding of him."

"Don't you believe me?" she turned on him, a wild paranoia in her eyes.

"No, I mean, yes, I wasn't saying that. God, no," he stuttered.

"When he finally had me where he wanted. When I began to realise that was the way it was going to be. That no one was coming to find me. That I was going to be kept prisoner under lock-and-key and under twenty-four hour observation. With all that came a very slow and numb acceptance. It was as if someone had given me the absolute worst case prognosis. That I would never speak or walk again. That I was paralysed. That my life was over as I knew it. That's how it felt. Like I was left living inside a shell. And alone, Joe. Utterly alone."

"But your mother…"

"What, Joe? My mother what? Don't you think she was being subjected to the same sort of psychological abuse by then? It was like being brainwashed. He would use all manner of intimidation or flagrant language to humiliate and degrade us. Of course he would prey on her mental state. I don't know why 'damaged goods' sticks with me or his claim that no one would ever want me more than being called 'Daddy's little cum slut' but it did because in the end even he didn't want me. His little cookie had become overdone."

Joe watched as she broke into a tiny display of withheld sobs. He didn't understand why she seemed more upset than angry.

"Was he rough with you?" he couldn't help asking.

"He raped me," she said stonily.

She was right. It had been a stupid thing to say.

Ellie began rooting around in the baby bag again for more tissues to blow her nose. Swapping little Jimmy around from one crook in her arm to the other. Joe thought against offering to hold the kid. It was something he hadn't factored in. Not the kid. Not her story. Not any of it. He had never allowed himself to think that she'd forgotten about him and got married with a family of her own which not only would have been the more logical assumption but might have stopped him obsessing over the date of their pact year in year out. Listening to her story had been harrowing of course but testifying to his own, out loud, for the first time, suddenly left Joe doubting himself.

"He thought he was making love to me," she barely whispered, her whole body beginning to shake. "I mean, he thought he was showing me his love."

"What happened if you tried to resist?" he persisted. Because there had to have been force. As hard as he tried he couldn't envisage it any other way.

"There was no 'resistance', Joe," her voice hardened, almost uncoiling out of her chair like a snake ready to strike. "Haven't you been listening? I told you I can't explain why I let it happen or why I didn't run away. I'm as much to blame."

"You can't seriously believe that," he baulked.

"I don't expect you to understand. I don't expect anyone to understand. That's why no one will ever want me."

"It's not your fault," he said.

"Don't," Ellie cut him off. "You sound like the psychologists."

"Well, they're right."

"Then why didn't I stop it, Joe? Answer me that. It doesn't matter that I wasn't allowed out of my room when the postman came. Or that there was no landline and my father had the only phone. Or that only he could drive. It doesn't matter about the threats. That if I ever tried to leave he would put all the evidence of us out there on the internet for the perverts to trawl before killing himself and leaving me and my mother to deal with it. I should have found the strength…"

"Jesus," Joe had covered his face with his hands in horror. "I didn't know… I mean, I just don't know what to say to you, Ellie."

"Of course you don't. No one does. Not the psychologists. Not the police. Not the doctors. It doesn't matter anyway," her voice instantly softened. "Actions speak louder than words. You came on the day of our pact for eight years. No one would have done that."

Joe's phone began to flash and tremble.

"Why don't you just answer it?" Ellie asked, trying not to read the name on the screen.

"I wish I'd known," he blubbered, "I so wish I could have saved you."

"You're here now, aren't you? That's what you said earlier," she took a deep breath and reached over to touch his hand. "No one would have done that. You are my dragon slayer. I don't care what you say."

"I don't deserve that," he shook his head and looked away. "Not after what you've been through."

"Listen," she hushed him. "I wasn't allowed anything. Any little thing I requested whether it was something to read, or to watch a television show, or some new clothes from the mail order, anything at all, came with a price," she nodded at him so that he should understand. "He took my virginity. My innocence. My life. But he couldn't take the one thing I never let go of. The one thing he never knew about and couldn't sully. That you would still be waiting for me."

"But how could you have known?"

"You're asking me?" she exclaimed, wide-eyed and disbelieving.

He shook his head and started to grin, feeling slightly better about himself.

"Kiss me, Joe," she said.

He leaned over and closed his eyes. Their lips slightly apart. Her breath had a faint metallic whiff. He tried pushing away the thought of all the things that mouth had been made to do or had done without refusal or argument or perhaps even willingly.

"This can't be happening can it?" she murmured, beginning to plant random kisses around his lips.

"No," he said, and laughed nervously.

When the baby stirred she pulled away, blowing him another kiss in the process and leaving Joe feeling all at once warm and wanted and special. For a long while he was content just to watch the mother in her jiggle and cajole the baby back to slumber.

When another message came through Joe picked up his phone. He was close to completing a chain of sales but there had been a hitch when one of the buyers suddenly wanted another fifteen-hundred off the agreed price a day before signing. The seller was having none of it and now the whole deal threatened to break down. Joe resisted returning the call even though he knew he should and continued to watch Ellie instead, trying not to think about the baby's origin and feeling a sudden compulsion to finish his story and tell her everything.

"I would have thought the last thing the high street wanted was another estate agents," he said after a while.

"What do you mean?" she looked up from dealing with little Jimmy, barely registering an interest.

"The shop," he watched her with an amused smile.

"This shop!" she perked up.

He nodded and smiled broadly as she hurriedly moved things around and made herself comfortable. Her features softened with an eager readiness as she settled down to listen.

"Just one thing," she said, and leaned forward with the baby dangling to plant another kiss on him.

He watched her mouth open. The tip of her wet tongue resting just inside her bottom lip. Joe didn't have that much experience but she kissed like a woman. Like they did in the movies. She kissed with all the expertise of a three-times divorcee going in for number four and be damned if she wasn't going to make this one work. She kissed as if it was all she had ever known, he couldn't help thinking.

"Year nine," he tried pulling away as she bit down lightly on his lip.

"Yes, sorry," she sat back, giggling. "Year nine," she repeated, nodding obediently like a first-year pupil.

"By then, what with the property market the way it was – the way it still is, in fact, a lot of people with some spare cash were buying to let which is what we dealt in specifically."

"We?" she sounded puzzled.

"Yes," he said patiently. "I got a job there, well, here."

"Here?" she repeated, "you mean here?"

"Yes," he smirked, wondering when the penny was going to drop. "These exact premises."

"You worked here again?" her eyes widened in surprise.

"Yes," he laughed. "That's what I'm saying."

"You worked here again so that…" her face began to distort between joy and heartbreak.

"Yes," he urged her to understand.

"So it wasn't just eight years. It was longer?" her voice filled with awe.

"Another two years longer," he smiled. "At least until one of the big heavyweight coffee chains moved in."

"So…how long has this place been here?" she asked, still not quite believing.

"This place? This café? About a year," he shrugged.

"That's ten years you waited," she whispered.

"Eleven," he corrected. "That's if you include me turning up here today. You want to hear something stupid? I was even going to apply for a job here. Just part-time. So that I could be here all day. On this day."

"So you have been here every day on the date of our pact," she looked at him. "One way or another. Under all those transformations. For the last eleven years?"

He nodded.

"You've waited eleven years for me?"

He nodded more vigorously.

"For this moment?"

"Yes."

"Are you sure?" she hesitated.

"Yes!" he laughed.

She looked away and began chewing the inside of her cheek, the enormity of his efforts suddenly so hard to take in.

"What if I hadn't come, Joe?" she looked at him in all earnest, becoming seriously concerned. "I mean it. What if I had never come?"

"But you did," he smiled simply.

"You could have wasted your entire life just waiting. It doesn't bear thinking about," she uttered. "It was selfish of me to even think that you would."

They'd been kids, yes, she thought. But had she really believed it even then? In all the insanity of that shut-off world of degradation and abuse at her father's hands Ellie had known it was just a fairy-tale. That Joe would never be waiting. It was just something to cling on to the way a life-sentenced prisoner might – worse, the way someone held captive in a dark and dank dungeon might with all hope lost, of ever being saved or found. It was too much to ask. She knew it had been too much to ask. But just thinking that he might walk past the shop and remember her had been enough.

"I haven't wasted a moment waiting for you if you think about it, Ellie," he smiled and looked around before hunkering down and dropping his voice. "Listen, your Dad thought I wasn't good enough for you because I came from a different background and wasn't educated privately. Like father like son? What with my Dad being a tradesman and having no apparent business acumen? Well, I know from experience how money can make money. It was just that my father didn't have the capital to lose like your Dad did. I was up at four-thirty every morning putting in a hard day's shift at Ozzie's for very little pay. That taught me a good work ethic. Then trying my hand at hairdressing gave me confidence beyond my imagination. Learning something different like that, going to college and meeting like-minded people, I would never have done that. I couldn't wait to drop out of school as you probably remember. And when I applied for the job at the estate agent's the manager said he took me on more for my diversity and the fact a guy with little education had kept himself so busy. He said he knew he wouldn't have to be concerned about my desire, effort and ability to learn. And he was right. I am now area manager of four branches and have made some money out of the property market into the bargain. What… What is it?" he asked, realising he'd lost her attention.

"You can't possibly still believe our fathers fell out over business matters," she looked at him incredulously.

"Well, I…I just always assumed…"

"He paid off your parents not to talk, Joe. Christ, he paid your sister off, too, and God knows who else down the years. That's what people in a position of power do when they fuck up."

"You mean, Charley?"

"Yes of course Charley. Charley, me, the trainee. He's lucky he only got relocated and didn't get locked up years ago. At least then I wouldn't be sitting here."

"So…your father. He's in prison?"

"Yes, Joe. Where do you think he is? Acapulco? If they hadn't come and arrested him I would still be there. Maybe with another baby on the way."

"Are you going to tell me?"

"About the father?"

Joe nodded.

She shook her head and seemed to take a long time thinking about it.

"He…my father, after he didn't want me anymore. After he'd left me as 'damaged goods'…once I got too old and my body was fully developed he started getting involved with a ring of other men on the internet. Men who were advertising their daughters or step-daughters or who knows who they were? They'd exchange mostly photographs and videos at first. But the thing about my father's sexual craving was that it was only ever satisfied for so long. So one day a man came to the house. I never saw him. I was tied to the bed and blindfolded. He had a northern accent and smelt of cigars and I could feel his bushy beard up against my skin. Everywhere…" she trailed off.

"Didn't you…didn't you try and call out or scream?"

Ellie looked straight through him. He wasn't listening. He didn't understand. She'd been too numb to scream but the other girl in the next room had put up a fight. She sounded much younger. Ellie could hear her struggling and crying until she fell quiet under her father's familiar soft and reassuring soothing voice as Ellie imagined him forcing himself upon her. Telling her everything would be alright. Just the way it had been for Ellie. She couldn't describe the reasons for her jealousy at hearing the sounds but in some sort of warped retaliation had done whatever the man wanted her to do without offering any resistance. He untied her so she could accommodate him even further. She bent over so he could take her from behind. She felt his probing tongue and fat fingers inside her. She took him in her hand. Her mouth. All the things she'd been shown. She even orgasmed loudly in the hope her father would hear and remembered wishing for the pregnancy at the time which is something her father had always been careful not to let happen.

"When the police came early one morning to arrest him they took away his computer and interviewed me for days. I wasn't allowed to speak to my mother. She's not really in a home. I don't even know if she has dementia. She's in a psychiatric unit. She's had some sort of nervous breakdown. Those little notes she used to make? I came across them after in more detailed form in an exercise book she kept hidden with all her tuition papers. They were documented details of my father's absences that dated back years. She clearly suspected him of something. But to this day I don't know if she recorded them to incriminate him or if they were to be alibis. Not that any of it matters. My father's threats all came to fruition in the end. My mother's lost her marbles. Naked pictures, videos of my father having sex with me are out there on the internet."

"Is that how he got caught?" Joe pressed as gently as he could.

She nodded and sipped at her coffee.

"It was a countrywide operation. About twelve men were connected. Mostly for being in the possession of illegal images. They found thousands downloaded on my father's hard-drive. Thirteen, fourteen, fifteen-year-olds. Along with that my father is standing trial on two counts of raping a minor. One of them being me. I haven't seen him since that day."

"When is it?" Joe asked. His words were thick and furry.

"It starts today."

"This day?" his mouth fell open.

She nodded stiffly. Her eyes hardening.

"Shouldn't you...I mean, shouldn't you be there?"

"I had somewhere else to be, Joe," she said, and flickered a bitter smile. "Besides, I won't have to testify for weeks. He's going down for life."

"Well, thank God for that," Joe breathed a sigh of relief.

"I don't think God has anything to do with it," her tone turned hard and cold.

"I didn't mean it like that."

"That's what you said. 'Thank God for that,'" she insisted.

"Sorry," he stammered.

"'Thank God for that,'" she repeated. "Thank God? So what is it exactly that I should be thanking God for, Joe? Tell me that. Tell me where God was all that time when you seemed to be doing so well for yourself. You might have something to thank God for, Joe. You might have God to thank for my abduction and imprisonment and years of sexual abuse when all you had to do was turn up here once a year to alleviate your conscience but don't you dare thank Him on my behalf. You think I didn't pray? You think I didn't ask for God's help? Fuck you, Joe. Fuck you and your success on the back of my misery."

"I wasn't saying that. I wasn't saying that at all."

"Let me remind you that while you were waiting tables at Ozzie's and...and cutting hair and selling houses and giving yourself a slap on the back. All the years you were building a career I was kept prisoner in a cold, empty bedroom, tied and starved and mentally tortured into sexual submission on a daily basis by a demonically incestuous man I can't even bring myself to call a father. Until I didn't know anything different. Until every day became the same. Trust me, Joe. God had plenty of time to fix it."

"I'm sorry," Joe said. "I don't know what to say."

"Then don't say anything if it's going to be something stupid."

"I'm sorry," he said again.

"All the time I kept thinking that I must have done something terrible in a former life," she spoke through him, as if addressing someone over his shoulder. "Karma, right? Isn't that what they say? Isn't that what they say about people who are born deformed? I would have been better off God cursing me deaf, dumb and blind than what I've been through."

"Do you really believe that?"

"And you. What did you do in a former life to have prospered out of my abuse? You must have been a fucking saint or something I don't know."

Joe watched in dull disbelief as she began to get her things together.

"What are you doing?"

"What does it look like?"

"You can't go. You can't just leave."

"I shouldn't have come. There's something wrong about this. Believe me, I've developed a good instinct."

"For what? Mistrust? Of course you have. That might never heal. But you have to give yourself a chance, Ellie," he seized her wrist. "Listen, I have a flat ready and waiting for us. You wouldn't believe it. You can move right in. Are you listening? I've done it all for us, Ellie. I've been waiting for us."

Out of the corner of his eye he saw a young guy in a leather jacket stand up and begin showing some concern.

"Who's that?" he saw her looking. "Do you know him?"

"What? Get off me," she retorted.

"Sit down," Joe jeered at him. "You come in here for a coffee once in a blue moon when I've been coming here every year? Worked here every year waiting?"

"Joe!" Ellie insisted. "You're making a scene."

"What have I done?" he tore his gaze away and pleaded.

"Nothing," she said. "It was a mistake that's all."

"So that's it?"

"We made a pact. We kept it. Don't ask me why," she shrugged. "Don't ask me why my father's trial starts today of all days. I should have listened. I should have read the signs?"

"What signs?"

"Why are you here, Joe?" she suddenly wanted to know. Her eyes roved over him with suspicion. "Why are you even fucking here? Give me a straight answer without sounding like some…some fucking weirdo who's wasted his life on a dream? On a stupid pact. An obsession."

He could feel his mouth moving silently.

"That's what I thought," she said.

Joe watched helplessly as she clipped little Jimmy into the pushchair and put on her coat. He had to move out of her way with all the bags. It looked like she had old clothes in there.

"Do you have somewhere to go?"

"Don't worry about me," she said.

"You never asked me about the missing eighteen months," he called to her as she reached the shop front.

For a moment he saw her hesitate.

"When the shop was closed," he said, walking slowly towards her.

Someone had just vacated the prime seats. Soft leather sofas in the front of the window, their cushions still flattened and sighing under the vanishing weight. Olga appeared beside him, excusing herself and clearing away the table of its empty cups and plates.

"You are staying, yes? Two more lattes? One in a cup?" she snickered.

Ellie slowly nodded.

"Yes?" Olga asked Joe, encouraging him with a brisk nod.

"Yes," he said, his eyes locked on Ellie. "Both in a cup, please."

They sat down opposite each other almost simultaneously. There was more room for the buggy at the front of the shop and Ellie was perched on the edge of her seat slowly pushing it back and forth as Jimmy slept. She would listen and leave, Ellie thought. She would tick off every month of every year of her hell because Joe was the only calendar she had of her disappearance. All that time she had cared less about the media world and what was going on outside than the life she was missing out on. Listening to Joe had been like coming out of a coma. Of course things had changed. Of course he deserved his success. What had she been thinking? Hadn't she come to the shop today in the faint and utterly hopeless expectation of seeing him? So what frightened her so much to find him still here just as she had wished and dreamed he'd be?

Olga came back with a tray and set the coffees down with some little cubed samples of cake. She waved away his gesture of paying. "It is on me. He is in here always…waiting," she smiled at Ellie as if sharing a secret. Somehow the grudging romantic in the east European girl seemed to know what was going on. Joe looked at Ellie and raised his eyebrows in a hopeful attempt at reconciliation.

"Don't go, Ellie, please," he appealed to her softly once Olga had left them alone.

Ellie blinked and stopped pushing the chair. She put her hands in her lap and remained on the edge of the seat as if ready to leave at any moment.

"If you go now what have we been waiting for? You say you're damaged but what about me? We made a pact to meet on this day whether it was last year, or the first year, or another eleven years from now. What has happened in between, whatever you're thinking, that I've somehow led this fortuitous life at your expense was because you made me swear to you in the pool that day to meet you here on this date. And I've thought of nothing else since," he said, inching slowly forward. "You don't think I know I owe you everything I've achieved? But you also have to ask yourself where the strength came from."

"What strength?" she mocked him and looked away.

"Not just in me but you," he continued hurriedly. "The resilience. To have endured such unspeakable horrors for so long at the hands of someone who was supposed to be there to love and protect you. What kept you going, Ellie, when there must have seemed no way of it ever ending?"

"I don't know," she sighed.

"Yes you do," he nodded at her intensely. "Yes you do, Ellie."

"All right, then. The pact," she said reluctantly after a moment, dropping her head.

"That's right," he said softy. "The pact that now seems to suddenly scare you. The one thing you dared hope for. If we hadn't made that promise to each other I don't think you would have made it. Real or imagined. With not one single ounce of proof that I would still be here. You had to believe it because there was nothing else. Just as I had to keep on believing and preparing for this day."

She began nodding slowly, reaching for some more tissues and blowing her nose, her eyes clearing as she allowed his words to flood in.

"Tell me about when the shop was shut," she said. "When you couldn't work here."

He stirred his coffee thoughtfully. Not knowing how to say it.

"Joe?" she asked. "What happened in the eighteen months? You have to tell me."

"Well, I made sure I came back here on the date of the pact," he wavered.

"Yes, yes I know, you said that," she began to grow impatient. "But what about the rest of the time? What were you doing all the while the shop was shut? Before it became an estate agents? Before you worked here again? Did you find someone else? Is that it? Is there someone else, Joe? Is that what you have waited to tell me?"

"There's been no one, Ellie. Do you believe me?"

The enormity of his loyalty seemed suddenly overwhelming. She had no right to have expected that of him even though she hadn't known what she was saying at the time. They were just kids. Fourteen-year-old kids. It was puppy love. What else could it have been?

He looked at her for a long moment, his emotions threatening to engulf him.

"I'm so sorry, Ellie," he uttered, lifting a trembling finger to trace his hairline. "I'm sorry I couldn't find you."

"What do you mean?" her expression faltered, feeling slightly afraid. She'd been waiting for the other shoe to drop from the moment they'd started talking. She knew it was all too good to be true. That something bad was coming. That's why she found herself suddenly wanting to leave. She didn't want to hear it.

"After everything you've told me…" his voice trembled. "I would have… I might even have knocked on your door…"

"I don't understand," she said, sliding back into her seat. A growing look of alarm appearing in her eyes.

"I came to look for you, Ellie," he tried explaining.

"But…how, where? You didn't even know where I was."

"All I knew was Devon," he shrugged his shoulders. "After that, Somerset, Cornwall, Dorset. I searched all over the West Country looking for you. I carried copies of your picture around with me everywhere. I taped them to every tree and lamppost in every town with my phone number asking if anyone knew of your whereabouts. I scoured every street of every map and knocked on every door. I spoke to everyone I encountered. I worked with migrants on farms. I got casual labour in pubs and tea rooms and B&B's and masqueraded as a gardener and handy man and all sorts."

"But no one ever knew I was there," she uttered incomprehensively. "No one knew I was there, Joe. Not even the postman. I was barely allowed out into the daylight."

"That's what I'm saying," his mood began to plummet. His gallant efforts to find her suddenly seeming foolhardy and hopeless. "I might have knocked on your door. I might have been so close. I can't stand to think of it."

"My mother and I were forbidden to answer," she recalled with a whisper. "In the world we had retreated into a knock on the door was regarded as a threat. He made it that way. He didn't even answer the door himself most of the time. He didn't want anyone snooping around the house or getting friendly."

In a weird way Joe could relate to that. He had so many old photographs of Ellie around the house that one work colleague had mistaken them for his previously unmentioned niece or little sister. He didn't invite anyone round anymore. Joe was only twenty-five but having pictures of a bikini-clad fourteen-year-old girl in every room at his age was hard to explain even if you knew the story. Even if it really had been his niece or baby sister.

"What is it?" he asked, catching himself smiling whimsically and looking up to see Ellie staring at him strangely.

"I was just wondering," she frowned. "I was just wondering if anyone knows about all this."

"What do you mean?"

"Have you told anyone about me? When you worked here. Did you tell anyone about me? Did you tell anyone why you took jobs here? That you were waiting for a girl you made a promise to years before? A fourteen-year-old girl?"

"I stopped telling people a long time ago," he admitted.

"Why?"

"Well, because…"

"Because they thought you were crazy?"

"Yes."

"Obsessive?"

He shrugged.

"That you were wasting your life?"

"Yes, yes, all of that!" he snapped. "What do you want me to say?"

"Didn't you think at any point they might have been right?"

"But it doesn't matter now though does it? I was right, wasn't I? You're here, aren't you?"

"Unless it's all been for nothing, Joe," she uttered ominously. "Did you ever think about that?"

"Don't say that," he shook his head and smiled painfully, suddenly feeling the need to cry.

"Why, Joe?" Ellie persisted.

"Why, what?" his features flickered annoyance.

"Why did you wait?"

"I…I don't understand what you want from me?" he began to shift in his seat restlessly. "You know why. Haven't we discussed all this? Isn't that the reason we're here?"

"You said I had to believe in the pact to give me strength to carry on and you were right," she said.

"Yes," he nodded eagerly, feeling a surge of relief. "That's what I'm saying."

"But the truth is, deep inside, I didn't believe it. No more than I thought God was listening to my prayers."

"I…don't get it," his face fell.

"It was just something I made myself believe in. Hope, Joe. That's all it was."

"Well, what's the difference?"

"The difference is that you did believe it in the same way a religious fanatic or a suicide bomber believes they are going to a better place. And I have to say that frightens me a little."

Joe sat shaking his head in silent disagreement. Jiggling his legs and trying to keep his patience. He wasn't asking her to believe in God. Just to keep faith in him. Of course, it was never going to be the same after what she had endured. They could never have picked up where they'd left off and in that sense he totally understood her fears. He just had to convince her somehow.

"I'm sorry, Joe," she said, watching his phone begin to vibrate and flash again.

Eleven years, Joe's mind kept repeating, hesitating at the point of picking up the phone. Eleven years he had waited. Had they really become so different a person after committing to each other for all that time and in circumstances that would have broken even the most devoted couple?

"Take it, Joe," she said. "Take the call,"

"Yes, I should. It's important," he stood up and said, looking around uncertainly and smoothing out the creases in his jacket. "Sorry, but I have to go outside. The signal isn't very good and the noise in here… Will you wait for me, Ellie? Do you promise to wait for me?"

She watched him leave the café and stand on the street with his finger in one ear. He would glance back at her every few seconds and smile unsurely. She couldn't shake the feeling that there was something desperate, almost unhealthy about the way he had waited so long. Why hadn't he just got on with his life? Why hadn't he believed she was getting on with hers? He might have waited forever, she couldn't help thinking. She didn't like the burden of that responsibility or to think he had troubled for so long in preparing a place ready for them to live in. That he had worked in the same shop all that time. Waiting and believing. Ellie looked all the way down the cafe to the corridor past the toilets and the back door that led out into the alley. She had been a prisoner to her father's domination, she began to think with growing anxiety. Wouldn't this just be the same thing? Joe might never let her out of his sight again after all this time and the thought of that terrified her.

Like a rudderless boat Joe had drifted further and further down the street trying to find a quiet shop doorway to speak and just wanting to get the conversation over. It seemed that both the buyer and seller were not prepared to budge and Joe was close to offering to pay for the repair of the guttering himself if it meant he could get off the phone and go back to Ellie. If she could just see the house, he thought. If he could just get her to spend a few nights she would realise how much effort had gone into preparing for her homecoming. From the photographs that had kept her memory so vividly alive in the early years when he would watch from the window of the shop searching every passing face, to the recently purchased personalised pillowcases and bath robes. Since owning his own property on the night of the pact Joe liked to prepare the rooms with flowers and scented candles and a trail of rose petals leading from the threshold to the bedroom all in the undying hope of her return and this morning had been no different except that at last he hoped more than anything not to be walking back through the door alone. And he couldn't wait to give her the stack of unsent Valentine, birthday and Christmas cards with all their heartfelt sentiments. The love letters that had piled up year after year with nowhere to go. It wasn't the perfect set-up but even little Jimmy was a ready-made fit for the nursery he had lovingly prepared long before in the everlasting belief that they would one day settle down and start a family of their own. She was just going to take some convincing that's all even if it meant keeping her in the basement flat he'd had soundproofed until she learnt to trust him. The one tiny window was blacked-out and barred. The only entrance door heavily secured with three mortice locks. He'd told the builders he wanted to convert it into a recording studio but there was no musical equipment down there. Just an en suite bathroom, a TV, a fridge and bed and a twenty-four-hour surveillance camera linked to his computer. Almost as if reading his thoughts Joe lifted his head and smiled crookedly in acknowledgement at a man on his phone inside the shop until he had the unnerving sensation of realising he was looking at his own reflection. As if he was back in the empty premises of the café. Still held hostage by the pact, by today's very date in fact. As if he was still watching. Still waiting.

NEXT WEEKEND

He had been on a training course that week, he said. He was taking his time about going home because he didn't have much to go home to. That's what he said. His wife had left him and taken the dog. An adorable black and white bundle of a papillon with panda-patched eyes and a snaggletooth on the left side of his pointy little snout that made it look like it was continually smirking. Or so the many pictures on his phone revealed. All mostly in the arms of his wife. Or being kissed and snuggled by his wife. Or even out-vied by his wife. With the dog barely in the frame but for one of its black, semi-erect butterfly-wing ears that appeared to bow at the very top under its own fluffy and seemingly disproportionate weight. Look at me, his wife seemed to be saying. Aren't I adorable, too? Aren't I just the cutest thing? There were no kids involved which made a family photograph even harder to imagine with an attention-craver like that.

He and his wife had argued over getting another papillon, he said. He even admitted to feeling a little excluded at the thought, to which they both laughed and bought another round of drinks, feeling that warm flood of shared intimacies that can sometimes happen between strangers because you think you will never see them again. But they had stayed talking and drinking at the bar of the hotel where he had finished his conference with increasing insouciance. Both knowing where it was heading. He had made several references to his sleeping alone that night already. The mini-bar. Even the porn channels. They discovered they both had a mutual like of porn. And of oral sex in particular.

But in the end there wasn't any need for more alcohol or some sort of sexual stimulation. Desire took hold the moment they were behind the door of his room. Pushing up against the wall. Clawing. Pawing. Panting and sweating and moaning like whales. They shredded each other's clothes like wet tissue. Searching to find the skin beneath the skin. Buttons popped. Seams teared. Almost as if they had lived a sexually charged and tormented lifetime of denial from being around each other. The utmost forbidden love. Scarlet letter lovers. All at once that tension-trembling dam of withheld and agonizingly illicit lust finally erupted into a near-pure ecstasy of euphoric relief. A saliva-devouring orgy of frenzied sex. And when they were done their still-palpitating and dehydrated lips stuck upon each other's face and mouth and ears as if moulding into one. Still licking at each other like mother mammals to their young. Whispering as if to reveal unspeakable secrets in the gloom from the lit bathroom door where there was just enough light to see the whites of his eyes staring up at the ceiling. The almost comic-book hero delineation of his face. The iron-hard contours of his chest. And their limbs, locked as if rope-bound, both inescapably and fatally entwined.

It had been special from the start.

They never slept. In that one night they shared their childhoods, their loves, their dreams and disappointments. All their shit and baggage. Everything. Emerging the next morning like old friends when casually chatting and sharing jokes over the incongruously put-together 'continental' buffet that consisted of croissants and English ham. *Dairylea* triangles and *Kellog's Frosties*. They were in hysterics about it and making the other guests openly uncomfortable in the cutlery-chinking silence of the cheaply put-together breakfast lounge with their snorting laughter and open criticism. Anyone who might have been in on the joke was ignored otherwise they were oblivious to the surrounding disapproval. Both knowing things didn't happen the way they had very often. You didn't just meet someone and connect like that. Yet there they were. Glowing in periphescence for all to see. It was impossible not to think of a whole future opening up before them. He lived over an hour away so, yes, that could be a problem in the beginning. There was the glaring age difference given his comparative youth but that he nonetheless seemed unconcerned about. He was of course still technically married and one of his confidences the night before had been that he was sex-starved. Apparently, his wife hadn't been very adventurous in bed and he had for a long time suspected she might be frigid. He had lived his whole six-year marriage like that, he said. And whenever the subject came up she would just freak out. Calling him all sorts. A disgusting pervert. A dirty dog. That he just wanted her for sex. That she was just there to accommodate his hard-on. Like a job. Like a *job*! He repeated incredulously and exploded with laughter. Then suddenly turned serious as if the joke was on him. But not a fucking blow job, he uttered darkly. Not even a fucking hand-job. He desired her but it simply wasn't reciprocated. She didn't understand him, he said. And just seemed to grow more disillusioned as he sat there shaking his head. She was cold, withdrawn and loveless, he looked up finally and shrugged.

They arranged for him to come up the following weekend and stay. He liked the apartment upon entry. He filled the doorway with his impressive frame, as if he might not even fit through. He held a suit protector slung across his shoulder for work the next week and carried a smart leather Louis Vuitton gym bag. He gazed around and began nodding approvingly with that big square-chinned smile. He might have been a potential vendor who clearly had a good vibe about the place.

The apartment was up high on the twelfth floor of a new development with a part-sea view. He set down his stuff and ran his broad hand along the furnishings going from room to room. The gleaming grey granite kitchen top. The sumptuously cushioned edges of the sofa. I'm going to enjoy this bed, he said, sitting and bouncing on one corner, smiling ambiguously when their eyes met and creating a frisson between them that he seemed to be able to do almost at will.

The bed was a *Tempur Pedic*. One of the best money could buy. It was obvious he liked nice things. His overnight bag. His Rolex. His Cole Haan shoes that could only be bought in America or Canada. He'd alluded several times to his business travels. Watching him, taking note of his attention to detail, it felt a little strange having him back. He appeared slightly taller and his eyes seemed a lighter colour brown. Almost hazel. Making the weekend before feel like a dream. Or something that had happened long ago and the memory had become fuzzy. He was perfectly happy moving around the place and making himself at home. Hanging his clothes in the walk-in wardrobe. Sniffing and trying out cosmetics. He touched everything the way a blind man might, feeling the quality, smelling, pushing fabrics up against that beautifully chiseled face. When he found a rogue toothbrush in the toilet he held it up quizzically, somehow knowing it didn't belong there. They jokingly dismissed it as if any old stray was welcome to come back but it was his first warning that he was laying down the law. That he wasn't prepared to be shared even in his uncertain circumstances. He was a good-looking man and he knew it but not in an arrogant way. He appeared comfortable with himself which created a relaxed air and made him easy to talk to. But he was in control. He would be the one calling the shots. That was tacitly established from the very beginning.

It went on like that for a couple of months. He would arrive Friday night and leave early Monday to beat the motorway traffic and drive back up to London to work. They spent every hour of the weekend together. And it wasn't about going out and having a good time. He made it clear he liked to cuddle up on the sofa and watch movies. Take a bath together. Spend long mornings in bed slowly rousing, reading the papers and drinking coffee and watching morning TV. He preferred to stay in, he said. It made the weekends together seem longer. Apparently, he had always been the homely type. It could have begun then, but when they agreed to take turns in cooking, he would send ingredients to be picked up with random, almost officious and increasingly loveless texts when only weeks before he would bring his own fresh produce.

The emojis and kisses dried up quickly.

His messages became matter-of-fact. The romance was melting. He didn't like to talk on the phone, he said. Claiming that work filled his day. And in the evenings he was too tired to call. The red flags were there right from the start. But the next weekend was never really very far away.

Upon reflection the panic of losing him had set in from the very beginning. He was too good to be true. Which is why he had been allowed to get his own way. Fifty-one percent in his favour quickly became fifty-five, then sixty... Every weekend when he turned up at the door seemed like a miracle. Increasing the growing sense of inequality between them. He could talk over you or interrupt or yawn just as easily as if he had not been listening, which was the worst feeling of all. As if he was somewhere else. As if he had somewhere else to be.

His boredom began to manifest in little ways too. In sharp bursts like slamming down the newspaper as if he had spontaneously made a decision to go out. Or his addiction to playing games on his phone where he would periodically sigh or chuckle to himself and create a rude and uncomfortable air of exclusion between them of which he seemed either cruelly unaware or deliberately uncaring. And then there were those gut-churning mood-swing moments that came out of nowhere when he would get up without a word and take himself away and stand on the balcony with the glass door shut and just smoking - a habit that appeared to have accelerated with his wife's leaving and certainly in the small time they had known each other. A sneaked peek between the blinds would see him just staring out at the part-sea view for long periods, alone and impenetrable, as if just wanting away from there but not knowing how to say it. That's what he could do. He appeared oblivious to the conjectures he could conjure just by a single gesture. A distracted scratch of his face. A long and vacant dull-eyed stare before all at once coming back to life and responding to a question. Or his habit of asking you to repeat yourself. Which was soul-destroying in its regularity. As if he was being nagged. As if he had more important things on his mind.

Yet the moment he brightened and suggested something to do the atmosphere changed and the madding tension that may or may not have ever been there began to subside. Until the hours ran down the clock again to its slow, inevitable, seventy-percent-in-his-favour and hopelessly unstoppable and insidious return where he could be found back on the balcony smoking again. Alone with his thoughts or whatever it was that seemed to permanently occupy him.

The first time he made an excuse to go early one Sunday afternoon a great black hole appeared in the ensuing hours. It was frightening the void he could leave. His power. His all-consuming addiction. To suddenly wake up and find yourself so cripplingly dependent upon someone was spirit-crushing. An ongoing turmoil of emotions raged day and night. Festering paranoia battled the still small voice of reason. Blind faith fought against the seething, bubbling, deadly unpredictability of white-hot outrage. All self-control was vanquished by a darker side wrestling to be heard in another tongue. And with it came a creeping sickness spreading through every inch of your exhausted vessel from the stomach to the throat. Your limbs left sapped and lifeless. Your muscles jellied. Every tunnel of sleep invaded. Each and every waking independent thought corrupted.

Five days.

What had not so long before been only a delightful skip through the park, an increasingly exciting and blissfully carefree hopscotch of days until the weekend - until Friday, now appeared a huge impassable cold blank wall. And that was only Monday. There was no point calling him. His phone was always off and he had quickly stopped responding to text messages and even when he had the language became hurtfully obligatory. As if he had a whole number of people to respond to. Quite possibly he had two phones. Or even more. That didn't auger well. Only deceptive people had two phones. Shadowy businessmen, serial adulterers, drug dealers. Trust was something that could only ever be built from within. Yet he appeared to just assume it. That he could turn up and the door would open. That the weekends were there at his disposal. That he could pretty much come and go as he pleased. It was hard not to think that way when there were still four days to go, but by Wednesday the frustration and anger began to soften towards the expectation of seeing him. Like that song by The Cure. *'Thursdays I don't care about you, but Friday I'm in love.'* It was crazy to become obsessed about that song. That an attraction could have such an effect. But there was a whole host of songs that had been burnt on a disc devoted to him and that would be surreptitiously slipped inside his overnight bag before he left on Monday morning - songs that now appeared at will on the radio, or in bars or in soundtracks to films. Songs. He had even infiltrated songs that weren't written for him. That they hadn't even shared. It was suffocating. There was no escape. He was everywhere.

When he didn't arrive on Friday night it seemed the miracle of that moment was over forever. He could never be trusted to turn up again without at least a confirmation message or phone call. That would have to be insisted upon in future. Ever since they'd met they had parted with his usual twinkly-eyed, leave-taking. "See you next Friday." Which is why it really had seemed like an act of God to get through all those days and hours to be able to arrive at that point again. That heart-in-the-mouth, daring-to-believe moment at the sound of the doorbell chiming around seven-thirty the following weekend and opening the door to find him standing there just as he said he would, but with no contact in-between. It wasn't a natural arrangement of course. Alarm bells were going off all the time. The warning signs were there. He had never revealed his address or place of work. There were now only brief, acrimonious references to his wife. He didn't like to talk about those things. He came to relax, he said. To be together. I just want something of my own, he said. Can't I just have something of my own? And as a consequence, and the longer it went on, it began to feel like holding something precious you were scared to drop. Scared - even, to take a breath. No one should be made to live that way.

He turned up unannounced on Saturday lunchtime instead. He seemed unimpressed by the aloofness in which he was greeted. But what with the previous Sunday the weekend had now shrunk by half. He never did go on to explain why he hadn't come the night before and there seemed no point in bringing it up now that he was here. He saw the disc on the side with his name drawn on it inside a heart. What's this? he asked. Is this for me? He went to the PC and put it on and on came Robert Smith and the band. He stood listening for a long time. *I don't care if Monday's black...* Slowly grinning at the irony. It suddenly seemed a small thing to have got upset about. He could, after all, have had an accident or something even worse - but he was here now, thank God, holding out his arms to dance, a flickering fire in his eyes. You're such a diva, he said. And the whole afternoon seemed to stretch out in front of them and making the time so much more important not to waste on some misunderstanding that had already happened.

The next weekend he turned up around the same time on Saturday, making the song completely irrelevant by then. He walked in as if it was to be expected and looking back his parting words the weekend before had been rather questioning: See you next week? A self-hatred began to set in at being so accommodating but the alternative that he never came at all - or ever again, was unthinkable. There was nothing to cook so unusually they went out. He always seemed a little on edge about being seen out in public. Avoiding any physical contact and keeping a slight distance between them. But when they got to one of the bars and he got a few drinks down him he would start to relax and become increasingly loud and flirtatious, jokingly writhing his hips on his bar stool and waving his hands above his head as if he was getting in the mood. The sharp angles of his film-star face were more apparent in the phosphorescent glow-stick light of the club. His cheek bones became hairpin mountain bends. His jawline a crafted axe-head. He consistently swept back his lustrous black hair which was just long enough to fall into his line of vision, and undid yet another button on his shirt to teasingly reveal his newly-waxed chest-plate to one and all. It was hard not to notice that shadowed rivulet between his pecs. The first fruit-sized ripple of his abs. His almost unspeakably gladiatorial armour.

He was God-like and gorgeous.

He did just about everything but get up and dance, which he would never have done in any case. In fact, by contrast he openly struggled with his inhibitions but nevertheless it was hard to keep his attention from wandering. His eyes glittered green with lubricious curiosity. As if they could change colour. As if, like his masquerading there was more than one side to him. They roved everywhere and upon everyone. His nods and smiles almost always reciprocated. He spoke to fellow revelers as if he knew them. It was part of his amatory charm. He was just letting his hair down, his outer-skin, his mask. He was patently out of his comfort zone which was his biggest attraction to any would-be suitors. Yet there was nothing to feel threatened about. He always made it clear they were a couple if he was ever hit upon. He always introduced both of them by name. Outside of his moods he was respectful and had impeccable manners. He just liked to ask a lot of questions. He was a bit of a watcher, that's all. Sometimes he could be lost in conversation with someone for half-an-hour but they always left together and would go home and end up laughing about it and then make love passionately. He loved to be licked around the perineum. It was as if the whole experience had turned him on.

He never did come on a Friday again, claiming that he was always working late and just wanted to go to the pub for a drink with his colleagues and unwind when he finished at the end of the week. Apparently, his wife used to go on about him getting home all the time. It was much better to come down on a Saturday morning feeling refreshed and when there was no rush-hour traffic, he tried explaining with a suspended lift of his shoulders. He held the pose as if a coat hanger had got stuck inside the back of his jacket. Unconvincing and out-of-the-ordinary gestures like that had started to creep in. Elaborate shrugs that begged understanding, quick tight smiles, loud empty laughs, a testing stare down of the eyes. They had got to know each other so well and so quickly in such a short space of time yet he might as well have been breaking the habit of a thirty-year marriage with his guilty behaviour. He was hiding something. He was lying. The fact he wasn't any good at it was probably the only true self he had revealed. He was a fake after all, it was dismaying to admit. He was a wolf in sheep's clothing. A false advertiser. His pellucid facade was becoming a pathetic joke. And so, true to type, he began to turn up later and later. A short spell of potentially relationship-resurrecting and semi-romantic Saturday brunches drinking Mimosas with salmon and scrambled eggs at a discreet sea-front hotel with a spectacular view lasted just a couple of weeks. Then there were one or two wine-bar dalliances as his arrivals got later and later. Until they were reduced to a series of tawdry local pub lunch meetings where he felt inclined to drink too many pints, appearing not only overtly conscious of the raucous football audience in for the live TV game but developing a sudden change of body language in a seemingly nervous need to integrate. But he could never settle in a public arena. He was always looking over his shoulder.

So after they would end up in bed as he slept it off and then he'd wake and be out of sync for the rest of the evening which meant they would just sit up into the early morning hours watching late night chat shows and the tail-end of old movies eating any old comestible from the fridge. Or whatever fast-food service was prepared to deliver. Then one Saturday night when they had arranged to go out to a karaoke club he didn't turn up at all even though they had tickets and a VIP suite with a group of friends he was supposed to meet for the first time. It was obvious he hadn't been comfortable about the idea from the beginning but he had promised he would be there which, as he admitted, was the least he could do given his recent erratic behavior. But he just seemed to be using words now. Words that he thought were the right thing to say and were so much more insulting to the intelligence than his increasingly laughable thespian attempts at pretending he still wanted to come down. It was done. It was over. There had to be more to life than this. But within a day or two the unexpectedness of the next weekend began to loom. Is that what it was then? The rush, the adrenalin and utter madness and penance of the not-knowing. And to what end? How much more could he expect? Seventy-five percent had become eighty. Eighty had become eighty-five… Why hadn't he just severed it and put them both out of their misery? Why did he continue to come? It took him over an hour to drive there. Long weekends, long days had become half-days. Then hours. Then spontaneous snatched moments of temporary satisfaction. Are you in? I need to see you. Can I come round? His prone to impulse was never far away. He was becoming a cliché. But then, it really wasn't that uncommon in men his age. Sometimes he would just walk in and leave wordlessly after getting what he craved. That first night lying in bed in the hotel room he had hesitantly admitted to leading a double-life of sorts, before going on to divulge in increasing detail how that a rising curiosity for his own sexual-orientation had took such a hold over time that he began going to certain known public areas to sit in his car and watch men routinely park up and get out to go meet in bushes. Then he learnt about other places. Toilets, lay-bys, car parks. It was funny how certain types knew how to find each other. He paused to share a significant look. Lorries, vans, commercial and public service vehicles. It didn't matter, he'd said. Until it became an all-consuming, fully-blown and ultimately fruitless and time-wasting obsession. Hours upon hours spent sitting in his car pretending to talk on the phone or hiding behind sunglasses whilst pruriently watching the sordid activity of men of all descriptions covertly ducking into some public lavatory or roadside scrubland to emerge a short time later. Usually with that same hurried amble. Looking directly ahead as if with a gun to their back. Suddenly trying to be invisible to any would-be suspicions. The gauntlet run and almost out of danger from their own deviant urges. Until the next time...

Now and again he would be approached on the pretense of some casual enquiry or sometimes they would just get straight to it. Did he have the time? What was he into? Do you mind if I get in? Did he have anything interesting on his phone to look at? Did he have somewhere to accommodate? I bet you go bareback, don't you? He went on to share each revelation with a knowing grin as if he couldn't believe what he was saying himself. Men would surreptitiously peer into his car to see what he was doing. Others would try and make lude and sometimes chilling eye contact or offer subtle gestures or openly rearrange themselves as they passed by under the act of a casual stroll or in some cases just loitered openly with a fondling hand inside their pockets and a barely-concealed leer. Several penises had been flashed to him, he confided. Old. Young. Scruffy. Smart. There was no stereotype. Gay. Married. Curious. It didn't matter. They were the faces of both bin men and teachers. Criminals and accountants. A next door neighbour. A gym member. The guy down the pub. Your friend. My friend. Somebody's husband. Somebody's son. All of them driven by the same indiscriminate and primitive urge. Yet it was remarkable how so few tried to disguise themselves with so much as a hoodie or hat, he'd said. Most of them wore some sort of accessible jogging attire or tracksuit bottom with a cord tie or elasticated waist. Which was always both a give-a-way and a sign.

Other men who sat for long periods in their cars would leave only to arrive back again within five minutes as if daring to be followed to some preferred or more secluded spot and many times he too had been pursued until it became obvious he wasn't interested. But even then the possibility so unexplainably excited him that he would delay going home and follow them and just drive and drive until they or he disappeared from the rear-view mirror. In time he began to recognize some of the more habitual offenders and in doing so they must have taken him to be some fellow cottager but of a seemingly more discerning disposition. At the very least he must have developed a reputation as some sort of voyeur. Which is exactly what he was or had become, he admitted. But there were others like him too who never left their vehicles. Clearly exposing themselves or openly masturbating and who would sometimes roll down the window and allow one of the other deviants to watch on the pretense of having a chit-chat. Sometimes a lingerer's persistence paid off and would be allowed to lean or perhaps reach in, or be encouraged to get in the passenger seat where the pair would sit staring straight ahead on the look-out for the occasional cruising police car. Their hands out of view. Not that the police didn't know, of course. Everyone knew. There were signs everywhere warning against anti-social behaviour. In parks. At the entrances to men's toilets.

Cars would randomly toot when driving by. Sometimes insults were hurled. Lorry drivers would peer down from their elevated positions but that could have meant anything. It didn't matter. It didn't stop the meetings. Driving rain, freezing cold never stopped them turning up. There was always someone waiting in their car. Even if it was only him, he'd said. Which was even harder to explain if he was never going to act upon the mindless compulsion that had driven him there in the first place. All those irrational detours to and from work or on his way home. Every excuse for an errand or trip to the petrol station or supermarket run. Whenever his wife was out of the house. Sometimes even at night when she slept. Only to have his legs turn to lead every time he moved to get out of the car and satisfy the mind-fueled and heart-racing sexual fantasies spying upon such blatant and depraved behaviour provoked in him. He knew it made no sense just sitting there watching all that time. But he was scared, he said. Scared of getting caught. Scared of being recognised. Scared of committing. Scared of catching a disease. But most of all he was scared of himself. There had been a distant terror in his eyes when he said that. I don't know who I am, he confessed, and turned his head face-on. For a long time after he didn't even blink.

A few more months passed without any contact when on a shopping trip up to London as the cold, darkening days of Christmas neared a man who looked very much like him was sitting in the misted window of a café talking to a group of people. It looked like some sort of casual out-of-office meeting. Laptops and smart phones were on display. They were all dressed in business attire but some with their ties loosened or their jackets thrown over the back of chairs. It was only four o'clock but quite possibly they were finished for the day and had something to feel self-satisfied about. A woman with her legs on show sat on a stool beside and above him. She had far too many teeth for a mouth and even from the street you could see that the back of her high heels were scuffed and peeling.

Trollope, in other words.

The warm interior lights and festive decorations made the scene appear very cozy. You could tell he was the one holding court not because he was doing all the talking but by the way his colleagues were focused around him. He had them under his spell. They were all looking in his direction. All laughing along as he spoke. The men. The women. (And we know he didn't mind which). All falling for those war-hero looks. Those chameleon eyes. It was said Venetian's first wore masks to disguise their social standing. Oh, to walk in and strip away that veil now in front of all of his friends. To reveal him for the false face he really was. Of course, he didn't take any notice of someone on the other side of the glass watching him from the street. Neither did his team members. Why would they? It was all right for some.

They were all wrapped up in themselves. In their lives. Probably they all had other halves waiting for them to come home to. Loving texts coupled with emojis sent in anticipation of their evenings. A chilled bottle of wine in the fridge waiting. Their oh-so-precious weekends. All except for him. He wouldn't be going home anywhere soon. Not someone like that. He had distractions. His world was arcane. He had admitted that first night how prey to impulse he was. It would be the easiest thing in the world to follow him.

One by one the group got up and left until he was sitting there alone. As soon as everyone was gone he got another coffee and began diligently going through his phone. Scrolling. Checking. Texting. To phone him now would give him a shock. But the line just went dead. He had changed his number or was indeed that serial player he had made such a poor attempt at hiding. There was a sudden heart-stopping moment when he appeared to stare directly out. As if he had known all along he was being spied upon and had just been waiting for everyone to go. They say if you stare at someone long enough that person will eventually turn and look at you. Had his sixth sense told him exactly that? Was there still that special connection between them? It was hard not to smile or lift a hand and wave in acknowledgment at him. But it was dark now and shoppers continually surged past and anyway the next time the café came into view his seat was empty.

That fear of not so long ago. That awful terror in the night that they were never to be felt like an anxiety bomb just waiting to go off. A throng of customers began blocking the doorway to the café in bovine disorder. Bumping and shuffling as they tried to make their way in and out. What had been the chances of ever seeing him again in a metropolis like this? He couldn't go. He just couldn't leave again. Cold-nosed faces buried in scarves and upturned coat collars and warm woolly hats swarmed past and around and ahead like shoals of human fish. There was everywhere and nowhere to look. Then suddenly he was standing right there as if ready to speak. His eyes lit like lanterns. Before brushing past without a hint of recognition.

After he detoured off Regent Street and began weaving his way through the tight mazy streets of Soho it was just a case of keeping close behind or losing him to the night forever. He had on a long flowing mack that he wore open and unbelted with his hands pushed deep into the pockets. He stopped off at a pub on the corner of Wardour Street and went in only to return moments later with a pint in his hand and stood outside smoking. It was a gay bar but he distanced himself from the other groups of men and didn't appear to be cruising though he was certainly getting some attention and not just because he was beautiful and supremely self-confident but because one gay man can usually tell another and right from the beginning he always kept you guessing. After his second cigarette he hurriedly pulled out his phone as if it was red hot and had a quick conversation that ended in the most crushingly warm and affectionate laugh. He threw back his head, revealing that rocky jaw line and plumb-sized Adam's apple, before switching it off and shaking his head in amusement. Some of the other men caught his eye and he lifted his head and smiled back with the utmost pleasantry. Turning them into mush. Into giggling schoolgirls. You really had to be a victim of it to know it.

This time his walk was idle, as if he had time to kill. He lit another cigarette along the way. Dawdling. Reading over the illuminated menus of restaurants. He was waiting to meet someone. That much was clear. A deeper dysphoria began to stir. For all the not knowing the actual knowing now suddenly felt sickening. He was his own man, of course. That had been an instant attraction. The only person with a legal claim to him was his wife. It wasn't right to follow someone like this. To meddle in someone else's affairs. But a smouldering curiosity had taken over. He had stayed in the apartment after all. Weekend after weekend. He knew everything. He knew where the spare batteries were. The clean towels. The coffee filters. Yet after his initial revelations he never wanted to talk about his life. Not his marriage or work or anything remotely recreational. As if he was being pried upon. It just wasn't natural. He quickly became suspicious of giving out any personal details. Apart from espying his pin code and being able to jot down the numbers in his phone's contact list there had been few opportunities to rifle through his pockets while he slept. He carried no ID and only ever used cash. It had never been fair or equal. Fifty-one percent accelerated into ninety. An all-consuming one hundred. There was no respect. It was completely one-sided. He couldn't be like that with everyone. So what the hell did that mean?

By the time he reached his destination a burning anger had taken over and it had been hard not to just make a running jump at his back and expose him for what he was. To gouge out the self-seeking popinjay inside. To wildly claw at his face and hair whilst screaming hysterically and bringing his sham to all the world's attention. Except that nobody cared. To hang on a little longer and get a chance to at least reveal him to the person he had come to meet would be more fitting.

It was a pay-at-the-door, neon-lit club with a camp cabaret act advertised as *'Elisa. The Horrible and The Incorrigible'*, and with a mostly gay clientele which was hardly surprising. It was filling up quickly so had been easy to infiltrate and find a place at the bar where he could be observed unnoticed. Almost as if he belonged there he found a corner seat of a black leather sofa that continued in a sweeping wave around one-half of the purple-lit stage edge. He had taken off his coat and loosened his tie, appearing visibly relaxed. Now and again someone came up and spoke to him or shook his hand. For a surreal moment it was as if he had swapped with a body double in the full knowledge he was being watched. Yet not once did he look over or appear furtive. Quite the opposite. The area wasn't roped off but had obviously been set out for a VIP and it seemed he was it. He didn't even mind when the sing-along drag queen act picked him out for a lude joke to which he exchanged some muffled banter and brought about a ripple of laughter from the crowd. The entertainment carried on. It was all in good spirits. There was an air of nostalgia about the club. It had an old Soho feel. Not so many years before it might have been smoked-filled and the act barely visible through the blue haze but Elisa stood large as life in front of a huge projector screen that appeared suspiciously dormant. Clearly more was to come. He, that was, *she,* (apparently it was appropriate to use the female pronoun when drag queens were performing) wore a flowing red chiffon dress whose hem brushed the stage as she went through her sixties medley courtesy of some sort of music sequencer operated by a laptop in the shadows, revealing just a sparkle of pearly footwear and matching scarlet toenails. Even her blonde beehive wig that tumbled to her overly broad shoulders in waves and curls inspired a yesteryear look as she appropriately broke into a Dusty Springfield number. And still he sat there quietly clapping along and smiling as if for all the world he couldn't care less who was there or who might see him.

Then something quite unexpected happened.

A beautiful woman appeared and touched him on the shoulder. She was tall and blonde and wore a tight–fitting silver sequined dress that shimmered like crystal under the mood lights, producing a kaleidoscope of colours. He stood up and smiled. They kissed and hugged. She fitted against him like a spoon. He moved a chair from the table set out in front of them. Some drinks were brought without him appearing to order. They were a perfect match. A magazine cover couple. There was one thing for sure though. It wasn't his wife.

Suddenly an immense power took hold. Sliding off the bar stool and crossing the floor in front of the cabaret act and feeling awash in the lilac luminescence felt almost like an out-of-body experience. The anxiety and hurt and depression of the last year just peeled away like shredded skin. His time of nemesis had arrived and it felt good. He turned his head and their expressions met. His eyes sharpened a little but that was it. A flame appeared to die. They were just ordinary eyes after all and almost certainly not periwinkle as the club lighting made them out to be. There was nothing to be enchanted about. No going back. No way out for him. To his credit he didn't seem alarmed, just resigned. Like a criminal who knew that his time was up. He passed comment to Cinderella. It looked like a warning. Brace yourself, he seemed to be saying or something like that. But by the time she had asked him to repeat himself his voice was in earshot.

"This is the guy I was telling you about," he said, jerking a thumb.

What did he mean by that? Was it some sort of bluff? Was he already thinking on his feet like the duplicitous character he was? Cinderella frowned and adopted a manly pose because as beautiful as she appeared to be from a distance she was, or at least had once been, a man.

"Hello, Alex."

"Sit down, Philip," Alex said coolly, and called for a chair.

The chick with a dick continued to look at him with disdain. Her dress sparkled as if dusted by fairies. She had man's hands. Philip hesitated. It wasn't quite going as expected. Where was the fear? Where were the cracks in his oh-so-smug façade?

"What are you doing here?" Alex asked.

"Well, the same could be said of you," Philip replied prissily. "What about your wife? What about the papillon? Do they know you're sitting here in a club with a transvestite?"

"I'm not a tranny," Cinderella replied off-handedly, albeit a little gruff. "I'm transgender. There's a difference."

Her glitter-dappled cleavage testified to that.

"And I'm not married," Alex responded, sitting back in his chair with his hands behind his head."

"Well, of course you wouldn't have the pictures of your wife and dog on your *new* phone, would you? You're one of many *other* phones."

"You mean these?" Alex said tiredly. He reached for his current mobile and pulled up the pictures and there she was. The attention-seeker dominating the frame. Look at me! Poor snaggletooth never stood a chance. She was all but elbowing the dumb mutt out of the way. Philip didn't know why he'd expressed such an interest in the dog at their first time of meeting. He hated animals. Especially dogs. Dogs stunk. Dogs made his nose turn up. He just couldn't believe all the signals he'd been getting from Alex at the time. That they would end up in bed together. Thinking of that now made Philip recall how Alex had said that his wife was frigid and all the rest of it. Spinning that typical hard-luck slime ball of a married man's story that Philip had eaten up gleefully. Yet still that night in the hotel seemed like only yesterday. Their wet mouths and rock-hard cocks. Alex's wonderfully responsive tumescent cock.

"It's my sister," Alex explained. "Look close enough and you'll see the resemblance."

"Only in the self-promotion," Philip turned his nose up as if encountering a bad smell and handed back the phone.

"Don't be a bitch, Philip. Don't pull your stinky face on me you sneaky little coxcomb. Why do you always have to be such a diva?"

"Do you sleep with your sister then? At least that might explain why she's so passionless towards you." Philip responded tartly, throwing a shoulder "It wouldn't surprise me. Nothing would surprise me knowing what I know about you."

Philip shared a look with Cinders as if he, she, should know. But Cinders only blinked disinterestedly at him with her long, false eyelashes.

"Is that some sort of threat, Philip? You'd like that wouldn't you? Thinking you had some sort of hold over me. Sit down for fuck's sake and stop drawing attention to yourself. Stop being such a sad little man."

Philip was visibly taken aback by the remark. Was Alex showing off in front of his new friend? For a moment he was speechless and could only feel himself dutifully sliding into the chair.

"I use it as cover when I first meet someone," he shrugged.

"It's true," Cinderella chipped in, and cleared her throat deeply. "I thought he was married for months."

Philip sat up and looked incredulously from one to the other. It was like talking to a two-headed gorgon.

"That way I can keep guys at arm's length unless I choose otherwise," Alex simply smiled.

"Or for the weekends," Philip's response was picky.

"Or weekends, yes," Alex conceded with a half-nod.

"Or half-weekends, or half-days or hours or minutes or however long it took to give you a fucking good blow-job!" Philip shrieked.

"Calm down Philip," Alex warned. "Make one of your prissy little fucking scenes here and I'll have you removed."

Philip threw his head to one side and pouted.

"Just take it easy, okay? Come on, let me get you a drink."

A round of drinks came. It felt so good to be up close to him again. To hear his voice and smell his musky Tom Ford cologne. What happened? Did he get bored? Was none of it even real?

"I just got put-off," he said after a moment, as if reading Philip's thoughts.

Cinderella's eyes lit up with interest. She reached over and put her gorilla pad on Alex's leg.

"The endless texts, Philip. The overload of emojis. The *missed fucking calls?* And that was only in the first couple of weeks."

"But..." Philip stuttered. "You wouldn't answer. You wouldn't respond."

"One day I had eighty-seven missed calls," he casually commented to Cinderella. "You know how I love to cook?" he asked her.

She/he nodded.

"Well, we were supposed to take turns each weekend and within one *month* it had all changed. Philip's idea of me cooking was to pick up some ingredients on the way down or 'involve' me by buying them. Fuck that.

Why should I? I soon gave up the culinary competing. It wasn't worth the tantrums."

Philip looked aghast at the pair. Why was he sharing stuff like that with her – with *him?* Oh to fuck with the pronouns, thought Philip.

"Do you know he has sex with men in bushes?" Philip told Cinders in retaliation, sitting back in his chair and crossing his arms and legs. He screwed up his nose and gave a sharp nod of affirmation.

"That's his stinky face," Alex remarked casually.

But Cinderella only shrugged and would have no doubt raised her eyebrows a little higher but for the substrata of Botox cementing her features. Talk about masks. Her forehead shone like eggshell. Her eyes stretched like elastic bands making her look slightly Oriental. There had been work done in that department as well as everywhere else, Philip felt sure.

"Obviously you've never lived in Clapham," Cinders quipped, reaching in her matching sequined clutch bag for a vanity mirror to check herself.

"Also, I never acted upon it," Alex reminded Philip with a wag of his finger. "How many times do I have to tell you that, Philip?"

"Because how would I know if it's true or not? Let's face it nothing else you've said is the truth is it, Mr Whoever-you-are? "

Alex took a long sip of his drink before considering Philip the way a parent might a rebellious child.

"Babe, have you seen my lip gloss?" Cinders interrupted. She began scouring around the seat. "Oh, it's okay I found it," she said. And pulled it from between her big fake tits. They exchanged a knowing look as if it was always happening. Then incredibly they leant in and kissed.

Philip couldn't believe what he was witnessing.

"Well," Alex said, turning his attention back to Philip. "For a start I did find it a cause for concern to discover you going through my pockets the first few weekends I came to stay. I didn't say anything. It could have been innocent. At first I thought you were even going to put on some washing. Or were just folding my clothes the right way out. You know how OCD you are, darling. But you didn't. You were snooping. You thought I was asleep. So I began to leave little traps like lying my clothes in a certain way. Or zipping my overnight bag to the last ten teeth. You always fell for it. You couldn't be trusted which is why I found it necessary to conceal as much as I could from you. But you found enough didn't you, Philip? More than enough you unscrupulous little ferret."

"Oh my *Gawd*, he went through your stuff?" Cinders said quietly, clearly engrossed. The alcohol was releasing her real accent which Philip guessed to be from around the East End. She drank from her glass in big gulps like a man does at a call for last orders.

"I didn't know why you felt the need to know," Alex continued. "I mean, I was there wasn't I? That's all that mattered."

"Well… well, because it wasn't natural," Philip protested.

"But it didn't stop at that did it, Philip?" he asked.

The conversation was interrupted by the drag artist who began to go through her stand-up. Alex and Cinders stopped to give the act their full attention, leaving Philip with his back turned to the stage feeling suddenly isolated and vulnerable. The pair laughed along and chipped in with the occasional heckle while Philip just stared ahead drinking his cocktail and refusing to participate. What was different from when he and Philip had gone out in public together was that Alex didn't seem on edge. Yet there he was in full view of everyone on the prime table with a man that dressed as a woman. Or had become a woman. Philip didn't much care for that type. Philip was an old queen. Everyone could see that. But freaks like Cinders had their own party politics. Their own rules about what to be called and what pronouns to use. They looked upon today's social ignorance and misunderstanding of them as if it was a new thing but it was gay men of Philip's age who had taken the ridicule and abuse and paved the way towards a more acceptable tolerance and appreciation for any of today's would-be outcasts. Nowadays kids as young as three or four felt empowered enough to declare themselves homosexual or that they had been born the wrong gender. But it was the likes of Philip who had changed the law. It was the likes of Philip who had lived with and exposed the discrimination. It was only after that everyone else came crawling out from under their stone. But when Philip next caught himself building up into another icy stinky-faced glare towards Cinders he all at once realized she'd been nodding at him to respond to the drag artist who had centered her show upon them all.

"Yeah, I'm talking to you, Elton," Elisa said in a gruff amplified voice.

Philip winced and turned and shaded his eyes towards the spotlight that was suddenly focused on him. For an excruciating moment everything went silent followed by a slow, nervous tittering of laughter that was clearly at his expense.

"I bet you've blown a candle or two in the wind haven't you, sweetheart?" Elisa the drag queen's voice was course and gravelly. Her cold black eyes flicked like a lizard's from behind all that clown make-up stuck inattentively to her five o'clock shadow. She began scouring the crowd as if she had some personal agenda not just with someone but perhaps everyone, causing Philip and others he noticed to shrink back in fear of being verbally set upon. The audience continued to laugh apprehensively and someone at the back whistled.

"What's the matter, mate. You lost your dog?" Elisa called out.

She laughed to herself at the joke and coughed into the mic, producing a bit of feedback.

"Don't mind me," she muttered. "I'm only playing..."

But along with the sidelong glance she gave Philip it had a strange sound of forewarning. Like a storm was rolling in. Then suddenly as if to wake up the crowd she spoke up proudly as if for all the world to hear.

"I've been doing these gigs for more than forty years!" she roared like a man.

The crowd chipped in with lots of whoops and cheers and a steady round of applause as Elisa pretended to fan herself with her hand.

"Thank you," she responded in an attempt to appear humble. "Thank you," she repeated with an approaching darkness.

The entire club had fallen into a hushed and expectant silence.

"Back in the day, when it was more ris-que," she quietly rhymed and chuckled to herself, her voice rumbling through the speakers. It might have been a catchphrase. It might have been part of the act, but the menace was palpable. Philip shifted in his seat, recalling Elisa's tagline on the posters as he'd walked in.

The Horrible and The Incorrigible.

"I don't mind people talking when I'm doing my thing," she started. "In fact, I cut my shiny eight-hundred-pound-a-piece veneers in places smaller than this, I can tell you. Northern working men's clubs mostly. Miners. Shipyard workers. 'Dockers', as they used to call them back in the day...when...it...was...*ohhh*...so...more..."

"RIS-QUE!" the audience shouted as one and roared laughter.

"You're so kind," she grinned wolfishly, her eyes constantly searching and roving. She took a deliberate moment to lope comically man-like to the side of the stage where a glass of something clear and iced awaited her on a high table. Strangely, Elisa was anything but camp. She was slightly hunched. She had long arms that swung by her side like a primate. When she took a slow sip of her drink someone made a noise as if the worst was yet to come. Her eyes were sharp as flint to the sound.

"You *should* be worried, mate," Elisa said in a plain male voice. Then lifted her head like a bear on the scent of something and making the entire audience take a trepid step backwards as if they had all stumbled upon a cliff edge.

"Fe-fo-fi-fum," she stomped towards them. "I smell the funk of someone's bum!"

The crowd erupted into raptures and took a good minute to die down while Elisa just trained those obsidian eyes on some poor unfortunate at the back. Creating ripple after ripple of laughter as everyone died down.

"I told you that you should be worried, mate," Elisa grinned manically.

The chuckling audience began looking around for the victim, whoever he was, hiding in the shadows.

"Why is it?" Elisa suddenly shouted as if to change the subject. "That when people say they're only joking they're usually making a point?"

An immediate and appreciative roar of laughter came to which Elisa only disregarded with a cynical look.

"My wife does it all the time," she took an exaggerated draw of breath and nodded to someone else. The crowd laughed nervously. "Yeah, I've been waiting a long time to throw that one in."

She used the little clicker in her hand and a women's face from the audience was suddenly lit up on the screen, looking embarrassed and shaking her head and hiding her eyes.

"Far be it from me to make a discriminatory assumption but you look like a relatively heterosexual female, luv. So what are you doing here amongst all us…'chimeras'?" she breathed deeply into the mic for accentuation and shared a wink with everyone else, "sorry, darling. Didn't catch that. You're what…?" she chuckled and asked the woman to repeat herself.

It took a moment for the woman to control herself. Elisa continued to smile politely and shrugged nonplussed at her tittering followers but with a look that suggested that this might be fun.

"Because I am… I'm your wife," she called back. "Your newly-wedded wife!" She continued to giggle and bury her face into a man standing next to her. She must have been about twenty years Elisa's junior but still a little too old for a pony-tail.

There was a sudden gasp of surprise and then a loud round of applause.

A snapshot appeared next on the big drop screen of a man in full motorcycle attire. A glossy black helmet painted in flames in his hand. Posing on a Harley.

Philip did a double-take. It was Elisa. There was no wig or make-up or anything remotely give-a-way to his profession. He had let his grey beard grow. Those gleaming ice-white veneer teeth bounced back against the light. Underneath all that disguise was a very handsome man probably in his late fifties. It made Philip want to shift around in his seat.

"That's me in my heterosexual mufti," she turned to admire herself.

There were a few wolf-whistles. One or two gasps of appreciation.

"Yes, people will always make assumptions but I like to keep my private life private outside of the bitchy glamour industry I choose to work in," she adjusted her wig and pouted for comedic effect. "You'll never see me in the newspapers. Chance would be a fine thing," she pulled a face and flounced.

The crowd laughed and clapped.

"I love you, baby," Elisa suddenly said, and blew a kiss to her wife, her eyes gleaming.

"Love you, Daddy!" she called back, jumping up and down on the spot like a teenager at her first concert. "Love you sooo…so much." She blew kisses back at him.

It really was a tender moment. Their hands reached across the crowd as if separated by water. Their sincerity for each other was palpable. Why should a fifty-odd-year-old man dressed in drag and a woman young enough to be his daughter have it all? Philip couldn't ever remember feeling so dismayed. It had to be part of the act.

"Ahhh," the crowd sighed in unison.

It took a moment for Elisa's eyes to stop shining towards his wife and turn his attention back to the audience.

"So…" he appeared to take a big emotional breath. "As I was saying, I don't mind people talking when I'm doing my routine. You're all here for a drink and a chat and a good time. I don't expect everyone to sing along. Less music and more muzak. That's me," she admitted brightly. "That's elevator music to you, honey. Not some new health food," Elisa leaned forward and said to someone at the front. "No offence but you look like you're into all that shit," she growled.

"I am!" the guy made the mistake of replying.

Elisa did a double-take as if she wasn't used to being addressed.

"Yeah? Well, it aint fucking working," she chirped. "Not being funny mate but I've seen better skin on a dried date."

This brought about a roar of laughter and applause.

"And the date was eighteen-hundred-and-fucking-ten!" she announced with an exaggerated prance around the stage a la Mick Jagger courtesy of a blast of 'Brown Sugar' from the music sequencer.

The club erupted into laughter for a full minute or two as Elisa stood patiently waiting, clutching the microphone with both hands and smiling and nodding at individuals in the audience as if she knew each and every one of them until it eventually subsided into a smattering of titters and giggles.

"It's alright," she said, adopting a high-pitched voice that was obviously supposed to be an impersonation of Elisa's wife. "I'm only joking!" Another explosion of laughter. Elisa's eyes twinkled. She gave a reassuring wink to her victim then blew another kiss to her wife.

"Daddy!" she could be heard calling.

It was clear Elisa was enjoying herself.

"Talking of making a point," she said, a little breathlessly. "I wish I could stick to mine. Where was I? Oh, yes. People talking while I'm singing or whatnot," she waved a hand irrelevantly, flicking her bracelets back down her thick wrist. Then suddenly brought her attention back to Philip with a big flouncy turn. Philip's face appeared on the screen.

Oh…my…God, Philip thought. And turned away.

"So, as I say, people come here to have a good time. I can't always be the centre of attention, I know. That's fine. I get it. 'What can I expect but a cuff or a blow'," she suddenly quoted John Hurt's adaptation of Quentin Crisp in *The Naked Civil Servant*. "When I say 'blow' that's physical not oral, sunshine," she looked at someone else in the audience with a judgmental frown.

Another burst of laughter.

"But what I can't stand is having someone's hairy old worn-out fundament, his sagging 'sphincter' turned towards me while I'm doing stand-up. I mean, that's just plain disrespectful, innit?" she asked, adopting a street accent with a fishwife's teapot stance. "He's not even getting a drink at the bar. I mean, does he even know I'm speaking to him?"

Philip could feel himself beginning to cringe. He hated being exposed like this. To have everyone watching him on that screen. For at least thirty seconds Elisa just stared at the table where Philip was seated. A mounting tension of amusement rose in the audience. Alex continued looking at him with an expression of quiet retribution, a flicker of a smile at the corners of his mouth. Those thick full sensual lips. Plump as ripe fruit. Philip could sense what was happening. Someone else was going to get a licking. And that someone was him. He hadn't come here for this. Why didn't the old has-been of a drag queen just stay out of it and mind her own business?

"What's going on with that little menage-a-trois over there anyway? That's what I want to know," Elisa finally called. "It's an unlikely looking trio, isn't it?" she resounded breathlessly into the microphone and asked everyone. The invisible camera panned out to show all three seated at the front of the stage. "What are you Elton their little gimp or something? Oi, Elton! You old candle blower. I'm talking to you. What's going on?"

"Nothing," Philip called desperately over his shoulder.

"He actually answers to the name of Elton," Elisa said in wonderment and paused, before wandering around the stage in an apparent confused state.

The crowd began to snigger but once again not without a certain amount of tension and uncertainty.

"It's like a cheap celebrity look-a-like convention on that table, isn't it? You got Elton and his Norma Jean there and…and…*hmmm*, who can we liken that handsome brute to. Anyone?" she invited the audience.

"Rock Hudson!" somebody immediately shouted.

"Rock Hudson," Elisa repeated, putting the tip of her false-nailed ruby-red index finger between her puckered lips as if to contemplate. "I know what you mean about keeping it in the same era and all that. Yes, I like your thinking, mate. I'm going to go with that. Especially as I can work it into my next joke… as old as it is," she confided out of the side of her mouth in a half-whisper. "Rock Hudson it is then. So…Rock Hudson," she announced loudly, and turned towards the sea of expectant faces held under her spell all with ready-made grins. From Philip's angle they looked like a horde of stupid-faced Disney minions. "Hollywood's beefcake who, as it turned out… was actually a cupcake."

The crowd guffawed as one. Even stony-faced Cinders. Even Rock Hudson threw his head back and sat for a long time shaking his head and chortling, sweeping his glossy dark locks from his two-tone eyes.

Everyone laughed but Philip.

"My wife and I love playing that game, don't you?" Elisa continued. "Sitting at an airport or whatever and spotting look-a-likes. Back in the day-"

"…when it was so RIS-QUE!" the crowd swooped.

"No," Elisa held up a hand and began chuckling uncontrollably. "I really meant it that time." She took a moment to compose herself. "Seriously, you are so kind. And may I take this moment and say thank you once again for turning up in all your supportive droves, I love you all!!!"

"Daddy, I love you!" Elisa's wife could be heard calling again amongst all the whoops and whistles.

Elisa's eyes shone brightly and for a moment looked genuinely moved.

"Sooo…so much, Daddy. With all my heart and soul."

Again, Elisa appeared emotional to the point of tears and blew another fond kiss towards her.

"I'd cut off my pinky for you!" she exclaimed.

The crowd roared and cheered and whooped.

"Two pinkies!" she continued.

"Baby…" he held up a hand and tried calming her with a warm smile that was so outside of the Horrible and Incorrigible it almost melted the crowd into a reverential silence.

All the while Philip just felt himself wanting to crawl away into a hole. He didn't know if it was the cosy contentment of Alex and Cinders sitting in their VIP spot, the obnoxious drag queen and her adoring young wife or the almost familial togetherness of the club that for some reason seemed intent on excluding him. Every joke directed at him so far had been homophobic. That wasn't funny. Everyone in the room should know that. He had lived the life of an outcast for most of his years and yet in a place where he should have experienced acceptance he was being made to feel like some sort of social pariah.

"In my mufti I once got mistaken for Roger Moore," Elisa continued, nodding and looking pleased with herself.

"You mean Demi Moore!" Elisa's wife called out. "You're beautiful, baby!"

"Actually, I think it was my safari suit that did it but I'll take either any day of the week," Elisa smiled as the laughter subsided. "So…any other celebrity look-a-likes in tonight?" she called.

"Will Smith!" someone called out.

Elisa spun on her heels. Shielding her eyes towards the voice. Someone was pointing to their friend. They came up on screen.

"Racist," she muttered dismissively.

The audience erupted as one.

Elisa stood cupping the mic like a chalice. Nodding and smiling at people in turn until everyone settled down.

"Of course, Norma Jean, who as you are all no doubt aware was more famously known as Marilyn Monroe, was rumoured to have died her pubic hair with bleach so that the carpet would match the drapes. So…what about it, Norma?" she suddenly asked Cinders.

The crowd gave out a rumble of suppressed laughter. Someone snickered loudly.

"Wouldn't you like to know," she replied, making a big statement about crossing her legs.

A few people whooped and cheered in her defence.

Elisa blinked and made a pretense of hiding her blushes. "Wow! What just happened there? Talk about a Sharon Stone moment. I'm not sure if that was a trick-of-the-light, a quivering bush or if you're still awaiting the operation."

Elisa nodded and winked as Cinders gave her the finger.

"Something moved in there I swear," she engaged the audience with an affirmative nod as they fell into hysterics.

It was like a fucking self-appreciation society in here, thought Philip. Who at least was glad the attention had been turned from him.

"Of course, no one has pubic hair anymore, do they?" Elisa spoke seriously as the crowd died down. "No one really has a 'bush'," she whispered, tittering like a naughty schoolgirl behind her hand. "Hmmm, it's gone a little quiet so I'll tell you what. Hands up here who isn't shaven," she spoke up loudly. "Come on, don't be shy. I'm genuinely interested in your disgusting clock-spring pubic hygiene. You know you shred it, don't you? In your bed, in your clothes, in whatever orifice you partake in. I can't remember the time I last got one between my teeth or at the back of my throat because I just won't go there. It's a put off. Frankly, people like you are just apes and belong in a fucking museum. Fucking hairy-armpit, privet-hedged, Europeans have got a lot to answer for. And don't even get me started on circumcision. There's a reason the French make the best cheese, you know."

More raucous and nervous laughter.

"You'll never look at Roquefort in the same way again will you, sweetheart?" she addressed another woman in the crowd.

The crowd began to look at each other suspiciously. If they weren't shaved or circumcised they suddenly wanted to be or say they were.

"Look, I have no problem with a bit of topiary. A Brazilian or a Hitler. But just fucking keep it under control," Elisa advised sagely.

"Why don't you put your hand up, Philip?" Alex asked lowly amidst the stirring clamour.

For a moment Philip had forgotten that he was still sat there quietly watching him.

"What?" Philip turned to see both Alex and Cinders studying him like a swayed jury.

"Put your hand up," he repeated darkly. "You're not shaved you hairy old cunt so put your fucking hand up."

"What? *Why*? No," Philip hissed.

"What's the matter, Philip? Don't like people knowing your business? Put your fucking hand up or I'll say it," he said menacingly. "He has a grey bush!" Alex suddenly announced and pointed.

"Yes!" Elisa announced gloriously. "Our own Silver Daddy with his disgusting silver bush. I bet he has a silver back, too, doesn't he? The old lycanthrope." Elisa lowered her voice and nodded furiously as if it was just between Alex and her. "Hmmm… though, I suppose you know what my next question is to you now don't you, Rock?"

"How do I know about his silver bush, Elisa?" Alex projected his voice deliberately.

"Yes, how do you know about his big curly disgusting unshaven silver bush whose tiny uncircumcised frog of a cock has never seen the inside of his flies let alone daylight, Rock, if…you don't mind my asking," Elisa answered sweetly, and fluttered her eyelashes at the audience.

What the hell was happening? Philip plunged his face into his hands amidst the near-hysterical laughter.

"I don't mind you asking in the slightest, Elisa," Alex answered. "Well, let me see now. For a start he has bombarded my sister with enough pictures of it for one thing."

Philip looked up at Alex mortified. Why would he even *admit* to that?

"And anyone else in my contact list," Alex added. "Describing in detail what I thought were intimate moments between us. Shared pictures forwarded by hundreds of emails to work colleagues. Clients. Just about everyone on my phone. In particular, he likes to tell people I meet men in bushes for sex. Which, incidentally, I don't. He's sent graphic texts to my mother and my poor frail ninety-year-old grandmother who I only bought a mobile for last year so we could all keep in touch. He didn't know who he was contacting. He didn't care. My family didn't even know I was gay.

Though they've probably suspected it. As you say, Elisa. I prefer not to talk about my private life. That should be my prerogative. Anyway, they sure know now. Everyone does," he laughed to himself, reaching over and squeezing Cinders hand.

The laughter had turned to shock. The audience sounded aghast with near horror.

"He has stalked me for the last six months. He has found out where I work and live. He knows everything about me. I knew he was off. I knew he was possessive. I finally left when his previous lover contacted me. A man he is still so obsessed with he keeps his toothbrush in a jar waiting for his return. That's me now. He still thinks I'm coming back. Anyway, this guy before you, Philip – it's Philip not Elton, his ex, saw us out one day and tracked me down. We went for a drink. The poor man has had to change his address three times. Philip always finds him. That's been going on for nearly ten years."

Philip spun round and glared hatefully at Elisa who was making a mockery out of being shocked. Bringing a hand to her powder-puffed face and encouraging the audience with her wide-eyed, false-eyelash outrage.

"But surely the police…?" Elisa left the sentence trailing.

It was a set-up, Philip began to realise. The VIP table right by the stage. The way the two were interacting. Even an overhead microphone had dropped ever-so-cautiously down from the shadows on a mechanical arm so that every word could be amplified. Philip could see people in the audience holding up their mobile phones. This could go viral, he recoiled in horror.

"He, Philip, has several convictions for harassment I was to discover. He has at this very moment a restraining order to keep away from me but which of course he has failed to do by following me in here and as I know, dear friend, you will happily testify to. Usually he just waits outside my office, my places of lunch, my train rides. My *home*. And of course, the constant abuse through the network. If I didn't have very understanding employers, supportive friends and family he could have done to me what he did to the other guy. And that was to ruin his life."

"Fucking freak," Cinders chipped in lowly. Her carefully pedicured hands had curled into tight bejeweled fists. Philip feared he/she hadn't been taking enough MTF hormones. Just the thought of violence made him nauseous and want to run.

"Booooo!" the audience started to roar. "BOOOOOOO!"

Philip covered his ears to the sound.

"He trashed my car."

"You mean this car?" Elisa flicked the tiny remote held in her hand and an image flashed up on the screen of a white Mercedes daubed in red painted words: PHONY LYING PHANTOM.

"Hmm…'phony, lying, phantom.' Could be the name of a new heavy metal band. PLP. It has rather a nice resonance to it, don't you think?" Elisa continued to whip up the audience. "I have to admit though that apart from the distress it must have caused you and the blatant criminal damage, I've been called a lot worse in my time, Rock."

Elisa pulled a face to a suppressed wave of laughter.

Alex conceded the point with a nod.

It was an act! Philip's hysteria began to escalate. It was all a fucking act!

"I agree," Alex said, "but when the same words are applied to a crazed, intimidating rant over the phone you might think otherwise."

He held his mobile up to the overhead mic.

"Go fuck yourself!" Philip's shrill, helter-skelter-like rage quickly reached an ear-piercing fever pitch of abuse. "You motherfucking fuck! You cock-sucking dick! Get out of my life! You King of Liars! False advertiser! Phony phantom FUCK! Go sell your bullshit to some frigid lonely housewife with snaggletooth pups. Go back in the bushes! Maybe you'll get lucky. I beat my head against a wall all week and for what? A cum-swallowing five minute blow-job? Never speak to me again. You hateful, evil, spiteful motherfucking cunt of a man! Man's too good for you. Bitch-man! That's what you are. You fucking disgraceful arsehole! Hateful motherfucking fuck! There's no going back now. It's over. You've sealed your coffin. Forget me. Damage done. Cunt bitch!"

A shocked hush descended upon the crowd.

"Well, very colourful, I must say," Elisa gushed and fanned herself as if flushed with embarrassment. "But apart from the fact he sounds like he spends too much time watching Tarantino movies what the hell was that about, Rock?"

"Obviously, I have volumes of this stuff," Alex answered with a heavy sigh. "But this particular one was in response to a text I sent him apologizing that I wouldn't be able to make a karaoke night with some friends of his. I honestly quite intended to go right up until the last minute. I didn't want to let him down but I also knew it couldn't go on."

Philip was crouched down in his seat and peeked out at Alex between his entangled arms like a five-year-old. Was that even true?

"He looks harmless enough sitting there but anyone who has ever lived with something like this will tell you the same thing," Alex offered a brief look of compassion towards Philip and then sat up in his chair and raised his voice. Talking directly to the gathering as if it was a referendum of some kind.

Why didn't he just shut the fuck up?

"It shreds your nerves. It saps your confidence and eats into your self-esteem. Every day is a concern. You are ever anxious, ever watchful and ever fearful. It's worse than anything you can imagine. It is overwhelming and the truth is I don't even think he knows what he is doing. Philip is sick. I've no idea whether he knows it or not."

But that's how I felt each time you left me, Philip wailed inside, hugging himself. Torturing me with your long absences. Your unreturned texts and calls. Your absence of emojis when I sent you pages, reams, overloaded megabytes of them. Sweet patterns in heart or flower shapes. But you always only ever responded with one. A stupid wink. A blown fucking kiss. They're fucking free you know! You stupid fake cunt!

It took a moment for Philip to realise the club had fallen completely silent and appeared to be waiting for him to reply. No one was laughing anymore. He peered over his elbow, feeling like a cornered animal. All eyes were agog. There was a chink of glasses over by the bar. Elisa looked down upon him disapprovingly with her arms crossed and the mother of all stinky faces. It was as if Philip had brought a happy wedding ceremony in full flow to a standstill with one crass and inappropriate comment in a speech about the bride.

Slowly, he untangled himself and got to his feet. Standing up straight and patting himself down.

"Well," he coughed, taking a moment to look at his overblown image on the big screen. He looked like an unctuous, giant, sweaty fat toad. "It appears I have outstayed my welcome," he uttered almost inaudibly.

Alex crossed his legs and arms and watched him go.

"Never contact me again, Philip," he called. "You asked for it. It's over."

Philip kept his head down as the audience silently parted to let him through.

"Loser," someone said.

"Fucking sad case," said another.

"Crawl back under your stone."

Philip made it into the late night air never feeling so relieved. Oh, the indignity of it all. The opprobrium. The contrivance! When he looked over his shoulder as he hurried down the street he thought someone had followed him out. Perhaps even to give him a good beating. It felt strange to think he had sensed some homophobia in a place like that. But he had, oh yes. At least Philip knew who he was. He couldn't say the same for Alex, or Cinders, or Elisa. That plotting triumvirate. He rushed towards the station shaking his head. Pulling his coat tight around him. Talking to himself.

"You alright there, mate?" someone stood in his way as Philip brushed past.

"Piss off!" Philip hissed.

"Whoa!" the guy held up his hands as his friends suddenly roared laughter.

"Faggot!" one of them called after him.

"Takes one to know one," Philip called over his shoulder, cocking a snoot at him.

But the group of young men just literally collapsed in hysterics, folding in on each other like a house of cards, coughing and choking. It seemed the joke was always on him. Philip's hateful gaze told them he wished he had each and every one of their phone numbers and emails and friends and families addresses. They wouldn't be laughing then. And almost as if they sensed something, they gave up and moved on. If it hadn't been for the buzzing night crowd of London and everyone streaming to or from the station Philip might have been more fearful. He'd been on the end of a good kick-in or two just for being who he was and he knew a few friends who had got it worse. One had died with an internal brain hemorrhage. You had to keep your wits about you.

Once he reached the busy concourse crowded with late-night drinkers he saw he still had twenty minutes to wait for the last train. He looked around for the men's toilets and felt an old stirring. Thirty-pence to take a leak was an outrage. But of course it was just another deterrent along with twenty-four-hour attendants and security cameras upon entry. Nothing was the same anymore. Apart from hugely trafficked areas like stations and airports and shopping malls public toilets hardly existed.

In the old days men's lavatories were prime meeting places for quick and anonymous sex. They all had the same smell of piss and bleach. They all looked like fairy-tale cottages with their pitched rooves and tiny illuminated leaded windows and equally a mystery always awaited within. In the cubicles scrawled messages on the walls leaving dates and times to meet were commonplace. Phone numbers. Graphic graffiti depictions of oral and anal sex. Sometimes tiny spy holes or even bigger glory holes had been bored out for mutual relief of some description.

Philip's first experience had been as a sixteen-year-old. He had been on his way to school to pick up his GCSE results. There had been a recent local newspaper article about the public toilets in the park reporting that a father and his two-year-old son had walked in on two men having sex. After Philip had read that he always walked through the park and stopped off at the toilets to and from school.

Encountering strangers in there had been his sexual awakening.

He paid his money and went through the turnstile. The toilets were bright and clean and empty. The attendant was hidden behind two-way glass. Philip walked to the back of the toilet and found a urinal in the corner lingering as long as he dare. No one came down. The evening's whole ordeal had left him strangely frustrated. His chemicals were stirring. His heart fluttered a little. He could feel himself growing in his hand. He wished for one more weekend with Alex. Or to have that first night in the hotel room with him all over again. Perhaps he should just write him a letter apologizing for everything and hoping they could stay friends. That maybe they could meet up once in a while or for a weekend. He stroked himself a little more and then moved to the sinks and began washing his hands. At that point a young guy with long dark hair and carrying a backpack slung over one shoulder entered and their eyes locked in the mirror above the hand-basins. Philip hesitated. Not daring to hope he had caught a fish at the first time of asking. He knew he had loitered long enough. That the invisible attendant might already be getting suspicious. But Philip continued to massage his hands slowly. Watching the young man in the reflection who had already half-turned his head once in Philip's direction. Another few seconds passed. Philp could feel his throat going dry. He wanted for all the world to move up alongside him but he couldn't be sure and his legs had turned to lead just the way Alex had told him his would do when watching men disappear into bushes and fighting the desire to follow them. Philip waited and waited and then there it was. A full-frontal exposure as the man turned to zip up. A nice size, Philip noted. A good girth. Unshaven but circumcised, incidentally. Dark red pubic hair. He shook himself long enough for Philip to take in all the details. Staring at Philip all the time. When he finished he casually walked over to the sinks and pumped the soap dispenser more than was necessary so that a huge puddle of the semi-transparent liquid collected in his palm. He gazed at Philip again. His dark brown eyes softer this time.

"Have you had a good evening?" Philip surprised himself by asking.

The man was a boy. A few years younger than he'd first thought. Maybe twenty. He had a scruffy growth of beard that grew in patches. His eyes twinkled as he pulled his mouth into an ironic smirk. "Well, I've missed my connecting train," he shrugged.

"Oh dear," Philip replied.

"Oh dear is right," he repeated. "I'm on my way back to university and now I have nowhere to sleep. I can't go home again."

"Why not?" Philip tried enquiring in a casual tone, but already his mind was racing.

"I had a fallout with my Dad," he sniffed. "He doesn't agree with my…'lifestyle'. It seems I have disappointed him. That's the last time I go home for the weekend," he added, then jerked his head at the attendant's cubicle. "Do you think anyone's in there?" he called loudly. "Pervert!" he shouted and laughed.

Philip flinched at the sound and then laughed a little nervously too. He'd been cautioned on more than once occasion by transport police for loitering.

They hung around the platform chatting like old friends. The boy didn't appear to want to leave. Philip discovered they lived in the same area. They knew the same pubs and clubs. The places to go. He even knew the apartment block where Philip lived. Nice view of the sea, he said. Half-view, Philip corrected. And they both laughed. He told Philip he had slept in the same bedroom all his life. A box room in a three-bedroom semi with a view of the street and a bus stop where he still couldn't stop playing his childhood game of guessing how many people stood waiting just before he looked. We've probably walked right past each other at some time or other, he reflected. They both nodded and held each other's gaze for a time. You should stay, Philip said spontaneously. Or at least that's how it sounded. In truth he had been desperate to say it from the moment they had started to talk. But he shouldn't come across too eager. The boy smiled and hitched his backpack further up his shoulder. They both knew what the invitation meant. Did you like what you saw? he asked Philip boldly. Philip felt his loins tingle. Very much, he answered a little breathlessly. The boy smirked and gave Philip a sidelong look as if he was still contemplating the offer. He reminded Philip of his younger self. How much braver he would get each time he visited the men's toilet on the way to and from school. The regulars quickly got to know his routine. He began visiting it in his lunchbreak and the wait for the next weekend when he would be out all day became unbearable. Then there had been the long summer holiday of that year. They all wanted the young boy. Philip's eyes grew glassy at the memory. Sometimes there were groups of them. Mostly old men. It excited him to be desired. To be abused. He let them do anything they wanted. They pushed him around from one to the other. Urging each other on in croaky whispers. Both aroused and disgusted by him. Disgusted by themselves. Before going back to their families or whatever lives they led. The floor left spattered in semen. He got high on the danger of being caught or what might happen to him. He didn't care. He continually fantasised about it. Sometimes one of them guarded the door and they would strip him naked. They forced themselves in him. He wanted it. He wanted their love. He wanted their rough and depraved and secret sex. He craved the attention and craved it still. As old as he was. Except that now the shoe was on the other foot. He wasn't in control anymore. He was despairing and lacking and lonesome and frightened of being left on his own. Of being marginalised. Of growing old and never finding love. Most of all love. He had old pictures of himself that had amazed Alex. When he had been lithe and young with a good head of hair. When all manner of men had wanted him. When he was the one who could pick and choose much like Alex. Much like the boy standing right next to him with the power to say yes or no.

Where have you been tonight? the boy wanted to know. To see an old friend, Philip replied. The boy stood nodding. Have you got a spare toothbrush? he asked. Philip smiled slowly. Several, he said.

FRANKLIN STREET (THE BEAUTY AND THE PAIN)

'Google knows everything…'

It was the song that brought her round. It was playing over and over in her head. Or at least that's what she thought. She was going to wake up with a song in her head and it was going to annoy her for the rest of the day.

'But Google doesn't know a thing
About the way I feel for you,
Baby.'
Wake up.

She tried opening her eyes. They felt leaden and ever so sleepy. She was coming round from anaesthetic. That's what it was. She knew the feeling. She must be in hospital. It would come back to her why she was in there. She just needed a little more rest. A little more sleepies. Shleepies. That's how she would send Kimberly off to bed when she was a baby. Shleepies… Where was Kimberly? But the song wouldn't stop. It sounded so familiar. Where had she heard it…?

If Adam had just made up any old lines to the song she might never have even known it was him. It was the closing act to a chat show. Her six-year-old daughter, Kimberly, had asked to stay up and watch the band. As it was the weekend Zoe had agreed, getting up without the slightest interest to empty the dishwasher as the music started. She didn't listen to the charts anymore and old songs just made her feel, well, old. But the unmistakable refrain lured her back into the living-room like a charm. How long since they had split? Eight, nine years ago now? With her accusing him of being a loser and having no intention of ever settling down and starting a family or getting a proper job (he had a business studies degree), of going back on all the things he had promised, commitment, mostly - instead of dreaming away his life about being a singer in a band.

Come on, really?

When she walked back into the living-room, Simon, her partner, and Kimberly were perched on the edge of the settee, holding hands and swaying along to the chorus as if they had front row seats at a concert. He looked across his shoulder at Zoe and just shrugged happily. His and her daughter's earlier spat apparently forgotten. Simon could get a bit heavy-handed about playing the paternal role and had threatened to send Kimberly to bed twice already in the full knowledge that she had asked to stay up. He could get a bit heavy-handed about a lot of things since he'd moved in and began contributing towards the rent and the bills and allowing Zoe to work part-time and be able to pick her kid up from school. He had a successful roofing company and they had been together for two years so it was a natural progression and it did at least make her life easier but sometimes she just wasn't sure it was worth the extra attention he demanded of her. She never used to be so accommodating. It wasn't in her nature. She used to stick up for herself. If not for her child's lifestyle being improved as a result Zoe might never have even agreed to it. Most of all she just wanted Kimberly to grow up with some sort of father figure in her life. But Simon behaved more like a child himself with his incessant needs and immature behavior around her daughter.

"Who are – what are these called?" she raised her voice over the noise and squinted her eyes towards the screen. It was a four piece band with the classic format of lead and bass guitarists, a drummer and vocalist.

"Shhh, Mum," Kimberly responded. "Let me hear them."

And then she and Simon broke into the chorus again.

'Because Google knows everything
Oh yeah
Big brother Google
Thinks it knows everything
But Google doesn't know a thing
About the way I feel for you,
Baby.'

And then there he was. A close-up on camera. Almost unrecognizable with his dark scruffy beard and shoulder-length hair. He had lost weight, too. By at least a couple of stone which he had always been self-conscious about and thought it made his front-man aspirations even less likely. His dress sense had got worse. She was always trying to tidy him up and get him to conform. Her father had been a banker. Her two older brothers were traders. Likewise her earlier boyfriends. She'd grown up around sharp-suited men and at first Adam's casual indifference to his appearance had been part of the attraction. He wasn't preened or perfumed or proud. But the torn vest and ragged jeans and fingerless gloves he wore on TV made her want to laugh out loud. He looked like an overgrown skateboarder. His entire right arm was a tattooed sleeve now. He looked straight at the camera as the music came to an abrupt halt, those watery blue eyes glittering as if sunlit the same way they did when he would talk passionately about his writing. His 'work'. Zoe would mock him when he called it that. Being raised in a conventional household with men using their brains for business instead of investing so much time and effort in what she only saw as some glorified hobby. But she knew the next line even before he uttered them to the adoring audience in the studio. To all the Simons and Kimberlys in all the living-rooms all over the country.

For a moment it seemed his special look was just for her. She silently mouthed the words along with him.

'We live in a must-know society.
But isn't it all about the not knowing.'

He lamented rhetorically and dropped his head for effect. Taking one step back from the mic but still holding it outstretched with his emblazoned arm.

The studio audience cheered rapturously. Kimberly squealed and clapped her hands in quick succession. Simon sat back and announced gruffly: "I keep hearing that in the truck. They're good. That song's got Number One written all over it."

Simon could say some stupid things but he was right about that. It stayed at the top of the charts for six weeks all over the summer.

The host came on and struggled to wrap up the show over the noise so began shouting as the credits rolled up.

"So it's good night from me and all our guests and a big good night from Franklin Street. You heard them here first!"

"Didn't you live on a street called Franklin, Mum?" Kimberly spun round and asked excitedly.

Zoe was still in too much shock to answer. She nodded dreamily. It was him, she thought. It was Adam. And he had used the very same lines of a poem he had sent her years before and turned it into a song.

Simon stood up and yawned and brushed past her, whistling the chorus.

"'Google thinks it knows everything...'" he wiggled his eyebrows, appearing in an unusually good mood. He rounded on her, his eyes giving off a familiar glint that was less about rousing desire these days than clinical expectation and triggered off a creeping sickness in her. He had recently started to shave and polish his head to a billiard ball sheen. He could make her skin crawl. That wasn't right. That wasn't good.

He jumped back round the other side as if to take her by surprise with his arms outstretched, smiling and singing at the top of his off-key lungs. "But they don't know a thing about how I feel for you, Baby!"

"Google doesn't," Kimberly corrected.

"What?" Simon said, frowning, his arms still about to embrace Zoe who could already feel herself tightening. It was his big stevedore chest and almost abnormally swollen biceps that had first appealed to her but now they just made her heart race with apprehension each time he expanded himself in such a way. As if to swallow her up like some monstrous clam. Just the weight of him on top of her was enough to leave her fighting against panic. Knowing that the more she did the more he seemed to like it.

"It's 'Google' doesn't know a thing – not 'they,'" Kimberly said.

Zoe gave Simon a confused, distracted look as he appeared to be waiting for her to play the arbitrator, but she hadn't been listening. Adam's song still filled her head. The words might just sound like corny, trite pop sentiments to anyone else but only she could know. All his poems had come from the heart. She loved to receive them. It was her best memory of him.

"Isn't it time for little girls to get to bed," Simon's jocular mood suddenly changed to one of irritation.

"Yes, go to bed, Kimberly, there's a good girl," Zoe said automatically.

"You can't just say it because he said so," she pouted. "He's not my dad."

"Yeah, well why don't you call your dad and ask him if you can stay up then, eh?" Simon jeered, a case in point he was apt to use and one which could normally bring Kimberly to tears. But the little girl's face just reddened in frustration, clenching her fists and thumping down on the settee cushions as if about to combust. Simon laughed to himself and nodded at Kimberly to Zoe as if she should join in on the teasing.

"She'll be bending her fingers back next. See if I'm right, babe," he encouraged Zoe. "Oh, hang on," he prowled around Kimberly with his hands on his hips. "I forgot. You haven't got your dad's number because you don't even know where he is."

Sure enough the little girl began to bend her fingers back so hard her palm went white.

"Stop it, Si," Zoe said under her breath, knowing he wouldn't be happy until he had made Kimberly cry.

"You don't even know where he lives," he whined as if to mimic her.

"Ahhhrghh!" Kimberly growled. She jumped up and bent them harder as if to prove that she meant it. Red blotches began to appear.

"Si…" Zoe warned. "Leave her alone."

"Anyway, you're lucky I'm not your dad. I wouldn't have you talking like that to me or your mother if you were my little girl. You'd be over my knee in a second young lady getting a good spank-"

"Go to bed!" Zoe suddenly erupted. "And stop threatening her with violence. I don't hit my kid. Just shut up the pair of you. I'm sick of your constant arguing."

Zoe stormed off and went up to the bathroom and locked herself in, hearing the soft creeping shocked silence from downstairs as both of them tiptoed up the stairs and went quietly to their rooms. She turned off the light and sat on the seat and hugged herself in the dark, rocking to and fro.

What was the matter with her? Why was she reacting like this after all the time that had passed? She felt sick. Zoe knew this feeling from long ago. The all-consuming anxiety. The inability to concentrate. She and Adam would fall out for weeks. She'd been strong in those days, but that strength could lead to an irrational recalcitrance. They both believed in what they wanted. And then, more often than not, he would send her a poem, and she knew he had been thinking and hurting and feeling the same things as she. Hearing that song, turning them into lines, had sent her rocketing back in time. He could bring her back with his words. He had always been able to bring her back. The poem had been called, 'I Didn't Know'. The subject being about the first time they had ever met. He called upon all the twists of fate and chance and coincidence that had brought them together on that first night. He romanced it. He had made it sound meant. But then, he could make you believe a lot of things with his words. After all, they had only met in a bar like a lot of people do.

Leaving him had been the hardest thing she'd ever done.

Probably he'd had a flashback and the phrase just fit the song, she began reasoning.

'Google knows everything...'

Yet already she could feel a deep, age-old anger burning as if they were in the midst of one of their ongoing altercations. Rows that could go on for weeks with neither one budging. You have commercialised a poem into a pop song you wrote for me! She wanted to scream.

'But Google doesn't know a thing...'

It was written to her.

'About the way I feel for you...'

About his feelings for her.

'Baby.'

Zoe knew where the poems were. But she couldn't very well go rooting around for them now. She had to calm down. They were his words after all and so ultimately his property, she supposed. Probably he just remembered the phrase, she told herself again. It was quite a clever gimmick using Google when you thought about it. Everyone could relate to it. She could see that now. In fact, it had been a gimmick using it on her, she was suddenly dismayed to admit. Which didn't make it a very romantic poem at all. If he could turn it into a song how did she know he hadn't used the same phrase on other women? And with that thought in mind, she went to bed.

Wake up.

But she didn't want to. Not yet. She was aching. In a way that you knew to move might hurt or cause more serious injury. Why didn't the nurses bring something for the pain? She opened her mouth to speak but realised she was just dribbling instead. No sound came. She managed to force one bleary eye open. She must be dreaming. She was in her bedroom. Face down on her bed with her head turned on the pillow. She looked around the room as much as she could. Everything was normal and in its place as far as she could see. Everything was normal but she somehow knew that everything was not.

What quickly became apparent, however, was that all the words in the song were taken from the poem. Not only that, the song was entitled 'I Didn't Know,' and not anything to do with the catchy chorus she had only heard that first night and just assumed involved the line 'Google knows everything.' She hadn't thought about it. It hadn't occurred to her that he had turned the entire poem into a song. The first he had ever written her.

'I didn't know you when I walked in the bar
I didn't know the match score either,
I knew I wanted a beer and a burger
But couldn't find a place to sit amidst
The football fan fever
'"The football fan fever…"
"Football fan fever…"

All right, those last few lines sung like a supporters' chant hadn't been in the original poem and she didn't know whether to be mad about him for sullying the text or not. Even if it did have the desired effect and had everyone joining in the mantra infectiously as if roaring on their team from the stands. What was most strange was hearing her daughter sing along to it. Or driving in the car to the supermarket and hearing Simon's caterwauling strangulation of the heartfelt prose she had once read over and over and that she had come to learn off-by-heart. Many times when moving she had deliberated over throwing them away. But she couldn't. She didn't think anyone could. People still found love letters in attics written a century ago. And that's what they were essentially. A beautifully open declaration of his love for her.

And then of course she continued to hear it everywhere else she went. In cafes and bars and then most surreal of all, the first time she saw the video of Adam when she had been working-out in the gym. There had been no dressing the thing up. He had re-enacted their first meeting with unsettling and precise detail. Except that the girl in the film wasn't her and the set only a mock-up of the crowded sports bar full of TV screens that had been at the end of the street where she used to live. Then there were the St. Patrick's Day pennants (the owner was Irish). And the one vacant stool at the end of the counter where he was filmed entering on his own before going through the act of not noticing her at first. Ordering a beer and craning his neck to watch the match before striking up a conversation with her friend, Phoebe, to his right, the girl she had been with on the day and had since lost contact with. Then, when the seat next to Zoe had been vacated he moved himself round next to her to get a better view of the TV, but even then went on to become engaged with the guy to his right (which had been the way it was), as they began silently gesticulating about the match for the purpose of the video. The camera then focused on the two actresses playing Zoe and her friend, with Phoebe deliberately nudging Zoe on to initiate a conversation with him, which, again, was pretty much the way it had been. Except that since that time Zoe had cut off all her long wavy auburn hair.

'I could never have known
I would be calling you 'Missy', then
I didn't even know your name
Not then…'

Missy. His name for her from the very beginning. It arrested her every time she heard it. And she must have heard the song ten or twenty times by then. A jolt would go through her body, causing an involuntary flinch or shudder and she would stop what she was doing, sometimes drifting off into a deep trance and hearing his voice, his laugh, a thousand different conversations reverberating through her mind. Missy. He used it endearingly, reprovingly, lovingly. Behave yourself, Missy. Hearing it in the song evoked even the tiniest, faintest flashbacks and snapshots and (she might have gone the rest of her life not knowing this) the all-but-forgotten little sweet-nothings that lingered deep in her memory. Just be a good girl, Missy. It was like she'd been hypnotised. She used to like the inside of her arm being stroked while going off to sleep just the way her father used to do. She still did. But it had to be done right. Feathery. Light. And brushed with the back of the fingertips. Simon prodded her like a laptop but Adam was an acoustic guitarist at heart. He could send her off to sleep in minutes. Circling her back with only the slightest pressure of his fingernails (which she also liked), massaging the nape of her neck or gently playing with the contours of her ear. He had once leaned in and asked in a low whisper how it was that you could come to adore every single part of someone. I love you, Missy…

Wake up, Missy.
Missy? She opened her eyes again but an evening light now filled the room. All the time her arms had felt like dead weights by her side but she discovered she could move them. That they weren't shackled or paralised.

Likewise she kicked out her legs. She wasn't in hospital. But something was wrong internally. She could feel it. Down below and in her throat where a fire raged continually. Something had happened to her. She remembered something happening to her. But her mind was a fog. An impassable thicket of drowsy confusion. She lifted her head unsteadily and called out for Kimberly but she could only emit a strangulated noise as if she was trying to shout in a dream.

Did Adam mean the song to be dedicated to her as had the poem? Was he hoping she was out there somewhere listening, perhaps reminiscing with a smile at the video? It could not have crossed his mind that she would not. She really wanted to think like that but part of her believed it might also have been an act of revenge for her leaving him. That he had waited a long time to have his say. To show her what she had missed out on. That he had made it in spite of all her doubts and accusations of him being a dreamer. Even though he had never been in the slightest way vindictive. But if he had wanted to send her a sign, if that's what it was, if he had wanted to tell her that she was still in his thoughts, that he still in fact loved her, if he was still so sure she would at some point hear his music, why turn it into a pumping anthem that had everyone talking? Why not a love ballad? That would have been the romantic thing to do. And he was a romantic. Anyone who wrote had to be a romantic. She truly believed that. Even so, she still didn't know what to make of any of it. Perhaps the beat represented his still-simmering anger. It was the beat that was the song's strength. Was anyone really listening to the words? Why couldn't he have just made up some other lines instead? What was she supposed to think other than that he must have wanted her to know?

For all her demands of him, her craving to settle down and lead an ordinary existence independent of his pipe-dream of stardom, or at the very least some sort of tenuous career in the music industry, Zoe's life had not turned out the way she would have liked. For a start she hadn't planned on getting pregnant so early. Adam had made an effort to keep in touch despite the way she had ended it. But she had wanted to make a clean break so had cut all ties. It was the only way. She didn't want him luring her back with his words like so many times before and return to that feeling of her life just drifting so the first thing she did was to change her number. At the time her landlord was becoming increasingly difficult and Adam was always doing small gigs around the country (another bone of contention with her when he would be gone for weeks) so the next time he went away she moved without leaving a forwarding address. By then she'd been with Adam for three years. She was twenty-six. He found her in the end of course through mutual contacts, but in the mean time she had tried getting him out of her system by getting back in with a band of old friends and began dating other guys. That was the advice she had been given by everyone. Even her mother. And especially her father and brothers who just thought of Adam as a waster even though he'd always supported himself one way or another. Once Adam heard about that he backed off completely and she knew he had gone for good. She would have done the same. Adam wasn't vindictive, but he could become hard-nosed to the point of obstinacy if he thought he was right or that she had somehow wronged him or let him down. And if she was the same he would only put it down to her childlike determination for not being able to get her own way rather than any point of principle she might have. In the early days she almost enjoyed their battle of wills confident in the knowledge that she would eventually win. Then over time when Zoe knew she would have to come around she began to develop a grudging respect for his strength and the way he handled her. Zoe wasn't used to that. Until she met Adam she was always getting her own way. Even if she had to shout and scream and stamp her feet for it. Even if she had to bend her fingers back like Kimberly. Being the youngest and only girl in the family she had been allowed a lot of license. She'd grown up spoilt and indulged. Yet despite the warring with Adam and the break-ups the trust between them had never been an issue. It was wonderful being able to feel like that given the men she had been with subsequently. There were times when she even suspected Simon. He had a secretive side about him. Just little things that didn't add up. The signs had been there for a long time and she was just as guilty for ignoring them. She didn't want to rock the boat whatever that meant. An unspoken compromise had crept in. She had started to choose her arguments much like she had seen other couples do. Much like she had watched her mother do with her father who'd provided everything but also frustrated her with his distance and lack of affection. She and Simon were becoming like everyone else. They were an unhappy couple in the making. The future looked miserable. She longed to get out of it. Yet she and Adam never used to worry about their commitment to each other no matter how long they were apart or fell out for. They always knew they would come back and sometimes it was just what they needed given the intensity of their love. The beauty and the pain of it all and the almost unbearable existence between.

After she left Zoe felt his hurt for a long, long time.

Kimberly. This time a confused panic aroused her as if she had overslept a crucial appointment. Zoe raised her head groggily and slid out from beneath the top blanket and sat up on the edge of the bed. It was nearly dark. If it was a week day her daughter would need picking up from school. She shivered involuntarily and looked down at herself. How had she ended up in bed naked under the top blanket? She always wore something even if it was only an oversized T-shirt. She tried to focus and looked around the room. Her throat was so dry she must have slept with her mouth open the way she sometimes caught herself doing when she had been drinking too much. But she didn't really feel any of the symptoms of a bad hangover. Just the worrying inability to stitch together the events of the day before.

As Adam's notoriety grew by being the lead singer of Franklin Street, the TV interviews, the magazine articles, the song – 'I Didn't Know', in particular, that had stayed top of the charts to haunt her all summer, so Zoe felt her life was being increasingly spotlighted and subject to unwanted outside attention. Her mother contacted her claiming to have always thought Adam a 'nice boy'. Zoe's father and brothers remained conspicuously silent. Damn them to hell, she thought. No one had ever been good enough which was behind the reason her family had never met any of her boyfriends since. Not even Kimberley's father. Wherever he was now. And certainly not Simon. The whole scandal of being a single mother only deepening the estrangement between them all. In trying to leave her past behind she still used social media until old friends began to come out of the woodwork asking about Adam and she felt compelled to shut the sites down. But she had started to question herself if that was more in fear of Simon coming across something which she began to hate herself for. Then one day she was spotted by someone she used to know and who couldn't wait to stop and talk to her about Adam's success. It was a woman from the gym who hadn't spoken to Zoe in years but now felt perfectly at liberty to corner her in the changing rooms and cross-examine Zoe for a full ten minutes on her past relationship with Adam and if she still had any contact with him. For the life of her, Zoe had no idea why she made up a story that she still did. Or that it had been on the tip of her tongue to say the song had been written about her, which at least would have been the truth. She felt desperate to tell someone because the song, the poem, all the poems that she had kept safe and gone back to read again and again had left her thinking about Adam obsessively all through the day and deep into the night. Summoning up old memories and trying her best to spurn Simon's advances which of course he took as a challenge. Another game to get him excited. Lately he had been encouraging her to talk about other men during sex. What they would do to her. What she wanted them to do to her. So she lay there and imagined Adam, feeling only the betrayal to Adam as Simon grunted and moaned and uttered contemptuous abuse at her until he came.

Every morning she would wake up to that same familiar sickness. The one she had felt when he would go off touring. 'Separation anxiety' she had called it. A constant feeling akin to some terrible foreboding stirring deep in the pit of her stomach. A state of near-dread for the inevitable eruption of white hot anger that was never far away and she found so difficult to quell.

Behave yourself, Missy. But she didn't want to. She couldn't. Not by then. Not when she was on the point of exploding. She could say the most terrible things. She would let him have it. Both fucking barrels. It was over. She hated his fucking guts for doing this to her! For putting her through this every time. This isn't working. I'm done! And then for a while they wouldn't speak. But they would both continue to feel the lure no matter how long the silence or how far the distance. It didn't even have to be said. It could be days or weeks. Their love was a howling wounded beast tortured by frustration and anguish but that would not be slayed. And every now and then, in those most desperate and heart-rung and exhaustive and empty of moments, a handwritten poem would arrive...

Zoe stood up shakily and saw that her clothes had been discarded across the bedroom floor. Her partially buttoned blouse had been thrown into a corner. Her jeans were turned inside-out with her underwear still entangled in the legs as if it had been a struggle to get them off. Simon must have undressed her. Her bra lay by the side of the bed still clasped at the back. She would never have left her clothes like that. What had happened? Had she been such a dead weight that removing her clothing had proved near impossible - and if so why bother to undress her at all? Zoe hugged herself feeling suddenly vulnerable and fearful of her amnesia and began to try and think back to the last thing that she could remember.

Franklin Street's follow up single was a song called, 'Pictures' and at first Zoe assumed it had nothing to do with her. That Adam's summer hit had just been a one off. An accolade to an old girlfriend that she felt sure would one day come out in an interview if it hadn't already, or that like many songs the mystery person's identity remained there in the lyrics like an unmarked grave. Is that what she was to him now that he had got the whole thing out of his system, dead and buried? It shouldn't matter and in a way she was almost relieved that things had moved on and began to look back on the whole emotional episode as fun while it lasted. As if she'd just been through the highs and lows of a passionate but short-lived secret affair that had ended for the best and with no innocent parties hurt. She might even be tempted to tell Kimberly at some point but knew she could never reveal Adam's true persona to Simon who outside of his bedroom fantasies had a tendency to flip if she so much as made eye contact with another guy. Simon was six-years younger than her. She had been attracted to his body-builder physique more than anything but apart from his obvious insecurities he also wasn't very bright otherwise he might have made the connection long ago what with Zoe's previous address being the name of the band and the fact he knew she had once dated a musician called Adam.

She missed the intellect.

She missed those feelings that the song had aroused in her even if it had felt like she was truly dying half the time. As Lady Antebellum says, 'Guess I'd rather hurt than feel nothing at all.' Was that true? She had told Adam once that if it didn't work out between them she would never get into another serious relationship again. That it just wasn't worth feeling like that all the time. That it was too hard. Too difficult and that she would rather go through a series of casual flings if and when she needed human companionship than live in pain. And then... well, here she was. Eight years after. Pretty much following up on that prediction. Emerging into the blinking daylight from yet another transitory romance that had run its course but with Adam now living his dream in the background.

Was she supposed to have waited forever?

The song was actually called 'Pictures (of You)'. The parenthesis was important in that Adam was to later stress in a Rolling Stone article that he didn't want it to be confused or even respectfully compared to The Cure's hit. Or that at first thought his fans might think he'd already run short of ideas and produced a cover.

'I have a small collection
Of pictures of you
There are not nearly enough...'

Of course, she had been listening out for their second song like everyone else once Kimberly had told her about its imminent release. Not only out of curiosity but because she was and always had been an admirer of his writing. Or at least much more than his musical or vocal talents. She had genuinely come round to the belief that the first song had just been a one-off. At best a tip of the hat to her. An acknowledgement of what they had shared. It would have been sweet and typical of him. He always had been a warm-hearted and generous soul and she realised through that first song alone they had not only shared something very special but that she loved him still and that, perhaps, he still loved her. It had been a tribute at best and after all the inner turmoil of the last few months Zoe had finally settled down and begun to feel very lucky. Given his new, hard-earned fame, it was almost a privilege to have known him. Then she heard 'Pictures' for the very first time driving to work in her car.

'I love the folds between your breasts.
You won't
And no doubt don't.
But it speaks of an older
Woman I hope to know...'

This time it felt like a violation. She pulled the car over and started to shake violently. What the hell was he doing? Her shaking hand fumbled at the radio. Accidently changing channels. For the first time in she didn't know how long she needed a cigarette. But of course she knew exactly how long. Since she had last seen Adam. They had been bad for each other in that respect. There had been lots of drinking and smoking. Lots of great sex. Real rock 'n roll, she supposed upon reflection, laughing ironically. And now it felt like he was doing it to her all over again after years of separation. But this time reaching out through the air waves. Zoe threw her head back gasping for air and drew down the car windows whilst trying to steady her breathing. She was having a panic attack. What else could it be? Her heart fluttered. Her chest felt tight and burning. Her back ached. This was worse than anything they had put each other through. She fought against turning the radio off. Folding her arms and shivering and glaring at it. The song had started off so differently from their big hit. An acoustic ballad with what sounded like a mandolin, reminding her at first of The Stones' 'Lady Jane'. It wasn't what she'd been expecting at all. She hadn't known what to expect. Something new. Something different about his life and influences or points of view. But not this. Not something as personal as this. It had been the shortest poem he'd ever sent and, unusually, to inspire her rather than reconcile or persuade her back onto the rocky promontory of their love. She had lost her job and been feeling low. His timing had been immaculate. Christ, she had only been reading it the other day in another addictive scurry into the attic when Simon had gone to pick her daughter up from swimming club. It really was like having an affair. Just waiting for any opportunity for your partner's back to be turned. And the strange thing was, she felt almost as guilty.

'The mole near your belly button.
And, of course,
Your baby button.
Everything about you,
Baby.'

Baby button? Now he was telling the world about her baby button?
She had answered his poem by email telling him his words had brought tears to her eyes. That he saw her in a way she never could.

'That troubled angel.
You know the one,
With the sleeping frown…'

Those intimate, beautiful observations had been stirred up by a maelstrom of emotions and now the words swirled in her head like confetti. Why was he doing this to her after all this time?

'Baby girl.
I have a small collection
Of pictures of you.
There are not nearly enough.'

She leant over the steering wheel and finally let it all out. Not just what he was putting her through right now but way back then. Everything she had held in and tried to run away from. The frustrations and wrong-turns ever since. Was he calling or mocking her? She still couldn't be sure. It wasn't fair that he had the power to do this. He could have still tracked her down if he felt that way. If that's what he wanted. But she had left him and begun dating other guys even though they had been wholly committed to each other. He would never have been able to forgive her that. And so she came full circle again. These songs weren't accolades to her, she decided. He was cheapening the words she had kept close to her heart all this time by turning them into the sort of catchy pop that even had her six-year-old daughter singing along, and even worse – was profiting from them. It suddenly seemed cold-hearted and mercenary. Clearly the poems had become as much a merchandise to be exploited as Adam's image himself. (On his last appearance he had been wearing eye-liner and dramatically shaved the hair around his ears to reveal a tattooed braiding above each one whilst leaving a short of shaggy Mohican style and giving his eyes a mean, feral look that she couldn't quite distinguish but that might have been drug-related). Before she'd met him Adam admitted to having a weed and coke addiction but had worked hard at kicking it because he said it interfered with his creativity. Nevertheless, Adam talked about those days fondly and with an insouciance that prayed at the back of her mind whenever he was away on gigs.

She would be lying to herself if she couldn't admit that in her most desperate of moments she had wished for Adam back in her life. Or that she could go back to the way it had once been if only even for a short time. To feel the passion and love's suffering again. As bad as that could be at times. As wrung-out and exhaustive and heart-aching as that could be. But it wasn't like this. This was far worse. And what next? Zoe began to think. Would it never end? Was there another song waiting for her in the wings?

Now and then, if she had said something particularly bad in the heat of the moment, or because she was feeling spiteful and frustrated and just wanted to hurt him he would suddenly fall silent for weeks. She hated that. She hated not knowing what he was thinking. Or giving her nothing to feed on and keep her anger fuelled. Silence made her think too much. Silence screamed at her and eventually made her feel guilty. This time his silence had lasted for nine years.

Had he really waited that long?

Something wasn't right. She sat on the toilet for over ten minutes feeling bloated and constipated. It felt painful to even try. Her urine stung. Her colon ached. Her nipples were tender to the touch and slightly bruised but that could have been Simon. He could get carried away sometimes. Perhaps she had an infection. Everywhere felt sore and inflamed. She stood in the shower until the water temperature dropped, soaping herself softly with a sponge, rhythmical and trance-like. She didn't know how far back to go to start remembering. What had happened last week? A smokescreen filled her mind. She knew that the answers lay just beyond but didn't know how to push her way through it. Before the shower she had put on a dressing gown and made a cursory look for her phone. Going from room to room and looking for a note. Anything. It was late. The house seemed to be holding its breath. She found herself standing in the study. That's what it felt like. For a frightening moment she had no recollection of even entering there.

"Don't you think Kimberly's a little young to have an infatuation with a pop star?" Simon asked her after coming down from the shower. Zoe was preparing the evening meal and watched him out of the corner of her eye as he went to the fridge and helped himself to a bottle of beer. He popped it open and took a big swig from the neck and stood at the counter watching her. "Did you hear what I said, old woman?" he asked.

"I'm not sure what you mean," she tried not to flinch at his insult and continued to busy herself.

By the look of the wet patches coming through his T-shirt and joggers he had dried himself in a hurry. At Simon's insistence Kimberly was having her first sleepover at the daughter of one of his work friends. A little girl called Annabelle who was very sweet and the youngest of three but whose parents, Vicky and Vince, seemed a bit self-centred and were always having their children babysat from what Zoe could tell. She had been instinctively uncomfortable with the idea but Simon still liked to go out a lot and was always complaining about not spending enough time together alone which is when he would start attributing their lack of a social life to her age. That she was past it. That she couldn't hack it anymore.

He returned to the fridge and began busying himself and then surprised Zoe by moving in silently on her other side and offering her a glass of wine. His shiny scalp was peppered with beads of sweat. She much preferred to see the hair coming through. Or would once have done. She forced a smile and went to take it but he pulled the glass away, offering his puckered lips instead. She tried thinking of Adam but kissing Simon had become like kissing a stone wall. If he had ever mastered the art it was lost now in his increasing desire to force himself on her. It didn't matter about Zoe's increasingly cold and weary dispassion towards him. The less she initiated sex the more he seemed to like it. He uttered a long, drawn out 'mmmm' sound and reached around her waist with one of his big bear paws even though her lips remained sealed to his insistence and she tried pulling away.

"'Because Google knows everything,'" he nuzzled her neck and began murmuring in her ear. He was so strong against her thin frame that to struggle was useless. It was like she had been impaled to his body. The harder she fought the deeper the impalement. The more his arm took on a python hold. It took all her guile and coercion to escape this sort of mood in him because she knew all too well that to resist only aroused him further. "'But Google doesn't know a thing…'" he crooned, his grip tightening and pulling her up against him.

"What makes you say that about Kimberly, anyway?" she tried returning to the subject.

"'…about the way I feel for you, baby.'"

His singing of Adam's words had her head spinning surreally while the crushing together of their bodies only served to heighten her growing panic. He had put down the wine and mangled his fat ferreting fingers in her hair with his other hand, pulling her head back hard in an effort to make her cry out. But she only grunted, feeling the outbreak of his clammy flesh beneath his clothes, his stirring erection. He didn't like his cock to be touched until it was hard. He had a thing about it being soft. He would swat her hand away. Then steer it roughly towards it when he was ready.

I love the folds between your breasts… she heard Adam's voice then, as if trying to drown out what was happening.

Simon had settled on a routine which didn't much involve what she liked or even what she was comfortable with anymore. He wasn't particularly large in length but he could fill her mouth with his girth and only then did he want her to try and speak when gagged with his solid, warm, hard lump of flesh.

The mole near your belly button.

He would verbally abuse her. Try goading her into admittance that it was what she wanted. That she was enjoying it. That she would take two, three other men at once if she could. Say it you fucking slut! You fucking dirty bitch! If she didn't comply he would struggle with his erection which would only make him angry and resentful. So she said it.

And of course your baby button.

And then he would flip her over like a rag doll and take her from behind. Holding her head face down by the nape of her neck and leaving her gasping for air. It was something that she used to like. To be taken. To be dominated. But now it only ever seemed to be for his own personal pleasure. It didn't involve her. He was somewhere else. Living a dangerous fantasy that she sometimes worried about. As if deep-down he hated women. That he was capable of taking any woman against her will. Verbally abusing them right to the end the way he did her. Calling her everything. Every disgusting thing you could imagine a woman to be called.

Everything about you.

Baby.

So Zoe continued to talk, trying to keep the tremor from her voice and her body limp from resistance. She had become good at that. Like a hostage to their captor. Keep saying his name, she would tell herself. Ask questions. Make him think. "Come on, Simon," she attempted an empty laugh. "Is it even possible for a six-year-old to feel infatuation?"

"Huh?" he said irritably, his already stale beer breath panting in her ear.

Her neck felt vulnerable and exposed as he pulled on her hair. He could effortlessly close his hands right around it. She knew he wouldn't. She didn't fear for her own life. Just felt an unexplainable responsibility that if she didn't do what Simon wanted then he might take it out on someone else. A total stranger. The girlfriends and wives of convicted rapists and killers must have all felt answerable to their crimes to some degree. You shouldn't be with a man who made you feel like that. A man you were scared to make angry.

"Kimberly?"

He shook his head, growing annoyed. He didn't want to talk about it, she could tell. He didn't want to be distracted.

"Besides, Simon. Haven't you ever heard of weeny-boppers?"

"What are you even talking about, old woman?" he growled, pulling his face away.

For a moment she watched his eyes lose their glaze and come into focus. His hold on her lessened slightly. His hardness quickly faded.

"Well, there must be a reason you think she's obsessed," she continued to prod his mind.

"I didn't say she was obsessed," he frowned and shook his head. "It's just that she seems to be spending too much time looking at stuff on the computer about him. I think one of us should have a talk with her about it."

"How do you know?" she genuinely questioned him for the first time. "I haven't noticed anything."

"It was all in the history," he shrugged, releasing her and going back to the fridge for another beer. "And that's not the only time."

"Why are you checking history?"

"I'm being a responsible parent," he said.

She hated it when he called himself that. He made it sound like he would be around forever.

"Show me," she said.

"It's not there now," he only glanced at her across his shoulder.

"Why not?" she asked.

"I deleted it."

"Why?" she asked again, feeling that old suspicion surface.

"Oh, you know. Just cleaning up."

"Cleaning up what?" she asked.

"Its capacity," he said, when he turned to look at her his face had hardened into one of defiance.

"You know it's strange," she shook her head slowly and began to smirk. "But twice I've gone to find a website I had been on by checking back through history and twice everything had been deleted."

"It's an old PC," he said. "You need to manage the storage."

"Every day?" she exclaimed, and laughed mockingly.

He reddened a bit under her scrutiny.

"Are you hiding something?" she asked.

"Are you?" he erupted. His eyes bulged like eggs when he raised his voice. "Because if it's not Kimberly cruising sites about this Adam guy then it must be you. That was my second thought. Is it you?"

She laughed a little nervously.

"Is it me what, Simon?" she crossed her arms.

"You heard. Is it you obsessing about Adam what's-his-name?"

"Don't be ridiculous," she scoffed.

"I know," he admitted. "That's what I keep telling myself. But you've been acting different now for a long time."

"You make me sound like a teenager. I'm not a teenager."

"So what? Neither is he. In fact he's as old as you are. He's a virtual geriatric."

"Oh, really?" she glared at him.

"Is it you?" he asked again.

"What else was in history, Simon?" she asked.

"Is it you?" he demanded.

"Well, if you wanted to make a point about how many times a site about Franklin Street had been visited I don't understand why you deleted it all. So, I'm asking you what else was in history that you felt compelled to delete. Never mind what you think I or Kimberly have been looking at. What have you been looking at?"

She could tell he had gone dry-mouthed. He was struggling to swallow and wouldn't hold her gaze. His hand trembled as he took another swig of beer.

"Because I have a six-year-old daughter who uses that computer," she continued, "and if she ever comes across anything-"

"You think a guy like that would be interested in you?" he interrupted with a hateful sneer.

"I will call the police without a moment's hesitation," she warned, beginning to shake with rage.

"A washed up old hag like you? It's fucking sad," he said. "It's fucking pathetic. Go ahead. Join his fucking fan club or whatever's going on in that little fantasy world of yours. You might as well be obsessing over Mick Jagger for all the chance you've got. He's about your age, too."

She found her phone under the bed. Something must have happened to it because the wallpaper had returned to its default setting and when she typed in her code nothing happened. She stared at it for a long time feeling a deeper dread for her condition or whatever was or had gone on.

Of course, she had over-reacted because Simon had been right that all the research on Adam had been her doing. The information on him had been overwhelming even though she knew almost all of it. She read and watched all his interviews but when asked about the inspiration for his songs and the name of the band he only explained that he had set out to write about a 'virtual girlfriend' who had lived on a 'virtual street' to give his music identity.

Virtual?

What the fuck did that mean? That she didn't or had never really existed? Or that he was trying to protect her? Perhaps he thought she had some legal claim to his money as the songs had been written exclusively about her. About them. Every word so far had been about them. He displayed an air or reluctance to talk about the upcoming album, saying only that there was an ongoing debate between the band and the producers over which songs were to be recorded. He had written lots of songs, he added. By songs Zoe assumed he meant poems.

Was he thinking about her when he answered those questions? Zoe wondered. Was he even the slightest bit concerned about the impact it might be having on her or was he worried that she should reveal him as some sort of pop charlatan? A self-plagiarist or a thief of the most intimate possession one can bestow upon another? Poems that came from the soul. Dedicated and given to her alone. She had tried to read his eyes when he looked into the camera. It was him but it wasn't. It was as if someone was impersonating him. It was almost as if he had detached himself from the lyrics. That they were just words that made good songs to him. He'd had success with the first one and so had tried the same formula which was probably why he was being so cagy about the album. Perhaps his dilemma lay in producing something real and that had been created in the moment as opposed to something simply made up. Assuming he could just make something up and that the poems were not all the success Adam had left to rely upon.

Yet in the cold light of day Zoe had to accept that he must have written other poems for other women and that sooner or later a song would appear that meant not only nothing to her but which would mean he was singing about someone else and then the whole fantasy, as Simon put it, would come crashing down and leave her feeling naïve and foolish. She had left Adam nine years ago, she told herself again and again. Whatever remaining sentiment she still construed in the words had been diluted a hundred thousand times over not only in his record sales but to the hundreds of thousands who both listened and related to them. When she thought of it like that, it made her want to hate him.

'Do you want to fight or do you want to love?
We have always been clinging to the crumbling edge
Yet somehow supporting each other
When it was easier to plummet
And walk away from the fight
Than to fight for love.'

The new song was called 'Got You', which is what the poem had been called. He had asked her once early into their relationship if she wanted to fight or to love, and in that moment had defused an argument that had been sending them over the cliff edge. They often likened their torment to standing on a precipice. Each daring the other to take the leap. "Just jump then, if that's how you feel. Just go ahead and jump." Which is what she did in the end, of course. Somebody had to. The pain was too much. But many times before that, when either felt a heated exchange between them spiraling out of control, if one felt the other's hand slipping from their grasp, the other would be reeled back in by those words. 'Do you want to fight or do you want to love?'

For you, baby.
I get you
I got you
Like no other ever.

This time there could be no doubt. The third poem transformed into a beautiful melody. The song seemed far removed from his upbeat summer hit of the year before. It sounded like he was speaking to her and her alone. Kimberly found a live studio session of them performing on YouTube. Far from Adam's almost glam rock image he and the band had seemed to be heading in the direction of they all just sat around dressed down in T-shirts and jeans a bit like the old Adam. Gone was his make-up to reveal the dark bags beneath his eyes and a more familiar pasty complexion. He looked skinny and loose-skinned. He'd let the shaven side of his head grow out a bit so that it now hung in different lengths. She couldn't keep up with his body art anymore but nonetheless he looked relaxed and happy in his work. Aside from the other session musicians there was a trio of attractive female backing singers that stirred up an irrational jealousy in her. He must get unlimited attention from girls of all ages, she told herself. And tried pushing the thought far from her mind.

> Don't look down
> Or over your shoulder
> I get you
> I got you
> Like no other ever.
> For you baby,
> This song is for you.

Apart from the addition of the word 'song' in the last line it was exactly how he'd written it.

"Is this true?" she had asked him at that time. "Is all of this true? Because if it is you'd better remember it."

"I don't have to remember it, Missy," he answered. "You do."

"I love you for this," she told him.

"I love you for this," she whispered now at the computer screen, stroking her hand down and across it.

At that moment Kimberly walked in and mocked her mother for talking to the PC. How Zoe would have loved to tell her daughter that all Adam's songs had been written for her. To have taken down the box from the attic and showed her of other songs still to come. All at once she heard herself encouraging Kimberly to write to him on the pretense of getting a signed photograph. Even offering to draft the letter herself for her daughter to copy and making sure to include her own details in the text and in particular her full name and that she had once lived on a road called Franklin Street. Just one fan mail letter among tens of thousands Zoe felt sure, but in talking about Google she had done a search on her own name once and only three others had come up in the UK. It was highly unlikely all three would be writing to him. He must know who she was. Also, in a recent interview he had claimed to open all his fan mail personally and if that was true he would be left in little doubt who was behind the letter. Just the thought alone of contacting him thrilled her. All this time she had made up countless reasons to question his intentions but the one thing that hadn't occurred to her was that perhaps he'd been trying to maintain a respectful distance. That he may have even believed she could be happily married and settled down with a young family as she had always claimed to want, and that the last thing she needed in her life was an ex-lover publicly reiterating his love for her after all these years. It all made perfect sense to her now.

While Kimberly sat at the study desk diligently copying her mother's words Zoe turned to the computer and went to the band's website to read about a forthcoming announcement of dates and venues for their first UK tour accompanying the release of their album. Zoe felt her heart soar. Imagining all sorts of things. She saw him pick her out of the audience and pull her up on stage. She fantasised about him serenading her with 'Got You', pulling her tight to him and dancing to the music as the crowd cheered.

I get you
I got you
Like no other ever…

Or meeting him backstage. She would get VIP tickets. She would pay anything. It was crazy. She was acting like a lovesick sweetheart, she knew. But suddenly her reverie was broken by the sound of the front door slamming. Zoe looked up in shock. Simon was home early. An unexplainable feeling of frozen guilt took hold. Her hands began to shake. Her fingers fumbled at the keyboard. Kimberly looked up at her quizzically, sensing her panic.

"It's only Daddy," she said.

She tried pacifying her daughter with a smile that stuck to her face.

Recently she had deleted anything she had been looking at regarding Adam after Simon's previous suspicions. But when she clicked on history this time a whole list of sites appeared that she had never seen before. Her mind could barely take in the host titles she was reading. All of them times and dates of the night before. The middle of the night.

When Simon would sometimes claim he couldn't sleep because he was thinking about work and would go over his accounts in the study. Her mind produced a jumble of depraved images as she quickly scrolled down the list but in her haste she accidently deleted everything. Wiping away the evidence so that it might not have ever been there. But she knew what she had seen. She would never forget what she had seen. The words burned indelibly in her mind.

"He's not your Daddy," she whispered shakily.

"Huh?" Kimberly chewed at the end of her pencil.

She could hear him coming swiftly up the stairs. Taking two steps at a time. He appeared in the doorway with a fake smile, panting a little. He smelt of sawn wood.

"What's going on?" he breathed, his eyes roving over the desk, at the computer.

"We're writing a letter," Kimberly said.

"Oh yeah," he grinned crookedly. "Who to?"

"Adam," Kimberly replied thoughtfully.

He exchanged an unreadable look with Zoe. A look she'd never seen before. It might have been desperation or pleading or terror. But at the same time a calm sense of self-preservation quickly took hold. He looked around the room, nodding. The situation was under his control, he seemed to be reminding himself. It was just him and them. He appeared unconcerned about the letter.

"What are you doing?" he asked Zoe directly.

"Helping," she replied nervously.

She reached over and put a protective arm around Kimberly.

"What's the matter?" he asked.

"Nothing," she said, but couldn't hide her fear.

He stared at the computer again and she saw his indecision return. A glassy wistfulness that made his eyes shine. As if suddenly moved at the memory of something painful. The wallpaper screen showed a picture of them all at a theme park in happier days. The same one she had on her phone. More trusting and less dark days. Something had come between them. She knew that now and so did he. All this time she had been blaming herself. Her infatuation with her old boyfriend. His poems. The words that only deepened her regret and heartache for ever having left him. For spurning his love and of all the time wasted in-between. So much time.

"Are you going to be on there long because I need to work out some quotes?" he asked.

"Go ahead. I've only just switched it on," she replied.

Both knew each other was lying. Which on top of everything else was a new thing.

When Kimberly went to correct her Zoe hushed her daughter and began ushering her out of the room. "Come on we can finish this downstairs," she said. "I'll start dinner."

It wasn't her phone, she realised. It was the same phone but it wasn't hers. She looked around the bedroom feeling her mind trying to speak to her. Without thinking she slowly peeled back the top blanket on the bed to reveal the crumpled top sheet beneath uncertain of what she might find. There were dried sex stains and a tiny patch of brown blood but she couldn't remember the last time she had changed them. She didn't even know what day it was. She looked at her clothes again still left as she had found them. Something had happened to her right here in this room, she thought. Her jeans still turned inside out no longer looked like a drunk's attempt to undress themselves and she noticed several of the buttonholes on her blouse had been torn. At that moment she heard the whirr of Simon's diesel truck pull up to the house. She peeked through the curtains and saw him mount the kerb before staggering out into the street and looking directly up at the bedroom window. Zoe pulled away. Suddenly in fear for her safety and not knowing why. She tiptoed into the hallway looking for a place to hide. Outside she thought she heard Simon talking to someone. He sounded drunk. Then she heard him fumbling at the front door lock with his key.

That night she slept with Kimberly. Simon didn't ask why. They hadn't spoken a word all evening. He'd just sat there watching TV and routinely going to the fridge for a beer. The silence between them becoming deafening and accusatory. And when the next morning she returned from taking Kimberly to school and saw Simon's truck still parked outside the house her stomach performed a slow, sick roll of apprehension at the thought of a confrontation. She'd lay awake all night listening for sounds of movement. The creak of a door. The tap of a keyboard. Simon would usually start off by tossing and turning his big frame for an hour before settling into a steady snore. But there had only been silence. As if, like she, he had lain on his back all night wide awake and staring at the ceiling.

When she entered the kitchen she saw his keys and phone on the side. He was always out the door by this time. Something was wrong. The anxiety was never far away but this time she could feel it feeding off her fears from the night before. Filling her chest like a swarm of angry bees and making it difficult to breathe. She crept up the stairs expecting to hear him in the shower or find him still in bed but when she reached the landing she saw the small step ladders and the attic door open.

"Simon?" she called out hesitantly.

At first she couldn't think why he would be in the attic. It was all her stuff up there. Old baby clothes and toys mostly. Kimberly's high chair and first cot. She checked the other rooms, hesitating at the study door, fearing he might be on the computer. That he had seized the opportunity of her absence in the same way she would him when going up into the attic to read over Adam's poems. Except that she wouldn't be caught sitting there ambivalent or oblivious to his presence. Out of control. Naked or with his pants pulled down or whatever he did. Whatever men did.

Adam's poems...

But of course the little room was empty. The open blinds overlooking the long strip of back garden let in the bright morning light. Simon's files of invoices and other correspondence were stacked and organised. The desk was tidy. Even the waste bin had been mysteriously emptied which she now coolly regarded with new suspicion. She took a step forward and placed her hand on the back of the cheap office chair and began swiveling it from left to right all the while staring at the dormant PC. The portal to his other world might as well have been shut inside a tomb yet still a lingering insanity resided in the room. Something thick and living and almost palpably evil. What else could it be but a sickness of the mind to make him want to log into the sort of depraved websites he had in the dead of night? She had never known him. By comparison Adam would bear his heart but in the two years she and Simon had been together it seemed impossible to think she had never known him. She moved to open the window to let in some air, feeling the bile in her stomach stir. For a moment she couldn't understand what she was seeing. At the back of the garden Simon was standing over the incinerator by the garage he had converted into a workshop since moving in. It seemed a strange time of day to get a fire started and she couldn't think what he might be burning until she recognized the open box by his side and the papers he systematically took out and was reading over. Slowly letting each corner of a page catch alight before dropping it into the roaring blaze.

She brought a hand to her mouth and gasped. "No, please no" she whispered, and fled the room.

When Simon saw her coming up the garden path he began to read out loud.

"'So we lay there
Apparently oblivious
To the torrent of issues
That had raged between us
Not so long before-'"

"Stop it!" Zoe demanded. "Give me those."

"'Buried and forgotten," Simon held up a finger as if not to be interrupted.

"'Beneath the sheepskin throw
And marshmallow pillows
With legs entwined
And ankles brushing…'"

Simon's face suddenly started to crumble. When Zoe took another step forward he held the pages over the incinerator with a trembling hand. His eyes were red from crying or standing too near the flames. It was hard to tell. His voice continued slow and trembling.

"'Foregoing the stir of hormones
Baby,
Which
If are not ever-present
Then never
Ever
Far away.'"

The poem had been called 'That Afternoon' and evoked memories of a long weekend they had spent together one summer in a cottage in the Lake District.

"You think I didn't know?" he bellowed. "You think I didn't know about your little trips up into the attic? Do you think Kimberly didn't notice?"

"Give me those, Simon," she warned. "They are my property. You have no right."

"Wait," he warded her off with a hand. "There's...there's another bit that I like. I have to say it's pretty good actually. Just...just give me a second," he sniveled.

"They were written years ago," she said. "It has nothing to do with anything."

"Here it is," he ignored her.

"' I've said this before
I know
In so many ways
As to become boring
But
Top to toe
Inside out
Unconditional
(I know that now)
It has to be
Is there any other kind?
Really,
It's everything that's not to love
That I find myself loving about you the most.'"

He stood there nodding and wiped at his snotty nose with his sleeve.

"They read better as poems," he said reflectively, and looked up at her from across the flickering flames. "Have you ever felt that way about me? The things that are not to love you love the most?"

She held his gaze for a long time. The words sounded flat and stupid coming from him. The big oaf.

"I didn't think so," he said.

"I didn't write them. They were written to me, Simon. They were written about me."

"Do you want to be with him?"

"It's too late for that, Simon," she said.

"Is it?" he suddenly raged. "Does he think it's too late? Eh? He's...he's making fucking songs about you. Even now. How do you compete with that?"

He dropped the remainder of the pages into the fire and Zoe felt something in her die. No more escape. No more fantasy. Simon had killed the dream. She would never see Adam. She knew that now. In a way he had brought her to her senses. Her eyes turned to the box she had kept Adam's memory in all these years but the box was empty. Simon had just burnt the last of the poems. She looked forlornly at the curling black pages. Feeling the flames licking at her heart.

"Get out," she said, her voice low and guttural. She began to tremble with anger. "Get out of my house. Get out of my life."

"He did this to us," he pointed at the fire. "You can't blame me. He's the one who's come between us. I love you, babe. I really love you. Before that fucking song about Google we were doing just fine."

"I have known love, Simon. I have known both the beauty and the pain and I can tell you this isn't it. It has never been it. Before that first song I had ceased to exist," she replied softly. "Before that first song... all the songs," she paused, "before then, somewhere down the line, I settled for a whole lot less. Real love lasts forever and you just destroyed the testimony."

"What can I do to make it right? Just tell me, babe. We can move past this."

"You think love is taking a woman against her will, Simon? You think that's an expression of love? You've got a problem."

"What are you talking about?"

"Us. You and...and your increasingly weird demands."

"Come on," he tried joking. "That's just a game. I'm only trying to spice up our sex life a little so you don't get old and set in your ways. I can't write fucking poetry if that's what turns you on."

"And what about rape and torture and the mutilation of women? I've seen what you look at. It really is quite scary what's going on in your head. Will cutting off my nipples spice things up for you too, Simon? Is that what you'd like to do when you're raping me?"

"Rape?" he looked aghast.

"Well, that's what it feels like. That's what's going on in your head, isn't it?"

"But...I thought you liked it."

"Of course you did," she looked away, dumbfounded more by herself if anything that she should have let it go on so long. Since when had she become so passive?

"You've never complained before," he tried reminding her.

Maybe he was right. Zoe shook her head and shut her eyes at both what she had let go and what she had become.

Everything about you baby...

"Rape. What do you know about rape, anyway?" he jeered. "You should be so lucky. Who the fuck would want to rape you?"

He turned away and found a piece of wood and threw it into the fire.

"I should report you to the police," she uttered in disgust.

"They're all legal sites," he countered, but a hopeless misery had entered his eyes, as if he wanted to take the whole thing back.

"That doesn't make it right," she said, with a mocking laugh. "Why are you looking at them? What are you thinking about when you look at films of a woman's genitals being attached to electrodes? Are you thinking about me? Are you thinking about Kimberly?"

He looked up and appeared genuinely shocked.

"It's a fantasy, Zoe," he mumbled into his chest. "The sites are fantasies. They're not really doing those things. That's all it is. None of it's real. Not even normal...stuff," he tried stopping himself.

"A fantasy," she repeated in a low whisper. "You're a misogynist. That's the real word for it."

"You want to know something real?" he yelled, "your fucking boyfriend that's what's real. Those fucking poems that's what's real. Well, they're not fucking real now are they you fucking lying bitch?"

"You think burning those words will make them go away?" she asked him. "I know every line of every poem off by heart. I didn't then. Not when he sent them. They weren't meant for then whether I knew it or not. Whether Adam knew it or not. I didn't need saving then."

"But you do now..." he said, nodding his head and looking away and not waiting for an answer before suddenly kicking out at the incinerator and sending its cinders and ashes spilling across the path. Zoe took a step back and narrowed her eyes, fighting an urge to chase and hit him over the head with the first thing she could find.

"Get out of my house you fucking weirdo!" she screamed. "Get out of my life!"

She lay listening to the sound of Simon stomping around and calling out her name from under Kimberly's bed. "Fuck!" he kept shouting. "Fuck! Fuck! Fuuuuck!" He rampaged through the rooms but kept returning to their bedroom where she heard him grunt and groan and moving furniture about. When he entered Kimberly's room and switched on the light she retreated as far back as she could. She watched his feet pace quickly to the centre of the room. He had his work boots on. She could hear him panting but his breath was tremulous. For a moment she was convinced he knew she was under there and just deciding what to do but it seemed he was only taking a reflective moment because he eventually let out a heavy sigh and quietly left the room, switching off the light and silently closing the door as if he had found Kimberly herself lying in there asleep. The next moment she heard a man call Simon's name from downstairs.

"Have you found it?" he called.

"It's gone. She's gone," Simon replied hopelessly.

"What the fuck!" the voice screeched. The man mounted the stairs in what sounded like three strides.

"Are you sure?" he sounded hysterical.

"You dumb cunt," Simon began to sob. "You stupid, stupid dumb cunt."

She could hear them from outside the door standing on the landing.

"Well, hang on," the man gibbered. "Let's just calm down a second. She doesn't know my code. She can't get into it. You said you slipped her two...three...what is it, what's it called?"

"Rohypnol," Simon bleated. "What does it matter what it's called?"

"How long did you say she would be out for?"

"I don't know," Simon moaned.

"Well, you said you've done it before."

"Not to Zoe..."

"I know but other chicks, right?"

"I can't even believe she's up and about."

"Okay, so...so she's wandering around wondering where the last fucking day went, right? She's got my phone that she thinks is her phone. Her head's fucked up. She can't remember anything. She's probably walking the streets looking for Kimberly or something. Hang on, wait a minute. Just ring it!"

"What?"

Zoe's hands were locked around the phone. She fumbled at the screen button and the mobile illuminated under the bed. If it should ring now they would hear it.

"Call my fucking phone, man. It might still be in the house!" the man's voice grew agitated. "Or we'll at least know where she is and what she knows."

"Okay, hang on." There was a pause. "It's switched off," Simon said.

"Fuck," the man breathed heavily.

Zoe's shaking hands spilled the phone onto the carpeted floor and a new wave of fear took hold. Something she had never felt before in her life. She had a very real sense that she was in danger.

"Look I have to go back and get Kimberly from your place, Vince. That was the plan, remember? Zoe wakes up thinking she's been sick or something and I'm the hero who's been looking after her and taking care of Kimberly. She was supposed to wake up to me mopping her fucking brow not walking around town with your phone with films and pictures of her being fucking drug raped on it!"

And then there it was. Every question answered in a blink of a second.

Drug raped.

Zoe flinched and let out a tiny whimper at the words, bringing a hand to her mouth.

She shrank further back into the shadows like a petrified animal. A sudden sadness overwhelming her as she curled into a tight ball and began to silently cry. She could feel every burning penetration now. Every sordid violation. She had lost claim to her body forever. That's what it felt like. As if it had ceased to be her property. She would wear it like second-hand clothes. Like sackcloth.

She listened to them go. All the while comforting herself with thoughts of Adam sending her off to sleep by drawing circles with his fingers on the inside of her arm, or lightly scratching hieroglyphics into her back. He liked to strum his fingers through her hair. She could tell when he had a song in his head. He would absently play with her ear lobe like he would a guitar pic. More than love there was a kindness to his touch that told her he would protect her always. But that world, his words, now seemed a million miles away. She didn't know how long she stayed. She didn't want to come out. She might have even slept. It wasn't uncertainty or fear or even a feeling of safety that kept her under there.

It was a mortifying sense of shame and guilt that she might have been in some part responsible for what had happened.

Zoe never did send the fan letter to Adam or get to see them live at the arena near her. His band went on to win various awards including MTVs 'Best Newcomer' in the wake of the countrywide acclaim attributed to the single 'Got You', and which was due to be followed by their debut album entitled simply: 'Franklin Street'. Zoe felt her heart melt when she read a review of the playlist to find all the tracks were poems he had sent her. She hadn't known what to expect from the cover design after the personal journey of the last year but if there was ever any doubt she had somehow misinterpreted every lyric for words that had been written exclusively for her, then it was the cover's image of him standing at the end of the road where she used to live with the pub now boarded up and derelict. It had been at the end of a peninsula on the main high-street that split the road into two directions. She could just make out her old street sign in the backdrop above a corner shop. Zoe hadn't been back in years. In the shot Adam had his hands in his pockets dressed just in a white T-shirt and jeans, donning a full dark hipster beard flecked with grey and was peering down the road as if he was looking out for someone. He'd let his hair grow out and didn't look that much different from when they'd first met apart from the beard. Not at all her type, she remembered thinking. On that same night after they'd got talking and she'd discovered his line of 'work' they got onto the subject of their musical tastes and she remembered him telling her that Eric Clapton's Derek and the Dominoes lone studio album was a seventy-seven minute declaration of his love for Pattie Boyd, the then wife of his friend and neighbour George Harrison, the former Beatle. 'Layla', he went on to tell her, was a variant of Leila, a name of Arabic origin. It means "dark beauty," he looked at her meaningfully. Zoe had worn her hair long and wavy back then and he'd likened her eyes to a Sultan's, which was something she was sure she'd heard before in a song and only made her suspicious of his compliments at first. That he was just using lyrics he knew to woo her. "Can you imagine someone expressing their feelings for you in such a way?" he had asked her in all seriousness. He couldn't have possibly known. Not then. But maybe the idea had returned to him.

When Kimberly saw the cover she shrieked with excitement.

"Mum, is that really the same street you used to live on?" she asked dubiously. "Are you sure it's not just any old Franklin Street?"

"No. It's not just 'any old' Franklin Street, sweetie," Zoe grinned.

"O-M-G. Can we go there please? Will you take me there?"

"Well, there's nothing to see."

"Are you kidding? We can take a selfie with the street name and I can Instagram all my friends. Oh, please, Mum. We could go there on the same day the album's released. Wouldn't that be cool, Mum?" she began to jump up and down. "How cool would that be standing on Franklin Street the day the album comes out and sending pictures to all my friends? They would be sooo jealous," Kimberley rolled her eyes and spun on the spot. "They still don't believe me. I still don't believe you. Are you sure, Mum? Are you really sure that's your street in the picture?"

Zoe looked at the picture and nodded slowly. Suddenly unable to speak another word.

There was no doubt anymore in her conviction that Adam had not only masterminded the entire project from start to finish but that he had tacitly dedicated the entire album to her and their time together. But she still couldn't help but feel there was also an air of finality about it. Of completion. Did he already have another venture in the works? Was that all it had ever been? Nevertheless, for old time's sake she would give Kimberley a day off school and take her to Franklin Street for the last time and then move and get on with her life and try and forget about Adam just the way she had tried to do once before.

Despite still having no real memory of what had happened in those missing twenty-four hours Zoe hesitated upon taking the phone to the police in the fear she might be exposed to something she'd rather not remember. Things like that got leaked onto the internet all the time and then of course there would be the trial itself. She wasn't sure she could put her daughter through that and in court the defence could make you out to look like anything. An unfit mother, a willing party to a vulgar threesome that ended in regret. She hadn't been kidnapped. She hadn't been found wandering naked in a park. It had taken place in her bedroom and with her partner. She had to be in some way complicit. Even the truth was too publicly excruciating to bear. If nothing else she must be a gullible idiot for letting that happen to her and therein lied the shame. There was also another reason for not going public.

Adam.

So far the pills had done their job. She had since learned that Rohypnol was the so-called 'date rape' drug' and that due to the strong amnesia produced could leave victims with limited or even no recollection of being sexually assaulted at all. Every night she went to sleep fearing she would wake up and remember. But with each day that passed her sense of relief grew deeper. It was her secret to tell. Simon and Vince, the father of her daughter's friend, could live in purgatory the rest of their lives for all she cared. They knew she had the evidence. She told Simon she had left the phone with a friend with the strict instructions that if anything was to happen to her she should take it straight to the police. "You had better hope I live long and never read of something happening to anyone else like this," she added, knowing all the while that rape victims were always coming forward years after the event for much the same reasons as she. Maybe when she felt strong enough…

'Your siren songs
After the damaging words
The ones you don't mean
And asking me to brush it off
Just brush it off…'

At Kimberly's insistence they had listened to the album tracks all the way up on the train to Zoe's old stomping ground, sharing her daughter's headphones. Of course, 'Siren Songs' had been written about their many fall-outs and she found herself drifting into a reverie about those impassioned conflicts while being seduced by the rhythmic rock of the train. Was she really just looking back at those days through rose-tinted glasses? They had argued, yes. More than any other person she had ever known they had waged war with each other and both stood their ground. So what kept bringing them back together?

'Our must-have collisions
Inside our own collision
That freak of circumstance
Brought about by a single bar stool
In an otherwise crowded bar…'

That freak of circumstance. Yes. They were both supposed to be somewhere else that night. He was meeting friends to watch the match but was unfamiliar to the area and had gotten lost. She had given up on her intended evening because of public transport problems. Zoe hardly ever went to her local bar but her friend had been drawn by the testosterone atmosphere and Adam had just wandered in there because the match had started. A packed bar but for that one unoccupied stool next to Phoebe. And he had hesitated even then because of the view of the screen.

And the convoluted route
That led us there
And keeps us there…'

Yes, yes, yes! She remembered now. Zoe and Kimberly alighted from the train and began the short walk to Franklin. She hadn't met Adam the way she had old boyfriends or even other men since in a work place, say, or through some mutual friend or habitual haunt. It was and had always felt like providence. He shouldn't have been there. She shouldn't have been there...

They stopped to cross the road. But when Kimberly went to pull Zoe's hand her mother's body went rigid.

"What is it, Mum?"

Across the road she could see some shamrock flags fluttering in the breeze strung outside a pub with some patrons drinking outside dressed in green. Just the way it had been.

"I didn't know it was St. Patrick's Day," she said. "Is it St. Patrick's Day?" she asked.

"Oh, Mum. Come on," Kimberly insisted.

Zoe felt her heart skip a beat. Up ahead she could see the island of little enterprises that narrowed and divided the road with the old flat-iron looking premises of the pub looming into view but that had since been boarded-up with big sheets of graffiti-strewn plywood and appearing to be a place where drop-outs now hung. When they reached Franklin Zoe was dismayed to see that some of the older properties in the road also looked empty and ready for demolition. Development appeared to be going on everywhere. Soon the place would be unrecognizable. It made her question why was she even there. Probably Adam was celebrating his success on some yacht somewhere with tens of groupies or famous models and other celebrities because the alternative that he should have lured her here on this day of all days was not only too impossible to comprehend but made her feel like the victim of a cruel trick. He wasn't coming. He was never coming. What was she even thinking?

Kimberly let out a little squeal of excitement.

"Can you believe we're here, Mum? Can you believe Adam stood right there?" she pointed at the island. "Right next to the street where you used to live?"

"Don't point, sweetie," she said, pushing her daughter's hand away lest she should draw attention to the congregation of drug-addicts, alcoholics, homeless, whoever or whatever they were, should take offence. Zoe took a moment to look around. Her old street ended at a T-junction to the main road. It was now one-way only. Some of the small businesses in the high street had changed hands with the bigger chains. She hadn't known what to expect. It had been a long time. More than its appearance it just felt different. The yuppies were moving in, she thought.

"Are you okay, Mum?"

She hadn't even considered it until this moment but she had left the area because of Adam. Why had she even agreed to come back? What good was it doing? Would this malaise never end?

"Let's take your photograph, sweetie," she said, squeezing her daughter's hand. "Then we'll go and have some lunch."

"I thought we were going to stay longer," she pouted.

"But...why?" Zoe frowned and smiled.

"I just did."

"Look!" her daughter pointed to a downstairs bay window decorated with more pennants. "Why did you say that about St. Patrick's Day, Mum?" Kimberly chatted on. "What happened on St. Patrick's Day?"

Zoe knelt down and brushed the hair from Kimberly's face.

"One day I'll tell you everything," she said. "I promise."

'I get you
I got you...'

Stop doing it to yourself! Zoe could feel the tears welling up. Her vision swam. She took a deep breath and stopped at her old ground floor flat.

'Like no other ever...'

"This is it," Zoe sniffed.

Kimberly looked to the house and then back at her mother.

"Are you sad, Mom?" Kimberly asked.

"A little," she smiled tightly.

"Happy sad or sad sad?"

"A bit of both," Zoe breathed, her eyes brightening. "Happy sad, you know?"

Her daughter nodded somberly and Zoe took out her phone. It had been posted to her. But she couldn't look at it without going back to the scene of the crime. She had slept on the sofa every night since and had moved all her clothes into the study, keeping the bedroom door shut for fear of remembering. She'd already started to look at other properties.

Kimberly walked up the path to the door and turned and smiled and held out her hands.

"Can you believe you lived on Franklin Street!" she suddenly exclaimed, her eyes agog. "I mean, why would Adam name a band about a street where you used to live? This street?"

"I really don't know," Zoe said, and smiled to herself.

MORTAL LOVE

My mother sent me an old video of myself recently when I was only twenty-years-old. It had been on my birthday and my brother and his girlfriend, my boyfriend, Andy, and I were seated around the living-room as my father filmed and my mother held court before handing out the presents. At one point in her tipsy state she spontaneously broke into a dance routine to the background music and shimmied close up to the lens with an unlit cigarette dangling out of her mouth, on another she tried teasing me by waving one of the gifts around in her hand and then pretending to go off track and put it down and start talking about something else. I'd been used to that sort of provocation as a kid but my mood that day had been one of subdued irritation and mild embarrassment. I remember the time as if it was yesterday even if the only thing recognisable about myself upon seeing it after all this time was my begrudging outbreaks of laughter which could be overheard as my mother continued to entertain and make my father chuckle and cause the camera to shake in his hand. I recall everything about that day right down to the perfume I was wearing and the burning need to get the celebration over with and just leave and be out with my friends. We could jump the queue and breeze into any club in those days and I was usually the one at the head of the crew doing all the talking. I know it's an old expression but I was dressed to kill that night in a red mini velvet dress and silver heels and could still feel the tight fit of it against my body. In the footage Andy is looking on at me adoringly from the other sofa as I sullenly play with one of the diamond ear-rings my parents bought me for my eighteenth and doing my best to ignore my father's attempts for me to turn towards the camera and smile. People were always encouraging me to smile back then. Especially men. I was very aware of the opposite sex's attraction to me long before I should have been. I could stop traffic and attract wolf-whistles as a pre-pubescent. I had seen grown men gawk when I was just a teenager or turn into juvenile idiots or embarrass themselves with some inappropriate comment. I wore my hair long and straight which was streaked naturally blonde and hung all the way down my back. When practising my wiggle in passing shop window reflections I could make it sway like a shimmering silk curtain. Everything came easy. I had grown up with my eyes being likened to glittering sapphires and exotic seas and azure skies. I had heard it all. And when I began to develop a big breast size I would even catch close family members and friends ogling. An uncle once tried to tongue me. Another time I woke to find my older cousin groping me while I was asleep in my bed. But those experiences aside I knew I was lucky in lots of ways but knew also that of all things my looks and my body were to be my golden ticket in life. That's what my father told me anyway. He didn't tell me how or when that was supposed to happen but after reaching my mid-thirties and going through a series of serious relationships with good-looking boyfriends of perfectly good credential but all of which I eventually ended, I began to realise I was running out of time and so settled upon the idea of marrying a rich older man to look after me.

My phone was one of the last privileges Robert allowed me. After he saw the video he took it away telling me it was for my own good. In the half-light of the TV screen I awoke to find him sitting on the edge of the bed slurping his breakfast. I could hear the scrape of the spoon against the bowl. We hadn't slept together in a long time but he still felt at liberty to come into my bedroom with a pot of coffee and lie around with his feet up watching the news and price indexes as if everything was normal. Everything was not normal but he seemed to have accepted things for so long now that they have become so. It's as if only I remember.

"Turn it over," I said.

"It's all that's on."

"Put on my old movie channel."

"You know, normal people want to wake up and be informed."

"'Normal?'"

"I didn't mean it like that, baby," he sighed.

"Put it on my old movie channel."

"Really? At this time in the morning? Is that all you're going to do all day?"

"What do you care what I do all day?"

"I care," he said, and looked at me.

I didn't like to think of another world out there which is why I kept the curtains closed. I much prefer the past. Old movies. Old TV series and sit coms. Old music. But not, it seems, old videos of myself. When I felt the touch of a cold spoon against my lips I pulled my head back and asked what he was eating.

"Ice cream, pancakes and *berries!*" he announced with gusto, trying to life my spirits. "You need to keep up your strength."

"You're putting over one hundred grams in your mouth with each scoop. I hope you know that."

I swatted the spoon away feeling the early morning depression come on and began bracing myself against the coming highs and lows of the day.

"Come on," he insisted. "Why do we have to go through this every morning? You know you'll feel better when you eat something."

He was right about that. My blood glucose levels were already fluctuating just with that one sudden movement and left me feeling dizzy and weak which wasn't unusual after a heavy weekend's drinking. I watched Robert as he stood up and switched on the bedside lamp. He stifled a belch. Already grimacing at his heartburn and rubbed at his chest as if he might be suffering too and began looking around for what I thought at first to be his pills. But instead he just reached for the remote and began flicking through the channels until he found the tail-end of *Pretty Woman* where Edward goes back to get his girl.

On the point of waking there was always a moment before I recalled where I was. It was like reliving the most terrible realisation again and again. As if I had suffered an accident and had been left paralysed and bed-ridden. That I could only ever dream of strolling barefoot through the surf again or even walking out the door. That's what I thought about the most. Just walking out and never coming back. That was the objective I woke up to each and every morning. But each and every morning was the same. Each and every morning I could feel that old shadow of myself spiralling around inside my aching heart and calling for help. Each and every morning I cried for help. But no one was listening.

After a long marriage my parents had since divorced leaving my mother alone and which is why Robert claimed she was always sticking her nose into our affairs when he of all should talk coming from Italian descent and an overbearing matriarch that he still continued to visit almost every weekend as if she wasn't round the house enough. My father subsequently met someone else and moved away and started a new family at the ripe old age of fifty-five. My brother too, whose job took him abroad and now lives in Staten Island with his American girlfriend.

Robert is the same age as my Dad which took my family some getting used to. One can't help but make the comparison. My father has since had a stroke and is on blood thinners which forced him into retirement. He walks with a stick and has twice contracted gout and moans about his health all the time and how his gums bleed. His toe nails are the colour of a Lamborghini. Despite his age when Robert and I first married it seemed I had so much to look forward to even if my mother did give me every reason and more not to wed him. From the very start they never got on. She suspected his motives. She worried I would just be his plaything. His trophy wife. To be put in a cage high on a mantle like some exotic bird and taken down and let out whenever he felt. Of course I knew better. I was the one in control. He salivated at the sight of me. I made him beg for sex which in the end began to disgust me. I had a credit card with no limit. I didn't have to work. I moved into his mock-Tudor, six-bedroom house on the outskirts of a quaint little village in the Surrey greenbelt and woke up when I felt like it. I had carte blanche choice over redecorating and furnishing. Not that the house needed it. Every room was immaculate even if not given to my taste. It sat in three acres of land backing on to Epsom Downs and had a swimming pool and a tennis court. The gardener drove around on a quad bike. Calum, the cook, had trained under a Michelin star chef. But Robert's maid and cleaner, Martina, was also his sister and had given me problems from the very start. Not only that Robert had been married before and despite his reluctance to talk about it or even so much as produce a photograph of her I could feel his ex-wife's influence everywhere so set about changing things as soon as I could. He didn't care. He was and still is a financial consultant to the super-rich and could get so wrapped up in his work it sometimes took him hours to decompress when he got home, if not an entire weekend which is when the drinking would start. It seems a strange thing to say but if his job hadn't put him under so much pressure, if his mother and sister hadn't been around, we might have been genuine soul-mates. At least that's how he first sold himself to me. We seemed to have a lot in common despite the age gap which was mostly to do with his wealth and the fact he owned a fifty-foot yacht docked in Marbella. I'd never known anyone who had a boat. But we also liked to party. Had expensive tastes. Enjoyed the high-life and both had bon vivant eclectically epicurean appetites. It goes without saying that money was never an issue. Apart from sailing around the Med there were exotic holidays and skiing trips and the best seats at Wimbledon and Ascot. But I realise now these were all just distractions and that I was only ever superficially happy. He would catch me looking at younger men which being of Latin temperament would only drive him crazy. I don't know when it happened that I should be the objectifier instead of the other way around. I ached to be that girl in the video again. Maybe Robert was right to take it away and that my mother had sent it to me out of spite rather than motivation. I hadn't seen her for a long time but she knew even back then I could no longer look in the mirror. What should have been a happy and nostalgic bit of film only depressed me more than I had already become.

"Well, my mother's coming over tonight so I expect you to eat then or you know how she will take offence. Also, Martina will be making you lunch so I don't want you upsetting her either."

"Where's Calum?"

"He's on a pastry chef course so you'll just have to get your eye candy from watching all that reality crap you like," he wheezed, reading into my expression. "Besides, imagine all the different pies he can cook when he gets back."

He clapped his hands in genuine excitement and laughed.

The walk up to the bedroom seemed to have left him out of breath. He was dressed for work and smelt as if he had showered in citrus but had broken into a sweat which was seeping into his shirt and sat glistening on his big, broad, balding scalp and forehead. He sweated a lot. He was hirsute and could afford to lose a few stone and I had long since given up on wishing him dead and imagining everything left to me which had probably been the plan I had in mind. If his maternal side was anything to go by he would live a long life despite his hereditary blood pressure and weight problems. Sofia, his mother, had just turned eighty, was built like a tank and still going strong. His sister, too, was a heavyweight and older than me so it was like having a twin-headed disapproving battle-axe of a mother-in-law in the house most of the time. Only his father's life had been cut short by a scaffold accident when working on a building site many years before which was when Robert stepped up to the plate as head of the family and became ultimate provider. I'd been told all this. The red flags were there from the very beginning. Italian men's love of their mothers borders on the Oedipean. I knew what I was getting into but I chose to ignore them or, like most women, thought I could eventually change my man for the better if only under the threat of withheld sex or divorce or some other twisted form of eventually getting what I wanted. He was easy to manipulate right from the start which is why I ignored all my friends' warnings that you should never marry a mummy's boy. He cried when we rowed. He ran to his Mama before coming back and begging forgiveness. It's no wonder she and her daughter thought I was a bitch. But I came to understand that my capricious behaviour was only the early manifestations of a far deeper torment. That I was not or ever had been physically attracted to him. That I had to be recklessly drunk to have sex. That I had married him for his money and just tried to make the best of it. I thought I had it all figured out when in reality all I really felt was a growing disconnection from myself because it's true what they say. You can't put a price on happiness. Not my six-figure engagement and wedding rings that were to be handed back if we ever separated according to the pre-nup. Not the baby Bentley he bought me for our first anniversary. Not First Class travel or even a never-ending open cheque book. Certainly not a stupid pretentious yacht that he worried over like a precious pet. All of it. All of it just compounded my deepening regret that I had sold out to blind greed without a moment's consideration for something real and of substance and truth but most of all I had sold out to every girl's teenage dream of a love immortal.

At around ten Martina would bring me up her idea of a snack which was usually a milkshake and some cake. Sofia made great cake. Martina really didn't have that much to do around the house so would sit and watch *The Jeremy Kyle Show* with me for her own need of company more than anything else until I took the first of many naps and then she would return with lunch when *Loose Women* started. As usual I told her I didn't want any.

"You know its tiramisu cheesecake," she frowned at me with a little empty laugh as if I was just being silly.

"I know what it is," I looked across at it.

"Mama brought it over this morning. She was up all evening making it for you."

"We have a chef," I said.

"Well, he's not here now, is he?"

"Take it away," I said, because I already had hunger cramps and was feeling a little light-headed at the heavenly sweet scent of it. "I just want some coffee."

Martina cut a slice for herself and dropped a piece down her front she seemed in such a hurry to eat. She caught my gaze and giggled at herself and licked at her fingers.

"Not even a homemade ginger biscuit? Mama made those, too. I brought you some. I bet if I went to the shops and bought you a big fat iced bun round you'd eat that, wouldn't you? Or maybe a box of *Krispy Kremes?*" she tried tempting me.

But it wasn't about the quality of the cake and Martina knew it. Sofia's cooking was some of the best I've ever eaten. Even better than Calum's. Also, Martina was well aware I was starving despite Robert insisting I share in his gargantuan breakfast earlier to the point of being force-fed. Just having the cake in the room was a torturous and cruel thing to do. Already the tears were rolling down my face. I was a prisoner in my own body. Every day was the same struggle. But by the time she brought up a heaped serving bowl of spaghetti Bolognese for my lunch the cake was already gone and I was feeling strangely better. Dismissing my earlier gloom and telling myself that tomorrow was another day. Almost without my knowledge it was as if someone had stolen into my room while I dozed and sat there gorging on the gateau and licking every last forkful of it. Not a sliver. Not a healthy slice. But all six-inch in half-diameter and nearly two pounds of it.

One thing about Robert was I knew he loved me no matter what. He still does. Of course I was out of his league when we first met but the fact he could have bought ten of me evened things up a little. He saw my tits and I saw pound signs. I think we both knew that if we were going to be honest about it. Within the very first hour I'd already cosied up to him much to the amusement of his cohorts who all looked like a pack of drooling jackals ready to pounce should he so much as turn his back. We were in a pole-dancing club which obviously favoured male clientele and I always cruised the VIP sections which is when our eyes met and he instantly beckoned me over. There were ten or twelve of them still in work attire but looking relaxed with their ties yanked down and collared shirts open. They were spread around on leather sofas surrounding a low glass table with three magnum's of Dom Perignon sitting in ice buckets and already red-eyed and boisterous from drinking. I was out on a hen night as my last best friend was about to finally make it up the aisle. The other two already had kids. Inside I was starting to panic.

"Are you going to look after me, big baby boy?" I purred on his lap, for the entertainment of everyone. I already had my eye on another younger guy there who sat quietly looking on from the neon-lit shadows in unbridled appreciation of my body. I had seen that look many times. He would have fucked me in the toilets. But he was a player and no matter how rich he was there was no future in that anymore. I was done with worrying about being cheated on and dreamy empty talk of settling down in the years ahead and having lots of kids and a dog. Those years had vanished from me to the point I had begun to think about the breed of dog more than children's names. Big Baby Boy Robert seemed a far more long-term proposition having quickly established he was a divorcee and on the market once he'd asked about me and my friends' cause for celebration. After that it was easy to continue on the subject of marriage and commitment and failed relationships without sounding in any way desperate even if deep down inside of me that's how I felt.

With his big reassuring arm around me and deep chuckle, even his large belly, I was given to a paternal yearning that I hadn't felt since I was a child. Certainly not in the later years with my own father's selfish and increasingly weak and needy disposition. I realised I missed that and it only made me want to cling to Robert for protection. Also, his one and only real thing of notice to me that night was his friendly, sparkling light blue eyes which I normally find so attractive with a Latin complexion. I was and still am genuinely drawn by them but only in the same way you might the splintered ice-like hue of a timber wolf's or a husky. That's the best I could do. The best I could get to a term of endearment. A pet name. My Big Baby Boy. My Big Husky. But I heard myself say it every time. The way I heard myself testify to loving him. Unless you are comfortable lying about that you will never know how difficult those words are to say to someone who needs to hear it.

I was already building myself up to have sex with him. Something I'd never had to do before. I had plucked men like fruit in the past lured always by the mutual magnetic power of sexual attraction. It was always my choice. I always considered them the lucky ones. I was always the challenge. And when the magic died I knew it was time to go no matter how hard I tried to make it work or felt loyalty to the cause. When the sex has gone it's over for me so I couldn't envisage going to bed with someone I didn't have strong feelings for. Why should anyone? Well, finally I knew. I had played up to Robert. Teased and tantalised and held out as long as I could not because I was a good girl but because despite our budding courtship and love of the excess his hand on mine still felt like a stranger's touch, his tongue in my mouth like that of my uncle's, his groping hands an awkward, fumbling gorilla's that made me want to jolt and freeze. If the plan was ever going to work. If I was going to marry my rich man I would have to go through with it. I knew what I was giving in to. I still believed I could learn to love him if only because of our deepening friendship. He had done some good things for me by then. Wiped out a few debts. Got my father some health care. I truly admired and respected him for that but it would still be like going to bed with a family friend. My uncle. It made me feel sick just to think about it but most of all it made me sad inside. As if I had disappointed my own heart. I could feel it growing weary of expectation. Unfulfilled and beginning to slowly die. There's no escaping that part of yourself. It took nearly a whole bottle of the best tequila in short, swift shots the first time it happened. Perhaps the alcohol addiction had started then. The next morning I struggled to remember any of it.

"Do you know how I know you don't love me? Because I don't *feel* it," he would thump his fist against his heart passionately. "You are incapable of returning my love. I know it. I see it. I *feel* it," he would say over and over.

He was right. Pretending to love is the hardest thing you can ever do. But I wanted to. I really wanted to.

"You have to be drunk to even have sex with me."

"Yeah, and I fake it every time," I would retaliate, if only because sometimes it felt good to tell the truth even if it was disguised as sarcasm.

And yet deep down I was scared of losing him. Of blowing this one last chance I had of carving out some sort of future for myself. Robert was successful, wealthy and generous. He showered me in praise and affection. Sometimes it felt as if he really was my Daddy and I his daughter. He was kind and patient around my infamously difficult and headstrong temperament that had brought previous relationships to a head. Of course I've been spoilt. Of course I've got my own way. I'd been adored as an object all my life but never a person and that made me increasingly suspicious. As a child growing up I became acutely aware of my own father's need to show me off like a prize he had won and seemingly wanting to take all of the credit for. It certainly wasn't my brains he was parading. It felt like I had a sign round my neck saying 'YOU CAN LOOK BUT DON'T TOUCH'. He couldn't have cared less about how well I was doing at school or what was going on in my head.

"You won't need qualifications where you're going," he would assure me. "You can be anything you want. You've got the golden ticket!"

That might have been true if I'd been born a man.

Apart from the sex Robert genuinely didn't expect anything from me. I wasn't used to that. I'd had my guard up so long ready for disappointment I'd forgotten what feeling good about myself was like. We joked all the time. I could make him laugh out loud. We agreed on virtually everything and really hit it off to the point we spent all his free time together which I grew happy and excited to do even at the expense of my family and friends. My friends were all married and making families of their own anyway. My parents were divorced. My brother moved away. I'd never thought of being left on my own or that my looks would fade and when I started to gain a bit of weight along with my new and comfortable existence I was never in any doubt I could shake it off. But after we married it began to make me a little self-conscious and so I was more than happy to be away from the spotlight of people who had seen me in my prime. I felt myself beginning to hide and began to cover up around Robert who took it as just another indication of my coldness towards him. I stopped posing for photographs. Began to loathe the shape of myself in the mirror. I obsessed over the bear cub swell of my tummy, the sudden heaviness of my breasts. The roll of flesh beneath my chin and puffy eyes first thing in the morning. And yet if I could go back to that time now I know that it was just a matter of some extra pounds. Maybe a stone at the very most. But I had stayed the same size all my life. Had ate and drank whatever I wanted. It was like my metabolism had slowed down overnight. It was making me miserable not being able to wear the same dress size even if Robert was forever telling me that the girl stood in front of him was the girl he knew and loved. He was continually supportive. He'd done nothing wrong or so I thought at the time. He always said the right things and I wholeheartedly believed him when he said I was gorgeous and that my change in figure suited me but he'd begun to use words like curvaceous and voluptuous which to any woman just translates as fat. I'd become fat and there seemed no signs of stopping. Diet pills didn't work. Switching from beer and wine to vodka didn't work. Forcing myself to throw up after a meal just made me hungrier even if my love of food was the only thing that made me happy, however temporary that was. I was caught in a vicious cycle and it didn't help that Robert loved the same things as me and which was generally his answer to everything.

"You have to help me," I would plead.

"Start tomorrow," he'd say. "You have all day to diet or lay off the booze why can't you just eat and drink with me when I get home? You know how I have to unwind."

So I would eat for the pleasure and drink to block out the despair. Accusing Robert of liking my extra weight just so that men would stop looking at me. Well, men were still looking at me. But not the sort that I was used to. Not the young, fit, good-looking type I would reel in with a glance. They were older men. Men like Robert but without the money. Men who had once known their place in the pecking order. Men I used to intimidate. But now the butcher in the village, the postman, the creep who worked the counter at the post office all seemed perfectly at liberty to try their luck. Now it was all I could do to get Harry the gardener to stop with his innuendoes and harassment whenever the opportunity arose.

"What would it take?" he wanted to know. Harry always had a twinkle in his eye and was almost herding me into the potting shed as I walked around the grounds one day trying to shake off a hangover. "I mean, a woman like you. You're so hot. I mean it. You're the hottest woman in the village. Would you go out with a man like me if you wasn't married to Robert? What is it? Is it money? Is that what it would take?"

The hottest woman in the village didn't take much if the locals who drank in the pub were anything to go by. Harry was in his fifties, weathered and lined from his exposure to the outdoors all his life and walked with a slight limp but sported a distinguished grey goatee and slicked back his full head of hair with some such product that always smelt good so obviously he still thought of himself as worth presenting. Good for him. But apart from the audacity of abusing his position and hitting on me every chance he got what chance could he have possibly thought he had? Unless I was still thinking like the girl inside. The girl in the video my mother had sent instead of this new older me with what Harry described as my 'sensual womanly curves.'

I wanted to die.

"Get away from me, Harry," I pushed him, unsure if it was his idea of a joke. "Not only am I married, but so are you."

"Yeah, and I bet you're a real pain in the arse," he said brazenly, looking me over.

"I am. But I make up for it in other ways," I said, not only because I was desperate to feel good about myself and see his jaw drop but because it was true. My talents didn't just run skin deep. At least not until I married Robert. I ached to feel real sexual contact again. To command that power over a man. To be taken by near force. Sometimes I even dreamed about me and Calum. But he wasn't interested and even if he was I couldn't be sure I had the self-confidence to go through with it. It might have to be with the lights off. I might have to be drunk. What had happened to me?

Looking back I blame drink. It became the answer to everything. It didn't help that at the weekend Robert would pop open a beer for breakfast and our forty-eight hour bender would pretty much start from there. We'd both become functioning alcoholics but the difference was he still held down a job when on Monday morning all I had to think about was drinking out of sight of Robert's mother and sister, both of whom had keys to the house. I would go back to bed in the day feigning headaches or some other sickness that only enhanced my reputation as being of high-maintenance. But their continuing and often unexpected presence just made me feel like locking myself away. I would lay around in my bedroom watching TV and scoffing down last night's leftovers. Sofia never threw anything out and I had got into the habit of going back to the fridge for seconds and thirds through the night. A lot of it pasta based or rich, seductive desserts. I began eating for comfort. Because I was bored and lonely and because it was there. Sofia was always cooking and bringing stuff over in competition with Calum who Robert told me had originally been employed as some sort of part-time 'life coach' to get his mind and body in shape after he'd got divorced. Apart from Calum's health-driven culinary skills he had also worked as a personal trainer and yoga instructor. He was younger than me and easy on the eye and as lithe as a serpent. But from the very first time upon meeting him it was as if we could tell what each other was up to. Robert was easy prey and that remained understood until I started to lose shape and then I began to involve Calum in some more unconventional requests to help me lose weight that he was reluctant to go along with but seemed somehow tacitly complicit. We were both carrion feeding off the same carcass.

The temptation to eat was constant. Of course it was my choice but I began to suspect it was also a very subtle form of control instigated by my husband to keep me imprisoned at home. I rarely felt like going out anymore because I could feel women in particular staring or passing comment. When he socialised it was always after work which would only leave me feeling more alone and insecure that he had picked up a girl at a club with his cronies. Someone slim with firm breasts and on the prowl for a rich man. My former doppelganger self. Surely Robert could see what was happening to me. Not least his mother and sister. But of course they were all big. Martina never stopped stuffing her fat face. Upon the moment of first meeting them I could see the resentment in their stony faces. Their eyes roving over me with some warped disapproval or that I should be taking Robert for a ride. I could never be myself around them. And when they wanted to say something they spoke in Italian to each other which is not only rude but one of the worst humiliations you can go through. It makes you feel stupid and inadequate. Every day was becoming the same. I would go to sleep each night telling myself tomorrow would be different. I thought about leaving all the time. Of asking for help. I wanted to phone my mother and friends and tell them how unhappy I was without them having say I told you so but I was also very ashamed. I began to ignore all their messages to meet up because by then I was carrying almost twice my perfect weight and my self-loathing had gone beyond my appearance and was starting to eat into my mental state. I only slept when I was full or comatose from drink. I had loss all self-respect. I despised myself for being so weak and dependent. When Robert and I argued I blamed him for refusing to see it and for being the reason I was so unhappy but he only attributed it to vanity.

"Why do you want to look like that girl anyway?" he would seize a wedding photograph and thrust it in my face.

But I couldn't look at them anymore. They made me want to cry and he knew it. I could still feel the sickness in my stomach not only from that day but weeks and even months before. I wanted it but I didn't. I could still hear the voice inside my head telling me I was making a mistake. I couldn't smile properly for all the photographer's jolly coaxing that brought about ripples of polite laughter from the congregation. It just magnified the pressure. I felt like an overnight paranoid celebrity star unready for the bright lights. My eyes searched my family and friends for help. My mother going through the act of holding my father's arm who in turn had his other wife's arm and his walking stick hooked in his waistcoat. My brother and his big-toothed grin of an American wife who we had only ever pretended to see eye-to-eye on. Couldn't they see it or were they just glad to get me off their backs? I felt like I was being taken across a border to another land and would never return. I didn't love Robert. Not in the way he needed. I would never love him. I knew that. I had wasted my one chance in life. My golden ticket.

"For the same reason you wanted to marry her," I turned my face away.

"I married you for the person. Do you understand? I married you because I love *you*. But you wouldn't know how that feels, would you? All this…this cold, self-centred, frigid bitch of a wife wanted to do was buy a big diamond ring to show off to her friends," he stabbed at the picture and addressed the room as if in front of an audience. "All this conceited, gold-digging *cunt* of a wife wanted to do was to go on holidays and spend my money and threaten me with divorce every week or be so drunk to have sex she can't even remember what hole she's been fucked in."

"And you call that love, Robert?"

"If I can't fuck you when you're awake I will fuck my little drunken whore of a wife when she's passed out in whatever orifice is available to me because they have all been fucked before with everything and anyone and anything anyway. Isn't that right, baby?"

When he became abusive like that there was no reasoning. The conversation would lead to old boyfriends or the odd casual acquaintance I'd made the mistake of admitting to. He seemed incapable of accepting I had a past or that it was my choice who I'd slept with. Half the time I didn't even remember telling him. But he did. He recalled every story in detail to the point it began to feel he had such a hold on me I lived in fear of even referring to a time or place just to explain some innocent old anecdote. When he saw the video my mother sent me he was more obsessed by my boyfriend of over twenty years before than how I once looked. Of course, I'd told him all about Andy as he'd been my first real love but that didn't stop Robert from stealing into my room sometime after while I slept and deleting nearly every picture on both my phone and my iPad along with my entire directory. All my memories were on those devices. My entire digital life. I didn't care about the contacts. I hadn't spoken to anyone in a long time and when I did it was only to make an excuse not to meet them. Half the time they thought I was living the life of royalty anyway with a new circle of friends and may even have got above my station in life. Only my mother persisted. She worried at the sound of my voice over the phone. She read through my lies. She knew something was wrong but I would rather her believe anything than the awful truth. I hadn't seen my mother in over a year. Around the time my body mass index made me technically obese. She didn't have to say anything. In fact she said everything but. I knew then I couldn't see her again until I had sorted myself out. But it turned out to be just another day of false promises to myself.

Robert has since taken my devices away. He says I can have them back when I start taking responsibility for my actions but I know him. He would have made a note of all my old contacts before deleting them. Especially one or two ex-boyfriends who still kept in touch and would often message me with the odd request to meet up. I knew what that usually meant. I knew also that one of them married on the rebound from breaking up with me. I'd chewed up a few along the way. They all ended up limping off like hit-and-run dogs. Did Robert really think any man would be interested in me at the size I had become? The size he has slowly and systematically enabled me into becoming because of his self-destructive, utterly irrational insecurity. 'Enabling' is often a term used in the context of an addict and means to remove the natural consequences of someone's behaviour. Co-dependents often feel compelled to solve their partner's problems for them so what apparent well-intentioned desire was behind Robert's insistence to force-feed me each time I set my mind into losing a few pounds? When, if they hadn't strapped me down, I would wake to find his mother and sister sitting on my hands while he poured some revolting concoction from the blender down a funnel into my throat and then, to teach me a lesson, leave me lying in bed in my own vomit? Some sort of twisted Pygmalion story this had become. He had married me still at the peak of my years but couldn't cope with so much as the gardener looking at me.

With that thought in mind I heard Robert talking to Harry outside my bedroom window after just such an episode. Season after season had passed since I last saw Harry and I missed the walks around the garden and even his lascivious eye. A girl still likes to feel good about herself. I can't remember the last whistle I attracted. Sometimes I would hear Harry's quad bike but by the time I had shuffled towards the window he had gone and I was usually too breathless to call out and tell him they had started to lock me in my own bedroom. But this time he and Robert had stayed chatting long enough for me to reach the window seat before I began shouting down to Harry that I was being kept prisoner and could he please get help. Whatever I thought I had become. Whatever I had been scared to see in the mirror all this time was written through Harry's face.

I knew then what it was like to be a monster.

Moments later Robert came pounding up the stairs with his sister as they rushed towards me showing the sort of concern you might a sickly five-year-old found wandering out of bed and so tried ushering me back in.

"See what you've done to me?" I yelled, as much for the purpose of Harry who I hoped was still in shock and rooted to the spot outside.

"My baby," Robert was crying. "My beautiful baby. I love you."

But I knew he was only saying that for Harry's sake.

"You wanted me this size? You didn't like me the way I was? You wanted a big fat fucking wife the size of your mother and sister rolled into one because my body intimidated you? Because you couldn't even get your flaccid drunken shrimp of a dick up? Because you wanted to fuck a roly-poly just like your mother! You sick fucking mummy's boy!"

"Please, baby. Stop it. Please. I beg you."

He was sobbing uncontrollably. And then his mother entered and started getting involved.

"Holy Mother of God! What's all this disturbance now? Hush child," she hurried in and stroked at my brow before I heard her say: "Let's get her out of this mess."

"She's supposed to do it herself, Mama," Robert wailed. "You don't do what she is capable of doing."

"Well, she's not going to do it is she, Roberto?" Sofia snapped. "The poor baby's been sitting in it all day and night. I'm not putting up with anymore mumbo-jumbo. She needs changing and washing. Poor child."

"Yes, Mama."

He nodded and leant forward and kissed my cheek.

I felt suddenly too exhausted to push him away or even turn my head. It was all a show. I had embarrassed Robert in front of the gardener and now he was trying to cover up his neglect of me. They all were. I wasn't fooled for a minute by their looks of pity and concern.

The time I finally agreed to try counselling Robert got me there under the pretention we were going to talk about our alcohol addiction. But after just a quick lecture on 'managing our consumption', Robin, the counsellor, moved into more personal territory and I began to realise we hadn't come to talk about us at all. Looking around the room I had already seen what I presumed to be a mirror that had been taken down from the wall and left propped in a corner of his office facing away.

"What would be a typical day's diet for you?" he wanted to know.

"Diet isn't a word I'd use," I looked across at Robert and laughed.

"That's interesting you should pick me up on that. What do you think 'diet' means?"

"What is this, playschool?"

I glared at Robert to help me out but he remained stony-faced and staring ahead.

"Ok, well. What word would you use?"

"Well, look at us. It's obvious we don't survive on salads."

"Breakfast, for instance."

"I thought we were here to talk about drink," I frowned and looked from one to the other. "Oh, I forgot. We covered that. Go home and manage it yourself. What sort of advice is that? If that's your *modus operandi* for everything you might as well lock me in a bakery."

"And what would happen if I did?"

"What do you mean?"

"Ooh, I don't know," he formed a steeple with his fingers and tried adopting a friendly tone. "What do you think would happen if I locked you in a shop full of bread and cakes and delicious strawberry tarts?"

"Are you patronising me?" I wanted to know.

"Of course not," he smiled unsurely and looked at Robert.

We were both looking at Robert.

"Well, then you must be being cruel."

"He's just asking, baby," Robert said quietly.

"He's not asking he's insinuating."

"What am I insinuating?"

"That I'm obese. Morbidly obese. That's ok. But I'd prefer you just say it."

"I wasn't…"

"I'd prefer you just call me a fat fucking cow if I'm honest. If we're going to put our cards on the table and that's the real reason I'm here. It's what went through your mind when I came in anyway, isn't that right? I've grown used to that look. You might think you're above thinking those things because of a couple of online diplomas you've printed off but you're not. We're all conditioned to think like that in the same way my first impression of you was that you're probably gay, you can't grow a proper beard and that Robin's a name for a nancy boy."

"Jesus, I'm sorry-" Robert spluttered.

"That's ok," Robin held up a hand.

"Don't apologise for me," I snapped at my conniving husband for colluding into bringing me there. "He wants to know what I eat and then starts talking about strawberry tarts when he tells us to go back home and carry on drinking? We're fucking alcoholics for Christ's sake. We drink every fucking day. Everything that's happened to us is because of alcohol. We can't function without alcohol. You want admittance how about that?"

"What do you mean by 'everything that's happened'?"

"You want the truth?"

"It's a good place to start."

"Jesus, why can't you just answer normally? Why can't you just say 'yes'.

Beside me Robert shifted in his seat and sighed heavily.

"Yes," said Robin

It was on the tip of my lips. Everything that Robert knew but had never been properly said. I didn't love my husband. That I had to block out sex with drink. That I was dying inside. That I had to stuff my fat face because I was so unhappy. And that over the course of time Robert had knowingly encouraged that.

"I could show you some pictures of what I used to look like. You wouldn't believe," I hung my head and uttered. "That is until my jealous husband decided to get rid of them."

"Baby, you're still gorgeous," Robert said softly. "I just want you to get better."

"Then help me, Robert," I beseeched him. "Stop feeding me. How long does this have to go on?"

"You're husband loves you," Robin said. But there was a delicacy about his words. As if he was treading on eggshells. "He's trying to help but you have to recognise what's going on here as well or…"

"Or what? I'll clog up my arteries until I explode? You think I don't know that? You think I don't know I could get type 2 diabetes or coronary heart disease or have a heart attack or get any number of cancers? You think I don't know the consequences of my eating disorder?"

"So you admit you have an eating disorder?"

Beside me I felt Robert sit up.

I sighed and shrugged limply.

"Baby?" Robert said.

"Well, it was one of the deadly sins, right?"

"What was?" Robin leaned forward over his desk. "What was one of the deadly sins?"

"Gluttony," I looked at both of them.

What the counsellor didn't get to finish saying was that if I didn't get better I may have to go into hospital, or so Robert told me a few days after. I'd awoken to find him sitting on the edge of the bed watching me doze with a solemn expression on his face. He had opened a curtain. It was still light out.

"Good," I said, wearily. "Maybe I'll get some proper nutrition without having blended cookies and cream shoved down my throat in the middle of the night while you strap me to the bed."

"I've never put blend-"

"You think I don't know what's behind all this? You're so afraid of offending your Mama you have to liquidise a chocolate mud cake just so that you can say I've eaten some. Who cares about my calorie intake?"

"It's not that sort of hospital," he said, in order to shut me up.

"What?"

"Baby, I just want you to get better."

"Can you stop saying that. What sort of hospital is it, then?" I tried sitting up. "A rehab? You're going to stick me in rehab?"

"It's too late for that."

"What are you talking about?"

But his guilty expression said it all.

"You can't mean like a mental institution? Is that what you're saying? You're going to stick me in a fucking asylum?"

"Calm down. They don't call them that anymore."

"You're going to have me sectioned?"

"I don't want to. It would be a last resort."

"You can't have me sectioned," I began to laugh a little manically. "What do you think this is a Hitchcock movie? I'm obese not insane. You can't lock up people for being overweight or half the country would be in the nuthouse."

"They'll know how to look after you. I've tried. I've done my best."

"And all this on the strength of what some agony aunt of a counsellor says? I don't think so, Robert."

"Robin is more than just a counsellor. I've known him a long time. I trust his opinion."

"'Opinion'? *Opinion?* What the hell does that mean? I thought we were going there together. To talk about us. And now you're telling me what? That all the time I was being psychoanalyzed?"

"Assessed, yes."

"By Mr Tank Top? By Mr fucking CAMRA subscriber? Give me a fucking break, Robert," I looked at him. "You lied to me. We were supposed to be going there to talk about drink."

"And when was the last drink you had? Can you tell me that?"

"What does that matter? I can't hold out a hand for shaking. I'm scared that if I touch a drop I won't be able to stop. I'm scared that just a whiff of cooking sherry will set me off. That's an alcoholic, Robert."

He went to put his hand on mine but thought better of it.

"Aww, what's the matter, big baby boy?" I pouted at him. "Did your little plan backfire? You wanted a big girl so men would stop looking at me? You wanted a girl the size of your Mama but then you couldn't stop me from getting bigger and bigger just like that kid Augutus Gloop and now I disgust you so much you can't even touch me? You want to lock me in a cell and throw away the key so you don't have to look at your handy work anymore because locking me in my own bedroom isn't enough? Will your ex-wife be in the cell next to me? Did you feed her up, too? Is that what happened? Why won't you tell me about your wife? Why won't you show me a picture? Is she as hideous to look at as me?"

"I love you, baby," he closed his eyes and shook his head.

"It's true. I saw the revulsion on Harry's face. You know not so long ago he would have had me in the potting shed. Are you listening? Your gardener wanted to fuck me and he would have if I'd let him, if it hadn't all been such a tragic fucking cliché."

"Harry cares about you just like the rest of us. He asks after you every time I see him."

"I know what Harry wants."

"Will you just stop!" he suddenly yelled. "Why do you still insist on trying to make me jealous? Even now? I mean, what's the point? Listen. You're right, okay? I wanted you for my own but not in the way you think. I'm a jealous man. I have reason to be. Who wouldn't feel protective of you? But you're wrong if you think it has anything to do with my not being able to cope with some pictures of old boyfriends. I'm jealous that I'll never be able to make you love me in the way you did them. And you did. You've been sure to let me know about that in some detail."

"Then give me my phone back," I blinked at him, suddenly feeling the need to skirt the issue because he may have had a point. It became a defence mechanism of mine when we started drinking and I would feel Robert's expectations growing to bring up explicit stories of old boyfriends. For instance, my first beau, Andy, could control his climax to exactly the same point as mine so that we came together completely. It was the first thing we would joke about years after when we ran into each other. I would tell Robert these things not to make him angry but just to put him off. But of course in doing that it still made him angry. I just didn't know how else to deal with his advances no matter how much I drunk but to summon up some past and pleasurable fantasy in morbid preparation for sex. Given the benefits of marrying Robert I thought it would be easy. I thought I would get used to it. But sex with my husband was never like it had been with the men I'd truly loved or even hadn't. There was no animal arousal. No passion. No tenderness. It was brutal and invasive. I felt like I was being raped and just wanted the whole horror over with. It wasn't his fault. He might as well have been trying to mount roadkill. We should never have been together.

"You do know why I took your phone, don't you?" he tried patiently, as if we had been down this road before.

"I want my mother. I want my phone back before you get rid of what few memories I have left on there."

"I didn't get rid of them," he replied softly. "*You* did. And if you get rid of what's left for whatever reason I just want you to know I have saved the remainder onto the computer just in case you ever want them back."

"Are you trying to make me think I'm mad?" I gave him a curious look. "Is that what you're all trying to do? I may be a lot of things, Robert. I may be a depressed alcoholic. I may be a greedy fat hog but I'm not crazy."

"You're not crazy," he agreed patiently. "But you are unwell. *Very* unwell."

"I want to call my mother. You're not locking me up in some funny farm where you can forget about me. If you want a divorce just say so. We've been over this. You got your pre-nup. What are you still trying to protect? Just fucking divorce me. I'll walk away from here with just the shirt on my back. You hear me? I want a divorce!"

I sat back breathlessly.

"I can call your mother if you'd like," he offered, after a moment had passed.

"Why? So you can fill her head with all the crap you're trying to convince me of?"

"No, because the last conversation you had with her you ended up screaming down the phone and telling her that you never wanted to see her again. You accused her of deliberately trying to upset you by sending that old video of your birthday."

"I want to see it again," I said sullenly. "I want to see how beautiful I was. I want to see Andy. He was my first love. We could come together at the same time. Did I ever tell you?"

"You deleted it," he took a deep breath.

"Liar," I said, and crossed my arms. "Jealous of a twenty-year-old boy. Stupid. He's married now with kids. He probably doesn't even think about me."

"You deleted it like you did nearly all the other pictures because you couldn't stand to look at how you were and, I'm afraid to say, the life you clearly feel you missed out on. After that you told me to get rid of all the mirrors in the house or..."

"Or what?" I asked, remembering the mirror that had been taken down in the counsellor's office.

"Or...you would smash them all like the ones you did in this bedroom. Not just the mirrors but every reflective surface. That's pretty much the whole house. That's why your door is locked, that's why your wrists and arms are bandaged."

"These aren't bandages. They're straps for when you tie me down at night and force a funnel into my mouth."

"There's nothing to stop you from taking them off but you should be careful. The left wrist needed stitching. You hurt yourself. If you could bear to look in the mirror you would see that you cut your face quite deeply in places, too. You are in very great danger of hurting yourself again which is why you should be getting professional care."

"If you would just stop feeding me. If you would just let me lose a few pounds I could get through this," I began to grow anxious. "I know you think you are doing a good thing but you're just making it worse. I don't want this life anymore. We're done with the eating and drinking. I mean it, Robert. No more force-feeding. I don't expect to be that girl in the video again. I can live with a few curves. 'The girl before you is the one you know and love'? Do you remember saying that?"

"And it's still true," he replied with a soft smile.

"Then help me, Robert."

"Baby, I'm out of ideas. I'm at my wits end," he hung his head and began to sob.

I'd never heard him talk like this. He was beginning to frighten me. In taking his love for granted the one thing I never expected was for him to give up on me but that's what it was beginning to sound like. Could he get away with it? Could Robin the shrink or whatever he was really have me put away? As much as I had tried to hide from the world. As much as I didn't want my family and friends to see me like this I was going to have to enlist the help of someone I trusted. And that person could only be my mother.

My first experience of Robert's overbearing jealousy was in the early months of our relationship when we were texting each other back and forth like teenagers. It felt good to have someone back in my life again but for all the activity on the phone even then I kept waiting for something to happen. A spark. A tingle of excitement. Anything. But all I felt was a continuing foreboding in me to end it there and then and so I continued to play hard to get which naturally only seemed to further his interest. Ostensibly, it couldn't have been further from the truth that I didn't appear particularly impressed by his prosperity. Robert had a yacht. He was exactly the sort of man I had set out to find. And so I let him wine and dine me. I accepted his presents and yielded to his insistence on settling some outstanding accounts. We genuinely got on and shared the same sense of humour which was not only unusual for me but only made things more difficult because it was always at the back of my mind that if our relationship was to continue it would eventually lead to sex and by then I knew that I would only ever regard him as a friend. I told myself he had nice eyes. I told myself he was kind and generous and a chance like him might never come along again. It wasn't even anything to do with his physique. I'd dated heavier guys before. Rock that beer gut. I just didn't feel it with him and there was an increasing pressure in my knowing that he knew it, too. With each date I began drinking to excess through nerves alone and then one summer's day he text to ask what I was doing and when I told him I was sunbathing he asked me to send him a picture. By that time it shouldn't have felt like an inappropriate request but in feeling strangely self-conscious about doing so I instinctively sent one I'd taken the year before for a guy I'd had a hot and heavy fling with over the course of a few months. It was just a selfie of me lying in a skimpy bikini on a sunbed taken from over my shoulder. You couldn't see my head but my body looked good. There was the remotest exposure of a nipple. My stomach lay firm and flat. My smooth golden legs stretched all the way down to where my ankles crossed. My toenails pedicured that very day and painted a bright blush pink. I didn't even think about it. I sent the picture because even then I had begun to obsess on the few pounds I'd put on since meeting Robert and so just wanted to show him one of me looking my best. I'd put none of it together. But his growing silence after and refusal to answer my messages had left me feeling confused and slightly panicked until I could bear it no longer and for the first time since meeting him I acted out of impulse and went to wait for him in a wine bar in London outside his place of work that I knew he frequented at the end of the day.

In the event I was brought near to tears within minutes of seeing him. Not least because I felt so foolish for spending the day making an effort getting my hair and nails done and feeling good about myself. Only the stupefying shock of his behaviour kept my emotions in check though I shook and trembled within as if I had just been told the most terrible news. It was a warm evening and he was stood at the end of a deeply crowded bar so noisy you could hear it from the street. He'd only ever spoke about the haunt. I'd never been there. Robert was based in the financial district and I never really did get to know any of his friends very well but my interpretation of the kind he mixed with was that a lot of mutual back-scratching went on. Traders, bankers, consultants and fellow advisors. Money people. By the way he spoke and from what I'd seen I also got the impression very early on that there was a heavy drinking culture within the group. The best champagne flowed. Old Fashioned and martinis were the favoured cocktails and slugged down like shots. They all played hard outside of office hours even if by contrast Robert was quite misanthropic at weekends and just wanted to stay home but where of course the revelry would always continue. At the time I'd no idea what I was getting into. I'm sure I'm not the only one who felt a lot of peer pressure being around Robert. If he insisted on one more round then everyone usually complied. Because of that he'd adopted the nickname 'The Reverend' on account of the persuasive cases he could put forward as a reason to carry on imbibing, or, for that matter, any excess whether it was a gut-busting dessert or staying out all hours. To this day I really don't know how his addictive personality hasn't brought about repercussions in his career or at least reduced him to burn-out. "Yes, Reverend!" they would cheer in unison. "Whatever The Reverend says." And that joke carried on into our own relationship for quite a while until it began to wear thin with me and I realised the more sinister connotations of the title. Because it really was like being held under the spell of a preacher. His insistence could render you with a feeling of such powerlessness that you were virtually left unable to say no. You didn't want to let him down or have his love of you doubted and in that sense I found his character very charismatic in the beginning. But the deeper knowledge that I was turned off by the idea of having sex with him was always there like a crime I was on the verge of committing and still had serious moral reservations about.

Within seconds of seeing me he had pulled up the picture I'd sent him and started showing it round to his following much to the awkwardness of some but not all as if he had been waiting for that very moment to do it. I was mortified at being exhibited in such a way and so snatched the phone from some giggling cretin's grasp, my hands shaking so much I immediately dropped it and cracked the screen.

"Why would you care who sees it when it obviously wasn't even intended for me?" Robert announced. "The date it was taken is a year old. I'm assuming you didn't take a selfie of your tits for your own pleasure. I'm assuming that nipple shot was intended to titillate someone else."

"Wait, there was a flash of nip?" someone else leered. "I missed that."

"Yeah, well it's fucked now," Robert was looking at his phone. He only swore when he was angry. He already looked unsteady and sounded drunk and miserable. It still didn't seem like that much of a big deal to me but it had clearly upset him and I didn't know how to make it right in the presence of such a pathetically transparent testosterone-charged audience, most of whom were wearing wedding bands.

"Haven't you got some pictures on your phone you prefer to more recent ones?" I stood my ground.

"Not in a bikini I hope," the guy next to him said, but it sounded like he was trying to diffuse the situation. "Come on. I'm Ian. What would you like to drink?" he asked me.

"Who was he?" Robert wanted to know.

I was trembling inside. I'd never felt so humiliated or under such scrutiny. Not even in the days my father would show me off. I was also livid that I was being put under pressure to explain my past to a bunch of half-drunk males I'd never even met. The golden ticket never seemed so far from the truth. Standing there I felt like a piece of meat on parade but I also felt desperate to reconcile with Robert and get him away from his sickening circle of sycophants I instinctively didn't trust.

"It doesn't matter. He was no one," I said.

"When was the last time you saw him?"

"Can't we do this somewhere else?" my voice shook.

"When was the last time you fucked him?"

"Jesus, Bobby," someone said.

The mood had turned dark and toxic. Other people had started to watch.

"I don't know. When was the last time you fucked someone, Robert?" I jeered. "When was the last time you fucked someone who wasn't your wife?" I looked around at everyone.

"Fuck you, bitch," came a voice.

"What did you say to her?" Robert's husky eyes would turn aquamarine when he grew angry.

"Ok, calm down, big man," his friend Ian said and put a hand against Robert's puffed up chest. "Everyone just calm the fuck down."

"It's ok, I'm going anyway," I said. "I shouldn't have come."

"Wait, stay," Ian went to put an arm out.

"Let her go," someone else called. "Go find another mine to dig."

"Are we getting another round in Reverend or what?"

I got out of the bar and began walking in circles feeling dazed and confused. It was like I'd walked into a post and hadn't yet realised where I was. Suddenly I felt someone take my arm and guide me to a low wall by the river to sit on. It was Ian. He was tall and dark-featured and had a nice soft Scottish accent that I found very calming. He was a bit younger than the others and wasn't busting out of his suit. Maybe a bit too slim for my liking but I might have dated him for his Gaelic charm alone.

"Whoa, there," he said. "You're going to end up under a bus if you're not careful. Let's just sit down and take a breather for a minute, shall we?"

"I'm sorry," I said, without knowing why.

I could feel every passer-by cast an eye over me sitting on that brick wall dressed up in a tight top and skirt and with Ian reaching a consoling arm around my shoulder as if I had somehow let myself down. Like those young girls you see on the local news on New Year's Eve staggering around in heels in the inner-cities after a drinking binge and throwing up in the street with their knickers on show. I wasn't used to chasing men not least someone the same age as my father. What had I been thinking all these years? I'd been left behind. I was in a different arena. I was beginning to feel old and out of touch.

"Do you know he hasn't spoken to me for three weeks because of that stupid fucking picture?" I shook my head, feeling a wave of indignation. "Who cares who it was meant for? Don't we all have past photos on our phones? I shouldn't have to justify to him what I was doing this time last year any more than he should me. Weren't we all in another place once? He was married for Christ's sake. Not that I've ever seen a picture of *her*. Can you believe that? He hasn't even got one. That's what he says, anyway. He won't even talk about it."

Ian sucked in his breath, making a whistling noise as if I couldn't have touched on a more sensitive subject.

"What happened?" I asked. "Do you know?"

"It's not really my place, I'm afraid," he pulled a tight face.

"Are you telling me that lot you're with don't know or haven't talked about it behind his back?"

He conceded my point with a shrug. A huge roar of laughter erupted from inside the bar causing us both to look over.

"There's no loyalty in there," I said. "It's all bullshit. Let's all 'revere the Reverend.'" I quoted cynically with a sneer. "They must all be getting something out of him. Why can't he see it?"

"And what about you?" he asked.

"What do you mean?"

"Why are you here?"

"I like him," I said.

"I like puppies," he replied. "But they're not just for Christmas." He patted my knee and stood up. "Be careful with Bobby," he advised me with a look that was meant just for us. "He's been hurt like you wouldn't believe."

"Are you going to tell me or not?" I called out to him tiredly as he went to walk away.

He stopped and looked around as if to see if anyone else was in earshot but the area was teeming with after-work revellers and buzzing with expectation. Ian came back and sat down. A welcome light breeze was coming off the water but despite my anger I still felt shaken and anxious.

"You can never say you know," Ian warned. "It's up to him to tell you."

"Did she cheat on him?" I asked a little too quickly, because I had never understood Robert's reticence on the matter and now I was close to knowing I just wanted it told straight to me.

"I mean it," Ian scowled at me.

"Okay," I took a deep breath and nodded.

"She disappeared."

I blinked. Not fully understanding what he meant.

"It's as exactly as I just said it."

"What? Like a missing person or something?"

"Not quite. She took all her stuff."

"How does someone disappear?"

"She didn't leave a trace."

"Why?"

He shrugged.

"Well, you must have a theory, Ian."

"I guess it just wasn't meant to be."

"What does that mean? That doesn't mean anything."

"She jilted him at the altar," he said.

"Oh my God," I felt my mouth go limp.

"I was there."

"Oh my God, the poor baby," I felt myself want to cry.

"He's been broken," Ian put a hand on mine and squeezed hard.

"But he told me he was divorced."

"That's what he tells everyone. It's easier for him to say that even if everyone knows the truth. And aside from the real thing you don't come much nearer to a marriage and divorce than he did. It just all happened in a single day for him. Well, weeks I suppose. When it all eventually sunk in and he realised she'd gone for good."

"Didn't he try and find her?"

"She didn't want to be found. That's the point."

"Why would she do that?" I asked myself quietly. "There must have been a reason. Was there someone else involved, do you think?"

"Bobby drove himself crazy thinking like that for a long time. But deep down I think he knew."

I felt myself shudder. I didn't bother to respond because I thought I knew what Ian was going to say next.

"In a way, you sort of have to admire it. Bobby's a great catch. But all the money in the world can't make you love someone if you don't. She did him a favour in the end. She listened to her heart."

Robert didn't tell me until after what happened. Anything I got to know about his wife-to-be I learnt from his mother which wasn't much apart from the fact the woman was regarded as a pariah within the household. Sofia and Martina had both been sworn to secrecy but they also didn't like to see Robert upset and so it had become almost like a family tragedy. No one ever spoke about it. And if I brought it up it was only in reference to the fact he never did. Sometimes I genuinely implored him that it might be cathartic for us both to do so. Matrimony shouldn't have mysteries. But in reality there was part of me that didn't want it out in the open either because I had come to believe the root cause of his suspicious nature lay not entirely in his insecurities about my not loving him and which in itself became an exhausting lie, but that even a pre-nuptial marriage was no guarantee that I would not one day walk out of his life just like she had done. In fact, as time went on it just made it easier for me to do so because as I constantly reminded him when arguing there was nothing to even keep me there. And so he talked constantly about changing the agreement. That I had proved my love to him by signing it and now he wanted to prove his love to me by ripping it up. I can't say I tried to talk him out of it. But after a course of time I realised it was always just going to be the carrot on the end of the stick. That it was all part of his plan to keep me right where he wanted.

"You were right all along, Mum," I told her over the phone. "Except he didn't want to put me in a cage high on a mantle and let me out like a bird whenever he wanted. He did the opposite. He wanted to stuff me like a pig for Christmas until no one else would ever look at me. Until I can't even bear to look at myself. I'm just warning you before you come."

"I know, my darling girl," she sounded moved to tears. "I'm just so glad

I'm getting to see you."

"Aren't you listening to me? I'm not that darling girl anymore. I'm not that girl in the video."

"You'll always be my darling girl."

"Stop it. You sound like him. Always telling me I'm gorgeous. He wants me this way, Mum. He couldn't stop me walking away so he made it so I couldn't. I can't even get out of bed half the time. I've get an air flow tube up my nose. You can't let him put me away, Mum. They tie me down and force-feed me."

"I know, honey. I know. Robert's told me everything."

"What do you mean?"

"I was wrong about him. He cares very much about you. He loves you."

"What has he been saying?"

"We're going to make you better, darling," she said. "I promise."

Sometime later I awoke to the smell of meat frying. The room was dark but there was a light cast across my bed and I realised for the first time since I don't know how long that my bedroom door had been left open. I waited. Expecting Robert or Martina to enter to change the towels or bed linen but no one did. Downstairs I could hear the quiet murmur of voices amongst the culinary clatter of Sofia going about her preparation. Apart from the familiar seductive fusion of spices that was her trademark Sofia was an industrious chef. The kitchen was her domain. Things clunked and clanged. She chattered and fussed and bossed. She didn't want help but at the same time would find menial jobs for anyone lurking inside her jurisdiction until you didn't want to be there anymore or would eventually just be shooed away as if your presence was somehow hindering her concentration.

For a long while I just lay there trying to come to my senses convinced that the open door was just a lingering dream I'd had that would eventually fade away. But each time I tried opening my eyes the more convinced I became that I had been sedated and not just because I felt groggy and leaden and the noises from downstairs seeped in and out of my sleep with an irritating insistence that made me want to call out, but that the dull ache in my left arm I had felt upon awakening was due to an IV drip inserted into my wrist. I lifted my hand slowly and followed the trail of the tube up to the empty bag hanging overhead on the trolley next to my bed. Had something happened? As hard as I tried to think a growing panic began to take over that Robert had been feeding me against my will again. I hurriedly began tearing at the plaster and yanked out the syringe. Whatever weight-inducing cocktail he'd been serving me this time might have already been in my stomach for hours. So I pulled at the oxygen flow and sat up, all the time steadying myself against wave after wave of giddiness before taking a few short breaths and starting for the bathroom. But in a crazed urge to get it out of me I already had my fingers down my throat and so I just stooped over in the middle of the room and fell to my knees. I wretched and gagged against the two-legged squid I had forced deep into my pharynx for minutes on end but it was all too late. Apart from a few strings of transparent liquid nothing came up. In my fat, disgusting greedy body's desire to eat it was already in my digestive system like a plump and fully-formed rat deep inside the tract of a python. That's how it felt. Like a living thing that needed to be purged. Like that alien in the film. I didn't need mirrors to show me the grotesque reality of my appearance. I lived inside my mind's eye. I knew and could picture every morsel that had gone into my human garbage disposal of a mouth. I no longer kept notes about my diet. My brain kept a record. It warned me every time about the dangers of eating to excess. I knew the nutritional intake of just about everything. Half a cup of baked beans contains 6.51 grams of fat, 27.06 in carbs and 191 calories. And they're supposed to be good for you! Now you know that fact try gorging on just one bean and I swear it will sit in your stomach like a stone, like a grinning gremlin.

I laid down on the floor for a bit like you do when you've thrown up but without the slow feeling of relief that the worst was over. I could still feel whatever needed to come out deep inside of me. I could usually rely on Calum in a situation like this to sneak me in some laxatives. He worried about me like everyone else but when he said he wasn't prepared to bring me any more I told him I would tell Robert how he'd been supplying me for months on end behind my husband's back and so he reluctantly continued. Maybe he was away on a on a pastry chef course or maybe he wasn't. This house had long since been full of whispers. I was being treated like a hospital patient. Worse, a psychiatric case. But Robert had been suspicious of my relationship with Calum anyway. It hadn't been fair to involve the poor boy. The whole thing had become a needless drama but now it seemed everyone was in on the plot for as I rose unsteadily to my feet and began tip-toeing towards the door I could hear them all downstairs talking about me in low voices. I recognized the calm, patronising tone of

Robert's shrink friend, Robin. Had heard both Sofia and Martina chipping in with their manic gibber. And then came my mother's voice, sounding timid and frightened and coupled all the while with the reassuring baritone murmur of my conspiratorial husband. "It's for the best," I heard him say. "It's for the best…"

So they were going to go through with it after all. My mother, too. Without even speaking to me. Without so much as even *seeing* me. Probably the thought disgusted her as much as it did me and she couldn't bear to look at what I had become. Her once darling girl. The beauty in the video. That wasted golden ticket. Of all the things that's what I felt the worst about. If I could go back now I would have married Andy just for Andy. Or any number of my loves. I didn't know what I wanted then. But nothing was ever quite the way my father had made it sound. For a start Andy's only ambition was to be a sports coach. Danny had a stake in his father's haulage business. Ollie was a banker but also an untrustworthy gambler. And so it went on. I still think my idea about marrying a rich older man was for the best and what my father was also unwittingly trying to tell me from a very early age. Just maybe not with a man born in the same year as him.

Be careful what you wish for, Dad.

It was never my golden ticket it was his. Waving it in front of his friends' faces all the time. Look what I got! Look what I won! I used to think he loved me but he was only ever pleased for himself. He was never thinking about me. He was never interested in me. I was his toy doll. His geisha. His love was plastic. And so in turn he made mine. I had judged all my old boyfriends on their looks. Their bodies. It was only after that I slowly became bored with their intellect. Their sameness.

I couldn't remember the last time I had the freedom of the house. There were two staircases at either end of the first floor landing. One led down into the enormous open dining area of the kitchen, the other wound its way towards the entrance hallway and the front door. I hesitated upon fleeing. The conversation drawing me ever nearer along with the sickeningly enticing cooking smells that my increasingly acute olfactory sense began to clinically divide into individual ingredients. I could taste each and every nauseating one of them. Garlic and onion, paprika and cumin and tarragon. That rancid mingling of tomatoes and sugar smelt like a dead bird to me. Sofia made her own stock from the collagen of beef bones and just the suggestion of the resulting oil-like gelatine vapour lingering like a miasma throughout the house made me want to empty my guts and I would if I could have in a show of protest. But my stomach felt like it always did. A tiny twisted piece of dry knotted rope.

Robert's family hailed from Tuscany so the kitchen had always been the hub of the house. Stone-floored with a big open fireplace and a long pine table with bench seats that could have catered for a family of twelve or more. Italians love their food which had been my first mistake. We never once entertained in the dining room. We never once entertained. Robert was homely at heart. I was still young enough to have his babies when we married. Of course we talked about it. But just the daunting thought of creating them was never far away. That and the idea of putting on weight and losing my figure. You never came back from that I don't care what anyone says.

I heard my mother gasp as I emerged from the upper shadows of the staircase and saw them all seated around the table like some incongruous family get-together. Robin slowly reached across and squeezed her hand as if not to say anything. He had some papers set out in front of him. Robert also appeared to have been looking through a glossy brochure before slowly closing the folder and laying his arms across it. Martina, however, seemed to be no part of the agenda and sat away from the others at the other end of the table stuffing her face into a two-layer carrot cake. Everyone was drinking coffee except Robert who swigged nervously upon seeing me from a bottle of beer. Only Sofia stood behind the peninsula border of the work surface that cordoned off the kitchen from the rest of the room wearing her habitual red, white and green horizontally-striped apron. She tried hiding her alarm at my appearance with a shaky smile before turning to switch off the overhead stove fan and reducing the room to a sudden and silent air of absurdity that she really might be expecting people to eat.

"What's going on?" I asked weakly.

The heat of the room, the rank and stifling stench of cooking smells was making me unsteady and I almost tottered on the last stair.

"You shouldn't be out of bed," Robert scraped his chair against the floor and stood up.

Sofia dusted off her hands and came round to join the others as if the plan was for all of them to suddenly rush me.

I held up a hand.

"None of you come near me," I said.

"Darling," my mother pleaded.

I looked at Martina disgustedly as she reluctantly set her fork down.

When I looked at my mother I caught her wearing the same expression. The same look Harry had given me.

"If you finish eating that you'd have to walk thirty-eight miles to burn it off," I told Robert's pig-faced sister.

"Baby, please," Robert closed his eyes and sighed.

"One nine-inch slice contains nearly nine-hundred calories and half of that comes from fat alone. Still, it has carrots in it I suppose."

"Well, I don't care," Martina spoke with her mouthful. "I'd rather look like me than you, *freak*."

"Martina!" Robert reproached her.

"How long have I been sedated?"

"Oh, darling, no one's sedated you. You're weak and unwell."

"What did you slip into my arm?" I demanded.

"Nutrients," Robin said simply and shrugged. "Vitamins, minerals."

"I don't believe you," I said. "You could give me those in a pill."

"Your digestive system is impaired," Robin looked at me seriously. "You do realise what you've done to yourself, don't you?"

"What do you mean?" I hesitated at his sober tone.

"The use of an IV allows the nutrients to bypass your digestive tract and go straight into the bloodstream. Simple oral replacement can take months to have effect. You are seriously malnourished. I estimate you weigh around three stone. It's a wonder you're even standing up. But with several IV treatment therapies we can increase those deficiencies with a rapid delivery system."

Did I hear him right? He must have meant *thirty*-three stone. Or even forty or fifty.

"When was the last time you ate?"

"I...when I was force-fed. Tell them, Mummy," I pleaded. "Tell him about the funnel and what they've been doing to me."

"You needed to eat!" Robert erupted. "It was only smoothies. Good stuff. I didn't know what to do before contacting Robin. I wasn't going to just sit there. You were dying in front of me. You still are. You obsessed over every tiny bit of food. Every calorie."

"I know you see a fat person in the mirror," Robin continued patiently. "But you have to believe me when I tell you cases as severe as yours can result in death from a wide range of causes. In my field it's known as the slowest form of suicide because around 5% of people with your condition die from complications from up to anything like a ten-year period. From what Robert tells me your problems started around a year ago when you were gaining weight and discovered you were officially obese."

"Yes! Yes!" I pointed at my mother. "You remember seeing me then, don't you?"

But she wasn't listening. She was walking towards me with her arms out sobbing.

"Just let me hold you," she wailed. "You look like a little bird. You're a bag of bones. Barely unrecognizable. My baby. Look at you. You've cut your face. You've soiled your nightdress."

"You're scaring me, mother," I laughed unsteadily and gripped the banister head. "You sound like them. Don't listen to *them*! I'm not crazy. You make it sound like I'm anorexic or something. I'm not anorexic if that's what you're all thinking. I mean, how could I be?" I looked at everyone.

Anorexia nervosa often begins following a major life-change or stress-inducing event. In my case I think I can safely say that started when I married a man I didn't love and felt no physical attraction towards. For a long time I thought I could fake it. People do. At some point maybe even search out a lover. But that never happened. Each day just got harder. It wasn't as if we had fallen out of love and I had grown to hate him. That would have involved passion. My heart was utterly indifferent towards a man who so much wanted to be loved and would have given me anything just to feel and believe it was real. But I couldn't. And like the good person that he is Robert now feels responsible for everything that happened to me. He told me recently that the reason he could never confess about being jilted was because he had known all along that the woman didn't love him and that deep down he knew I felt that way too. He had been there before and now thinks he is unlovable when just plain 'unlucky' might be a better way of putting it. He should have looked out for himself after his father had died instead of selflessly providing for his mother and his sister, and then the jilter, and then of course, me. I'm too selfish a person to recognise real kindness because I only understand it as a weakness. I've never been slapped or beaten. Maybe I should have. I wouldn't give a beggar a penny in the street. Fuck them and their bum ticket ride in life. And yet it's amazing how two lives can come together and create something unique. The tragedy being that it just wasn't meant to be. Apart from his overwhelming generosity Robert has a big heart. It saddens me now to think that part of him has been left unfulfilled because if for no other reason I know what that is like. It took me to the age of thirty-five before I went against my own soul's natural need because I felt incapable of not just receiving love but giving into it which is something I have been accused of many times in the past. I simply never had to try. And even in the beginning of a relationship when my boyfriends all said they loved me just to get their own way I knew that even if they didn't they soon would and then that would ultimately be the end of them. Once I was in charge it was hard not to get bored even though I tried to stick it out with every one of them. I really did. I wanted it all like any girl. I wanted the kids and the dog and the house and school-runs and kicking round a football in the garden. But I also knew it was always about me whatever I ended up accusing my exes of upon walking away. The time I ended it with Danny I woke to find him sniffing me in my sleep he had become so obsessed and so I just got up and left him and afterwards he stalked me for months driving by my house and blaring out old love songs. Another time just a bad-tempered remark about being held up in traffic when being given a lift to work was enough for me to get out of the car and leave someone I had dated for two years. It didn't matter about the compliments and the gifts and the treats and most of all, the sort of overbearing affection and attention my father used to bestow on me in front of his friends and relatives. Parading me like a prize with his golden ticket grin. Just like Robert when I sat on his lap that first night in the club. He didn't know it then. Not even the all-knowing Reverend knew it. Laughing and joking in front of his adoring entourage. Thinking he'd landed the golden ticket. Look what just fell into my lap! He didn't know what was coming then. But my wicked heart did.

I spent three-and-a-half-months in Robin's clinic undergoing his nutrient therapy. They started me off with potassium and zinc. Apparently a lack of iron can impair the ability to smell and taste and yet to this very day I still gag at the sickening stench of Sofia's revolting recipe that last night. It wasn't until later that I learnt she hadn't been preparing a meal at all. That there was nothing on the stove except for a pot of coffee. I had imagined it all and so much more to the point of a very real and deeply troubling paranoia that still has me questioning if my senses are playing some sort of psychosomatic trick on me. I can only say that when my zinc levels improved I regained my appetite and renewed ability to taste as if for the very first time. After that came the introduction of amino acids which I was told are especially important because they affect the body's hunger and desire to sleep. I'd slept intermittently for the best part of a year. The TV was always on. Food left on a tray by my bed which Martina inevitably finished off. The curtains closed. Sometimes I wouldn't know one day from the other. Then came a host of other vitamins and acids or 'rocket fuel' as Robin liked to call them, improving everything from the functioning of cells in my nervous system and intestinal tract to aiding increased metabolism of protein (and, yes) carbohydrates and fats. The range of nutritional deficiencies and the time it takes to re-build those stores after what I had done to myself is still ongoing. Every part of your physiological functioning gets affected by starvation. Blood, membranes, nose, throat, lungs, ears, vision, skin, bones, teeth, nerves and cardiovascular systems, immunity and healing. It is beyond description the photographs shown to me later when I was first admitted in relation to that girl in the video my mother sent me. Emaciated just makes me think of a starving cat. Skeletal a jokey Halloween figure. I had by far progressed both and more. Something indescribably thin but somehow alive with every bone joint visible like a broken string puppet. My skin a wrinkled sheath on the brink of death with hollow, bulbous, watery grey eyes no longer sapphire-infused or alluringly azure. A sunken-faced wraith. A ghost of a girl. But worst of all. The thing that couldn't be seen or mended. A sad and shrivelled heart that had cheated itself.

Printed in Great Britain
by Amazon